Remembering Sarah

"Successfully combines elements of Jacquelyn Mitchard's *The Deep End of the Ocean* and Dennis Lehane's *Mystic River.* . . . A compelling premise enhanced by the presence of an equally compelling, emotionally tortured central character."

—*Mystery Scene*

"A frightful read—in the good sense."

—*Daily News* (New York)

"Mooney writes with sensitivity. . . . *Remembering Sarah* has a lot of heart, and a protagonist who never gives up hope."

—*Boston Sunday Globe*

"Mooney's work is dark and desperate, but filled with genuine human emotion, sympathetic characters, and intriguing plots. *Remembering Sarah* is his best book yet and is sure to bring this gifted writer to a much larger audience—exactly what he deserves."

—*Chicago Sun-Times*

"One of the best thrillers of the year. Never exploitative, always gripping, *Remembering Sarah* is a moving exploration of remembered loss and undying hope that should catapult its author to the forefront of the new generation of thriller writers."

—John Connolly,
New York Times bestselling author of *Bad Men*

"A masterful journey into the dark regions of the heart. . . . You won't be able to tear yourself away from this gripping, moving, and wildly successful thriller."

—Larry Brooks, author of *Serpent's Dance*

"At the core of this gut-wrenching thriller is something rare: a thoughtful, poignant examination of parental love and parental folly. Chris Mooney has written his finest novel, and that's saying something indeed."

—Dennis Lehane, *New York Times* bestselling author of *Mystic River*

"Riveting, enthralling, scary. . . . Simply impossible to put down. . . . Mooney is a fabulous storyteller [with an] ability to transform an everyday occurrence into an abject vehicle of terror."

—Bookreporter.com

"Deeply moving. . . . A harrowing tale with a real emotional punch."

—*Deadly Pleasures*

"An impressive psychological suspense thriller that is the most accomplished book—poignant, neat-handed, and hopeful—in this talented writer's burgeoning career."

—*I Love a Mystery*

World Without End

"[Mooney's] imagination leaves nothing to be desired. . . . You can't keep track of the psychopaths without a scorecard."

—*Publishers Weekly*

"Timely and thought-provoking. . . . Rings alarmingly true."

—*Booklist*

Also by Chris Mooney

Deviant Ways
World Without End

CHRIS MOONEY

REMEMBERING SARAH

POCKET **STAR** BOOKS

NEW YORK   LONDON   TORONTO   SYDNEY

This book is a work of fiction. Names, characters, places and incidents are products of the author's imagination or are used fictitiously. Any resemblance to actual events or locales or persons, living or dead, is entirely coincidental.

A Pocket Star Book published by
POCKET BOOKS, a division of Simon & Schuster, Inc.
1230 Avenue of the Americas, New York, NY 10020

Copyright © 2004 by Chris Mooney

Originally published in hardcover in 2004 by Atria Books

ISBN: 0-7434-6379-X

First Pocket Books paperback printing April 2005

10 9 8 7 6 5 4 3 2 1

POCKET STAR BOOKS and colophon are registered trademarks of Simon & Schuster, Inc.

Cover design by Carlos Beltran

Manufactured in the United States of America

For information regarding special discounts for bulk purchases, please contact Simon & Schuster Special Sales at 1-800-456-6798 or business@simonandschuster.com

Acknowledgments

Thanks to Dave Crowley for answering all the legal questions. Richard Rosenthal, Chief of Police for the Wellfleet Police Department, and John "Zeke" Ezekiel. All mistakes are mine. Big thanks go to Greg Jackson for all the stories, and to Kay Byram.

Thanks to Jen, Randy, Elvis and Pam Bernstein, who read through the early drafts and gave me the honest feedback I needed. For Sarah Branham for keeping me on track.

My deepest thanks to Mel Berger and the amazing Emily Bestler, for once again finding the story within the manuscript and pushing me until I got it right. Every writer should be so blessed.

What follows is a work of fiction. That means I made everything up.

For Jen,
Always

His memories would always be dominated by churches. The night before his mother left, Mike Sullivan sat next to her in the front pew of St. Stephen's. At least twice a week, when they needed a place to hide, they would come here, and after praying, if she had some extra money, they'd head over to the Strand, Belham's downtown movie theater where three bucks got you back-to-back James Bond movies. Most of the time they'd head over to the public library where his mother would check out her weekly fix of paperback romance books, all of them with titles like *The Taming of Chastity Wellington* and *Miss Sofia's Secret*.

It was the snow that had driven them back inside the church that night. They had been on their way home from the library when the light snow suddenly turned bad, the wind howling so hard that Mike wondered if the car would tip over. Traffic was backed up everywhere, so they pulled into St. Stephen's to wait out the storm. Belham was still shoveling out from last month's whopper, the Blizzard of '78; now, not even a month later, a weatherman on the radio was predicting another storm for northeastern Massachusetts. Mike was eight.

The church was packed with people waiting for the roads to be cleared. His mother picked up one of the three travel magazines she had checked out from the library and started to read, her face serious but relaxed, the way she looked when she prayed. She was a petite woman, so small that Mike would tightly clasp his hands around hers, afraid that if he didn't somehow keep her anchored to the ground, she'd blow away. She flipped a page in her magazine, her free hand caressing the beautiful silk blue scarf she wore around her neck, the scarf imprinted with ancient pillars and statues and angels and looking completely out of place against her bulky winter jacket.

"It's rude to stare, Michael," she said in a soft voice. Even when she was mad, which was hardly ever, her voice stayed that way.

"I don't have anything to read," he whispered. "How come the library doesn't carry comics?"

"You should have picked out a book on woodworking." She turned around in her pew so she could face him, the magazine still opened up on her lap. "That birdhouse you made me for Christmas, I saw you working on it in your father's workshop. Saw the care you took when you stained it."

"I did a good job."

"No, you did a terrific job," she said, and smiled. That smile made men stop and take notice of her. That smile reassured him that everything was going to turn out all right.

"Where did you get that?"

"Get what?"

"That scarf."

"This thing? I've had this for a long time."

His mother's lies were as easy to spot as her bruises. She was careful never to wear the scarf around Lou, putting it on only after she left the house, taking it off and stuffing it in her jacket pocket before she got home, and Mike also knew she hid the scarf, along with the photo albums, in a box marked SEWING in the basement. One early Saturday morning, after Lou had left for work, Mike had caught her in the basement, removing the scarf from the box—the same hiding spot for her photo albums.

She caught the question in his eyes and said, "The scarf was a gift from my father. He gave it to me our last Christmas in Paris. I just don't want anything to happen to it."

"Paris. Oo la la."

Smiling, she placed the magazine on his lap and pointed to a color picture that showed the inside of an old church. The walls seemed a mile high, made of cracked white marble, the domed ceiling painted with a stunning portrait of Jesus Christ exposing his heart to the world.

"This is the Sacré-Coeur church," she said proudly. *"C'est l'endroit le plus beau du monde."*

When he heard his mother speak in her native French, heard the way the words rolled off her tongue, it made her seem more like the exotic young woman he had discovered in the black-and-white pictures pasted in the photo album. Sometimes, when he was alone in the house, he would sit in the cellar and study the pictures of his grandparents, his mother's friends, her home—everything she left behind in Paris to come here. The way these people dressed reminded him of royalty. At night, Mike would lie in bed and dream of an army of Parisians who would come to his house and rescue him and his mother.

"The pictures really don't do it justice," she said, and then leaned in closer. "The first time I stepped inside that church, I knew God was a real presence that could be felt and could fill you with love. But you have to believe, Michael. That's the key. Even when life is bad to you, you have to remember to keep your heart open to God's love."

"This picture has gargoyles."

"That's Notre Dame. Amazing, isn't it?"

"Gargoyles on a church. That has to be the coolest church in the world."

"Michael, do you ever wonder what goes on outside of Belham?"

"Not really," he said, his eyes fastened to another picture of a gargoyle, this one with its fangs bared, ready to leap down from the sky and strike down mortal sinners who dared to enter.

"Are you curious?"

"No."

"Why not?"

Mike shrugged, flipped a page. "Everything I know is here. The Hill and the Patriots and all my friends."

"You could make new friends."

"Not like Wild Bill."

"William's an original, I'll give you that."

"Dad said the problem with Paris is that it's full of French people."

"Your father's not a brave man."

Mike whipped his head up from the magazine. "But he fought in the Vietnam War," he said, not quite sure why he was defending his father. Mike didn't know what the Vietnam War was—well, not exactly. He knew war involved guns and knives and bombs and lots of blood and lots and lots of dead people. Mike had seen several old black-and-white war movies on TV.

"Holding a gun or hurting someone doesn't make you brave, Michael. Real bravery—*true* bravery—involves the spirit. Like having faith your life will turn out better when it looks like it won't. Having faith—that's real bravery, Michael. Always have faith, no matter how bad it looks. Don't let your father or anyone else take that away from you, okay?"

"Okay."

"Promise?"

"I promise."

His mother reached into her jacket, came back with a black velvet box and placed it on top of the magazine.

"What's this?" he asked.

"A gift. Go ahead. Open it."

He did. Inside was a gold chain affixed to a circular gold medal the size of a quarter. Etched on the medal was a bald man cradling a baby. The man, Mike knew, was a saint. The halo was always a dead giveaway.

"That's St. Anthony," his mother said. "He's the patron saint of lost things." She took the chain from the box, put

it around his neck and then clasped it, Mike feeling a
shudder when he placed the cold medal under his
sweater, against the warmth of his skin. "As long as you
wear it," she said, "St. Anthony will keep you safe. I even
had Father Jack bless it for you."

"Cool. Thank you."

The next day she was gone. Her car, an old Plym-
outh Valiant with rust pockets mended with duct tape,
was parked in the driveway when he came home. Mike
expected to see her in the kitchen, reading one of her
paperback romances by the table near the window. The
house was quiet, too quiet, he thought, and a sense of
panic he couldn't quite identify brushed against the
walls of his heart. He went upstairs to her bedroom, and
when he turned on the light and saw the neatly made
bed, he bolted back down into the kitchen, opened the
door for the basement and descended the stairs, Mike
remembering how lately his mother sat down here in
one of the plastic patio chairs and lost herself in her
photo albums. When he hit the bottom step, he saw the
box marked SEWING in the middle of the floor. He removed the box top, saw that the photo albums and the
blue silk scarf she kept hidden in there were gone, and
right then he knew, with a mean certainty, that his
mother had packed up and left without him.

The Shape of My Heart

(1999)

CHAPTER 1

It was probably the weatherman's hyping of yet another potential nor'easter that triggered the memory of his mother. This morning, Friday, he and Bill had been in Wellesley, starting in on a two-floor addition and kitchen renovation for a newly divorced mother with too much money and too much time on her hands when a light snow started to fall. Bill flipped the radio dial over to WBZ, the all-news station, and heard the weatherman talking about a major storm-front coming in late tomorrow afternoon that, after it left sometime late Sunday night, would dump somewhere in the neighborhood of twelve to sixteen inches of snow over eastern Massachusetts. Bill heard that and gave Mike a look, and by two, they both decided to quit early and take the girls sledding.

The problem with the plan was Jess. Since last month's incident, Jess had put a ban on sledding. Yes, what happened was an accident—Mike hadn't seen the other sled until it had slammed into them. And yes, Sarah had tumbled across the snow and whacked her forehead on a patch of ice—not bad enough to warrant a trip to the ER, but they took Sarah there anyway, Jess announcing along the way that sledding at the Hill was over, end of discussion. If Jess wanted to live in a bubble, fine, that was her choice, but it didn't mean he and Sarah had to live that way too. By the time Mike pulled up into his driveway, he had a solid plan in place.

Jess stood in the kitchen, a cordless phone wedged between her ear and shoulder as she picked up the stacks of file folders on the island table and shoved them inside one of those cardboard filing boxes. She was dressed in some sort of power suit: black pants and a matching jacket, the wide collar of her white shirt spread out like wings to reveal the new set of pearls he had given her for her birthday. Jess was in charge of St. Stephen's Annual Spring Craft Fair to raise money for the church's after-school daycare program. Her partner and co-chair had dropped out at the last minute due to a family illness, and with the Fair seven weeks away, Jess was left to shoulder all the details herself.

Jess's eyes shifted up from her packing, puzzled as to why he was home so early.

"Finished early," Mike whispered. He kissed her on the forehead, then grabbed a Heineken from the fridge.

"I'll have to get back to you on that." Jess hung up the phone, looking frazzled.

Mike said, "Your meeting with Father Jack still on?"

"Still on. How bad is the snow?"

"The roads are fine. They're already out plowing."

Jess nodded, sighed. "Shirley's running late—car problems—and since you're home, I was wondering if you'd mind watching Sarah when she comes—"

"Go. What time will you be home?"

"Probably not until seven."

"Want me to grab dinner?"

"The steaks are already defrosted and in the fridge. I'll do the rest when I get back." Jess scooped up her pocketbook and coat and hurried out the back door to the garage.

Ten minutes later, Mike was sitting in the chair-and-a-half in the family room, reading today's *Globe* and working on his second beer when he saw Shirley Chambers's red Honda Civic pull into the driveway. Sarah was six, the smallest in her class, and as Mike watched her run up the walk to the front door, her Barbie backpack bouncing against her back as one hand waved goodbye to Mrs. Chambers, the other pushing her glasses back up her face, he wondered when his daughter's growth hormones would kick in, help her catch up to the rest of her first grade class.

The front door slid open and Mike heard Fang, the big, burly bull-mastiff puppy they'd given her for Christmas, come charging from upstairs. Mike got to his feet and ran to the hall just as Fang bounced off the bottom step and jumped up on Sarah, all forty-plus pounds of him knocking her flat on her butt. Her glasses fell off, skidded across the floor. Sarah screamed.

"It's okay, Sarah, I got him." Mike picked up Fang,

the puppy's tail wagging a mile a minute, snorting as he licked Mike's chin. Sarah whipped her head back and forth, searching the floor, her world a blur.

"My glasses, Daddy."

"Remember what I taught you."

"I need my glasses," Sarah said again, lips quivering. "I can't see without them."

He wasn't going to run to her. That was Jess's job. No sooner did Sarah's glasses fall off (and they fell often, sometimes five, six times a day), no sooner did she take a tumble or bump her head and Jess would be right there to scoop her up. Mike knew how much the world loved to kick you in the ass, and when it did, it sure as hell didn't offer you an apology or a helping hand. Sometimes it kicked you again. Harder.

"Daddy, help—"

"Do you want to go sledding with Paula?"

Her lips stopped quivering. Sarah sat perfectly still on the floor.

"Okay then," Mike said. "If we're going to go sledding, you'll need your glasses. Now they were just on your face, right?"

"Yes."

"So that means they've got to be somewhere close."

"But what if—"

"You can do this. Now just relax and do what I showed you. You're a big girl, right?"

Squinting, Sarah scanned the floor, patting the hardwood with her hands, and found her glasses less than a minute later near the closet door. She picked up her glasses and put them on, her face beaming.

"My girl," Mike said. He put Fang back on the floor, told her to watch one of her videos while he took a quick shower, and then headed upstairs, stopping to pick up the cordless phone off his nightstand in the bedroom.

"I just left the house," Bill said. "You want me to stop by and pick you up?"

"Let yourself in. I'm going to jump in the shower."

"See you in five."

The plan didn't include Jess coming back home. Mike was in the shower when she walked back inside the house for the box of files she'd left on the island table. When he turned off the water, he heard shouting.

"But Dad said we could go sledding," Sarah cried from downstairs.

"Sarah, I said no."

Shit. Mike stepped out of the shower, grabbed a towel and quickly dried off.

"But why?"

Tell her the truth, Jess. Tell Sarah that you don't like her going sledding, that you don't like her jumping off diving boards and doing cannonballs in the pool or hopping on the back of a jet-ski or snowmobiling because fun equals risk and risk equals danger and danger lurks on every street corner in the world, just waiting to take you out if you aren't careful. That's what happened to your father, right? If he had been paying attention to the road and the snow instead of fiddling around with the radio, he would have seen the drunk driver.

Jess said, "No sledding. That's it."

"But Dad already said—"

"One more word and you'll get a time-out, young lady."

Mike heard Sarah stomp out of the kitchen and into the family room. He put on a clean pair of boxers and was in the process of sliding into a fresh pair of jeans when he heard Jess's boots clicking down the hallway.

The door to the garage slammed shut. Mike buttoned his jeans and ran down the stairs, bare-chested and barefoot, and caught up with Jess just as she was about to back out of the garage. She glared at him as she rolled down the window of her Explorer.

"I should have known you'd try and pull something like this," she said.

"What happened last month was an accident."

"Michael, she almost split her head open."

"It was a bump, not a concussion. The doctor told us that, remember?"

"I don't want her at the Hill. It's too crowded, and she's too small. I told you how I felt about that place. You're not being fair."

"*I'm* not being fair?"

"You want to sled around the house, fine, but she's not going down to the Hill." Jess put the Explorer in gear and backed out of the garage.

Mike watched as she drove away, thinking about how, beneath the executive clothing she wore like armor lately, the pearls and designer shoes, Jess still looked like the girl he had fallen in love with back in high school. She still wore her dirty blond hair long and still looked great in a pair of jeans and despite their fractured history, she still could, with just her touch, make him feel as though he was the most important, vital man in the world. But as for the private battle taking place behind her eyes, he was completely lost.

Jess hadn't always been that way. There was a time when she liked to have fun. Take their first Christmas party here at the house. Sixty-plus people filling their basement and crowding around the pool table, Billy Joel pumping from the boom-box speakers—the old Billy and not the pussy-whipped Billy, the mad genius Billy who sang songs like "Scenes From an Italian Restaurant" and made you feel he forged them from your own heart. And here was Jess getting into the spirit of the night, singing along to Billy's "Only the Good Die Young" and hanging tough until the last person left; Jess still looking for fun and still looking real good at two in the morning when she sat on the edge of the pool table singing "She's Got a Way" as she unbuttoned her shirt with that wicked smile on her face that always made his knees buckle. That night she had kissed him, hard and hungry, like she needed something from him—something to help her breathe. Back then when they had made love, they walked away bruised and exhausted and *needing* to do it again, the sex filling them up, energizing them.

The first miscarriage came a few months after that, followed by another one a year and a half later, and by the time they had Sarah, the space between them had changed, Mike not knowing how or why it had happened but dead certain that when he hugged Jess he felt like he was holding something cold and hollow.

A yellow Post-it note was stuck to the island table, right next to his keys so he wouldn't miss it. NO SLEDDING, the words underlined three times.

Mike picked up the note and crumpled it in his fist. The Heineken bottle was on the table, and he picked it up and drained the rest of it, wanting to throw it across the room, swear—do something to purge the anger ringing through his limbs. Only he couldn't do any of those things, not with Sarah in the next room.

He dumped his beer bottle and the Post-it note in the trash and tried to rub the anger out of his face. When he was sure he was calm, he walked into the TV room.

Fang lay sprawled out on his bed, half asleep. Sarah sat in the oversized denim chair, her head tilted down, her fist holding a crayon like a dagger and whipping it across the page of the coloring book spread open across her lap.

Mike knelt down, ready to pretend what happened was no big deal and, if asked, offer up some lame but hopefully acceptable excuse as to why Mom lived in a constant state of anxiety. "Want to go outside and build a snowman?"

Sarah didn't answer him, but Fang heard the word *outside* and his sleepy head jumped up, his small tail thumping against his bed.

"Come on," Mike said. "We'll even take Fang out with us. We'll throw snowballs and watch him chase after them."

"It's not fair," she whispered.

You're right, Sarah. It's not fair we're prisoners in our own home. It's not fair, and I don't know what to do about it anymore.

It was the crying that got to him—not the tears themselves, no, it was the *way* she was crying: her mouth clamped shut to keep silent whatever words wanted to be heard, her face a deep, dark red as tears spilled down her cheeks. A normal six-year-old didn't cry this way.

No sledding.

I said no, Michael. NO.

"Hey Sarah?"

Sarah's bawling had eased into sniffles. "Yes, Daddy?"

"Let's go get your snowsuit on."

CHAPTER 2

Everyone who lived in Belham called it the Hill, but the official name was Roby Park, named after the city's first mayor, Dan Roby. Back when Mike was growing up, the Hill had been nothing more than a long, wide stretch of grass, and at the top was Buzzy's, the only place in town where three bucks bought you a large Coke and a burger on a paper plate stacked high with fries or the world's greatest onion rings, your choice. Buzzy's was still there, along with a liquor store and video store, and now the Hill boasted one of those fancy jungle gyms and a new baseball diamond with stands.

The real attraction was the floodlight. Winters in New England meant the sky turned pitch black by four, so the town splurged and installed a telephone pole with a floodlight that lit up every inch of the hill. Now you could go sledding any time you wanted.

Mike found a spot in the lower parking lot, the one

abutting the new baseball diamond. Daylight was gone, and the snow was coming down a bit harder than an hour ago, but still it was light and still enjoyable. He got out first, went around to the other side of the truck and helped Sarah out, then grabbed the sled from the back of his truck. He held out his hand.

"I'm not a baby anymore," Sarah said and marched off.

The place was packed. The right side of the hill, the less bumpy area, was for kids Sarah's age and younger; the left for the older kids, the snowboarders. Watching the snowboarders brought Mike back to the days when he came here. When his mother could cover up the bruises on her face with makeup or hats, she would join the other mothers and talk with them as she smoked her Kools, all of the mothers watching as their boys did stupid things like stand on their cheap plastic sleds and have races down the hill. Bill would crash into him or give him a good shove and Mike would go tumbling across the snow, laughing his ass off the entire time. Everyone did—including some of the mothers. Back then, it was okay for kids to horse around and fall. Kids got bumped and bruised and cut and got themselves back up and then got bumped and bruised and cut all over again.

"DADDY!"

Mike looked down at his daughter and saw that she had stopped walking and was now pointing at the hill. *"There's Paula, Daddy! There's Paula! Here she comes!"*

Here came Bill's oldest daughter, Paula, riding her blue snow tube, Mike about to call out and tell Paula to watch out for the ramp—too late, Paula was airborne. It wasn't a big jump—less than a foot off the ground—but Paula wasn't prepared for the landing. The snow tube bounced against the ground, and Paula lost her balance and fell off, tumbling hard across the snow.

Sarah said, "I want to go sledding with Paula."

"Let's go," Mike said and held out his hand.

Sarah swatted it away. "No, Daddy, just with Paula."

"Paula's eight."

"So?"

"So you're six."

"And a *half*, Daddy. I'm six *and a half.*"

"Peanut—"

"I *told* you I don't like that name."

Oh boy, she's in a mood. "You're right, I'm sorry," Mike said, and knelt down so he was eye level with her. Snowflakes had melted against her glasses, the pink snowsuit's hood wrapped tightly around her head, the white imitation fur lining it blowing in the wind. "What I mean is Paula's bigger than you. The big kids' hill is very bumpy, and some of the kids have set up ramps." He pointed to where Paula just wiped out. "If you hit one of those ramps, you'll go flying in the air."

"Like a bird?" Sarah seemed very excited by the possibility.

"Last time you fell off the sled you hit a patch of ice and got you a big bump on your head, remember?"

"Oh yeah. That hurt."

"So let's go down together," Mike said and stuck out his hand.

"No," Sarah said, swatting away his hand. "I want to go with Paula."

Seeing her act this way reminded him of last summer, when he was teaching Sarah how to swim—only she refused to wear her floaties and she certainly didn't want a helping hand from her father. So Mike let her do it her way and watched, unsurprised, as Sarah sank right to the bottom. No sooner did Mike bring Sarah up for air than she wanted to try it again—on her own. He was so in love with this part of his daughter, her stubborn, almost unbreakable need to fight to do things in her own way, that he had to do everything in his power to keep from smiling.

No, Jess's voice warned him. *Don't you dare let her go down that hill by herself. What if she falls and hurts herself bad this time? What if she breaks a leg or cracks her head open— Jesus Christ, Michael, look at how small she is. What if—*

What if she has fun, Jess? You ever stop and think about that?

Your mother never spoke up, another voice added. *You want to raise a girl to become a woman who's terrified to speak her mind? You let Jess kill off this part of Sarah, she'll end up marrying a prize like your old man. That the life you want for her?*

"Daddy, Paula's getting ready to go back up the hill, can I go *pleeeease—*"

"Sarah, look at me."

She heard the tone in his voice and snapped her attention to him.

"You go up the hill with Paula, you come back down with Paula, understand?"

"I understand."

"What did I say?"

"Up and down with Paula."

"Right. I'll be standing over there next to your god-father, okay?"

Sarah grinned, her top teeth crooked, the bottom two missing, that smile of hers blowing straight through him, scaring him for some reason. She gripped the rope for the sled and trudged through the snow, screaming for Paula to wait up.

You realize what you've done.

Yes. He had committed the worst of parental sins: siding with the child. And guess what? It was worth it. Real life, with all of its sucker punches and bone-weary bullshit, would always be there. You only got one turn in life to be six—excuse me, six *and a half*—and if that meant he had to spend some time in the doghouse, so be it.

Bill O'Malley stood alone, a good amount of space between him and the people who had formed small groups, talking to themselves and, Mike noticed, occasionally cutting sideways, nervous glances at Wild Bill. That Bill, people said with a shake of the head. Full of piss and vinegar. Soft in the head for sure.

Everyone in town knew the story of the time when Bill was twelve and decided to drive himself and his friends to school, a move that landed him on the Boston news, one of those cutesy "Kids Do The Darndest Things" segments. But it was the stunt he pulled during the all-conference playoffs his junior year that cemented his reputation.

The Belham High football team had their first shot at a championship title, and on a cold, overcast Saturday in November, it seemed as if the entire town had shown up at the football stadium in Danvers to watch Belham's own go up against the snot-nosed, rich brats of St. Mark's Preparatory High School. With thirty seconds and more than forty yards to go, the ref made a bad call that cost Belham the championship. Bill lit into the ref, got right in the guy's face, and by the time the coach ran over, Bill had ripped off the ref's toupee and was running around the field with it, holding it high over his head, everyone in Belham on their feet, cheering.

"When you grow up and get married, I hope you have twin girls just like you," a weary Clara O'Malley told her son after the game.

Come this spring, Bill would get twins—twin girls, according to his wife Patty's latest ultrasound. Paula O'Malley was the oldest and only at eight had inherited her father's crude sense of humor. Last week Paula got her first detention for bringing a whoopee cushion to school and placing it underneath the seat cushion of her teacher's chair.

Bill saw the familiar pink snowsuit slide up next to his daughter and then turned around just as Mike walked up to him. A plug of chewing tobacco bulged from Bill's lower lip, and his black Harley-Davidson baseball hat was pulled low over his head. A small gold loop earring dangled from each ear.

Bill leaned in close and whispered, "Seriously, does Jess ever get jealous when you wear her jacket?"

The jacket in question, a Christmas gift from Sarah, was made of black wool and cashmere. More importantly, it was clean and new—unlike Bill's faded blue Patriots jacket that dated back to the early eighties, Bill refusing to give up the old, ratty jacket with its grease stains and torn pocket until the Pats won the Super Bowl.

"What's wrong with it?"

"Nothing," Bill said. "All the prettiest girls are wearing 'em this year."

Mike removed the pack of Marlboros from his coat pocket, his eyes locked on Sarah, watching her and Paula chugging their way up the hill. "I take it you ran into Jess."

"Yeah. She told me sledding was a no-go. Glad she had a change of heart."

"One of us did," Mike said.

Bill spit into his Dunkin Donuts cup, didn't say anything. Now Mike was suddenly filled with the need to talk. *I can't take it anymore, Bill. I'm tired of living with a shell. I'm tired of living with a woman who is terrified of life and has made me a prisoner in my own home. I'm tired of having to fight for the simple things like taking my six-and-a-half-year-old daughter sledding. I'm tired and I want out.*

That last thought wasn't new. It had been floating in and out of his gray matter over the past year—only now it stuck around more, and when Mike was driving back and forth to work or doing some boring task like shoveling, he played around with the idea of leaving, a part of himself excited by the possibilities, this new life out there waiting for him, a new life without all these walls and barriers.

Mike glanced over to his right, at East Dunstable Road, where cars were piled up on both sides, and saw a taxi crawling west toward the connection for Route 1. Mike pictured his mother sitting quietly in the back of the cab, her twelve years of marriage packed up in one suitcase, the driver asking, "Where you headed? North or south?" And for the first time his mother would make a decision and a man would listen. When she picked her new direction, Mike wondered if that scream trapped inside her skull had finally died.

Paula's snow tube slid over to them.

"What's with the puss?" Bill asked.

"Jimmy MacDonald's up at the top pushing everyone around," Paula said.

Jimmy Mac was Bobby MacDonald's youngest. Supposedly, Bobby Mac was the kind of guy who liked to have litters of kids with different mothers in the Mission Hill projects.

"He pushed me down and then he pushed Sarah down," Paula said.

Wonderful. Mike flicked his cigarette into the air. "I'll go up and get her," he said. "You guys wait here in case she comes down."

"He's always picking on us," Mike heard Paula say as he walked away. "We were walking home last week from Stacy's house and Jimmy Mac saw us and blew his nose all over Joanne Finzi and she called him wiener face."

"Nice call," Bill said.

The cold air was charged with giggles, shrieks and laughs as Mike climbed the hill, brushing his way past the parents and kids lumbering their way up the walking path. The snow, Mike now noticed, had turned bad. He could barely see a few feet in front of him.

He stepped out of the glare of the floodlight onto the top of the hill. The cars parked along Delaney Road were trying to merge with the cars snaking their way down the curvy road from Buzzy's parking lot. Dozens of headlights were pointed at him. Mike shielded his eyes with his hand and looked around the crowd of bodies for his daughter.

"Sarah, it's Dad. I'm at the top of the hill."

Out of nowhere a group of kids rushed past Mike as if being chased—or chasing someone. Mike looked over his shoulder and watched as the kids bolted down the road, disappearing into the snow. He turned his attention back to the hill and moved forward, taking slow steps as he looked for the pink snowsuit.

"Sarah, I'm here at the top. Where are you?"

She can't hear you.

Right. He had wrapped Sarah's jacket hood so tight around her head she probably couldn't hear him over the wind, over the shouts and screams, the drivers with their fists planted on their car horns. He peeled his way through the crowd, searching for her, yelling out her name.

"Sarah, it's me."

"Sarah, wave to me."

"Sarah, where are you?"

The bodies disappeared and now Mike stood on the end of the Hill where the older kids went snowboarding and sledding. A few feet from the top of the hill, where the kids were lining up, was a long blue sled that looked an awful lot like Sarah's. Mike jogged over to it, knelt down and brushed the snow off the padded seat. SARAH SULLIVAN was printed in black block letters, in his handwriting.

Maybe she walked down the hill, chasing after Paula.

"Bill?" Mike yelled. "Bill?"

"Yeah?"

"Sarah down there?"

"Not yet."

Mike felt a flutter in his heart. He turned to his right. Twenty feet away there was an embankment with a steep drop-off. The place was well marked and sectioned off—and Sarah knew to stay away from there.

He looked back at the sled and searched around it for a pair of small footprints that matched Sarah's. At the end of the sled was a thin shaped piece of plastic sticking out of the snow. He picked it up, shook the snow off.

Sarah's glasses.

The flutter turned into a cold, hard lump that knocked against the walls of his heart. He stumbled to his feet, a scream rising in his throat:

"SARAH, WHERE ARE YOU?"

Please God, please answer me.

All around him cars were leaving the parking lots, waiting for their turn to merge onto the mess on East Dunstable, the traffic moving forward in inches.

She still could be here.

No, Mike said to that rising, panicky voice. No way. Sarah wouldn't leave here without me or Bill.

But what if she did?

Almost slipping on the snow, Mike ran up to a Honda Accord parked only a few feet from Sarah's sled. He banged on the window until the guy with the Red Sox baseball cap, a guy Mike didn't recognize, rolled down the window. The man's son, all of four or so by the looks of him, sat in the passenger seat.

"A girl in a pink snowsuit," Mike said. "She was standing right over there next to the sled."

"I didn't see her."

"You sure?"

"I can barely see the car in front of me."

"I can't find her. Help me look, would you?"

The guy nodded and tried to pull over to the side. Mike ran toward East Dunstable, dodging his way through the spaces between the cars, a tightness growing inside his chest.

She's here, Sarah's still here.

"Sully?" Bill called out. "Sully?"

An Explorer was about to pull onto East Dunstable when Mike jumped in front and held out a hand. Car horns blared as the driver rolled down the window, Mike seeing it was the guy from the lumber yard at Home Depot, Billy something.

"What's wrong?"

"I can't find my daughter," Mike said. "She's wearing a pink snowsuit."

"Haven't seen her. You want some help?"

Mike nodded, said, "Do me a favor. Block off this road with your car, tell everyone what's going on."

"You got it."

"And make sure you check the backseats and under the cars. She might have got hit or something."

People had stepped out of their cars and were swearing at Mike to get out of the road. Mike was about to stop the next car, a Ford Mustang, when Bill appeared out from a curtain of snow, Paula beside him.

"I found her glasses next to her sled," Mike said. "Paula, what happened up here? Tell me what happened."

Paula flinched at the sound of Mike's voice.

"Sully, it's okay, calm—"

"Sarah can't see without her glasses."

"I know."

"She's terrified when she can't see."

Bill put his meaty hand on Mike's neck and squeezed. "I'm sure someone saw her all worked up and had the good sense to bring her inside Buzzy's. She's probably in there right now pigging out on a burger and fries. Don't worry. We'll find her."

CHAPTER 3

With the foul weather and traffic, it took the police almost an hour to arrive at the Hill. The first unit—Patrolmen Eddie "Slow Ed" Zukowski and another guy Mike knew, Charlie Ripken—were relieved to see that Mike had the smarts to block off the Hill. The second unit that answered had blocked off the lower parking lot, the one where Mike was parked.

Slow Ed brought Mike next door to the Tick-Tack-Toe liquor store. Mike stood underneath a ceiling vent blasting hot air, melting snow dripping off his jeans and coat, forming a puddle around his soaked boots. He dried off his face and head with a towel the liquor store owner had given him.

"About what Sarah was wearing," Patrolman Eddie Zukowski said, and flipped to a fresh page in his notebook. Slow Ed's pie-shaped face was bloated, shaped by too many late nights and too much fast food, but his tall frame was in good shape, still as thick as a telephone pole and no doubt packing the same explosive power that had made him a football star at Boston College.

Mike said, "It hasn't changed since I told the dispatcher."

"We've got three kids next door wearing a pink snowsuit—one of who's a boy, go figure. What I need from you, Sully, are the details. The snowsuit, the hat and gloves—that stuff."

What Mike heard in Slow Ed's voice was the same listless quality of the two patrolmen who came around asking Lou questions about the whereabouts of his wife. What Mike also heard were the traces of dumbness that had defined Slow Ed's father's life, Big Ed Zukowski, a man who wanted to take his wife on a two-week cruise to Aruba for their ten-year anniversary and came up with the bright idea of robbing the bank across the street from the car repair shop where he had worked as a mechanic since high school.

The wind howled, rattling the storefront glass and door. Sarah was out there in this mess. She had wandered away from the sled, had, he was sure, slipped down the embankment and was now wandering somewhere around the woods that stretched all the way back to Mike's house, to Salmon Brook Pond and Route 4, Sarah lost in the blinding snow and calling out for him, her voice lost in that wind, Sarah blind and terrified without her glasses.

"I already went over all this with the dispatcher," Mike said. "You want the info, get it from him." He tossed the towel on top of a stacked column of Bud bottles, got maybe two steps before Slow Ed grabbed his arm.

"Sully, you're soaked to the bone."

"I'm fine."

"That's why your lips are purple and your teeth are chattering. Don't bullshit me, Sully. I've known you too long."

"I've got to get back out there. She's wandering around the woods without her glasses—"

"What glasses?"

Mike removed the glasses from his jacket pocket and slapped them down on top of the towel. "Sarah's terrified when she doesn't have them on," he said. "I've got to get out there before she stumbles off one of those trails and steps onto Route Four."

"Volunteers are already out there. Now tell me where you found those glasses."

"I'm going back out."

"Hold up." Slow Ed tightened his grip, moved his big round face closer. "We're going to cover every inch of this place, but with the visibility for shit, you can see why I need as much information as possible."

"I already did."

"You didn't tell the dispatcher about the glasses."

"So now you know."

"Where'd you find the glasses?"

"Next to the sled." Again Mike tried to step away but Slow Ed wouldn't let go, Slow Ed digging his fingers in just hard enough to remind Mike who was in charge.

Mike wanted to scream. He wanted to scream out

that sick feeling coiling its way through his gut, wanted to knock Slow Ed down with the strength of it. *Ed, you stupid shit, you're talking too slow and you're wasting time.*

"Sarah's six years old and is wearing a pink snowsuit," Mike said. "Pink snowsuit with blue mittens—they've got reindeer printed on them. Pink Barbie snow boots. What else you want to know?"

Slow Ed released his grip but blocked the path to the door. Mike ran down the list: Sarah's height, weight, eye and hair color, the Cindy Crawford beauty mark above her lip, her two bottom missing teeth and the slightly crooked uppers—he even mentioned the bruise on Sarah's rib. He had discovered it last night when he gave Sarah a bath.

"How'd she get this bruise?" Slow Ed asked.

"Ran into the coffee table. Least that's what Jess told me."

Slow Ed stopped writing, looked up. "You don't believe her?"

"I'm saying I was at work." Mike removed his pack of cigarettes, saw that it was soaked.

"Sarah's snowsuit have any unusual markings on it?"

"Like what?"

"Decals, prints. Along those lines."

Mike rubbed his forehead, then closed his eyes

(Daddy, where are you?)

(Jess's voice: *Get out there and search for your daughter, NOW*)

and tried to picture details, these stupid, meaningless details—what mattered now was getting back outside to find Sarah. But how was he going to get around Slow Ed?

"Her name's written on the inside tag in black marker," Mike said. "Jacket's got a small tear in the front pocket. Right front—no, it was the left. Yeah, the left. Fang did that."

"Fang?"

"Our dog," Mike said, opening his eyes. "That's all I got."

Slow Ed stopped writing. He fished out a plastic baggie from his pocket and with a flick of the wrist he snapped it open. "When's the last time you saw your old man?"

"Years ago. Why?"

"How much time we talking about?"

"I don't know. Three, four years. Last I heard, he was living somewhere in Florida."

"But he kept his house, right?"

"Ed, no offense, but what's this got to do with finding my daughter?"

"Lou's been spotted around town."

Then Mike understood.

"Sarah's never met him," Mike said, watching as Slow Ed used his pen to push the glasses into the bag. "He wouldn't come near her, and even if he did—he wouldn't, but if he did, Sarah wouldn't believe him because I told her that her grandfather died before she was born. Sarah wouldn't leave with him or anyone else. Sarah knows about stranger danger. She wouldn't leave with anyone but me or Bill."

"Kids do funny things when they're scared, Sully. Way the snow's whipping around out there, everyone's dressed different, got their faces covered up, you don't know who's who. Sarah probably latched onto the first person she recognized."

That sick, sharp-edged worry he had been carrying for Sarah formed a wiry, heated energy that made his skin tingle. Mike judged the space between him and Ed, thinking of a way to get around him when Ed's cell phone rang.

"You call home and check your messages?" Ed asked as he unclipped the phone from his belt.

"Did that right after I called nine-one-one."

"That was a good forty minutes ago. Call and check again." Ed brought the phone up to his ear as he walked away and stood in front of the door, blocking it.

Mike took out his cell phone and saw that the battery had crapped out, this being the time of day when he normally recharged it. He walked past Slow Ed and moved up to the counter where a big, round bald guy was pretending to read a *Herald*.

"Use your phone, Frank?"

Frank Coccoluto handed him the cordless.

After having two answering machines break in the past year, Mike had opted for the phone company's voice-mail service. He dialed the number for his voice mailbox and entered in the code, his hopes rising and then crashing when the prerecorded operator said, "No new messages."

The wind rattled the glass again and Mike pictured

Sarah up alone on top of the hill, Sarah trying to find her glasses in the blowing snow, everything a blur. Okay, Sarah was upset but she was also smart. Sarah knew all about monsters disguised as kind and smiling people who offered candy and told kids they had lost their puppies or kittens and needed help looking for them, so if someone came by and offered his daughter help, Mike knew that Sarah, even at her most hysterical, would be smart enough to go only with a voice she recognized, a friend or parent she knew from school, someone from the neighborhood, maybe.

"Ed's right about kids doing funny things when they're scared," Frank said. "Few years back, I'm in Disney World with my daughter and my eight-year-old granddaughter? We turn our heads for, I don't know, maybe three seconds and when we looked back, Ash is gone. Swallowed into the crowd, poof, just like that." Frank snapped his fingers. "The Disney people, they ripped up the park, I swear to God I thought I was going to have a stroke I was worried so much. Guess where we ended up finding her? Back in the hotel, in my bed, sleeping like an angel. Park security guy found her. Ash was so hysterical about being lost, all she could do was say the hotel we were staying in, room number three-twenty-one, so that's where they brought her."

Mike glanced at his watch. Almost ninety minutes had passed since he had found the sled.

Slow Ed snapped his phone shut and Mike felt his hope rise again.

"Goddamn lousy weathermen dropped the ball again," Ed said. "The blizzard scheduled for yesterday's about to head straight up our ass. Let's go, Sully. We've got to get a move on to your house. State's on their way with the search dogs. I'll explain along the way."

CHAPTER 4

Slow Ed talked about bloodhounds, about how these dogs had sixty times more scent power than German shepherds and could follow the scent of a person, no matter how faint, in the air or on the ground for days, even weeks, day or night, rain or snow, it didn't matter. Example: a convict who had escaped a prison in Kentucky thought he was smart by lying on the bottom bed of a pond, using a cutout section of a hula-hoop as a snorkel, thinking the dogs wouldn't find him. Bloodhounds were so smart, Ed said, they could pick up the convict's scent coming through the piece of hoop. There had even been a case of a bloodhound who had trailed a person being carried away in the trunk of a car, the person's scent mixed with the car's exhaust, the bloodhound picking right up on it, Slow Ed going on and on with more stories, his voice growing dimmer and dimmer as a singular thought took root in Mike's mind:

You called in the dogs when someone was *missing*. Not lost, *missing*.

They hit a bump and Mike felt the St. Anthony medallion bounce against his chest.

Always have faith, no matter how bad it looks.

It got bad, real bad, those first few months after his mother left, Lou so angry and so sure she was never coming back he took all of her stuff and burned it in an aluminum trashcan in the backyard. And while God had turned a deaf ear to that mess, He had been paying attention on a Sunday afternoon in late March, Jess coming up on the seventh month of her pregnancy with Sarah, Mike thinking—*believing*—that everything was going to turn out okay this time around when Jess felt faint, then dizzy, then started throwing up. They had survived two miscarriages—no, it was more like endured, both of them separately coming to grips with the possibility of a life without kids until Jess got pregnant for the third time, a girl, Sarah. Each day lived with a held breath, Mike hitting the pillow every night and thanking God for keeping watch on his family, Mike calling on God again as he rushed Jess straight to Mass General. By the time he pulled up to the ER, Jess's blood pressure had dropped, her blood already poisoned from, he was about to learn, a life-threatening condition called preeclampsia.

In the end, it always came down to faith. God or Buddha, Mother Earth or that private space you went to when you made love—whatever you believed, in the end it all came down to faith. Faith that your life would work out the way you designed it. Faith that the people you loved would stick by you and stick around long enough. So when the surgeon explained the situation and the possibility that one if not both of them might not make it, Mike thought about the St. Anthony medal around his neck and called in his chits— Mass every Sunday; he didn't cheat on his wife, both he and Jess generous with their time and money when it came to St. Stephen's Church; and hey, while we're at it, let us not forget all that time served with Lou Sullivan. Save them both, Mike said. Save both of them and you can take me, I don't care because I couldn't live through losing either of them.

That day God listened and came through, and as Slow Ed forced his way through the middle lane of traffic on East Dunstable, sirens wailing and lights flashing, Mike reached under his shirt, clutched the medallion in his hand and prayed for God to intervene a second time.

Slow Ed was saying, "Like that kid from last year, the three-year-old from Revere. Snowing like a bastard and the idiot mother went inside her house and left her kid unattended in the front yard. When she came back out, her son was gone, right? Dogs came in and five minutes later tracked the kid to a neighbor's garage. Kid was unconscious, pinned underneath the car. Old man didn't know he hit him and dragged the kid down the street."

Another success story to give Mike hope, to dim the growing collection of doubtful voices rising like a chorus in the back of his mind: *And if the dogs don't find her, then what? What will I do?*

Slow Ed shut off the siren and turned left onto Anderson, the storm having already dumped a good six to eight inches on the sidewalks and street. "We need something with Sarah's scent. When's the last time you washed Sarah's sheets?"

"Last Sunday," Mike said.

"You're sure?"

"Jess does laundry every Sunday morning. Strips the beds before we go to church." The kitchen and living room lights were on, Mike saw. He had shut them off before he had left. Jess was home. "Do me a favor and kill the lights and siren. Last time Jess saw a cop pull into her driveway, they told her that her father had died."

Slow Ed killed the lights and siren, Mike hearing the tires cutting their way through the slushy snow. Mike pointed over to a mailbox at the end of a driveway. Slow Ed pulled over and parked the car.

"You want me to come in with you?"

Seeing a blue uniform standing in her home would send Jess's paranoia into overdrive.

"No, I'm all set," Mike said and opened the door.

"Hold up. You got a recent picture of Sarah?"

"We do the Sears portrait thing every Christmas."

"A Channel Five news van happened to be in the area, on Route One, you know, doing the storm coverage. They agreed to come over, get Sarah's face on the airwaves. It wouldn't hurt."

Mike nodded, shut the door and jogged up the driveway, telling himself that Sarah wasn't missing, she was only lost. He was sure of it in the same way he had been sure that day in the emergency room, knowing that both Jess and Sarah would make it. Sarah had slipped and fallen down the embankment and was wandering somewhere in the woods, huddled against a tree, maybe, cold and scared out of her mind, and he knew by the time he got back down to the Hill, he'd find her cradled in Bill's arms or drinking a hot chocolate at a booth at Buzzy's, Sarah surrounded by smiling, relieved cops. Jesus, Sarah, you gave us all quite a scare.

Mike opened the storm door, then the front door, and when he stepped inside the semi-dark foyer, he was surprised to see Jess standing at the stove, dumping sliced potatoes from a cutting board into a pot of boiling water. A yellow Sony Walkman was clipped to her belt, the Walkman and headphones her signal to let him know she was in that area beyond pissed off and in no mood to talk.

Mike walked down the foyer, half expecting to hear Sarah's little feet come running across the kitchen floor, Sarah calling out his name and smiling and cutting that sick feeling of razor-wire that had wrapped itself around his heart. It was only Fang who came running. Mike stepped into the kitchen, Fang following, his tail wagging. The kitchen table, he saw, was set for three.

"What are you doing home?"

"Father Jack had to cancel at the last minute. An emergency," Jess said, her voice cold and detached. "Why don't you go upstairs and draw Sarah a bath. I'm sure she's frozen after sledding."

That razor-wire tightened around his heart. He was

secretly hoping someone might have called and left a message. Jess always checked messages when she came home. Nobody had called, and Jess didn't know what was going on.

He yanked the headphones off her head.

"What are you—"

"There's been . . ." What was the word here? Sarah wasn't missing—at least not in the way he defined the word—and what had happened wasn't an accident.

"There's been a what?"

"Sarah went up the hill with Paula but didn't come back down."

The color drained from her face.

"Listen to me," Mike said. "Everything's under control. The police—"

"The *police.*"

"She's just lost. The police are there to help find her."

"Oh Jesus."

"It's going to be okay. Ed Zukowski drove me here. He's going to give us a ride down to the Hill, but we need to grab Sarah's pillow— Jess, wait."

She had already moved around the island. Mike moved around the other side just as she scooped her jacket off the back of one of the island chairs. He went to touch her and Jess stepped back.

"I told you not to go down there, you son of a bitch."

"Jess, listen to me. They've got bloodhounds, they're these amazing dogs that—"

"What kind of father are you? What kind of father

43

would just leave his daughter alone out there in the freezing cold? She's somewhere out there terrified and maybe hurt and you just *left* her?"

Mike tried to think of some grouping of words that would calm her down. It didn't matter. She had stepped outside, the storm door being held open by the wind, snow blowing everywhere.

CHAPTER 5

Sammy Pinkerton sat in the backseat of his dad's station wagon, on their way back from the Hill and stuck in traffic and listening to that all-boring, all-the-time news radio station, the weatherman blah-blah-blahing again about how the snowstorm had already knocked out power over half of Massachusetts and could, by the time it was done, turn out to be the worst storm since the Blizzard of '78. Sammy tuned the guy out and instead thought about how he was only a few weeks away from turning ten—double digits, he was officially a man, baby—and how he only stuttered when he got nervous. That was almost always the case when he listened to his parents fight over who was going to get custody this weekend, and it was especially true when he got around meltdowns like Jimmy Mac-Donald.

Why did that skidmark have to show up at the Hill tonight? All Sammy had wanted to do was try out his new snowboard and there, standing just a few feet away, was Jimmy Mac and his jerk friends from the Mission Hill projects, all of them dressed in leather jackets and jeans and trying to act cool as they held their cheap plastic sleds, waiting for their turn to go down the hill. Only *that* was taking forever. The snow was coming down harder—not blizzard conditions yet, but it was sure difficult to see, the line for sledding backed up and crowded with people.

Jimmy yelled, "This line better start moving or I'm gonna start kicking some ass."

All Jimmy's ghetto friends laughing too hard, wanting to impress him, everyone laughing except the two girls standing in front of Jimmy Mac. Sammy recognized the taller of the two girls from school: Paula O'Malley. Her dad was Wild Bill, this totally massive dude with these totally rad tattoos that ran up and down each of his big arms. Sammy had met her dad once when he came to pick Paula up from school—*on a Harley motorcycle*. Dad who did that, like, had to be the coolest dad in the world.

"That's it," Jimmy Mac said and started pushing kids out of the way.

That was the signal to leave. Sammy had learned his lesson a couple of months back when he'd accidentally bumped into Jimmy Mac in the bathroom. A simple mistake, happens all the time, right? The meltdown grabbed Sammy, shoved his face into the toilet bowl and flushed, kept flushing, one of Jimmy Mac's goons clapping, saying, "Damn Jimmy, we got ourselves a major league floater that just won't go down." They left laughing, and Sammy counted to one hundred and then opened the stall door, hoping he was alone. About a dozen eyes stared at him as he scrubbed his face and hair with soap and water, then dried himself under the hand dryer.

"Hey!" Paula O'Malley screamed. "Get your hands off me!"

"The baby hill's at the other end, pee wee. Beat it."

"It's our turn. Come on, Sarah."

Jimmy Mac picked Paula up, grabbed her by the arms and shoved her down on the snow tube. The little girl in the pink snowsuit, Sarah, she tried to grab Paula, either to help her out or to stay with her, and Jimmy Mac put his big hand on Sarah's face and shoved her so hard she went flying backwards.

"You're in big trouble!" Paula screamed, but Jimmy Mac had already kicked her snow tube down the hill.

Just walk away, a voice said. As wrong as all of this was, this wasn't his fight, and he had no interest in tangling with Jimmy Mac again.

That changed when he looked over at the little girl sitting in the snow, crying the way little kids do, like they just got their arms chopped off.

It wasn't the girl's tears that made Sammy keep from running away, it was her glasses, the way they hung crooked on her face. She looked so defenseless sitting there like that, and before Sammy knew what was happening—before he could stop it, his mouth gathered up the words he had wanted to say that day in the bathroom and launched them at Jimmy Mac.

"I hope God strikes you dead, you ugly turd."

Jimmy Mac whipped around, staring down the crowd of faces.

"Who said that? Who *said* that?"

Sammy didn't run away. He wanted to—a part of his brain was screaming at him to haul ass *right now*—but something was keeping him from running, a new thought about that day in the bathroom. The thing that made him cry and shake with anger later that day wasn't getting his head dunked or having to walk back inside the classroom with dried toilet water on his clothes. No, the worst part, the thing he didn't understand until right now, was that he hadn't fought back. When you didn't stand up to a bully, they ended up owning a piece of you. They held it in their eyes and in their smile and when they saw you, they used that stolen piece of you and got off spearing you with it because they knew you didn't have the balls to stand up for yourself. Maybe it was better to fight back. Maybe the pain of a broken nose or a black eye or whatever Jimmy Mac could dish out was better than having to look away from people every day in the hallways, hearing them laugh behind your back, calling you names like Stinky Pinkie. Black eyes and broken noses healed. At least they told people you weren't a coward.

The little girl, Sarah, was back on her feet, pulling her sled, *oh crap*, she was heading toward the bad part of the hill, the place where if you slipped and fell you could crack your head open. It happened to a kid last year, Jay Baron. His sled slammed into a boulder and Jay went flying into a tree and an ambulance had to take him away. Sammy was about to make a move to help the girl when Jimmy Mac stepped right in front of him.

"Stinky, that you who mouthed off?"

"Y-y-you leave me alone."

"You know why you sta-sta-stutter, Stinky?" Jimmy Mac's eyes were bloodshot like they were every morning on the bus. A gold loop earring dangled from each ear, the newest piercing a big silver hook stuck through his eyebrow like a fishhook. "It's ba-ba-because you're a re-re-retard."

You don't stand up to bullies, they end up owning a piece of you forever.

Sammy's dad said that when it came to fighting, all that mattered was winning. Jimmy Mac may be taller and wicked strong, but there was one spot where he would hurt the most. His face burning, his stomach full of bubbles moving so fast through his body it made his knees knock, Sammy wound up and kicked Jimmy Mac dead center in his apple sack.

Jimmy Mac grabbed his crotch with both hands and dropped to his knees, his eyes tearing up like a girl's, his mouth forming a silent, quivering O.

One kick to the balls didn't seem like just punishment. Sammy wanted Jimmy to feel more humiliation, more pain—wanted to get even for all the other kids Jimmy tortured on a daily basis. Sammy saw that silver loop sticking out of Jimmy Mac's eyebrow and before he could stop himself, reached down and ripped it off.

Jimmy Mac howled, blood bursting across his forehead.

Sammy grabbed his snowboard and fled into the snow. He didn't see the little girl Sarah until he ran straight into her. For the second time in ten minutes someone had knocked her on her butt.

"I'm wicked sorry," Sammy said, helping her get back up.

"My glasses," the girl cried.

Crap. He couldn't leave her here without her glasses. That wasn't right.

"I'll help you find them, okay? Just stop crying."

Just like his sister, the girl kept on crying. Man oh man oh man, why did they always carry on like this?

"It's okay, really, stop crying."

Sammy was on his knees, searching the snow— where did those glasses go?—when a man, the girl's father, stepped up next to him.

"It was an accident, I swear," Sammy said. "I didn't mean to knock into her. I just wasn't looking where I was going."

The man wore jeans and had on black gloves and this big blue parka with a hood on it that covered his face, the jacket similar to the one Sammy's dad wore when he snowplowed the driveway, only this hood had fur running around the edge, the brown colors reminding Sammy of raccoon fur. A blanket was tucked under the man's arm. Without a word, the man reached down and grabbed the girl's hand. She yanked it away. Typical girl, being a brat.

"Her glasses fell off," Sammy said. "I think that's why she's crying. I didn't hurt her, I swear."

The girl's dad kicked the snowboard over to Sammy and then made a shooing motion with his hand, the signal for Sammy to beat it.

"I'm sorry," Sammy said again. Before he snowboarded down the hill, the last thing he saw was the girl's dad whispering something against her ear as he wrapped the blanket around her body.

The next morning, Sammy wasn't thinking about Jimmy Mac or the little girl; he was thinking about electricity. It came back on early, around nine, about an hour after the snow stopped. Sammy was deep into playing Tony Hawk on his PlayStation 2 when his dad, Officer Tom Pinkerton, came in and asked Sammy if he knew anything about a girl in a pink snowsuit named Sarah Sullivan.

Next thing Sammy knew, he was down at the police station. He had met almost all the policemen at barbecues and softball games. Normally they would stop and say hi, but this morning, their faces were serious, mad even, and they buzzed around the police station in a flurry of activity, answering phones, shouting questions and orders to each other. Abducted. Missing. Disappeared. Those were the words Sammy kept hearing as Detective Francis Merrick opened the door to his office and asked Sammy to come inside—alone. Detective Merrick shut the door and Sammy sat down in the chair across from the big desk, Sammy thinking, *I'm about to talk to a detective, man oh man, I'm in serious trouble.*

Tomorrow Never Knows

(2004)

CHAPTER 6

Friday morning, just shy of five A.M., Mike sat alone inside his truck, watching a light snow falling over the Hill. He wanted a cigarette badly but didn't want to ruin the smell of the lilacs. Every year, on the eve of Sarah's anniversary, he had them shipped overnight to DeCarlo's Florist, and now the lilacs sat wrapped in plastic on the passenger seat, the flowers' overpowering but pleasant scent filling the truck and taking him back to that one spring when Sarah—she must have been all of three at the time—had asked him if she could take some lilacs from the tree in the backyard and place them in her room, Sarah going on and on about how much she loved the way they smelled. He propped her on his shoulders, and after they filled up one of her beach pails with flowers, they headed upstairs and placed the flowers around her room.

No, Daddy, put the flowers under *the pillows, not* on *the pillows.*

Her exact words, but the voice was still wrong. It was Sarah's voice, but it was still stuck at six. He couldn't remember how she sounded at three or four and he had no idea as to how her voice might sound like now, five years later, at eleven—eleven *and a half*. Now her body would be on the cusp of puberty, about to begin that slow, awkward transformation from girl to young woman. He could see her trading in her glasses for contacts. Knowing her, the ponytail would be gone—too little girl—her new hairstyle one of those short, messy hairdos he had seen on a lot of young girls lately. Her ears would be pierced—just one on each ear, he hoped, simple and tasteful—and she'd probably be wearing some jewelry, not much, and she would be dabbling with makeup and taking an interest in clothes, seeing how they fit against her growing curves—all of these small changes pushing her down the road to boys. If he saw her right now, he wondered if there would still be some of the last, lingering traces of the little girl who thought a fun afternoon was tossing a Nerf football in the backyard.

Mike could picture all of these things crystal clear in his mind, but Sarah's face, as always, remained a blur.

Sure, he had pictures. He had the ones he had taken over her six years with him, and the National Center for Missing and Exploited Children had provided the new pictures, ones spit out by a computer showing, in dozens of dizzying combinations, what Sarah might look like today. But as good of a job as they did with Sarah's picture each year—and they did a damn good job—sorting through all of those possible combinations had only muddied his head. At night, he would lie in bed and try to form a face but all his mind's eye saw was his gap-toothed little girl with her crooked glasses. And now that was fading too. The only time he seemed to have a lock on her was when he drank, but he couldn't drink anymore because of the court order.

The sun was starting to rise behind the trees in the woods when Mike grabbed the flowers, opened the door and walked around the front of the truck. The floodlight was on, always on, always shining down on the empty, white hill. He walked over to the spot where he had found Sarah's sled and knelt down, balancing his weight on the balls of his feet, and placed the lilacs on the snow. The fragrance of the flowers was strong, even out here in the wind, and as he stared at the place where Sarah had last stood, he again thought about how the air had no beginning or end, how he liked to imagine the powerful scent of these flowers blowing through other cities, blowing into Sarah's room where she was sleeping right now, maybe even waking her up, Mike thinking that maybe his daughter would smell the lilacs and it would trigger a memory, Sarah remembering him and the room waiting for her back in Belham. Maybe today she would pick up the phone and call home. Totally ridiculous, maybe, but that was the thing about hope. It made you believe in anything.

*　　　*　　　*

Dr. Rachel Tylo's Boston office had gray walls painted the color of thunderstorms and a white couch and matching chair that were as stiff as her glass-top coffee table. With the exception of the two expensively framed degrees, both from Harvard, the only personal item was the oil painting hanging above her desk, a wide canvas full of the kind of drips, squiggles and blots found on a housepainter's drop-cloth.

The door opened and here Dr. T came, looking more like Mr. T, a teetering powerhouse of doughy flesh wrapped in a designer suit and clouds of perfume. Peeking out from the stack of folders clasped under her arm was the past Sunday's *Boston Globe Magazine*.

Dr. T saw him eyeing it and said, "Why didn't you tell me about it?"

"Not much to tell," he said. "When Sarah's anniversary date draws closer, I call up my contacts in the press and ask them if they can run a story. It helps keep interest alive."

"I was referring to the side story on your father."

"I had no idea the reporters were going to talk with him." Which was true. And Mike had to admit he was impressed how the reporter or reporters had managed not only to track Lou down in Florida but had somehow convinced him to talk.

She settled in her chair. "This is the first time he's spoken out about his granddaughter, correct?"

"I have no idea."

"What's your reaction?"

"I don't have one."

Dr. T's eyes were fastened on him, watching and gauging his reactions for what the court called his "anger-management issues." First came the anger-management course, followed by this, forty-eight mandatory sessions designed around the ridiculous premise of figuring out why he had attacked Francis Jonah, the man everyone knew was responsible for Sarah's disappearance and the disappearance of two other girls: five-year-old Caroline Lenville from Seattle, Washington; and Ashley Giroux, age six, from Woodstock, Vermont.

Lou had nothing to do with any of this, but Dr. T, man, she just *loved* to poke her nose around in this area. Mike had to fill up the time somehow, so he had thrown out some general stories about growing up with Lou, about how Lou started out as a thief, robbing houses in posh suburbs before graduating to the more sophisticated jobs: cleaning out warehouses of computer and electrical equipment, the armored car heists in Charlestown and Cambridge. Lou's old gang all dead now—all except Lou.

Dr. T used one of the yellow bookmarks, flipped the magazine open and found the page. "The reporter asks your father if he's talked with you since your daughter's disappearance, and your father says: 'Michael and I haven't talked about much since the day he got married. That's his choice. Some men need hate to get them through the day.'"

She looked up for an answer. Mike stared at the diamond ring, three carats by the looks of it. Ring like that, she probably had a live-in nanny and a house in some place like Weston where she lived with her husband (probably a surgeon), dog (a Golden or Lab, depending on what was "in" in Weston at the time) and 2.5 kids (boys with names like Thad and Hunter). Her Harvard-bought observations and solutions might have been a big hit with the bored housewives looking for a sympathetic ear and a chemical vacation from the monotony of their nicely polished lives, but it meant jack shit when applied to enigmas like Lou Sullivan.

"Any thoughts?"

"Not really," Mike said.

"I believe your father gave this interview because he's trying to reach out to you and possibly make amends."

Mike leaned forward and picked up his cup of coffee from the glass table. "My old man reaching out? All due respect, I think you're the one who's reaching here."

"The reason I'm pressing you on this is because I want to make sure you're looking at your father the way he stands now and not through a leftover filter from your childhood."

"A filter from my childhood," Mike repeated evenly.

"Yes. We tend to view our parents by their roles and not as people. I've noticed that you especially tend to view people in either-or terms—good or bad, smart or dumb. I can certainly appreciate your feelings regarding your father, and I'm not trying to placate you by saying that I have an idea what it was like growing up with a father who was not only a thief but was also unpredictably violent."

Don't forget murderer, Mike added privately.

"That being said, there's clearly another side to him, the one that raised you after your mother left, took you to sporting events. The side your mother loved at one point."

His eyes slid over to the wall clock. Forty minutes and then it was sayonara.

"If he was willing to share his feelings in print," Dr. T was saying, "then maybe he would be willing to open up and share the truth about your mother."

Mike thought about the pewter keychain in his front pocket, the keychain a circular disc containing an etching of St. Anthony holding the baby Jesus, the back an etching of a church in Paris, Sacré-Coeur in Montmartre. The keychain had arrived in a package to Bill's house a month after she left. Mike had read the letter so many times he could recite the words: *The next time I write, I'll have an address where you can write me. Soon you'll be with me here in Paris. Have faith, Michael. Remember to have faith, no matter how bad it gets. And remember to keep this quiet. I don't have to remind you what your father would do to me if he found out where I was hiding.*

The second letter never came, but four months later, in July, Lou had come home from a three-day business trip, called Mike out into the backyard and launched into a spiel about how his mother wasn't coming home. Lou made the mistake of leaving his suitcase open. Mike walked by Lou's bedroom, and when he saw the camera sitting on top of the opened suitcase, he went in, did a little investigating and found the envelope holding a passport and plane tickets to Paris. Only the tickets were under the name Thom Peterson—the name that ran under the slightly altered passport photo of Lou.

"Look," Mike said. "I know you're gunning for some type of Oprah moment where I have, I dunno, some sort of emotional breakdown. That's not going to happen."

"Are you aware that your voice changes when you talk about your father?"

Thirty-five minutes left. He had to fill up the time somehow.

"Cadillac Jack," Mike said. "I've mentioned him a couple of times."

"He's one of your father's friends, a gangster who ran a garage."

"The garage was really a chop shop. He also ran a numbers joint out of there. Everyone thought Jack Scarlatta got the name because he had a thing for Caddies. He did, only it was because he could fit two, three bodies in the trunk, take them out to this quiet place in Quincy and pop them. You know what 'getting popped' means, right?"

"Yes," Dr. T said stiffly. "Unfortunately, my husband insists on watching *The Sopranos.*"

"So you have an idea what I'm talking about. Cadillac Jack and my old man were good friends from high school. Went to Vietnam together, only Cadillac Jack came back first while Lou stayed over there for another year and served time in a bamboo jail as a POW—ironically enough, the only jail time my old man would ever serve. Lou came back, and Cadillac Jack was running the

Mission Hill gang. My old man had a talent for cracking safes. There's not a safe on the planet he can't crack. The two of them had a great thing going until about five, six years ago when Cadillac Jack introduced Lou to this FBI agent named Bobby Stevens. You remember reading that in the papers?"

"Robert Stevens was allegedly a corrupt FBI agent. I remember there was a big investigation."

"Now the thing you've got to understand about the Irish is that there's nothing lower on this planet than a snitch. You don't rat out your friends, and in Belham, you protect your own. You see someone get shot, when the cops come around asking questions, you keep your mouth shut. Now Cadillac Jack, he was playing this FBI agent—you know, dropping Stevens some tips in exchange for information on what Jack's competitors were up to. Jack was feeding the FBI guy false leads. But in my old man's eyes, it was only a matter of time until his best friend Jack ratted him out. You know what happened to him?"

"I'm afraid I don't."

"Neither do I. They never found his body."

"You're suggesting your father killed him?"

"The night before he disappeared, I heard the two of them arguing in the kitchen, my old man saying that they should go for a ride, get some fresh air and think this through. Jack never made it back home."

"Maybe he's on the lam."

Mike sighed. "You remember the armored car heists from about five years ago? Three cars were hit in

Charlestown and Boston? Happened about two weeks before my daughter disappeared? These guys walked away with close to two million."

"Vaguely." She looked bored now. "Those stories generally don't hold my interest."

"It was the old Mission Hill crew. Seven of them. A week later they found all seven bodies in the trunks of three different Caddys parked at Logan. They were poisoned with arsenic. Lou was in Florida laundering the money."

"That's a lot of supposition."

"You're right. I should have mentioned that point to the FBI agents who kept popping by the house."

"Your father is alive," Dr. T said. "It's my opinion that he will try and approach you in an attempt at reconciliation."

Jesus Christ, she just didn't get it.

"How you choose to deal with this, of course, is entirely up to you. I think it would be in your best interest to keep an open mind. I say this for two reasons. First, by opening a dialogue with your father, you may be able to shed some of the anger you still harbor. As you continue to be angry with him, you are, in fact, allowing him to hold power over you. Secondly, your father won't be around forever. Good or bad, he's your only link to the past. Maybe if you open up to him, he'll open up to you."

Mike checked the wall clock, managed to suppress a smile. "Looks like our time's about up."

"I'd like to talk about Jonah for a moment."

He felt the heat climb into his neck.

"The article mentioned he was dying of pancreatic cancer."

Dying. The word pressed against his chest like concrete blocks.

"You're wondering if Jonah's dying might suddenly prompt me to confront him again?"

"His impending death does carry a sense of urgency," Dr. T said.

"I'm sure the police are talking with him."

"As of today, you and I are finished with these sessions. You have another six weeks of probation. During that time, if you make contact with Jonah in any way, you'll be in violation of your probation, and this time the judge will have no choice but to send you to jail. It's not fair, but it's the law. The same is true of your drinking. Are you still attending meetings?"

"I work a lot."

"Still, you should make an effort to attend meetings."

"I've been sober for two years."

"I'm more concerned about when your probation period ends. You'll need a support system in place to help you deal with your alcoholism."

The anger had seeped up through his neck and was now working behind his eyes like coils of hot wire. When this happened—and it happened often when he sat in this chair—he stared at a spot on the carpet and started the visualization exercise he learned in his anger-management course. The image he used to calm himself was a variation on that final scene in *Misery* where a hobbled James Caan stuffed the pages of his charred manuscript into the mouth of his deranged nurse, Kathy Bates, Caan screaming, *That's it, choke on it. Eat it till ya choke, you sick, twisted fuck.* Only in Mike's version, he stuffed one dollar bills down Dr. T's throat 125 times, her hourly fee for this bullshit.

"Something wrong?" Dr. T asked.

"Just practicing one of those calming visualization exercises I learned in anger management."

"Really. And does it work?"

"Yes," Mike said. "It works amazingly well."

CHAPTER 7

His parole officer suffered from a major case of little man's complex and approached his job with a strict, by-the-book mentality. Thief, arsonist, rapist, murderer, drug user or pusher or the father of a missing girl who had beaten up the suspect believed by everyone to be responsible for his daughter's disappearance—in Anthony Testa's world you were all lumped together under the same label and fixed with the same level of contempt.

Testa propped his worn leather briefcase on the bathroom counter and clicked open the locks. They were standing inside the rest room of a Mobil gas station right around the corner from the Boston Garden (Mike refused to call it the Fleet Center; a bank, Jesus). Mike was about to head out of the city when his cell phone rang and Testa told him to turn around.

Testa handed him the cup and said, "You know the drill."

The terms of Mike's probation required him to urinate in front of him; it was the only way to make sure the urine sample was, in fact, his. Mike unzipped his fly, and when he started to fill the cup, Testa slid his cell phone back up to his ear and returned to the conversation, his chest puffed out as he paced inside the bathroom, pausing occasionally to check out the condition of his gelled hair in the mirror.

Inside Testa's briefcase was today's *Globe*. FIVE YEARS AND QUESTIONS STILL LINGER was the top headline; the story dominated the entire top half of the paper. The reporters hadn't used the computer-enhanced pictures of what Sarah would look like now, at eleven. Next to Sarah's smiling six-year-old face was a picture of Jonah dressed in a winter coat, holding onto his cane. The photographer had captured Jonah's frailty, the death pallor of his skin.

Sully, you're one lucky son of a bitch.

The voice of his lawyer, Jimmy Douchette. Nearly four years ago, on a cold afternoon in late March, Mike had been gutting a kitchen in Wayland when his phone rang and Douchette's secretary was on the other end telling Mike to drop what he was doing and to get to the office ASAP. Less than an hour later, Mike stepped inside Douchette's sixth floor office with its sweeping view of the Charles River and found the lawyer on the phone, Douchette coming up on sixty, with white, wispy hair and skin that looked like sun-dried leather.

Criminal. That word a constant hum through Mike's thoughts day and night. It didn't matter that Jonah owned a jacket that was an exact match to the one described by the witness, the boy, Sammy Pinkerton. It didn't matter that on the next morning, Saturday, when the storm broke around nine and the bloodhounds had followed Sarah's scent through the trails to an old, weather-beaten Victorian, the boyhood home of Francis Jonah—only Jonah was going by the name of David Peters now. It didn't matter that Jonah was a now-defrocked priest who made two other young girls with blond hair disappear. What mattered was evidence.

Evidence, Mike learned, was the Holy Grail. No evidence = no case. The Belham detectives had come in with all their collective experience and forensic teams and examined every inch of Jonah's house, his tool shed in the backyard, his van, and failed to come away with the two most important items: DNA and fiber evidence. That meant Francis Jonah could hold a press conference and play the part of victim, right down to asking the public to pray for the safe return of Sarah Sullivan— Jonah could, if he wanted to, stand at the top of the Hill and watch all the little girls sledding. Jonah was a free man and free men could do anything they wanted.

Building a case takes time, Mr. Sullivan. You need to be patient, Mr. Sullivan. We're doing everything we can, Mr. Sullivan.

The police were good men, he supposed, but they didn't understand. To them Sarah was just another file with a docket number and some notes. Sarah was *his* daughter, and to ask him to be patient while this asshole who knew what had happened went about his daily life—Mike couldn't take another day of dragging that knowledge from one moment to the next and taking it to bed with him at night.

That night Mike had been drunk, too drunk. He wasn't denying that, but swear to Christ he went over there with the intention of talking to Jonah. Reasoning with him.

Douchette hung up the phone. "That was Jonah's lawyer."

Mike didn't move. For the past three weeks, while Jonah lay in the hospital, recuperating from the attack that had left him with three broken ribs and a severe concussion, Mike had tried to wrap his brain around the concept of possibly spending five to eight years of his life inside a jail cell. Facing it now it still seemed more like a foreign concept than a reality—like he was being asked to pack up for a vacation to Mars.

But he didn't regret it. Even now, as he stood in his lawyer's office, Mike didn't have the urge to step back in time and rewrite history. About Jess, yes, he did have regrets. If he went to jail, she could cash out their retirement savings and pay down a big chunk of the mortgage but she would still have to get a job, probably back in her field, teaching, and that salary would barely cover the monthly expenses. In all likelihood, she would have to sell the house and then either get an apartment or move back in with her mother. As for his nighttime visit to Jonah, his only regret was that he hadn't learned what the son of a bitch knew about Sarah.

Douchette flipped open the folder. Mike's breath

caught in his throat, a feeling of dread wrapping itself around his skin.

"Jonah's decided to drop all charges," Douchette said. "And he's promised not to sue."

Mike exhaled.

"As for the exact reasons, I couldn't tell you. Jonah's lawyer wouldn't say, but if I had to venture a guess, I'd say it's about spin control. Doing this shows everyone he has compassion. How many monsters out there have compassion, right?" Douchette shook his head. "You're one lucky son of a bitch, Sully. But before you go ahead and thank me, you better listen to the terms of the deal."

Three years probation including a five-week stay at an alcohol treatment program. After that came random drug testing—fail a test, get caught having so much as a single beer and he'd be riding the bus to Walpole to serve a minimum of five years. Six hundred hours of community service at the head trauma unit at Mass General. Two months of anger management classes that met three nights a week; after that, twenty-four sessions of private therapy, $100 to $150 an hour, depending on the shrink. All of it paid out of Mike's pocket. Jess did end up going back to teaching. It was the only way to cover the bills.

Mike placed the urine sample on the counter, and after he zipped up, he capped the sample with the plastic lid.

Testa snapped his cell phone shut. "Still on that job in Newton?"

"Still there."

"How long?"

"End of the month," Mike said. Part of his probation required proof of employment. That meant showing Testa check stubs, receipts—anything the P.O. wanted. Testa liked to examine everything. Nothing was going to slide by him. No sir, no way.

"Breathalyzer's next to the briefcase."

Mike washed his hands, and after he finished drying them with a paper towel, he picked up the portable breathalyzer, blew into it and handed it back to Testa, who read the meter.

"Clear. No booze."

"Imagine that," Mike said. "Clean and sober at eight-thirty in the morning."

"Joke about it all you want, but a lot of alkies like to booze it up in the morning, figuring I won't catch them."

Mike thought about correcting him, saying that even at his worst, he had never taken a drink in the morning or slipped behind the wheel when he was loaded—hungover, definitely, but never drunk. In Testa's eyes, though, a drunk was a drunk and always would be a drunk, and Mike wasn't about to justify himself to a midget with a terminal case of assholeitis.

"We about done here?" Mike said. "Some of us don't get paid by the hour."

"What time you kicking off work tonight?"

"Around six."

"And after that?"

"I haven't really thought about it."

"Well think about it now."

Mike reached into his jacket pocket and came back with an envelope that contained a copy of his next contract, another addition in Wellesley. "You want to spend your evening checking to see whether or not I'm drinking, go ahead and knock yourself out," he said, and placed the envelope on top of his urine sample.

"Remember the last time you got caught boozing?"

Strike two: Mike had made the mistake of getting bombed on the eve of Sarah's third anniversary, Mike doing it alone, at home, when Anthony Testa rang the doorbell at ten at night for a random drug test. No jail time, but the judge ordered up another round of therapy sessions with Dr. T, another stay at an alcohol treatment program. Mike had to start at zero again, work his way back up.

"You get caught again drinking or if I find booze in your system, that's strike three, game over," Testa said. "You can either go to jail or you can get your life back. How you want to play it is entirely up to you."

Mike opened the bathroom door and stepped outside into the bright winter sunshine, wondering what life Testa was referring to.

CHAPTER 8

They spent the morning and early afternoon installing the windows for Margaret Van Buren's sprawling two-floor addition in Newton, one of the more posh cities located west of Boston. At two, they broke for lunch. The three guys who worked for them were all in their early twenties and single and talked incessantly about the upcoming weekend: the bars they were going to hit, the different girls they were seeing and dated and wanted to date; the ones they wanted to dump.

Bill picked up his lunch. "I can't listen to this anymore," he said to Mike. "I'm drowning in diapers and these guys are having hot tub parties with bikini models."

They sat inside Mike's truck, eating the subs Bill had picked up downtown, Bill talking about last night's escapades with the twins: Grace and Emma wide awake at two in the morning and coloring in their room when Emma decided to shove the red crayon up her nose.

"Check this out," Bill said. "Me and Patty took the

kids out last night to the Border Café up on Route One. There was a wait, so I went up to the bar to grab a beer and notice every guy's got their bone tuned to the broad in a black suit and glasses kicking back a beer and reading *The Sporting News*. It was Sam."

"Samantha Ellis?"

"The one and only."

Her name brought up one of the best periods in Mike's life—the summer after Jess's freshman year at UNH, a time when he and Jess had decided to see other people.

Bill said, "She moved back here a year, year and a half ago. She's working at a law firm in downtown Boston— one of those places with six names that when you're done saying it gives you a headache. Harrington, Dole, something and something. Middle age is treating her *real* well. Got this nice J. Lo thing going on."

"J. Lo?"

"Yeah, Jennifer Lopez. Don't you watch MTV?"

"I haven't watched MTV since Joan Jett was the big thing."

"You're missing out. With the rap videos, station's like soft-core porn now."

"Let me ask you something," Mike said. "That article in last Sunday's *Globe* magazine. You read the interview with Lou?"

Bill nodded, grinning as he chewed. "Your old man missed his calling as a comic."

"The ice queen thinks Lou's going to reach out. You know, try and patch things up."

"You serious?"

"She was," Mike said and took another bite of his meatball sub.

"You should have told her about Cadillac Jack."

"Funny you should mention that."

"And?"

"Not even a dent."

"Arrange a get-together. She spends a minute talking with him, I guarantee you she'll walk away feeling like she's got bite marks all over her skin."

Or he'd kill her, Mike thought. *Bury her someplace where nobody will ever find her.*

Mike looked out the window, thinking of his mother.

Bill said, "I got an extra ticket tonight to Grace and Emma's play. You should come along. Trust me, it's going to be a comedy show."

"Dotty Conasta called again. She has a couple of questions she wants answered before she signs. I was thinking of swinging by."

Bill grinned. "You haven't met her yet, have you?"

"No. Why?"

"I was over there two nights ago, about to go over the plans for the addition when she tells me to wait. She wants her husband to listen in."

"So?"

"Her husband's in an urn. That job's got Excedrin written all over it."

Mike's cell rang. Had to be Testa. The guy was going to go out of his way to break balls today.

It wasn't Testa. The caller was Rose Giroux, the mother of Jonah's second victim, Ashley Giroux.

With the news of Sarah's disappearance came the news of Jonah's identity, his background as a priest and his tie to the two other girls, all of it being played over the airwaves and newspapers. Rose Giroux, this warm beach ball of a woman with dyed blond hair and too much makeup, came to Belham to offer her support and share the mistakes she and her husband had made with Ashley's investigation. It was Rose who had explained the importance of using the media to keep interest alive. Jess embraced her. In the beginning, Mike did everything in his power to avoid her.

Lying underneath Rose's experience and well-intentioned advice and prayers and need to hug and cry and share every emotion was the unspoken fact that Sarah wouldn't be coming home. He'd hear that sorrow welded to her voice and make some excuse to leave the room. *That's not going to be me. There's still time to find Sarah.* A week turned into a month, into three months and then half a year and it was only then Mike felt he could talk with Rose.

"I was just calling to see how you were doing today," Rose said.

"I'm doing. And yourself?"

"About the same."

"How's Sean?" In addition to calling on Sarah's anniversary date and the sporadic calls throughout the year, Rose would write long letters to Mike, detailing the events in her family and the lives of her three other children as if to reassure herself—or maybe to show him—that it was possible to pick up and move on.

"Sean's going to Harvard Medical this fall."

"You and Ted must be proud."

"Yes. Yes, we are." Rose sounded detached, or maybe she was just tired. "I read the article, the one from last Sunday's *Globe.*"

The reporter said he was going to interview Rose and, hopefully, Suzanne Lenville. When Mike read the article, he saw that Ashley Giroux and Caroline Lenville had been reduced to bylines: Ashley Giroux had been missing for sixteen years, Caroline Lenville for twenty-five. Caroline's mother, Suzanne, had divorced a decade ago and had remarried, changed her name and disappeared. She didn't give interviews, didn't talk about what had happened to her daughter.

"I read about you and Jess," Rose said. "How long have you two been separated?"

From the time I came home and told her that Sarah hadn't come back down the hill. "About two years," Mike said.

"Ted and I went through a rough patch. We went to counseling, and that really helped. In fact, I have a list of several counselors who specialize—"

"It's over. We signed the divorce papers last month." And he was fine with that. Honest to God he was. After everything he put her through, she deserved a shot at a new life.

"I'm so sorry, Michael."

The call-waiting on Mike's phone beeped. He checked the caller ID. St. Stephen's Church.

"Rose, I've got another call. Can I call you later?"

"I'll be home. Before I let you go: Is it true about the cancer?"

"I'm afraid so."

"Are the police talking to Jonah?"

"That's the word." Although that hadn't come from the police; Mike had learned it from the reporter doing the article. "The second I find out anything, Rose, I'll call you."

"Thank you, Michael. God be with you."

"You too, Rose. Thanks for calling." Mike hit the TALK button and switched to the incoming phone call. "Hello."

"Michael, Father Connelly."

Hearing Father Jack's voice triggered a rush of memories: the beer and peanut smell of the old Boston Garden as they watched the Celtics in their heyday, Bird and McHale and Parish leading them to another championship; Jess in her wedding dress, walking down the aisle of St. Stephen's; Father Jack coming into Mass General to visit Sarah; Father Jack baptizing Sarah.

"I don't know if this is my place," Father Jack said, "but Jess just left here. She's . . . she's very upset."

"What happened?"

"I didn't have any other appointments scheduled. I had no idea he was going to be there."

Mike tightened his grip on the phone.

"She stepped out of my office and saw him in the waiting room," Father Jack explained. "I tried to calm her down—tried to get her to go back in my office and close the door. I told her I'd drive her home afterward, but she tore out of here before—"

"Why was Jonah there?"

"I don't know Jess's cell phone number. Otherwise, I would have called her."

"You going to answer my question, or are you going to keep avoiding it?"

Father Jack swallowed audibly. The silence lingered.

"That's what I thought," Mike said and hung up.

CHAPTER 9

The last time Mike had set foot in Rowley was about a year and a half ago, the day of Jess's mother's funeral. After the funeral, Jess thanked him for coming and invited him to stop by the house. He did, partly out of respect for Jodi Armstrong but more so for Sarah. It was around that time his memories were starting to blur. Maybe seeing a place where Sarah had spent so many weekends and holidays would stimulate that part of his mind responsible for holding onto her.

A light snow was falling when Mike pulled into Jess's driveway. He shut off the truck, grabbed the flowers from the passenger seat, got out, and jogged up the walkway and onto the porch, about to open the door and rush in when he remembered his new position in her life. He shut the door and rang the doorbell. A moment later, the front door opened in a *whoosh*.

For a half second, he didn't recognize her. Jess had blond highlights in her hair, had cut it short, thick and messy as if waking up from sleep, and while she wasn't dressed up by any means—she wore stone-colored khakis and a white shirt—he had the feeling that she was clearly expecting someone else. The smile on her face turned into a look of surprise, maybe even mild shock, when she saw him standing there with a bouquet of flowers.

"Father Jack called me," he said.

Jess's eyes dropped to her shoes as she opened the storm door.

"I tried calling you on your cell phone, then here."

"I shut my cell phone off and went out for a bit," she said. "I just got back a few minutes ago. Come in."

The foyer was warm and eerily quiet—no TV or radio was on—and filled with the unmistakable smell of spaghetti sauce, Mike remembering the pleasure she took from this task, an Irish girl making homemade sauce from scratch. Two black suitcases, gifts he had given her one Christmas eons ago, sat on the white-tiled floor, near the foot of the stairs.

She shut the door. Mike handed her the flowers.

"Calla lilies," she said. They were Jess's favorite flower. "They're beautiful."

"I just wanted to make sure you were okay."

The phone rang.

"Excuse me for a second," Jess said, and Mike watched as she walked into the kitchen, placing the flowers on the counter, then plucked the cordless phone from its wall-mounted base.

Confession. That was the only reason Jonah would

have stopped by to see Father Jack. Despite his defrocked status, Jonah was still a devout Catholic—Mike had heard that Jonah went to the six A.M. mass every Sunday at St. Stephen's. Funeral preparations could have been neatly handled over the phone, so for Jonah to stop by like that, in person, meant he must have wanted to receive the sacrament of reconciliation. You couldn't do that over the phone. To stop by like that, out of the blue, meant that Jonah knew he had only a few days left.

Or hours.

"Of course I understand," Jess whispered from the kitchen. She picked up her wine glass, took a long pull and quickly swallowed. "I'm fine, honest. Don't worry about it."

Mike knew that tone. Jess was angry but didn't want the person on the other end to know it.

"I'll just meet you at the airport. . . . Right, me too. Bye."

Jess hung up and walked briskly back into the foyer, doing her best to hide her disappointment.

"Going someplace warm, I hope," Mike said, pointing to the suitcases.

"Five-week trip to Paris and then Italy."

"Going with one of your sisters?"

"No," Jess said, her smile thin. "Just a friend."

The way she said *friend* meant a male friend, a boyfriend or something more serious.

"Good for you," Mike said, and meant it. Jess seemed uncomfortable, so he changed the topic. "Your mother always talked about going to Italy."

"My mother always talked about doing a lot of things. Last week, I was cleaning out the spare bedroom and found a lump under the carpet. Guess what I found? Envelopes full of savings bonds dating back to the fifties. I'm talking stacks of them. She could have bought and paid for this house three times over."

"Your mother always thought the next Great Depression was a day away."

"She was hoarding all this money and for what?" Jess blew out a long stream of air and shook her head. "I made lasagna. Would you like to join me for dinner? And no, you're not intruding."

He could tell by the tone of her voice that she wanted him to stay. He didn't want to have dinner with his ex-wife and revisit the life he once had. He started to sort through a list of possible excuses while another part of his mind calculated all the times Jess had picked up his drunk ass from McCarthy's Bar; the times she had cleaned up his vomit and all the broken fragments of the glasses, mugs, plates he had thrown against the wall because he was drunk, because he was terrified for Sarah and because his marriage was dissolving and there wasn't a goddamn thing he could do to stop it—and let us not forget the months she had stuck by him when it looked like they might lose the house, all the money they had saved now going to bail and lawyer's fees. Jess had any number of reasons to bail and she didn't. She had hung in there with him, and while she was entitled to half of everything they owned, she wanted only two things in the divorce settlement: copies of the pictures and videos of Sarah; and items that had belonged to her mother.

"Dinner would be great," he said.

A pan of lasagna was on the stove, the island counter-top set with a pair of crystal wine glasses, a bottle of opened red wine and two plates. Jess had been expecting company.

Mike took off his jacket and draped it over the back of one of the island chairs as Jess picked up the plates. Above the kitchen sink was a window overlooking the three-season room. The backyard lights were on, and Mike could see the monstrous jungle gym set, a birthday gift from Jodi when Sarah turned two. He stared at it, thinking how lonely it looked, neglected and forgotten.

"How's work?" she asked.

"Busy, as always. You still a secretary for that accounting firm in Newburyport?"

"Still there. The pay's better than teaching, believe it or not. And the politically correct term, just so you know, is administrative assistant." She smiled as she handed him a plate, and then opened up the refrigerator and came back with a cold can of Coke.

Jess sat down, picked up a linen napkin and spread it across her lap. She picked up her fork, put it back down.

"He held the door open for me."

Mike rubbed the back of his head and neck.

"He was standing there with this . . . this sick grin. 'You're looking real good, Mrs. Sullivan. Life in Rowley must really be agreeing with you.' Then he held the door open for me. I couldn't get out of there fast enough."

"Why didn't you call me?"

"What could you have done?"

"I could have driven you home."

"And if you came to the parking lot, you'd have been in violation of your probation. All Jonah had to do was see you through Father Jack's office window and they'd be hauling you off to jail. That's our great legal system at work."

"I'm sorry, Jess." Mike not quite sure what he was apologizing for: her visit with Jonah or for all of it.

She waved him off, telling him she was over it.

"You have any idea why Jonah was there?" he asked.

"You'd have to ask Father Jack."

"I tried that. He wouldn't tell me."

Jess picked up the wine bottle and poured the wine, the *glug-glug* sound reminding him of Jack being poured over ice, of those evenings where he couldn't wait to get home and have that first long slow burn hit his stomach.

She saw him looking at the bottle. "I don't have to drink."

"It's fine. Why did you go to see Father Jack this afternoon?"

"To say goodbye." She put the bottle back on the table and folded her arms. "I'm moving."

"Where?"

"New York. The city."

Mike put down his fork, fear brushing against the walls of his heart.

"A friend—a friend of a friend, actually—his business is moving to Japan," Jess explained. "He owns this beautiful apartment on the Upper East Side and is letting me sublet it for a few months. It's a beautiful place—and a rare opportunity."

"Sounds expensive."

"It is. But I have the money my mother left me, and now the savings bonds. The apartment's on the fifteenth floor and it has this amazing view of the city. It's just so beautiful."

Yes, you've mentioned that twice now. He said, "Why New York? Why not go to San Diego? Be close to your sister and the kids?"

Jess paused, licked her lips. "Do you ever feel like packing up and starting over someplace where nobody knows the first thing about you?"

"I've thought of it, sure." *In fact, that night on the Hill, I actually wished for it,* Mike added privately.

"So why don't you?"

He picked up his fork, thought about it for a moment. "One morning, it must have been about six months after your mother had moved in here, I was having coffee with her. I was telling her how much I liked the house and she said, 'There are no memories here, just echoes.' That always stuck with me."

"It's not just about people staring," Jess said. "When my father died, he left her two life insurance policies and a nice sum of money so my mother wouldn't have to worry. She bought this house, figuring me, Rachel and Susan would live close to her and keep her busy with grandchildren. Then Rachel moved away, and Susan, well, she never wanted kids to begin with, and when Sarah disappeared, my mother . . . she just kept wishing for a different life. I don't want to become that person. Being afraid all the time because I wished things were different. Can you understand that?"

"Sure."

"You think you'll ever sell the house?"

Mike shrugged. "Someday."

"She's never coming home," Jess said gently.

He picked up his Coke and took a long sip, feeling it burn its way down his throat. He was getting angry and wasn't sure why. It didn't have to do with her comments about Sarah or selling the house. She had said them before, so why was he getting mad now?

It was New York. His only remaining connection to Sarah was moving away.

Mike put his can back on the table, rubbed his thumb across the surface. "Can you still see her?"

"I haven't forgotten her. I think about her all the time."

"What I mean is, when you close your eyes, can you see her the way she would look now?"

"I remember Sarah the way she was."

"I can't see her face anymore. I can hear her voice just fine, and I can remember the things Sarah said and did, but her face is always a blur. I didn't have this problem before."

"When you were drinking."

Mike nodded. When he drank, he'd lie on Sarah's bed and close his eyes and he'd see her as clear as day, and the two of them would have the most amazing conversations.

Jess said, "Today I was in a bookstore and this boy, he couldn't have been any more than four, was in line holding a copy of *Make Way for Ducklings*. You remember the first time you read her that story?"

"Sarah was around three. You purchased the book as a Christmas gift. It was Sarah's favorite book."

"The first time you read it, Sarah begged us to take her into Boston to see the ducks, remember?"

Mike felt a smile reach his face. He remembered how disappointed Sarah was to learn that the swan boats inside the Public Garden weren't actually real swans. That disappointment had nearly turned into tears when Sarah saw the bronze statues of the mother duck and the baby ducklings. *These aren't the ducks from the story, Daddy. These ducks aren't real.* It was during the ride home that Sarah came up with an explanation: *I know why the ducks are made of metal, Daddy. It's 'cause so people can't hurt them. Those kids were sitting on the backs of the mother duck and baby ducks, and if I had people sit on my back all day my back would hurt too. They're made of metal during the day so they won't get hurt. At night when everybody's at home in bed sleeping, that's when they turn into real ducks and go swimming in the pond with the real swans.* Sarah had been sitting in her car seat in the back of the Explorer when she said those words. The back window was down, and the wind was whipping her blond hair around her face and Sarah wore a white sunhat and a pink sundress, both birthday gifts from Jess's mother, and Sarah had a chocolate stain on the dress. Sarah's face blurred again and started to fade, *no, please, Sarah. Please don't leave me.*

CHAPTER 10

Francis Jonah sat at the head of his dining room table, sucking in air from an oxygen mask. His skin appeared sunken, pulled tight against the bone, and the black cardigan sweater he wore looked two sizes too big. His hair, once gray, was now gone.

A thin woman with short brown hair parted in the middle placed a glass of water with a straw in front of him, Jonah nodding his thanks as the spidery fingers of his free hand reached across the table and clawed at the woman's hand.

Had to be either a private nurse or a hospice worker, Mike thought. Jess's mother had battled lung cancer, and when it was clear there was nothing more the doctors could do, Jodi opted to die at home, in her bed. A hospice worker, an overweight, patient man with a warm smile, had come in, his sole function being to relieve Jodi's pain, make sure she was comfortable.

Mike sat inside his truck parked across the street,

smoking a cigarette and watching as Jonah pulled his mouth away from the straw and started panting.

You need to turn around and leave.

Look at him. He could be dead tonight.

All he has to do is make one phone call and the police will haul your ass off to jail.

He knows what happened to Sarah. I can't let him take that into the ground with him.

The way Mike figured it, the human side of Jonah, whatever bit of it was left, if that side had been strong enough to seek out Father Jack this afternoon and confess his sins, maybe that human part of Jonah was still there, and maybe it was possible to tap into it again. Father Jack couldn't reveal what was said during the confession, but maybe he had mandated that Jonah, in order to be forgiven, had to confess what he knew and relieve the victims of their suffering.

Mike opened the truck door, got out and shut the door softly behind him.

The air was cold and raw as he walked across the street and then around the corner to Jonah's front gate. The porch lights were off. Good. He unlocked the gate, pushed it open and quietly moved up the walk and front steps and saw the same blue-painted door cut with the oval bubble of thick glass he had seen four years ago—only that night he had stumbled up these steps and banged on the door with one fist, the other punching the doorbell until the door swung open and there was Jonah dressed in a wrinkled pair of khakis and a yellowed undershirt, his gray hair tousled from sleep and sticking up at odd angles as he blinked himself awake.

Where is she?

I didn't have anything to do with what happened to your daughter, Mr. Sullivan. I'm innocent.

Innocent men don't change their names and go into hiding.

You're drunk, Mr. Sullivan. Please, go home.

Jonah went to shut the door and Mike put out his hand and stopped it.

You're going to tell me what happened to my daughter.

Only God knows what is true.

What? What did you say?

I can't give you what I don't have. I can't give you back your daughter, and I can't take away the guilt you feel for letting Sarah walk up that hill by herself.

When Mike snapped out of it, Slow Ed and his partner had him pinned to the floor. Jonah lay a few feet away, his body deathly still, his face swollen, bleeding and unrecognizable. As for how Jonah got that way, Mike was at a loss—still was.

Mike's cell phone rang, the loud, chirping sound cutting through the silent air, startling him. He had forgotten to shut the ringer off, turn it to vibration mode. He ripped the phone off his belt, about to power it off when he thought it might be his P.O. and decided to answer it.

"Hello," Mike whispered.

"You back off the porch right now, I'll pretend I never saw you," Slow Ed said.

Mike looked around the dark street for a patrol car.

Slow Ed said, "I'm giving you to the count of ten to get to your truck."

"He went to see Father Connelly today," Mike whispered. "You're Catholic. You know what that means."

"Ten."

"Has Merrick talked with him?"

"Nine."

"Ed, don't do this to me."

"Eight . . . seven . . ."

CHAPTER 11

"Daddy, I need you."

Sarah's voice crying out for him through the darkness of the house.

"Daddy, please."

Mike whipped back the sheets and marched down the hall, and when he opened the door to Sarah's room, he found it flooded with sunlight. Sarah lay in her bed with the covers pulled up around her face. The house, he saw, sat on a sheet of ice that seemed to stretch on for miles in every direction. The ice looked safe. It could support the weight of the house no problem.

One of Sarah's pillows was on the floor. He picked it up and saw a woman step up next to the window.

It was his mother.

"You can never trust the ice, Michael," she said. "You think you're safe and sometimes the ice breaks for no good reason. Once you slip underneath the water, it doesn't matter how good a swimmer you are, your clothes will weigh you down, you're going to drown."

Sarah said, "Why are you ignoring me?"

Mike pulled down the blanket. He couldn't see her face but heard her start crying again and she wouldn't stop so he placed the pillow over her face and held it there while his mother started singing the Beatles' "Tomorrow Never Knows," the song she always sang when she was upset.

He woke up from the dream, his heart twisting inside his chest.

The dream was still fresh in his mind but Sarah's face still eluded him. He kept his eyes shut, breathed deeply and tried chasing after her. Fang, all 130 pounds of him, snored beside him on the other side of the king-sized bed, the place where Jess slept, Sarah sometimes wedged between them when she had a bad nightmare. Man, did she have an imagination. She had somehow convinced herself that there were monsters under her bed and the only way to get rid of them was to take a flashlight, turn it on and leave it under the bed all night. Mike saw her body wrapped in her sheets, the purple Beanie Baby she carried with her everywhere she went lying beside her. Purple was her favorite color. One time Sarah dumped a Costco-sized container of grape Kool-Aid into a white load of laundry because she wanted all of her clothes purple. Sarah shoved a peanut butter sandwich into the VCR. Sarah snuck out of her crib and grabbed the permanent markers from his office drawer and used them to draw pictures on the wall above her crib, and he could see her standing in her crib, pointing at the wall that contained a stick-figured representation of the house that was colored brown and purple and had blue grass and a green sun and he still couldn't see her face at all and it terrified him.

Mike opened his eyes and stared at the ceiling.

"I haven't forgotten about you, sweets," he said to the empty room. "Daddy's just having trouble remembering."

Daddy.

The phone rang. Mike jumped, turned around and reached over for the cordless from the nightstand. Fang's head was up, sleepy-eyed and staring.

"Hello."

"I'm going to die in peace," Jonah wheezed. "You're not going to take that away from me, understand? Not you, not the police, not the press. You stay away from me or this time I'll send you to rot in jail."

Jonah hung up.

Mike yanked the phone away from his ear and stared at it as if it were a snake that had bitten him. He started to dial *69, then stopped.

The conditions of the restraining order were specific: no contact at all—and that included phone calls. If he called Jonah back, Jonah would call the police, and the police in turn would go to the phone company who would have a record of Mike's call. It didn't matter if Jonah called first. Jonah had that freedom, that right. Mike didn't.

Why did Jonah call? He had never called here before.

You're not going to take that away from me.

Take what away from him?

The phone rang again.

"Mike, it's Francis."

Francis Merrick, the detective in charge of Sarah's case.

"I'm sorry to bother you at such an hour," Merrick said, "but I need you to come down to Roby Park."

Mike's heart was beating in his throat. "What's going on?"

"It's best if I explain when you get here."

CHAPTER 12

Two police cruisers blocked the entrance to the Hill. A single uniformed cop stood out in the middle of East Dunstable Road, signaling the traffic out at this hour to keep moving. Mike pulled his truck over to the side, flung the door open and then ran over to the cop, the snow coming down in thick, heavy sheets.

The cop was Slow Ed's partner, Charlie Ripken.

"Merrick's at the top," Rip said, his gaze cutting away from Mike's and pointing past the cruiser's bursts of blue and white lights toward the Hill's floodlight. "Go on over."

Near the area where Mike had placed the lilacs early this morning were four posts sectioned off with yellow police tape. Two plainly dressed detectives stood behind the tape, talking to themselves, their flashlights and eyes fastened on the item behind the tape, an item covered by a blue plastic tarp.

Merrick appeared out of the snow, holding a golf

umbrella. As always, his black hair and mustache were neatly combed, and every time Mike saw him, he couldn't get past the image of the man he saw at church—the lumpy, pear-shaped man dressed in pressed khakis and a crisp shirt who walked the aisle, working the collection basket. Even with the nine-millimeter strapped to his waist the guy looked soft.

"Let's go over here," Merrick said, and Mike followed him over to where the two detectives were standing. The one wearing a Red Sox baseball hat nudged the other and the two of them moved to opposite sides of the yellow tape. Both of them, Mike noticed, wore latex gloves. Whatever was under that bag was evidence.

Merrick faced the blue tarp. Mike stood next to him, under the umbrella, and watched as the two detectives picked up the tarp at the corners, gently shook off the snow, and then lifted it up.

Mike saw a flash of pink and his breath died somewhere in his throat.

The two detectives stepped back, and Mike could feel the three sets of eyes lock on him.

Merrick said, "I need to know if that belongs to your daughter."

Sarah's pink snow jacket was zippered all the way to the top. The hood was draped forward, both arms standing straight out. A piece of wood stuck out from one of the arm cuffs—a 2x4 by the looks of it.

His daughter's jacket was on a cross.

This is a prank.

Early on, during those first couple of weeks when the

police had been investigating Jonah—hell, even well after Jonah became the prime suspect—Mike's mailbox was flooded with anonymous letters professing they knew what had happened to Sarah. A few were from prisoners doing serious time who were looking to trade information for a lighter sentence, but most of the letters were anonymous and completely bogus, except for that select few who, for reasons Mike never understood, insisted on mailing pieces of Sarah's clothing. Like her pink jacket.

It was all bullshit. Jess usually bought Sarah's clothes in pairs, Sarah being the type of kid who really did a number on her clothes and went through them quickly. The replacement snowsuit was sent to the FBI lab and the report came back with specifics: it was manufactured by a North Carolina company called Bizzmarket, the pink model one of the company's most popular and sold all over the northeast in stores like Wal-Mart and Target.

This was a prank, another case of some sick, bored asshole who hated his life and, for kicks, decided to come out here in the middle of the night and place a look-alike jacket on top of the cross.

The detective with the Red Sox baseball hat reached forward and with his latex-covered hands gently folded the hood and pulled it back so Mike could read the tag. The other detective clicked on a flashlight.

Mike leaned in, slow and uncertain, as if the jacket might suddenly reach out and hug him.

Sarah Sullivan was written in black lettering across the jacket's white tag.

"That's Jess's handwriting," Mike said, remembering the day at the kitchen table when Jess wrote Sarah's name on the fabric BIZZMARKET tag with a black Sharpie marker. Sarah's name on the inside tag was a detail that hadn't been made public. "What about the pocket?"

The detective in the Red Sox hat pinched the edge of the left pocket and moved it forward, revealing the small tear in the stitching—another detail that hadn't been made public.

Mike didn't know his heart could beat this fast.

Buzzy's was open. The lights were on and Buzzy's owner, Debbie Dallal, was busy restocking one of the corner shelves with Sno-Balls. She looked up when the door swung open, the bell ringing as Merrick stepped inside with his folded umbrella, Mike trailing behind him. Debbie straightened up, a weary smile on her face.

"I just put a fresh pot of coffee on the counter," she said.

"Thanks for staying open so late," Merrick said, brushing the snow off his coat. "We appreciate it."

"It's not a problem," she said, Mike catching the look of pity in Deb's eyes before she looked away.

The coffee area was set up on a long island in the middle of the store, across from the deli and grill. Mike poured himself a cup of coffee, remembering how Debbie had come in the morning after Sarah disappeared. The storm broke for a couple of hours, and Merrick used Buzzy's as a makeshift base of operations to organize the volunteers who went door-to-door and blanketed Belham, Boston, Logan Airport and the airports in New Hampshire and Rhode Island with color copies of Sarah's picture, her age, height, weight—her six years of life compressed into a single sheet of $8\frac{1}{2} \times 11$ paper, the word MISSING written in bold red letters up at the top, right above Sarah's smiling face. Mike had stood in this very spot, drinking coffee to stay awake and looking out the window at the search-and-rescue helicopter hovering in the blue sky above the woods, the chopper's infrared devices penetrating through inches of snow in search of Sarah's body heat as bloodhounds tore through the trails.

Mike slid into one of the red leather booths by the front window. Water dripped from his face onto the table. He grabbed a wad of napkins from the dispenser and was patting himself dry.

This wasn't happening. Your missing daughter's jacket doesn't suddenly show up five years later in the middle of the night—*on a cross*.

Merrick slid into the opposite seat with his cup of coffee. "How are you holding up?"

"I don't think any of this is registering yet," Mike said. "Who found the jacket?"

"Deb did. One of her refrigeration units blew around nine. By the time the service guy came by and replaced the engine, it was after eleven. She went to her truck and saw someone collapsed on the snow and walked up to him. She thought the person was hurt, so she ran back up the hill, got into her truck and called nine-one-one."

"Who's the person?"

Merrick's expression changed, and a white noise filled Mike's head.

"Jonah walks around a lot at night," Merrick explained. "During the day, he's pretty much a shut-in. As you know, some people who recognize him throw rocks, push him—a few months ago someone actually tried to run him off the road. I'm sure you've read the stories in the paper. So he goes out at night, bundles himself up and disguises himself."

"And visits the place where he abducted my daughter," Mike said, the words strangling the inside of his throat.

"I don't have a witness who saw Jonah plant the jacket and cross on the hill. Now we're going to—"

"Where is he now?"

Merrick put his coffee cup down, folded his hands on the table and leaned forward. "Listen to me."

"Don't say it."

"Jonah called nine-one-one about five minutes before Deb did. The police were already on their way."

"You've had five years, Merrick—five fucking *years* to build a case against him, and now you've got an eye-witness who can place him with my daughter's jacket. The fuck you waiting for? For Jonah to ring your door-bell and say, 'Hi, I did it'?"

"I understand you're upset." Merrick speaking in that same bored monotone he always used—especially in the beginning, when he spoke like he had a clue about kids, about what it took to raise them, what they tore from you every time they stepped out the door. Merrick had never married; he lived alone in a condo complex called The Heights, nice but nothing fancy.

"Do you know he called me?"

"Jonah did? When?"

"Right before you did," Mike said and repeated Jonah's words.

"You didn't call him back, did you?"

"Of course not. I know about Jonah's rights. And we wouldn't want anything to interfere with that, would we?"

Merrick's face remained impassive. Talk, scream, yell—share an intimate detail about yourself or break down and cry in front of this guy and all he would do was give you back the blank look of nothingness, like you were talking to him about how to make a ham sandwich.

Mike couldn't look at that face anymore. He was about to stand up when a voice piped: *You storm out of here—you throw a fit and Merrick will keep you out of the investigation.*

"You're aware that Jonah's dying," Merrick said after a moment.

"I am. Are *you*?"

"Where do you think he's most likely to talk to us? Inside a jail cell or sitting in his favorite chair in his house where he's comfortable?"

Mike rubbed his forehead and tried to wrap his mind around what was going on, the store quiet except for the occasional crinkle of cellophane, the sliding of boxes across the floor.

"The jacket will be at the lab first thing in the morning," Merrick said. "When I find out anything, I'll call and let you know. Go home and get some sleep."

"How long before you know anything?"

"Depends on how backed-up the lab is. I'll call you the first I find out."

Anger itched along the inside of his skull. Mike said, "He saw Father Connelly earlier today. You know that?"

"No. What happened?"

As Mike explained what had happened, Merrick didn't seem surprised by any of it. He wasn't surprised, Mike knew, because Merrick had cops like Slow Ed watching Jonah—only Mike couldn't mention that. If he did, he'd be in violation of his probation and off to jail he'd go while Jonah went to sleep in his own bed.

Mike said, "What about Jonah's hospice nurse? You talk to her?"

"How do you know he has a hospice nurse?"

"Word around town. Is it true?"

Merrick nodded. "Hospice has been called in."

"And?"

"I'm asking you to stay away from her."

"I'm pretty sure the nurse isn't part of my restraining order."

"This evening someone called the station and said a truck was parked across the street from Jonah's house.

Unfortunately, this person didn't get a good look at the driver's face, or his license plate. If you go near him—if you so much as say hello—all he has to do is pick up the phone and call us and you'll be on your way to serve five to eight. And this time, there's nothing I can do to stop it either."

"Guy with the best lawyer wins, right?"

"Thanks to O.J., we're all operating in a different world now." Merrick moved his coffee aside and then leaned across the table, his face serious. "The truth is you hurt our investigation. You hurt it big time. When all this went down, Jonah was cooperative and then you moved in and almost killed him and now he won't make a move without talking to his lawyer."

Mike didn't say anything.

"Jonah's running on borrowed time. I think I've got a way to get what I need from him, but to do it, you're to stay away from him, the nurse, all of it. Let me do my job and worry about Jonah. Just go about your normal life."

"I don't have much of a life anymore," Mike said, "and I can guarantee you what's left over is anything but normal."

CHAPTER 13

The bar was on the edge of town, near Chelsea, and aptly named The Last Pass. The place always reminded him of a black-and-white drawing he had seen in a catechism book back in his parochial grammar school days—souls denied entrance to heaven lay in hospital beds, their faces twisted in pain. They seemed no different from the bar's patrons, a collection of the lost and angry and rejected who cashed in their Social Security, disability and welfare checks to spend their days drifting from one bar to the next, places with dim lighting and a constant haze of cigarette smoke.

The bartender was young, somewhere in his early twenties, with a shaved head and a blue muscle shirt with the sleeves cut off to show off the barbed wire tats that crisscrossed each bicep.

"Shot of Jack with a draft on the side," Mike said.

"What kind of draft?"

"I don't give a shit."

One drink. That was all he was asking for, one measly drink. Normal people came home from work after busting their hump all day and unwound with a drink, their reward for putting up with the daily grind. Just one drink to dull his nerves and help him sleep. No way his P.O. was going to call or stop by at this hour.

The bartender came back and placed the shot and draft on the bar. Mike stared at the shot, running his tongue over his front teeth.

You're feeling sorry for yourself.

Let's say that was true. So what? Where was the harm in indulging in a moment of self-pity? And why was he bound to a set of rules that dictated his every moment while that piece of shit got to go wherever he wanted?

Mike picked up the shot glass and brought it to his lips, the smell of booze filling his nostrils.

Just one drink. One drink to help him sleep and he'd go home.

One drink's going to turn into two and then three and four and five and you'll get good and drunk and then drive back to Jonah's. You want to knock that shot back, go ahead, but at least be honest with yourself.

Mike put the shot glass back down on the bar, unclipped the cell phone from his belt and dialed the number he knew by heart.

"You ever wonder about the difference between purgatory and life?"

"Father Jack?" Bill asked, his voice thick with sleep, groggy. "I swear, I haven't been touching myself in my bad place."

"They found Sarah's jacket at the top of the hill an hour ago." Mike took in a deep breath, swallowed. "It was on a cross."

"Where are you?"

"Staring at a shot of Jack and a draft at The Last Pass."

"That dump? Christ, Sully, if you're going to fall off the wagon, the least you can do is do it in style."

"I saw him tonight."

"Who?"

"Jonah," Mike said, and filled Bill in on what had happened.

"So Slow Ed did you a solid," Bill said. "He's a good guy. Came to visit my mother when she was in the hospital."

Mike watched the beads of moisture running down the beer glass. On the other end of the phone, he heard what sounded like a car door slamming shut, followed by a car starting.

"Get it out of your head, Sully."

"It's been an hour, and I still want to kill him."

"Leave him to the reaper. It's not worth it."

"Jess is moving to New York."

"Everyone's leaving Belham. Check this out. Tonight after the play, I took everyone out to that steak joint on Route Six? Guess who I ran into? Bam-Bam and his new gal-pal Nadine. You meet her?"

"Not yet."

"She's dumber than Anna Nicole Smith."

"That's impossible."

"Nadine thought pork came from a mushroom. And next Sunday's Pats game is out, by the way. Seems Bam's taking an unexpected trip to Arizona. Now guess why?"

"I take it it's not to see the Grand Canyon."

"Try day spa. Nadine wants Bam to drop some serious pounds, so she's taking him for a week to a spa. He's going to be eating wheat-germ pancakes for breakfast, doing yoga, taking mud baths and getting rock massages and enemas."

Mike was rubbing the shot glass between his fingers. "People do funny things when they're in love," he said, thinking about Jess's moving to New York, a move he was sure at least partly had something to do with the new man in her life.

"The fat bastard even got his teeth bleached. I says to him, 'Bam, why didn't you just pay two bucks for a bottle of Wite-Out, paint your teeth just like you did before our senior prom?'"

Mike let out a dry chuckle.

"See, that's funny. But Nadine? She just stared at me. I swear a thought in her head must be like a canary flying around an empty room. Hang tight, Sully, I'm almost there."

CHAPTER 14

When you use the media, they end up using you. Rose Giroux had drilled this fact into Mike's head early on. *What they're after, Michael, are your tears. That's all they care about. They want you to cry for them, to scream, swear—they want you to have a breakdown on camera, and the only way they can do that is by asking the questions meant to provoke you. When they ask them—and they will, over and over again—always remember to keep your focus on your daughter. Remember that behind every dumb question are cameras and tape recorders that are going to run Sarah's story and Sarah's picture. The longer you keep Sarah out there, the higher the chance someone will come forward with information. You stand there and be as nice as pie because there may come a time when you need them.*

For the next five days, no matter where Mike was or what mood he was in, he dropped whatever he was doing and in a strained but pleasant tone answered the same mind-numbing questions over and over again. Yes,

I'm sure it was my daughter's jacket on top of the hill. No, I can't explain why Jonah called 911 and reported finding the jacket. No, I don't know what's going on with the jacket. No, I don't know why the police haven't arrested Jonah yet. I don't know anything. You'd have to talk to the police. Go to the police. Speak with the police.

Merrick held two press conferences—smoke-and-mirror shows of "We're working on several leads" and "No comment." Merrick was holding his cards close to his chest; he wasn't going to give away any information. When the cameras and microphones were gone and it was just the two of them, alone in a room, he treated Mike to the same lip service. Be patient. We're making progress. Merrick never elaborated on exactly what that progress was.

By the end of the work week, with nothing fresh to feast on, the media went into a temporary state of hibernation. They were lingering around Belham, mostly around Jonah's house, hoping to catch a picture of the dying recluse. And sometimes they'd drive by Mike's house and knock on the door looking for an exclusive interview—only Mike wasn't there. He and Fang had moved temporarily into Bill's house. Anthony Testa popped by the job site for another pee and breath screen and left in a huff. Mike had forgotten to cap the sample and had accidentally dropped it inside Testa's briefcase.

Every morning, from five to six, even in the dead of winter, Father Jack Connelly ran the track at Belham

High School. Mike knew this because back in high school, he used to run the track in the early mornings to keep in shape for football. They often ran together and talked about any number of subjects, Father Jack not at all shy about voicing his thoughts on Lou Sullivan.

On a drizzling Friday morning Mike found Father Jack doing laps around the track, the priest alone and dressed in his gray sweats and a hooded navy-blue sweatshirt. He rounded the corner, and when he looked up and saw Mike standing next to his gym bag, he slowed to a walk.

"You should really give those up," Father Jack said, and pointed to the cigarette in Mike's hands.

"He molested the first girl and the church buried the story."

Father Jack stopped walking. He stood there with beads of sweat running down his face, his breath steaming in the cool air.

"The church moved him to another parish and then Caroline Lenville disappears," Mike said. "Her mother was late picking her up, so Jonah gave her a ride home. The police believe him because they don't know about the molestation charge, but the church did, and after the dust settled, you guys moved him to Vermont and then Ashley Giroux disappears."

Father Jack leaned forward and removed a towel from his gym bag.

"You held Sarah in your hands," Mike said. "You baptized her. You ate at my house."

"You want me to say it again, Michael? That I think

Jonah's a disgrace? That I'm ashamed at what the church did? How they ignored and betrayed the victims afterwards? You know how I feel about everything that's happened."

"Why did Jonah come to see you last week?"

"You know I can't tell you that."

So it was a confession. And since confessions were sealed, no cop or judge or court order of any kind could make Father Jack reveal what had transpired.

Mike flicked his cigarette into the wind and stepped in closer, his face inches from the priest.

"Whatever you say, I promise it will stay between you and me."

Father Jack looked out at the football field.

"Just point me in a direction," Mike said. "Tell me where to look."

"I know this has been an incredibly painful and difficult ordeal for you. Try and remember, God has a plan for all of us. We may not understand it, it may anger us at times, but He does have a plan for us."

"We're not in church. How about telling me as a friend?"

"It's in God's hands now. I'm sorry."

Mike felt a thick, bulging wetness in his throat. "That's the thing," he said. "I don't think you really are."

Ray Pinkerton stood in his kitchen and spoke slowly as he tucked his patrolman's shirt into his blue pants. "I'm sorry, but I can't." He had a soft, almost feminine voice that didn't go along with the hard, almost muscular fat of his big, wide body. "Not after the week Sammy's had."

"I know it's been a rough week for him," Mike said. He wasn't feeding the guy a line. Mike had witnessed the media's relentless pursuit of Sammy Pinkerton on TV this past week; reporters setting up camp outside of Sammy's house and skulking around the grounds of St. John's Prep high school in Danvers, taking pictures of him as he rushed to classes, bolted to his father's car.

"Nothing's changed over the past five years. Everything Sammy saw that night, he told Merrick, and Merrick told you."

"As far as I know," Mike said.

Pinkerton let the comment slide. "Why do you want to talk to him now, after all this time?"

It had something to do with wanting to place Sammy next to Sarah that night on the hill—and that by doing so, maybe Sammy could bring Sarah closer to him. And maybe, just maybe, if he heard Sammy talk about what happened and saw it through Sammy's eyes, maybe it would trigger some new thought or new direction.

"I'm not trying to be difficult here," Ray Pinkerton said. "I know you've asked to talk with him before, early on, and I said no." He sighed and ran his palm over his shaved head. "He blames himself for what happened, you know? That time, he wasn't sleeping at all, wouldn't eat. I got him into counseling and he finally worked his way out, and now with everything that's happening, I can see him slipping back."

"Dad, it's okay."

They both turned and saw Sammy standing in the hallway.

Seeing Sammy up close like this—Sammy not a kid anymore but sixteen and real tall and real thin with a buzz cut and patches of beard trying to come together and form a goatee—it rocked Mike back to that morning he had stood on the hill and wondered what Sarah would look like now, and he realized that Sarah could walk right by him and he probably wouldn't recognize her.

Ray Pinkerton was about to speak up when Sammy said: "Honest, Dad, I'm fine."

But Sammy didn't sound fine, he sounded scared. Looked it too, Mike thought. Sammy wouldn't look him in the eye.

"I didn't have anything to do with it," Sammy said, his voice barely above a whisper. "I found out about Neal's blog yesterday."

Ray said, "Blog? The hell's a blog?"

"It's like an online journal," Sammy said, and then shifted his attention to Mike. "That's why you're here, right?"

"I wanted to talk to you about that night on the hill."

Sammy grew still, a guy wishing he could shrink or turn invisible. He stuffed his hands in his jean pockets and studied the floor.

"Neal," Ray said. "As in Neal Sonnenberg."

Sammy nodded and Ray mumbled something under his breath.

Mike stood there and watched as Ray and his son exchanged glances. Then Ray said, "Neal lives here in Belham. Across the street from Jonah." Ray turned back to his son. "What's this blog business?"

Sammy shuffled back into the hallway, and Mike heard feet pounding up the stairs. Mike slid his attention to Ray, who now looked as nervous as his son, like he wanted to disappear.

"Something going on with Jonah?" Mike asked.

"I haven't heard anything."

He's lying, Mike thought. *He's either lying or stalling— or both.*

Sammy came back downstairs with a laptop. He set it up on the kitchen counter and then removed the phone jack from the phone and plugged the wire into the back of the laptop. He turned it on, and as they waited for the computer to boot up, Mike noticed the tension in the kid's shoulders, the nervous way he kept swallowing.

Less than two minutes later, Sammy had logged onto the Internet, and on the screen was a site called Neal's Place. It was filled with photos of a lanky kid with spiked black hair posing with women of varying ages on beaches, at football games, in parking lots, at Hooters. All the women were insanely good-looking and wore either tight or revealing clothing, and in every one of them Neal wore a lottery-winning smile.

Sammy double-clicked on a picture at the bottom

and a screen popped up asking for a name and password. He filled it in and hit ENTER.

A new screen with a headline in big, bold letters: HUNTING THE BOOGEYMAN. Mike saw a picture of himself placing the lilacs on top of the hill and to the left of the picture, Sammy's friend Neal's commentary.

Ray said, "Jesus Christ."

Sammy went on the defensive: "I didn't know about it until yesterday. Neal has it set up so you can only access it through a password. And you can't find it through a Google search. The only reason I know about it is 'cause Barry Paley told me about it and gave me the password to get on."

"How long has Neal been doing this?" Ray getting angry now.

"I don't know. A year, maybe." Sammy turned to Mike, looking for forgiveness or at least some measure of understanding. "I swear to God I'm telling you the truth," Sammy added, his voice trembling, about to break. "I swear to God."

Mike was staring at the laptop's screen. All he could see was the other picture, the one of Jonah standing on top of the hill, holding the flowers in his hands, inhaling the scent of the lilacs.

Neal Sonnenberg's online journal was a six-page rambling narrative of what time Jonah left the house, where he went on his walks and what he did. After Mike read it, he printed out the text and pictures and then left the Pinkerton home, hopped in his truck and dialed information. There was only one Sonnenberg listed. Mike was on his way to the house when his cell phone rang.

"You know the terms of the restraining order," Merrick said. "You come over here, you'll be violating the terms."

Ray Pinkerton must have called Merrick.

Mike said, "How long have you been there watching Jonah from the kid's house?"

"When I find out anything, I'll let you know."

"Like the website, right?"

"You read the kid's online journal. There was nothing there."

"Maybe you didn't see the picture of Jonah standing up on the top of the hill holding the flowers I left, or the pictures of him walking the trails near the back of my house."

"I asked you politely to stay out of this, and yet you keep screwing with my investigation."

"Maybe if you did your job I wouldn't have to."

"You come here, you're going to jail," Merrick said. "That's a promise."

CHAPTER 15

Mike had left an important set of plans for an upcoming addition inside his office, so he swung by his house, relieved to find no reporters. People had stopped by and placed flowers, cards and pictures of Sarah across his front lawn. He parked in the garage and grabbed the mail satchel he had picked up earlier at the post office. Mike had put a hold on his mail the day after Sarah's jacket was discovered.

It was just after eleven. He was wide awake and decided to go through the mail here. The shades in the TV room were drawn. He grabbed a Coke from the fridge and the garbage pail from the kitchen, turned the TV to ESPN, and then started sorting through the mountain of envelopes, packages and catalogues.

So far, none of the letters were from crazies claiming to have planted the jacket on the cross or saying that they knew what Jonah had done to her. Those letters, when they were found, were put in a special pile for

Merrick. Most of the letters were prayer cards from people he had never met or letters from psychics, like this one written on pink paper: MADAME DORA, INTERNATIONAL PSYCHIC. The woman in the attached color brochure looked like Bill in a blond wig. Mike crumpled the paper into a ball and tossed it at the garbage pail set up in the corner.

Sarah's jacket was at the lab. Latex-covered hands were reading their microscopes and slides, preparing to pry the jacket of its secrets.

So what made Jonah decide to, after all this time, not only reveal the jacket, but to put it on a cross?

The question came at Mike again and again and he still couldn't make sense of it. Of course, that didn't stop any number of retired FBI profilers and so-called experts on the criminal mind from getting their face-time on TV. A local big-shot criminal psychiatrist who specialized in psychopathic personalities was quoted in yesterday's *Herald* as saying—and Mike was paraphrasing here—that Jonah was, in his own, perverted, psychopathic way, telling the police he was ready to talk. He knew he was dying and felt he should confess, but see, he couldn't just pick up the phone and do it. No, he had to be forced, so he planted the evidence and now it was up to the police to play their part.

Someone knocked on the front door.

Mike went over to the window, pulled back the shades and peeked outside. No TV van or car, so it couldn't be a reporter.

Maybe it's Merrick.

The knock came again as Mike walked into the foyer. He opened the door and stared at the face on the other side of the storm door.

"Polite thing to do is to invite me in," Lou said.

Mike thought about it for a moment, then opened the door. Lou stepped inside the foyer. Mike checked for a car, didn't see one. Had Lou been following him?

"You're looking good, Michael. Lean and mean."

The same could be said of Lou. He was lean, always had been, the meanness and hair-trigger rage somehow preserving him. His hair was grayer, his tanned face a bit more weathered from decades of baking in the sun, but there was no question that Lou still possessed the confident, youthful swagger of his former self, a successful street fighter who knew how to hit you so you couldn't stand for weeks.

Or make you disappear, a voice added. *Let's not forget about that particular talent.*

Mike shut the door. "Police know you're back in town?"

"No, and I'd appreciate it if you kept it quiet," Lou said. He was dressed in a black suit and a white shirt, his black shoes shined and spotless. "I take it you're still buddy-buddy with that cop there, the one who looks like Mike Tyson, what's his name? Zukowski?"

"What do you want?"

"Came by to talk." Lou lit a cigarette with the gold lighter embossed with the Marine emblem on the front, the lighter a fixture in the house as long as Mike could remember. The flame jumped across Lou's face, then disappeared. "We gonna just stand here or can we sit down?"

"Here's fine."

Lou took a long drag of his cigarette, his face emotionless as he looked around the rooms. "Dr. Jackson lived here. Used to hold poker games right in there." He pointed to the dining room. "Decent enough guy. Had a bad gambling problem though."

"That the guy I saw you work over with a pipe on Devon Street?"

Lou picked a piece of tobacco off his tongue and examined it. "All this time, your circumstances, I thought it might have made you a bit more forgiving."

"St. Stephen's is in the other direction."

The words didn't register, just fell through Lou's eyes like stones down a well.

"You know Jonah's dying," Lou said.

"Everyone does."

"I mean he's going to buy the farm any day now. His nightstand and kitchen table are full of all kinds of medicine—morphine, Demerol, Prozac, you name it. I'm amazed the son of a bitch can still walk."

Mike started to speak then stopped.

Lou knew about the medicine because he had been inside Jonah's house.

"Lot of weird shit going on in there," Lou said. "Guy's got Christmas lights and decorations hung around his bedroom, his living room—he's got these toys all over the place. Phil told me—"

"Phil?"

"Phil Debrussio, one of Jonah's bodyguards. There's

two of them. Press has been all over Jonah since Sarah's jacket was found."

Sarah, Lou saying her name like she belonged to him too.

"This business with Christmas decorations and the toys, it's called regression," Lou said. "Jonah's hospice nurse, this broad Terry Russell, she said that can happen when a patient is dying. He goes back to happier times in his life, know what I mean?"

"She told you this?"

"Course not. She won't talk with me, and she sure as hell isn't going to talk to you. Broad's under strict orders from Merrick not to say a word to you, as is that kid who did that website on Jonah." Lou paused, letting that comment sink in for a moment. He took another long drag from his cigarette. "When Jonah's lucid, he talks a lot to his lawyer," he said in a plume of smoke. "He's terrified of dying in jail. Lawyer keeps telling him not to worry."

Jesus. He's bugged the place.

"I think it's time Jonah talks," Lou said, Mike hearing that effortless, magnetic confidence in Lou's words and remembering how his mother had responded to that voice time and time again, believing that the next time he'd keep his anger in check, promise not to drive his point home with his fists.

"I'm not asking you to get involved," Lou said, "but if the police come around and start asking questions, I may need an alibi."

Not once had Mike crossed that line into Lou's other

life. Growing up, if Cadillac Jack or any of the other lowlifes stopped by to play cards or talk business, Mike would leave for Bill's or, if that wasn't an option, he'd close his bedroom door and turn up the volume on the black-and-white TV or the radio.

Mike said, "Let the police handle this."

"That what you want?"

"They know what they're doing."

"How do you think Jonah got out of the house that night without being spotted?" Lou grinned, then added, "Next time you see your buddy Zukowski, ask him why the guy they got watching Jonah keeps falling asleep."

"You do anything to screw this up," Mike said evenly, "and I'll tell Merrick about this conversation."

Lou's eyes took on a disturbing vacant quality. He stepped forward, the cigarette dangling from his mouth, and Mike felt like a kid again, his attention automatically shifting to Lou's fists, watching to see if they would clench up, the sure sign that a beating was on the way. Those hands had loved Mike's mother, had beaten her and, Mike was sure, had buried her.

"That night I bumped into you at McCarthy's. I woke up the next morning and found out you put Jonah into a coma."

"That was an accident," Mike said, looking up. "I didn't plan on it."

"That what you tell yourself when you look in the mirror?"

Mike held his father's gaze. "It's the truth."

"The police are doing such a great job, why'd you drop by Jonah's last Friday?"

"Stay away from this."

"Jonah talks a lot in his sleep. I haven't been able to make out much, but he's said Sarah's name a few times. You change your mind, leave a message with George at McCarthy's. He'll know how to get in touch with me."

CHAPTER 16

The first Friday of every month, Mike knew Slow Ed got together with some of the guys from Highland Auto Body to play poker. Mike swung by the garage, and after a ten-minute conversation with the owner, found out where tonight's eight o'clock game was being held.

Mike pulled out of the garage, with one hand on the steering wheel, the other on his cell, dialing Bill's number.

"How'd the procedure go?" Bill had undergone a vasectomy earlier that afternoon.

"It's been four hours now and my giblets are still the size of cantaloupes," Bill said. "Minor swelling, my ass. Can you pick me up some more ice?"

"Sure. Anything else?"

"Two gallons of skim milk. Grace just dumped the last gallon into the tub—don't ask. Oh, and pick up some Rolaids. Patty's making turkey meatloaf for dinner."

"See you in a few."

"Hurry. I'm surrounded by mental patients."

Mike drove downtown. Even now, in the most complimentary sun, downtown Belham had the grimy feel of the forgotten. High TV, the electronics store where Mr. Dempson used to repair VCRs and TVs, was boarded up, just one of the many victims of the disposable mall mentality; why fix it when you can pitch it and buy it newer and cheaper and faster? Kingworld Shoes couldn't offer the same low mall prices and was forced to close. Two years ago, a fire had gutted the hockey rink where Sarah had attended several birthday parties along with the empty store next to it, Cusiack Fabrics (WORLD FAMOUS SINCE 1912 the sign had once read). The Strand, the old movie house he had gone to with his mother, where he had taken Sarah to see *E.T.,* was going to be torn down next. The only building that had survived was the public library. Lou, if he had been in a generous mood, would drive them to the library, Mike sitting on the front steps with him, listening to Lou blabber about how if he could have back the half of his life he spent waiting for women he'd live to be well over a hundred.

Collette's Grocery was also on the chopping block. Come next year, the store would be transformed into one of the big brand-name super grocery stores complete with pharmacy and film developing. The landscape around him was changing and yet nobody seemed to notice or care, he wasn't sure which.

Mike decided to pick up some items for himself

while he was here. He pushed the cart to the dairy, where he spotted Father Connelly dressed in jeans and a sweatshirt, examining the yogurt selections. Mike wondered if he should turn around. Too late. Father Jack had spotted him.

"Michael."

Why does he look nervous—and why is he looking over my shoulder?

Mike turned around.

Francis Jonah was pointing at a carton of orange juice, his other hand gripping his cane. Two guys in suits stood next to him—the bodyguards, both of them thick and wide. The guy with the shaved head picked up the orange carton and added it to the handcart. The other guy was short and had a buzz cut and a single diamond earring in his left ear. His eyes were fastened on Mike.

"Come on, Mr. Sullivan," Buzz Cut said. "You know the drill."

Mike didn't move, watching as Jonah slid his attention away from the orange juice selections and pulled the oxygen mask from his face.

"You heard the man," Jonah wheezed. "Leave."

Mike's mind filled with an image of Sarah, her vision terribly blurred without her glasses, crying out for help as she swatted away the strange hands eager to touch her.

"You're in violation of your probation," Jonah said. "I have a cell phone, and I have witnesses. Right, Father Connelly? Go ahead, Chucky, make the call."

Father Jack gripped Mike's bicep. "Leave him to God," he whispered.

Jonah licked his lips, his eyes gleaming.

Reggie Dempson still lived in the same ranch house where he had grown up with his three sisters and their mother, Crazy Alice, a woman who used to make her kids sleep with tinfoil on their heads to keep the UFO that circled their house every night from reading their thoughts. Slow Ed's champagne-colored Honda Accord was parked in the driveway.

At a quarter to ten, Mike parked across the street, shut off the truck and pulled out a fresh pack of Marlboros, smoked and waited.

Half a pack later, at ten-thirty, Slow Ed emerged from Dempson's front door, his massive frame plopping down the front steps as he waved goodbye to Reggie. Mike started his truck and rolled down the window just as Slow Ed reached his car.

"Not a good idea to drink and drive, Officer Zukowski. Let me give you a lift home."

"Talk to Merrick," Slow Ed said, opening the car door.

"Your boss seems to have a problem returning his phone calls."

"Maybe he's afraid you're going to go postal on Jonah again."

"So Merrick has something on Jonah."

"You said that—not me."

"Come on, Ed, I'm just asking for a progress report. You must know something by now."

"Like I said, talk to Merrick."

"I hear the guy you have watching Jonah's house has trouble staying awake on the job," Mike said. "I hope the press doesn't find out about that."

Slow Ed straightened, and then lumbered over to the truck, propping one arm on the roof as he leaned in close to Mike's window.

"I like you, Sully. I've always considered you a solid guy, which is why I decided to help you out the first time. I tell you we're looking at this guy Jonah, about his background and name change before he came back here—I tell you all of this in confidence and you thank me by turning into Wyatt Earp, remember?"

"I never told Merrick what you and I talked about."

"But he *knows* it had to have come from inside the department. Care to guess which cop had a microscope shoved up his ass that year?"

"How many more times you want me to apologize? I was drunk at the time. I don't drink anymore."

"I'm not talking about your drinking, I'm talking about your anger-management issues. The other night on Jonah's porch? What was that about? You're welcome, by the way."

"You were watching Jonah's house from that kid's house, right? Neal Sonnenberg. Had the website with the photos."

Slow Ed didn't say anything.

"I read through the kid's online journal," Mike said. "How much of it did Merrick edit?"

"Not a word. The kid did it to impress his friends."

"So why's the website down?"

"You want those pictures showing up in the papers and on TV?"

"It's coming up on two weeks and I haven't heard a thing."

"Merrick's busting his ass on this, Sully. That's the honest to God truth."

"I'm at my breaking point here. Please."

Slow Ed drummed his fingers on the truck's roof, his breath steaming in the night air.

"Just give me something to show you guys are closing in on him, and I swear I'll back off."

Slow Ed stopped drumming his fingers and perched his other arm on the roof. "I got your word?"

"You've got it."

Slow Ed paused for a moment, then said, "Merrick's been talking with an FBI profiler. They both agree that the way to unlock what Jonah knows is to confront him with the evidence. You know, show him that there's no way out."

"There is no way out. He's dying."

"My point. Once Merrick has the evidence in black and white, he's going to give Jonah an option: tell us what you know about the girls or you can die in prison. Jonah's terrified of dying in jail. Now which option you think Jonah's going to take?"

"You get the lab results yet?"

"Just preliminary stuff—emphasis on the word *preliminary*. Now the lab guys have got to do their thing, and when the results come in, Merrick's going to close in on Jonah."

"And how long we talking?"

"Depends on the lab."

"Can you give me an estimate?"

Slow Ed thought about it, then said, "If I had to guess, I'd say another week, max."

"He'll be dead by then."

"You don't know that."

"Have you seen him recently?" Mike asked, thinking back to the way Jonah had looked earlier, at the grocery store: twigs wrapped in loose clothing.

"That *CSI* stuff you see on TV is bullshit. You don't dump the evidence on these guys and have DNA and fiber evidence in an hour."

"You have DNA?"

"I didn't say that. Look, our goal here is to get Jonah to talk, and I'm pretty confident we'll get him to open up. Try and hang in there."

Mike draped one arm over the steering wheel and looked out the front window.

"It's not right."

Slow Ed said, "If Jonah hadn't placed that nine-one-one call—if someone caught him banging the cross into the ground or saw him holding Sarah's jacket in his hands, yeah, it'd be a different game. Maybe he'd confess right then, I don't know. We're dealing with the hand we've got."

"I'm talking about the way everyone's treating Jonah. Like he's a human being."

"We're doing everything we can, Sully."

Mike was thinking back to the grocery store. Turn around and leave, Jonah had said. And Mike did, like he was Jonah's bitch.

"I want him to burn, Ed. Swear to Christ, that son of a bitch is going to burn."

CHAPTER 17

The gig couldn't have been simpler: babysitting a Q-tip a breath away from being worm food. Chucky Bresler had practically grown up in the business, starting off doing security for his dad's bar in Southie before moving off to the major clubs on Lansdowne Street. Breaking up fights between drunks didn't bother him. All it took was a firm hand and a little muscle and you were good to go.

Usually.

The problem was the posers. Sure, they were easy to spot—guys wearing muscle shirts and gold chains or gang gear and flashing a lot of green and sauntering their pretty little selves around the club, acting like they owned the place and itching for trouble. Back in the day, before clubs made it mandatory for you to pass through a metal detector or get worked over head-to-toe with one of those handheld devices, these posers would think nothing of pulling a knife or worse, a gun.

Chucky never had a gun pulled on him, but one time, this group of Mattapan punks decided to get into it at the club, and by the time Chucky broke it up, he had all three of them down for the count. He also had a switchblade stuck in his lower back.

The doctor had to cut him open to repair the punctured kidney. Thank the sweet Lord for painkillers. While Chucky lay in the hospital recouping, doped up on Percodan, this *humongous* black dude dressed in some seriously expensive threads waltzed in and said how impressed he was by the way Chucky handled himself the other night at the club. Dude's name was Booker and he owned a private security company in downtown Boston. You interested in a full-time salary with health bennies, paid vacations and gym memberships? Hell yeah.

That was almost a decade ago, and during that time, Chucky, now forty-three, had carved out a nice life for himself, the only steady woman in his life a white pit bull named Snowball. Once in a while, when movie stars came to Boston to promote their latest piece of crap, Chucky would sometimes be called in for body detail for one of these cushy crowd-control jobs. Most of the time, though, he was called in to provide protection services for Mark Thompson's clients, guys out on bail who basically needed a babysitter—like this dude Francis Jonah.

Since six P.M., Jonah had been sitting in the rocking chair with an afghan draped over his lap, staring out the window overlooking his backyard. It was now one in the morning and he was still up, still rocking and staring out the window. What was the point of sleeping when you knew you were dying, right? One look and you could tell the guy was on his way out: air tubes in the nostrils, portable oxygen tank on the floor, veins bulging from beneath his egg-white skin, that VACANCY sign already hanging in his eyes. Chucky had seen that look so many times throughout his professional life he instantly recognized it.

"Get you something to eat or drink, Mr. Jonah?" Phil Debrussio asked. He was Chucky's partner. When it came to these gigs, you always worked in pairs.

Jonah mumbled something under his breath.

"What's that, Mr. Jonah?"

No answer. Not surprising either. Jonah liked to speak silently to himself, not hearing you or ignoring you, Chucky wasn't sure which. The guy was probably praying. If you knew you were on your way out, you probably tended to pray your ass off, talk to the guy upstairs and make sure everything was in order.

Only this guy could pray twenty-four seven and it wasn't going to make a lick of difference. After what he did to those three girls, this guy was destined for hotter climates.

"I'm going to make myself a sandwich," Phil said to Chucky. "You want anything?"

Chucky shook his head and Phil stood up, walked down the hallway and disappeared into the kitchen. Chucky turned back to an article about the pros and cons of breast implants. The article was written from a medical perspective, interesting as hell, sure, but there was no mention about which kind men preferred.

"Your sister's Sheila Bresler," Jonah croaked in a wet voice.

Chucky shut his *Newsweek* and made sure his face was blank before he looked up. Jonah had stopped rocking; his head rested on the back of the rocker, his face turned to the side, Chucky sure those dreamy, faraway eyes were staring straight into his soul.

"That *Globe* article," Jonah wheezed. "That was your sister. She died of a heroin overdose."

The interview had run in the *Globe* about a month ago. The reporter was a buddy from the neighborhood who wanted to talk about the heroin epidemic in Southie, and Chucky had jumped on it, wanting everyone to know that his sister was more than a junkie who had died in a motel room.

"I understand. Sometimes the hurt can be too much for us to bear. The Lord understands that. The Lord doesn't condemn, He *embraces*. Don't hold onto the hurt. If you let it go, the Lord will free you. The Lord will heal you. Trust me."

Chucky tossed the *Newsweek* on the end table and stood up, his knees cracking, and without a word walked out of the living room and into the kitchen.

Phil put down his sandwich. "What's up?"

"Just stepping outside for a smoke." Chucky picked his black Navy peacoat from the coat rack and shoved his arm in the sleeve, found it too small.

Not his coat; it was Jonah's.

Right. Jonah had a similar coat to the one Chucky wore.

Phil said, "You're as white as a sheet."

"Can you take him up the stairs yourself?"

Phil looked insulted. "Chucky, the guy barely weighs a buck."

"Grab some shuteye if you want to. I'll take the first shift."

Chucky picked up his coat, put it on and stepped out onto the back porch. Later, while he was in the hospital and after the doctors had stabilized the pain, he would think about how life could take a series of small and ab-solutely meaningless events and turn them into one big torpedo that seriously fucked up your life.

Morphine-induced psychosis. Jonah had trouble remem-bering where he left things like his glasses and keys, but his mind could, at any time, cough up memories from his childhood and month-old newspaper articles. Weird. Chucky had seen it happen before, to Trudy, his saint of a stepmother. When the breast cancer had finally taken hold of her organs, she'd sometimes have trouble re-membering Chucky's face. Then, out of nowhere, she'd start listing off the ingredients of a recipe she read in *Good Housekeeping.* The morphine just spit up these ran-dom bits, mixed them together, somehow made it a memory.

Good Lord the air felt good, so cool and sweet and clean. Spend an hour in that house, the windows shut and that baseboard heating percolating all of Jonah's sneezes and coughs, and you started to appreciate fresh air. Right now, it was nice and quiet, no reporters parked on the street—at least none that he could see. For the moment, the stream of reporters had pretty much petered out. Last night, around this time, Jonah had decided to go out for a walk. Again he refused to use his walker. It sat where it always did, in the corner near the top of the stairs.

Chucky leaned forward, grabbed it and stretched out his back. First time Sheila overdosed, she was so weak she had to use a walker to get to the bathroom. She had undergone every kind of detox and gimmick under the sun; but in the end, she always went for the needle, loved the needle, and Chucky knew that. Deep down he knew it was only a matter of time before he had to say goodbye, so he prepared himself, thinking that early grieving, if there was such a thing, would somehow spare him from whatever horror was waiting for him down the road. Wrong. In the end, you still needed to grieve. You still had to make room for your losses and find a way to carry your love for that person without drowning in it. Chucky Bresler didn't hear the dry flick of a lighter or see the jumping flame, but he did hear the solid crunch of footsteps running across snow. By the time he looked up, the glass bottle had shattered against the railing, splashing gasoline on his clothes and face, engulfing him in flames.

CHAPTER 18

"Homemade Molotov cocktail," Merrick was saying. "A glass bottle hit the porch and sprayed the guy's face and clothes. Lucky for him, he immediately dove into the snow and started rolling around."

Mike lifted his toolbox into the back of the truck. They were standing in Margaret Van Buren's driveway in Newton. It was Saturday, sometime after one, and Mike was wrapping up a half day of work.

"The bodyguard wasn't the target though," Merrick said. "He had a coat that was similar to Jonah's. Someone unscrewed the bulbs from the sensor lights out on the back porch. Bresler's out there in the dark, same height as Jonah, wearing a similar coat and standing near the walker, it could have been Jonah. If Bresler had noticed that the porch lights hadn't kicked on, he probably wouldn't be clinging to life inside a burn unit at Mass General."

Mike slammed the hatch shut.

"I'm sorry to ask you this," Merrick said, "but I need to know where you were last night."

"What's the deal with my daughter's jacket?"

"Still waiting for the lab results."

Mike fished his keys out of his pocket, Merrick's voice picking at his brain.

"So you don't know a thing."

"Not yet," Merrick said. "I should know something soon."

Mike felt a barely suppressed scream rising in his throat. He brushed past Merrick, opened the door to his truck and climbed inside the cab. Merrick stepped up next to the opened window.

"I asked you a question."

"I think I'm going to follow Jonah's lead," Mike said. "What do you guys call it? Getting lawyered up?"

"You care to explain the bug that's stuck up your ass?"

"I'm sorry, but that's a question for my lawyer."

Mike started the truck, wondering if Merrick might slap the cuffs on him, drag him down to the station. The guy looked pissed enough to do it.

"I suggest you go home," Merrick said. "A detective will be waiting there with a search warrant."

"There's a key under the mat on the back porch. Knock yourself out, Kojak."

WBZ news radio had the story in heavy rotation.

"In what police are calling a deadly case of mistaken

identity, Charles Bresler, one of two bodyguards hired to protect Francis Jonah, is listed in critical condition after suffering third-degree burns and inhalation injuries resulting from a fire-bombing attack during the early morning hours. Francis Jonah, the former priest police believed to be responsible for the disappearance of three young girls, the most recent Sarah Sullivan of Belham—"

Mike clicked off the radio and gripped the steering wheel so hard his knuckles formed white half moons. *Fucking Merrick. Guy hunts me down, runs right up here to get his questions answered and expects me to drop what I'm doing and then lies about the lab results.*

And what about Jess? She had to have known by now what was going on. The story of Sarah's jacket was everywhere—*USA Today*, CNN. They had *USA Today* in Paris, right? They sure as hell had CNN, and CNN had the story in heavy rotation the first two days. And even if Jess wasn't reading the papers or watching TV, one of her friends knew what was going on and must have tried to contact her in Italy or wherever she and her new boyfriend were honeymooning.

Mike came to a stop at the light. Sweat had gathered beneath his clothes; a dry pasty coating lined his mouth. Across the street was a bar. He stared at the neon sign and the big, dark window facing the street when his cell phone rang. It was Slow Ed.

"Have you lost your goddamn mind?"

"You actually think I did *that?*"

"You tell me. You were the one talking about wanting Jonah to burn."

"You know what, Ed? Go fuck yourself."

"Then what's this shit I hear about you getting lawyered up? Merrick just called over here to get a search warrant going."

"Merrick came by the jobsite with all these questions about where I was last night."

"Right. It's called a police investigation, Sully. Someone tried to turn Jonah into a candlestick and got the wrong guy. Given your past history with Jonah, you're what we call a prime suspect."

Mike squeezed the phone as he stepped on the gas. "I love how you guys expect me to drop whatever I'm doing and answer your questions, but when I've got a question, you turn into a bunch of mutes."

"Sully, we've already been over this."

"I asked Merrick about the lab results."

Slow Ed didn't say anything.

"I didn't tell him about last night or anything you said," Mike said. "I just wanted to see if he was—"

"I can't believe I'm hearing this."

"—telling me the truth, and as usual, Merrick denied—"

"You've got a serious hearing problem, you know that?"

"I've got rights here. You guys keep forgetting that this is my daughter we're talking about."

"Yeah, you're right, Sully. We're all a bunch of heartless pricks. That's why we kept you in the loop the first time around, only *you* had to turn around and beat the shit out of the main suspect because you felt we weren't doing our job."

"If you guys had done your job five years ago, Jonah would be behind bars. At least I'd have that satisfaction. He's out and about doing his thing and the cop you have watching him fell asleep at the wheel and I have to schedule time and pay money to piss in cups."

"You ever stop and ask yourself why Jonah hired bodyguards? Why he's got panic buttons installed all over his house? You think he's scared of us? The media?"

Mike heard his blood slamming against his eardrums, felt it pounding across his forehead and behind his eyes.

"Merrick shows up to your jobsite—he comes to you so you don't have to make a trip down to the station and deal with this media shitstorm—the guy's doing you a favor and as usual you turn around and kick a two-by-four up his ass. The *fuck* is your problem, Sully?"

"*My* problem?"

"Yeah, you're the problem. You're the one with the goddamn attitude. You're the one—"

"They found my daughter's jacket hanging on a cross—on a *cross*, Ed. I'd love to see what you'd do if the one person you loved more than anything—" Mike's throat froze up. He tried to clear it and felt his love for Sarah burning in his chest, his hope rising and falling, rising and falling, and then he thought about the jacket on the cross and thought that if given the opportunity, he'd gladly cut off his own arm if that meant discovering what had happened to her, because knowing whatever nightmare she had endured, alone, without him— knowing it had to be better than what he felt right now. It had to be.

"Finding Sarah's jacket is supposed to mean something, Ed. I've waited five years. I've done my time. You try walking around with all these weights piled high on your chest, see how long you can go."

"Sully."

Mike pulled the phone away from his ear, wiped his eyes with the back of his hand, Sarah still there in his chest, telling him to keep fighting.

"Sully," Slow Ed said, his voice a bit softer but still clearly pissed.

"What?"

"Just tell me where you were last night, and don't bullshit me, okay?"

And then Mike felt that need to fight for Sarah dry up.

"My dog's at Bill's house," he said. "His kids have been watching him for a few days. I had dog food in the truck so I swung by his house and ended up staying the night."

"What time you get in?"

"Around eleven-thirty. Bill saw me come in. He was up with one of the twins."

"Good," Slow Ed said. "The other bodyguard said Bresler went outside for a smoke at one. This is good. Bill know you talked to me?"

"I gave you my word on that, remember?"

"Hold on a sec."

Mike heard mumbling and then Slow Ed came back on the line, his voice a drawn out, heavy sigh. "Where you at right now?"

"On my way back to Belham."

"Meet me at Highland Auto Body. You can park your truck there, and I'll take you in and you can give your statement."

"I just told you where I was last night."

"I know, but word just came down. The bodyguard died. We're dealing with a homicide, and right now you're the prime suspect."

CHAPTER 19

The name Samantha Ellis would forever take him back to the kind of lazy days spent on the beach where the only cares you had were making sure your beer was cold and whether or not you liked the music pumping from the speakers. Mike wouldn't have met Sam at all if Jess hadn't decided to spend the summer after her freshman year working in Newport, Rhode Island, with her roommate and new best friend, Cassy Black; Jess wanting to see other people, to find out if what they had between them was real and meant to be and not the mutually shared neediness of two teenagers afraid of adjusting to life after high school.

In a weird way, he'd felt relieved. True, he had grown to love the predictable rhythm of their relationship: driving an hour north every Friday night to spend the weekend with Jess at UNH and hanging out with old friends from high school, guys like John "Bam-Bam" Bamford. Bam was riding a full boat scholarship for football, and

Chris Mooney

his coach had hooked him up with a sweet summer job working as a house painter, only the guy who owned the business needed more hands. Did Bam know anyone who was interested?

Every Saturday morning, they'd drag their hangovers north to get a good spot at Hampton Beach, home of the neon bikini and Lee Press-On nails, and hang out with a group of girls working as bartenders and wait-resses—the Aqua Net Chicks, Bill called them. Fun, bubblegum-smacking gigglers with teased hair who wore lots of gold—chains, bracelets, anklets, rings, you name it—and liked to rock out to the king of the hair bands, Bon Jovi.

Except Samantha Ellis. Sam, as she liked to be called, wore her brown hair straight, tied back in a ponytail, and unlike the other girls, Sam didn't feel the need to show off every inch of her skin. She read books by Hemingway and Faulkner and drank Tanqueray and tonic while her friends read *Cosmo* and *Glamour* and did shots with names like Screaming Orgasm and Titty Twister. The other girls tolerated her when she was around, but the second she left, they tore into her. Just because she's been to places like France and Italy and goes to Smith she thinks she's better than everyone else. I don't even know why she's up here working—her parents have a home on Martha's Vineyard, you know. A girl from Saugus called Sam "that stuck-up Jew from Newton."

It wasn't dislike; it was discomfort. Sam didn't have to put on makeup or buy fancy clothes to look good because she always looked good. She didn't have to struggle to make herself interesting because she *was* interesting. Having Sam around was a reminder of their limitations. They envied her. The only shot they'd have at Sam's future life was to marry up. Sam could afford to be choosy.

On the last Saturday in July, a storm swept through and roughed up the waves. Mike went bodysurfing and an hour later stumbled back up to his blanket and saw everyone playing volleyball—everyone except Sam. She sat in her beach chair, sipping a Coke as she alternated her attention between the sunset and the volleyball game. One of the girls screamed. Bill had dropped his shorts and was mooning her.

"You should tell your friend to try Clearasil," Sam said. "Clear that problem right up."

"I don't think he cares."

"And that's what I love about him." Sam cocked her head to him, squinting in the remaining sunlight. "How come you're not playing?"

"Surf's too good to waste. What about you? Afraid of getting mooned?"

"My mother told me to never waste the opportunity to watch a sunset. You never know when it's going to be your last."

"You sure you're not Irish Catholic?"

Sam laughed. Mike loved the contagious sound of it, the way it moved through him. A thought flooded his mind and turned his mouth dry, made his heart beat a little faster.

No way, a voice warned. *Not in a million years.*

But it was summer. He was having fun and hey, the mood felt right, so why not?

"Sunset's better down by the shore," he said. "Want to go for a walk?"

"Sure."

She lived in Newton, a city he had always associated with money and status. Both of her parents were Harvard-educated lawyers and worked at the same law office in downtown Boston. Her father had arranged a clerking job. An internship at a law office would look good on a resume, her father said.

"So what brings you up here?" She did seem more suited for a place like the Vineyard.

"Because my father would never be caught dead in a place like this. What about you?"

The one thing he knew about himself was that he wasn't good at pretending. So he told her.

Come September, he was going to drop out of community college and start a contracting business with none other than the pimple-assed William O'Malley. Mike liked working with his hands. It was a skill that had provided Bill's father, a guy with no college diploma, with a good house, his pick of trucks and every three years a brand new Ski-Doo snowmobile. What was the point of taking out loans to attend classes that, when you got right down to it, added up to nothing more than an expensive hand job that left you feeling unsatisfied and totally ripped off?

"Congratulations," she said.

"For what?"

"For being real. For being eighteen and knowing who you are and being so sure about what you want to do with your life and having the balls to go after it. Most people spend their whole lives pretending to like a job they hate. You should feel relieved."

They slept together three weeks later. Years would pass, and yet Mike would always be able to recall the way Sam looked as she took off her clothes, the curtains swelling around her; the cool air filled with the smell of fried seafood wafting up from the restaurant below; the electric touch that made his skin quiver; the way she stared into his eyes in that final, heart-twisting moment, Mike knowing that she was sharing more than just her skin.

It should never have ended, but it did, during the last week of summer. Jess had come home from Newport in tears, saying that she had made a mistake and wanted to get back together. He said yes.

He waited until Sam went off to college before he told her it was over. He did it over the phone, and when she asked why, he said he was getting back together with Jess. Sam didn't buy it. When she kept pressing him, he started dodging her phone calls. Maybe he was afraid of acknowledging the truth: that his shared history with Jess was comfortable and familiar and predictable. Besides, how realistic was it to hope that someone like Sam would stick around for the long haul with a blue-collar guy without a degree? He was going back to life in Belham, and Sam, well, she could go anywhere she wanted.

On an early Sunday morning, right before six, Mike woke up to Sam banging on the front door. He begged Lou not to open it.

"It's a big deal when you give over a piece of your heart, Michael. If you're going to shit all over it, then at least have the guts to look me in the eyes and tell me why."

Sam waited for ten minutes and then jumped back in her Jeep and peeled off down the street.

"Must have been one hell of a ride in the sack," Lou said with a grin. "The ones full of piss and vinegar usually are."

"Mr. Sullivan?"

The slightly feminine voice belonged to a pencil-thin, twentysomething man wearing black pants and a black shirt. His skin was deeply tanned, and although Mike was certainly no expert in such matters, he was pretty sure the guy had his eyebrows plucked or shaped. He had certainly done *something* to them.

"Hello," he said, extending his hand. His handshake was about as firm as wet toilet paper. "I'm Sam's assistant, Anthony. Sorry to keep you waiting, but it's been like, *so* incredibly hectic in here today. Follow me."

Mike followed Anthony as he navigated his way through hallways packed with suits and skirts. Some looked up from their law books and shot a look of mild curiosity at his clothes. Mike had been driving back from the jobsite when the idea hit him. He remembered the first two names in the law office, and the patient lady from Verizon had filled in the rest.

Sam stood in the archway of her door and still looked every inch of the smart, confident girl he had fallen in love with that summer in New Hampshire.

Bill was right. She looked good. Damn good.

"Michael Sullivan," she said. "What's it been? Fifteen years?"

"Something like that. Thanks for squeezing me in on such short notice, Sam."

Anthony said, "Mr. Sullivan, what can I get you to drink? We have Pellegrino—"

"Coffee's fine," Sam said. "Come on in, Sully."

Sam's office was roughly the size of his TV room. Cherry bookcases ran the length of one wall, but the most impressive piece of furniture was the desk—or the desk and a half. It was as long as the bed of his truck and held a computer, printer and fax machine and still had plenty of room left over for all her papers and books.

"Wow," Mike said. "You even have your own private bathroom."

"With a shower. This is what you get in exchange for working ninety-hour weeks and having no social life."

Sam sat down behind her desk. Mike took a seat in one of the two cushy black leather chairs arranged in front of her desk. Anthony came waltzing back in with a tray holding two china cups and a decanter full of coffee. He placed the tray down on the corner of the desk and asked if there was anything else she needed. Sam said no, thanked him and told him to go home. Anthony bid them *adieu* and shut the door behind him.

Sam put on a pair of tortoise-framed glasses and, coffee cup in hand, settled back in her chair. "I'm assuming this isn't a social call."

"I wish it was. I take it you've been following the news."

Sam nodded, her face growing softer. "Bill told me what happened when I bumped into him," she said. "I'm so sorry."

"My daughter's jacket has been at the lab for two weeks. Every time I try and talk to the detective running the case, this guy Merrick, he keeps stalling me."

"Maybe he doesn't have the results back yet."

"He's sitting on them."

"You know that for a fact?"

"Someone working close to the case told me. My question is—why I came to see you—can he legally do that? I mean, if Merrick knows something, he just couldn't keep it from me, right?"

"First off, I'm not a criminal attorney. I do mainly contract work. Mergers and acquisitions—don't worry, I won't bore you with the details. What I can tell you is that Merrick is under no legal obligation to share anything with you. I know that sounds cold, but homicide detectives are, by and large, a cold bunch. That being said, they're not heartless, so I would think Merrick would want to keep you up-to-date with the progress of the case—unless he has a legitimate reason not to."

His run-in with Jonah was being rehashed all over the papers and TV.

"Merrick thinks I may go after Jonah again," Mike said.

"It's a legitimate cause for concern on his part. If I had to guess, I'd say that he's afraid you're going to blow his case and, frankly, closing the case is all he cares about."

"If that's true, then he should have Jonah behind bars."

Sam nodded sympathetically.

Mike held up a hand. "Sorry, I'm not trying to unload this on you."

"Your frustration is perfectly understandable."

"Sam, do you know if there's any way to find out what's in the lab report?"

"You'd have to talk with a criminal attorney. What about the one who handled your criminal case?"

"He died about a year ago."

Sam thought about it for a moment. "We have a criminal attorney here named Martin Weinstein. He's the best in the state. He's on vacation, but I believe he'll be in toward the later part of next week. I can give him a call then."

More waiting. Mike could manage the sleepless nights, dragging his exhaustion like shackles with him throughout the day along with his growing need to drink, but the waiting was maddening. People like Merrick and Sam weren't holding onto threads. They did their jobs and clocked out, left for their other lives, their real lives.

Sam said, "Mind if I ask a personal question?"

"Not at all."

"Why me?"

"You mean why did I come to see you?"

Sam nodded. "Surely you must know other lawyers."

"Actually I don't. You're the only lawyer I know. And the ones I've met over the years are generally full of shit."

"It's a job requirement."

"Not with you. You never pulled any punches."

"You could have told Anthony what you wanted on the phone," Sam said. "I could have called you back."

"I wanted to talk to a face, not a phone. And honestly, I can't stand all this waiting. Bill mentioned he saw you, mentioned your firm, and I decided to give you a call, figuring that if there was a lawyer out there that could help me, it would be you."

Sam nodded, fixed him with a cool gaze. "I have Martin's cell phone, but I can't promise anything. Where can I reach you?"

Mike placed the coffee cup and saucer on the edge of her desk and then removed a business card from his wallet. He wrote his home number on the back and handed the card to her.

"Thanks," he said.

"You won't be thanking me when Martin sends you his bill."

She walked him to the door, opened it for him.

"Bill also told me about you and your wife," she said. "I've been through it myself. It's rough in the beginning, but then it gets better. Dating is certainly more interesting this time around. Two months ago, a guy flew me to Europe on his private plane."

"That must have been nice."

"He flew me there to see a David Hasselhoff concert."

"That's not so nice."

"More like yuck. Hang in there, Sully." Sam smiled and patted his arm.

Ten minutes later, when he started his truck, he could still feel the touch of her hand. Fifteen years, he thought. Maybe it wasn't possible to go back in time, but it certainly was possible to go back and revisit those moments you once held close to your heart.

CHAPTER 20

Fang suffered from a major case of colitis, so when Mike heard that high-pitched yelp, he threw back the covers and, dressed only in a pair of boxers, rushed through the semi-dark house and found the dog whimpering in the family room, his nose practically pressed against the sliding glass door.

Mike opened the door and Fang ran down the porch steps, disappearing into the thick, white mist that hung in the predawn light. Mike yawned, listening as Fang moved across the backyard, sniffing the grass as he searched for the perfect spot to relieve himself. Didn't matter how badly they had to go, dogs still had to search for that perfect spot—

Fang barked, a loud, deep rumbling sound that ripped through the quiet morning, and before Mike could call him home, the dog bolted into the woods.

Mike rushed upstairs, threw on jeans, sneakers and the flannel shirt he had worn last night, and then headed out through the screen door and ran up the trail that led into the woods. Somewhere in the mist he could hear Fang's barking, branches snapping back as he ran.

The trail opened up to a main road made of packed dirt that would later be nothing but mud. This wooded area was the last remaining section of undeveloped land in Belham, part of a nature conservatory or something, and during winter weekends, Salmon Brook Pond was crawling with small kids learning to skate, teenagers organizing hockey games, adults getting together, talking and catching up. Mike banged a left and jogged up the road, the mist thick and Fang's barking loud enough to wake up half the neighborhood. It had probably woken up his neighbor, Bob Dowery, a retired airline pilot who had anointed himself the neighborhood watchdog. Mike knew for sure that Bob would pop over later wearing that humdrum look of bad news on his face just before he launched into a lecture on how to be a responsible dog owner.

The barking stopped. Mike slowed to a walk, and a few minutes later spotted Fang's tail wagging back and forth in that windshield-wiper-caught-in-a-storm way that let the world know he was in doggy ecstasy. A man was lying on his stomach on the edge of a steep slope. It had to be a man. A woman wouldn't wear a Navy peacoat and a bright orange hunter's cap that fastened around the ears.

The man groaned. His legs, Mike noticed, were splayed at odd angles.

Fang had done this. The dog and his hundred-plus pounds had knocked the guy flat on his ass.

"Fang, come!"

The dog was too busy sniffing the man. Mike scooped up a snowball, and once he had the dog's attention, tossed it toward the main road and away from the pond. Fang tore after it, and Mike turned his attention to the man.

"I'm sorry, he bolted off before I could grab him. Are you hurt?"

The man waved him off. He propped himself up on his hands, his head bowed forward and his face out of view, and crawled through snow, heading in the direction of his cane and a small red plastic tube—an asthma inhaler. Mike reached down and scooped the inhaler off the snow, about to hand it over when he saw the liver-spotted hands, the spidery fingers.

"Give it . . . to . . . me," the man wheezed.

The sound of that panting, wheezy voice tore through Mike's brain like a bullet. He stood up straight, took a step back.

Put the inhaler in his hand and walk away.

Yes. The terms of his probation clearly stated that it was his responsibility—no, his duty—to hand over the inhaler and walk away. Put it in his hands and run back to the house and call 911 and then Merrick. It was an accident, Detective. The dog did it, I swear. I picked up the inhaler and put it in his hands and walked away and called 911. See what a good do-bee I am? See how I kept my anger in check, Dr. T. Go ahead and give me that breathalyzer, Mr. Testa, I'll pass with flying colors.

Then Mike remembered Jonah's slick grin of pleasure from the grocery store. I own you, that grin had said. I own your daughter, and now I own your life, and there isn't a goddamn thing you can do about it.

Put the inhaler in his hand and walk away.

"What are you doing out here so early?"

Jonah kept his head bowed, clouds of breath steaming around his face. "Sunrise. I came out here to see . . . a sunrise before . . ." Each word came out strained, as if some horrific amount of weight was piled against his chest. "My inhaler . . ."

Mike knelt down, balancing his weight on the balls of his feet, and pinched the inhaler between his thumb and forefinger.

"Look at me."

The former priest slowly lifted his eyes and met Mike's gaze.

"You're going to tell me where Sarah is," Mike said. "You're going to tell me and I'm going to give you your inhaler."

"I can't . . . breathe . . ."

"Good. Now you've got a taste of how I've been feeling every day for the past five years."

Panic bloomed on Jonah's face. His lungs made a sick, whistling sound that made Mike think of wet cement being poured through a pipe.

"I . . . don't—"

"What did you do to her?"

Jonah's mouth kept working, trying to draw in air. Jonah's windpipe was closing and Jonah was drowning in all this fresh air and Mike was vaguely aware that a part of himself was warming to the sight of this, the building terror in Jonah's eyes and voice.

Mike wiggled the inhaler in front of Jonah's face. "One puff and you can breathe again."

"I . . . I can't . . ."

"You can and you will."

"Please," Jonah begged, his eyes growing hungry and desperate.

"You want to die out here?"

Jonah lunged for the inhaler. Mike closed it inside his fist.

"Nobody's coming to help you," Mike said as Jonah's bony fingers worked furiously to pry open Mike's fist. "You're going to tell me what happened to Sarah and those two other girls, and you're going to tell me now or you're going to die out here."

Jonah wouldn't answer. Mike pressed his thumb on the metal tube, and the inhaler made a hissing sound as it released the medicine into the air.

"I . . . can't . . ."

Mike kept pressing the tube, Jonah watching, on the verge of tears.

"Tell me," Mike said through gritted teeth. "Tell me and I'll let you live."

Jonah collapsed against the snow, his face red from

the exertion. Mike straddled him, grabbed him by the front of the jacket collar.

"You have to tell me. You were a priest, remember? You need my forgiveness." Mike shook him. "Tell me what happened to my daughter."

Jonah worked his mouth but no sound came out.

Mike placed Jonah's body back against the snow and then leaned his ear close to Jonah's mouth, Mike close enough to smell the sour bile and funk baked in Jonah's breath. It was the smell of rot. Death.

"Our Father, who . . . art in heaven . . ."

Mike whipped his head around. Jonah stared up at the sky, his lips bloodless and dotted with spittle, wheezing through phlegm and whatever fluid was clogging his windpipe.

". . . hallowed be . . . thy name . . ."

Mike shook him again. "You need me to forgive you."

". . . thy kingdom come . . ."

"Make it right. I'm giving you a chance to make it right, now tell me, you son of a bitch."

". . . earth as it is in heaven . . ."

Mike rattled him. "*Goddamnit,* tell me. *TELL ME!*"

Jonah's eyes had a dreamy, faraway look. The mist had started to clear, and on the periphery of his vision, Mike could see Fang across the road, sniffing along the edge of the pond. *Twirly-birdy!* Sarah had said as she pointed to the TV where this peanut of a girl skated across the ice and then jumped in the air, twirling around before landing back on the ice. *I want to learn the twirly-birdy, Daddy.* And he had taken her to this pond, had put on her skates and laced them up and stacked two milk crates, putting her small hands on top of them, telling her how to push off, how to keep her balance, Sarah going along with it but wanting to know when he was going to show her the twirly-birdy jump and it was possible she had grown up and learned how to do that, oh yes, it was possible, anything was possible as long as you had faith, as long as you believed and kept believing and were good and said your prayers and God would protect you because God is love is faith and light and—

"*TELL ME.*"

The puffs of steam forming around Jonah's mouth had almost disappeared.

He's dying.

Let him die. I don't care.

If he dies out here, he takes his secrets with him.

Mike stuck the inhaler in Jonah's mouth and pressed down on the aerosol container. Medicine hissed out of the tube. Two, three, four more blasts and Jonah's mouth came alive, greedily sucking on the plastic nozzle like a hungry newborn.

A moment later, Jonah's eyes refocused.

Mike stood up, panting. For several minutes, they stared at each other, the last two men to have touched Sarah.

"Tell me if she's alive," Mike said. "At least give me that."

It took another minute for Jonah to regain his breath.

"Only God knows what is true."

Out of the corner of his eye, Mike saw the cane. His eyes shifted to Jonah's knee, saw the cane coming down on it, shattering bone.

Mike dropped the inhaler and stumbled away. He thought he heard Jonah weeping and forced himself to keep walking.

CHAPTER 21

Later that day, Sunday, Bill threw a barbecue. Mike stopped by early in the morning and helped Bill set up. He didn't tell Bill about his encounter with Jonah.

Two kegs were set up on the corner of the sprawling deck, and music from the Rock of Boston, WBCN, pumped over the deck's wall speakers. Mike drank ice-cold cans of Coke and forced himself to smile and act gracious, tried like hell to lose himself in the conversations as he mingled with the crowd of friends and Bill's neighbors while, in the back of his mind, he heard Jonah crying.

Maybe Jonah's near-death experience from this morning had forced him to confront the fact that his demise was days, possibly even hours away. Maybe getting his life back, whatever was left of it, maybe it had forced him to dip into whatever small chunk of humanity he had left.

I shouldn't have turned around, Mike thought. I

should have waited longer. He would have told me something, and I blew it.

A few more minutes wouldn't have mattered.

I should have tried.

And when he didn't give you what you wanted, then what would you have done? Tried using the cane on his kneecaps?

Mike didn't know what terrified him the more: the calm willingness he had felt at watching Jonah struggle for air, or the almost yawning ease with which he had slipped back into the shadow of his former self, the one he was convinced, at least until this morning, could only be accessed by booze. The rage was always there, he realized, on the skin instead of being buried underneath it, the booze the lame excuse he used to ignite it.

He looked at his watch. It was after three. Maybe Merrick knew something.

Mike took out his cell phone, moved to a quiet corner of the backyard and dialed Merrick's direct number at the station.

Ring.

Jonah's going to die.

Ring.

You can't change it.

Ring.

But you're going to have to face it.

Merrick's voice mail clicked on. Mike left a message, asking him to call immediately, and snapped his cell phone shut. His heart was beating faster than it should, his face shiny with perspiration.

That last morning, he had walked into Sarah's bedroom and kissed her on the head, the same ritual he performed every morning, and it always amazed him how this small person who was a part of him and yet not a part of him or like anyone else in the world could, just by the very sight of her, fill him up with equal amounts of love and fear. And it never went away. You didn't know that kind of love until you had a child, until you changed diapers and walked around with them during the night and lay next to them when they were sick—until they looked into your eyes for the first time and smiled, you couldn't understand how rare that kind of love was, how it changed you. That morning he had looked at her sleeping and knew that this was enough. If this was all he had in life, then he would be happy. And he had meant it.

That life is gone. You can't have it back.

She was born premature and had survived all the odds and had grown into this wonderfully, beautifully stubborn little girl who—

You've got to let her go. You've got to grieve and move on.

Move on to what?

You'll figure it out.

I don't want to figure it out. I want my daughter back.

That life is gone.

And it had been gone for a long time, hadn't it? And the life he was leading in the interim was coming to an end too. And Jonah was going to die today, tomorrow—it didn't matter because Mike knew Jonah was going to take his secrets to the grave, and he'd be left with Jonah's voice, and it would live forever in his mind, forced to share the same rooms with his daughter.

Mike went to take a drink and found his cup bone dry.

He navigated his way through the backyard and deck and to the kitchen island table where the bottles of soda were set up along with the bottles of Jack Daniel's, Absolut and Captain Morgan.

He was alone in the kitchen.

He was eyeing the bottle of Jack when his cell phone vibrated against his hip.

Not Merrick. It was Sam.

"Good, Sully, you're there. I just left a message for you at home."

"What's up?"

"I asked the private investigator we use to do a little digging and, well, I've managed to get a copy of the lab report on your daughter's jacket. I know it's short notice, but can you come into town in the next hour?"

"I'm on my way."

CHAPTER 22

Sam wasn't kidding about the long hours. A gorgeous Sunday afternoon and the law firm was humming with activity. It wasn't as packed as it had been the other day—people weren't running around with that same end-of-the-world urgency, for one—but the hallways and offices were bustling with a good number of people moving around with a wired, under-the-gun energy. And Sam's desk was in the same state of disarray as the other day, her wastebasket full of paper bags of takeout food. Mike wondered if she spent most of her nights here too.

Seated at the head of Sam's conference table was a pleasant-looking woman with short, messy blond hair wearing a gray zippered Black Dog sweatshirt. She blew out a long, pink bubble and popped it as she stood up.

Sam said, "Mike, this is Nancy Childs."

"Howareya," Nancy said. All one word. Probably still used words like *wicked cool* and *pissa,* Mike thought as he shook her hand. For a secretary, her handshake packed a lot of punch.

"The private investigator on his way?" he asked Sam.

Nancy said, "You're looking at her, big guy."

For some reason, when Sam had mentioned the words "private investigator," his mind had formed an image of a guy in his late fifties, an ex-cop or ex–FBI agent with a bad comb-over who wore suits from Sears—maybe even a Robert Urich type like in *Spenser: For Hire,* but definitely not a gum-smacking middle-aged graduate from the Revere Secretarial School.

"Let me guess," Nancy said with a grin. "You thought I was the secretary."

"Sorry. I guess I didn't know what to expect."

"Don't worry. Happens all the time. Sam and I are used to it, only Sam gets it less 'cause she speaks and dresses better than I do. You're right, Sam, I've gotta stop chomping on the gum and wear a big gun on my hip."

Nancy shot Sam one of those men-are-such-dopes glances before she sat down. Sam sat on the opposite end of the table, and Mike took the chair next to Nancy. The overhead canister lights in her office were dimmed, and soft jazz music played on the bookshelf speakers.

"Sam said you managed to get a copy of the state lab report," Mike said.

"Sure did. I had to call in some major favors to get it."

"I can't tell you how much I appreciate this."

"Reason I bring up the favor thing," Nancy said, "is

to impress upon you the importance of keeping this information to yourself."

"I understand."

"Do you really?"

"Do I really what?"

"Understand. Word is you're a hothead. My experience with hotheads is not only do they lack impulse
control, they always end up ramming you straight up the
old glory hole."

Mike sat there, his mind busy trying to untangle
himself from her words. Out of the corner of his eye, he
saw Sam shift in her chair.

Nancy said, "Sorry for being blunt, but I'm not good
with small talk, and I'm not good with BS. A lot of men
have a hard time with that, which may explain why I'm
still single. Another thing Sam and I have in common,
you know, besides the chick thing." Nancy smiled but
she wasn't joking.

"Any particular reason you're busting my balls?"

"Last time somebody helped you, you turned around
and used Jonah as a punching bag. Sorry, but I don't
need that kind of publicity."

Her whole Bill O'Reilly attitude should have bothered him and might have too if he hadn't been numbed
by his weekly verbal wrestling session with the queen of
the ball breakers, Dr. T. Nancy Childs just another part
of the same cold machinery that employed Dr. T and
Testa and Merrick, Nancy with her gum-snapping
brutal-honesty spiel and I-Can-Piss-Like-A-Man chip
on her shoulder just itching for him to flash a little

anger or throw a fit so she could pack up her files and march out the door, sorry Sam, but I don't do business with hotheads and boozehounds.

"I ran into Francis Jonah this morning," Mike said.

Nancy chewed her gum, waiting for the rest of it or not really caring, he didn't know which.

"My dog ran into him and knocked him flat on his ass—that's the honest-to-God truth," Mike said. "There was Jonah, lying in the snow and gasping for breath, I mean really struggling. He dropped his inhaler and he needs it to breathe, and the inhaler's right next to me. I pick it up and then the idea hits me: trade the inhaler for information on my daughter. He'll tell me what happened to Sarah, and I'll give him the inhaler so he can breathe. Now tell me, Nancy, what would you have done in that situation?"

"Hard to say."

"Go ahead, think about it," Mike said. "I'd love to get your take on it."

Nancy clicked her nails against the table.

Mike shook his head. "See, that's what I don't understand. Everyone tells me what I *should* have done—you know, play Monday-morning quarterback and judge me after the fact. But when I ask them to put themselves in my situation, they shrug or, like you, they clam up. So I guess what I'm trying to say, Nancy, is that if you have a problem with what I did out of the love of my daughter, please, by all means, take the lab report, wrap it around your attitude, and feel free to ram it straight up *your* glory hole because frankly—and I say this in the spirit of total honesty here—frankly, I'm sick and tired of explaining myself to people who are clueless."

Several seconds passed. No one spoke.

Nancy reached down and grabbed a leather satchel resting against her chair leg. Go ahead and leave. Fuck it. He was tired of begging.

She didn't leave. She removed a blue file folder, placed it on the table in front of him and flipped it open.

An 8x10 color photograph of Sarah's jacket. A ruler had been placed next to the jacket for measurement purposes, and the hood was open.

"What's that?" Mike said, pointing to the three quarter-sized black smudges on the left side of the hood.

"Those are bloodstains."

Mike felt like his heart had been dunked in ice water.

"They ran the DNA test on the blood and matched it to the sample they had on file—the hair they took from Sarah's brush when she went missing," Nancy said. "Both samples match."

He didn't remember seeing blood that night on the Hill.

You couldn't see them. The detective folded back the hood, remember?

Yes. The detective with the Red Sox baseball hat had folded back the hood—on purpose. Merrick didn't want him to see the blood and hadn't mentioned it because if Mike had known about the blood, there was no way he would have—

Mike looked away from the picture, thinking back to this morning's run-in with Jonah.

"Anything about the jacket stand out?"

He saw loneliness and fear. He saw defeat.

Nancy said, "The jacket's in good shape, wouldn't you agree?"

She was right. With the exception of the blood, there wasn't a blemish on the coat, a rip or a tear anywhere, and the white fur lining the outer rim of the hood, Jesus, it looked *clean*.

"He stored it," Mike said.

"For the jacket to be in this condition, yes, it would had to have been stored somewhere. Now we know a forensic team from the Boston Police Lab came in and tore up Jonah's house when Sarah disappeared. And we know they walked away empty-handed, which is why they couldn't build a case against Jonah. The thinking now is that Jonah must have hidden stuff at an off-site location, a storage facility, maybe even a safety-deposit box."

"I thought Merrick already checked into that."

"He did—under Jonah's real name and his fake one. Your daughter's jacket pops up, so now Merrick thinks if Jonah had one fake identity, who's to say he didn't have another one? Word I hear is that Merrick has been digging deep into that area."

"I don't understand why he'd keep the jacket. That's evidence."

"Some serial offenders often keep souvenirs of their crimes so they can, you know . . ."

"No," Mike said, looking up at her. "I don't know."

"Owning a piece of the victim's clothing, a piece of jewelry—they're called trophies. Some serial offenders often keep these items so they can relive their crimes. It's another way of maintaining control over their victims. From what I hear, Merrick has been investigating that angle for years. That's why, when your daughter's anniversary date rolls around, he puts people on him. Merrick's even searched through Jonah's garbage, tracked phone calls—he hasn't given up. The problem he's facing is that Jonah's highly intelligent. His IQ is off the charts, for one, and, unfortunately, he knows how to cover his tracks.

"Now let me answer your next question: Why would Jonah put the jacket on the cross and risk going back to living under a microscope—especially when he's dying and wants to die in peace?" Nancy said. "Perfectly rational question. The problem is that there's no rational answer. With the Jonahs of the world, normal, everyday logic doesn't apply. I talked it over with a few forensic psychiatrists I respect and the overwhelming theory is that Jonah wants to get caught. As crazy as it sounds, a lot of them do. Some get caught and want to brag. Some make it into a game—like Ted Bundy, for example."

"Jonah was dying this morning and wouldn't talk."

"Why does that surprise you?"

"You weren't there. He was terrified of dying. I could see it in his eyes."

"Of course he was terrified. You attacked him once. Suffocate or get beaten to death. Which one would you choose?"

Mike said, "You find anything else?"

"Lab found two fibers, both of them synthetic. One of them matches that imitation raccoon fur on Jonah's jacket hood. The *coup de grâce,* however, is the single strand of hair the lab found stuck to one of the cuffs."

"Jonah's."

"Bingo. Based on my sources, Merrick's going to move on Jonah with a search warrant any day now. With this evidence, I'd be willing to bet Jonah won't be going home."

So there it was. Five years and now he had a piece of concrete evidence linking Jonah to Sarah.

Mike stared at the picture of the jacket. All this time, all this energy into fighting and he expected to feel . . . to feel what? Vindicated? Was that it? If it was, then why'd he feel so hollow?

That hollow feeling is shock.

"I'm going to keep this folder," Nancy said. "If someone saw you with it and it got back to Merrick or someone else tied to the case, my ass would be in a lot of hot water."

"Thank you." Mike felt dazed, out of sorts.

"You're welcome." Nancy stood up, satchel and file folder in hand, and left the room, shutting the office door behind her.

Mike leaned back in his chair and rubbed his hand across the smoothness of the table as he looked out the window at the half dozen or so buildings dotting the Boston skyline.

"I'm sorry Nancy was so abrasive," Sam said after a

moment. "She's a good person. She just has a hard time dealing with people who drink. Her father and brother are alcoholics."

"Least you know where you stand with her. Thanks for arranging this, Sam. I owe you."

"Is there anything I can do?"

Mike shook his head and shut his eyes. As he rubbed them, trying to get some wetness going, he pictured Sarah's jacket stuffed in an evidence box, taped shut and locked away in some dark cabinet.

When he opened his eyes, Sam was staring at him, her face open and vulnerable, the way it had been all those years ago during those nights on the beach when they sat around and shared their disappointments and hurts. Back then, she had listened to his stories of his father and hadn't judged him, and Mike was willing to bet she wouldn't judge him now.

"I keep having these dreams," Mike said. "Sarah sleeping in her room and she's crying. She won't stop crying." He took in a deep breath and continued. "I grab a pillow and hold it over her face. The other night I had another dream where we're in a car and Sarah was crying and I kicked her out. Me. Her father. Why would I be having dreams like that?"

CHAPTER 23

Later that night, Sarah came for him.

She stood on the edge of Salmon Brook Pond, her pink jacket zippered to the top but her hood down, her face clear and bright. Her mouth was open, and the tip of her tongue was out, rubbing against her bottom lip.

"Look, Daddy, look!" she screamed, borderline hysterical as she skated across the pond in that wavering *tap-tap-tap* and "Oh-God-I'm-about-to-fall-on-my-bum" shuffle of all young skaters, her arms standing out by her sides, flapping like wings.

Mike skated up next to her. It was a perfect winter day: sky a hard blue, air cold but lacking that angry bite that drove you indoors. The kidney-shaped pond was packed with kids and parents. Down at the far end, away from the crowd, a group of kids was playing a heated game of hockey, the sound of their sticks *thwacking* across the ice echoing through the air.

"You're doing great, Sarah."

"Come skating with me."

"Can I hold your hand?"

Sarah had to think about it for a moment.

"Okay," she said, still *tap-tap-tapping* forward, "but we have to do the twirly-birdy jump."

"You know I can't do that, sweets."

Sarah stopped skating, looked up and pushed her glasses back up her nose. Here, out in the sunlight, every feature on her face seemed magnified: the dimpled cheeks on her pale Irish skin; the blueness of her eyes.

"But that's how the judges judge us," she said.

He frowned, trying to think through her thought process.

"On TV, Daddy, remember? The man and woman skated around and then they got numbers."

"Oh, you mean the figure skaters."

"The man picks up the girl and holds her up in the air and the judges give out the numbers."

"Now that I can do. You ready?"

"Ready," she said, and gave him her hand, its smallness reminding him of the early hair-trigger days Sarah spent in Mass General's NICU, the hospital's unit for preemie babies, all four pounds of his daughter being monitored by wires hooked up to all sorts of computerized gizmos, Sarah fighting to breathe on her own because her lungs were underdeveloped and then fighting off an infection that had almost killed her.

"Daddy!"

"Yeah, sweets?"

"You're not paying attention. The judges are watching us. They're waiting for you to pick me up and hold me out front."

He did as instructed, holding her out front—not difficult since she barely weighed forty pounds, Sarah still so tiny for her age.

Sarah spread apart her legs and arms, forming an X.

"Starfish! Now you do one."

He lifted Sarah up, placed her on top of his shoulders, and then wrapped one arm around her shins and hugged her legs close to his chest. He took his other arm and pointed it out in a straight line.

"How's that?"

"Call out what you're doing, Daddy!"

(Wooo-Woof!)

"Arrow!"

Sarah said, "The judges won't like that name."

"Well, what would you call it?"

"Fighting fish!"

(Fang barked again: *Woo-woo-WOO!*)

Mike's eyes cracked open. Moonlight flooded the bedroom. Fang wasn't in bed. Mike turned over and saw the dog standing next to one of the opened windows overlooking the backyard, his snout pressed against the screen, snorting at the air, his tail lolling back and forth.

Probably a raccoon or something. The upstairs windows were open, and all kinds of scents were blowing through the house.

"Fang, come on."

The dog wouldn't move. Mike stood up, feeling Sarah's face starting to fade, and quickly grabbed the dog by the collar.

"Daddy."

Mike jerked back from the window and almost tripped over the dog. Startled, Fang whipped around and started barking.

Sarah's voice. It was Sarah's voice and it had come from outside.

It's the dream. The dream's still floating around in your head and your imagination, it hiccuped it back up.

A rush of wind blew back the curtains. His heart climbing high in his chest, he got down on one knee and looked past the window screen. A full moon hung over the darkened tops of the pine trees, the moonlight turning the remaining patches of snow a light, neon blue. He scanned the backyard, waiting.

You're hearing things. You ran into Jonah today and had the dream and now—

"Daddy, where are you?"

"Woo-WOO-WOO!"

Sarah's voice. It was Sarah's voice and she was calling for him.

Mike scrambled for his jeans and put them on, his hands shaking as he worked the button and zipper.

"Daddy?"

He shoved his bare feet into a pair of sneakers and ran down the stairs and into the family room, Fang following behind him, barking. Mike's shaking hands worked the lock on the sliding glass door and then slid it open and the dog rushed out into the night. Mike took the trail, the overhead branches and limbs fanned with pine needles and leaves blocking out most of the moonlight, the woods growing darker and darker as he ran, Fang bounding somewhere ahead of him, barking, branches snapping back.

"Daddy, where are you?"

Sarah's voice, it was Sarah's voice, and by some miracle of God she had come home and was now lost in the woods and he was about to see her and bring her home.

"I'm here, Sarah. I'm here." He ran faster, almost tripping.

Mike stood at the edge of where the trail opened up onto the dirt road, lit up by moonlight.

"Sarah, I'm out here in the woods with you."

The wind whistled through the trees, shaking the limbs overhead. Mike waited for her to answer, his eyes were wide as they took in every shadow and shape. His legs were shaking and he kept swallowing.

"Daddy?"

Her voice coming from straight ahead, from deeper into the woods.

"Hold on, Sarah, I'm coming." Mike stepped off the trail and worked his way down the slope, the rubber treads of his sneakers slipping against the half-frozen ice, thinking about Sarah's voice, how wonderfully calm and patient it sounded, that was good, so wonderfully, beautifully good.

It was nearly pitch black down here at the bottom,

and the terrain was uneven, with swift, sudden dips, bumpy with large rocks, downed branches and limbs. Mike moved deeper in the woods, walking quickly but carefully, branches whipping past his face, cutting into his hands and arms and face. Up ahead, in a patch of moonlight on the snow, he thought he saw Fang's big, bulky frame tear up the side of a steep embankment.

"I can't see you," Sarah called from somewhere above him, Sarah still patient but starting to get scared.

"I'm right below you," Mike called out. "Just stay where you are. I'm coming up."

Mike made his way up the steep slope, grabbing branches for support. It was slow going; with his sneakers, he couldn't get any traction.

"Daddy?" Sarah was on the verge of tears.

"Don't panic, honey. Just talk to me. I'm almost there."

Mike continued making his way up the slope, sweat pouring off his face.

"Where are you?" Sarah called again.

Fang barked.

Both sounds above him, louder now, and closer.

"Just listen to the sound of my voice, Sarah. And those other sounds you hear, all those branches snapping—that's Fang. He's come out here to see you too. We've both missed you so much."

"Daddy, where are you?"

"Honey, I'm right—"

The voice was wrong. It was Sarah's voice, no question, but it was her old voice—her six-year-old voice.

Sarah was eleven now. Her voice would be different now. It wouldn't have that high-pitched, reedy quality to it. It would be deeper, maybe.

"Sarah," he yelled up the slope. "Tell me the name of your dog."

No answer.

"Tell me your favorite color."

Fang barked.

Finally, the slope leveled off. Moonlight trickled inside the area of woods where Mike now stood, and he could see the main road and beyond it, part of Salmon Brook Road. Fang had his snout pressed against the ground, sniffing around the base of a massive, sprawling maple.

"Daddy, where are you?"

Mike turned around. Resting on top of a rotted tree stump was a portable stereo, what he used to call a boom-box. The speakers were pointed in the direction of his house.

"Daddy?" Sarah cried from the speakers.

Mike wasn't looking at the radio anymore. His attention was locked on the same thing that held Fang's attention: Francis Jonah, hanging from a limb of the maple tree.

Remembering Sarah

CHAPTER 24

Francis Jonah was buried on Friday, the first day of spring. The former priest's last will and testament called for a private funeral service—absolutely no reporters. That job was left to Father Jack Connelly. The well-respected and much-loved priest had a lot of pull in the community; he managed to convince the police, a good majority of them Catholics themselves, to leave judgment in the hands of God and honor a man's final wishes.

What Father Jack couldn't contain were the leaks. Someone had tipped off the media, and they had set up camp in front of the church.

The front doors of St. Stephen's opened and the pallbearers, four young men on loan from McGill-Flattery Funeral Home, stepped out with the casket, not expecting to see the small group of reporters crowding the front steps. Flashbulbs popped and cameras clicked. The police detail moved into action, starting to clear a path to the hearse.

Mike sat in the passenger seat of Slow Ed's cruiser parked across the street, his eyes covered by sunglasses and scanning the faces of the hundred-plus crowd of people.

"Cemetery's going to be just as bad," Slow Ed said. "Probably even worse."

Mike didn't respond, just sat there, staring, a thin, slowly dissolving membrane of separateness dividing him from the rest of the world.

Slow Ed started the cruiser and pulled away from the curb.

"We can keep the media out of the cemetery, but we can't keep them from holding their cameras up over the cemetery wall. They set up shop on Evergreen. They're standing on the roofs of their vans to get a better view of the gravesite. You told me you wanted to keep your face off the tube. You go in there, your face will be playing on all the news cycles."

Downtown traffic was light. They pulled onto Parker Street and climbed the steep hill, and when they passed Evergreen, a long street of tract housing for the terminally jobless and lost, Mike saw some of the residents gathered out on their front steps, their faces drowsy with sleep and pinched with hangovers, their hands trembling as they lit cigarettes and drank coffee and watched reporters fix their hair and makeup. Vans were parked up on the sidewalk, satellite feeds extended into the air.

"If the reason you're going there is because you want to see Father Jack," Slow Ed said, "I can turn around and drive back to his office. You want, I'll wait with you until he comes back."

Slow Ed giving him an out. There really was no reason to go ahead with this—no logical reason Mike could put into words. He had tried. Slow Ed had asked, and so had Bill, and Mike couldn't explain the reason for wanting to be at the cemetery to either of them or himself and yet this need was still there, this throbbing, unexplainable compulsion that told him he needed to be at the cemetery when Jonah was buried. Maybe this sudden need had to do with the dreams of Sarah and the new ones where Jonah lay on the cool steel table, his last words still on his tongue—Mike could see them, Jesus, they were right there, let's pick them up and sort them out. But nobody wanted to do it. They started to sew Jonah's mouth shut and he'd scream at them to stop and they would ignore him.

The dreams, Mike felt, were a signal to keep digging. Or maybe he just wanted to punish himself. He had, after all, set all of this into motion.

Slow Ed hooked a left onto Hancock. Two cruisers were set up by the entrance. He rolled down his window and waved, and a patrolman opened the gate. They drove into the cemetery and when Slow Ed pulled over to the side, Mike saw, up on the hill and in clear view, the section of dirt where Jonah was about to be buried and felt a well of fear rise up in him that tore through that protective membrane like a bullet.

"I know you are—were—close to Father Jack," Slow Ed said. "That's why I don't think he'll have a problem with you being here. But if he asks you to leave, we have to respect that."

Mike nodded, got out of the car. The sun was warm on his face as he walked up the slope of damp grass, heading toward what looked like a utility shed and to the right of it, a small patch of trees that hadn't been cleared.

When he reached the top, Mike moved behind a tree and saw the contraption that would lower Jonah's coffin into his final resting place. No trees out there; no shade. The gravesite was exposed and it worried him for a reason he couldn't explain.

Several minutes later, the hearse and limousine pulled onto Evergreen. A half dozen or so blue uniforms directing traffic cleared the area to let the vehicles through. A moment later, the hearse and limo had pulled up against the curb, and the young pallbearers got out and carried Jonah's coffin up the slope, Father Jack dressed in his priestly robes in line behind them.

The pallbearers placed Jonah's coffin on the lowering device and stepped back. Mike wiped the sleeve of his sweatshirt across his forehead.

Father Jack opened his Bible. "Let us pray."

"Michael."

Wide awake with that middle of the night terror that tells him something's wrong with the baby. Jess is coming up on week twenty-two of her pregnancy with the girl they're going to name Sarah and now something's wrong.

The keys and wallet are on the nightstand so he doesn't have to hunt for them in the middle of the night. He scoops them up, sits up in bed.

"It's okay, Michael. Give me your hand."

He does, and she places it on her belly.

Kicking. The baby was kicking.

"Can you feel it?"

He did. Sarah was kicking up a storm. Jess lies back down, and he relaxes, eases himself against her back, his hand never leaving her belly, that feeling of life forming beneath her skin. Just give me this, God. Just give me this and it will be enough.

A rumble of gears and Mike saw the coffin being lowered into the ground.

Jonah on the morgue table, fighting to free the words from his lips.

Only God knows what is true.

The gears stopped working.

The coffin lay in the ground now, waiting to be buried.

"Amen," Father Jack said, and closed his Bible.

Mike dug his fingers into the bark of the tree. It kept him from screaming.

Mike paced the lawn around the cruiser, trying to work the knocking sensation out of his knees. His cell phone vibrated against his hip for the third time in the past two minutes. Mike checked the caller ID again: OUT OF AREA. Probably a reporter. Mike clipped the phone back on his belt and saw Father Jack walking this way.

The priest stepped up to him. "I'm sorry, Michael."

"Did he, you know . . ."

Father Jack bowed his head and studied his shoes.

Mike's cell phone vibrated again. He pulled it out from his back pocket, checked the caller ID. It was Bill. Mike answered it.

"Jess just called me," Bill said. "She's trying to call you on your cell and just called and said she hasn't been able to reach you."

OUT OF AREA—those calls were from Jess.

"Thanks," Mike said and hung up, Father Jack's eyes locked on him now.

"Francis was a bitter man. Bitter and very angry. He was in denial." Father Jack shook his head, sighed. "I tried."

Mike felt a thick, bulging wetness in his throat that he couldn't swallow back.

"I'm sorry," Father Jack said.

Okay. Okay, so Father Jack didn't know anything. There was still Merrick to talk to, and the nurse, Terry Russell. One of them had to know something. There was still hope.

Mike's phone rang again.

"Michael?" It was Jess, her panicked voice having an odd echo to it.

"I can barely hear you."

"I'm calling you from France." Her words came out hurried to the point where she sounded breathless. "I just found out. I've been staying out on a farm, there's no TV or—it doesn't matter. I just booked a flight and will be home tomorrow afternoon. Are you okay? Where are you?"

Mike's attention ran up the hill, stopped at Jonah's headstone.

I can't take it anymore, Bill. I'm tired of living with a shell. I'm tired of living with a woman who is terrified of life and has made me a prisoner in my own home. I'm tired of having to fight for the simple things like taking my six-and-a-half-year-old daughter sledding. I'm tired and I want out.

His words, spoken in an almost silent prayer that night on the Hill.

"Michael? You there?"

"I'm at Jonah's gravesite," he said.

"What? Why? Why would you do that to yourself?"

The need to cry and scream was building inside his chest. He wanted to reel it in, wanted to look away from the gravesite and couldn't.

"You've got to stop doing this to yourself. How many times have I told you—remember that time in the grocery store? Sarah was with me and I turned my head just for a second and she was gone. They tore the place up and five minutes later I found her outside talking to that woman. Sarah thought it was the mother of a friend and she had followed her out—"

"You don't understand."

"What don't I understand?" Jess sounded on the verge of tears. "Please, let me in. I want to help you."

That night on the Hill I let Sarah walk up that hill by herself because I was pissed at you. That night I prayed for a way out and for once God was listening.

"Talk to me, Michael. Don't shut me out again. Not now."

Mike opened his mouth to speak and a moan escaped his lips. The guilt, the anger, the love he still carried for his daughter and the life they had once shared, everything he had carried for the past five years was ripped out of him in sobs.

CHAPTER 25

Slow Ed pulled the cruiser into his driveway, where Mike's truck was parked.

"Jonah's nurse, Terry Russell," Mike said. "She say anything about Jonah talking in his sleep about Sarah?"

"I never heard anything along those lines."

"What did she tell Merrick?"

"I don't know specifics. You'll have to talk with Merrick about that. He's in Maine. His father's not doing too well from what I hear. Alzheimer's. He's supposed to come back today, so I'll have him call you, I promise."

"What about the autopsy report? Something show up there?"

Slow Ed shifted in his seat, the springs creaking. "Sully, why don't you come in? Sheila made this kick-ass chicken parm."

"Sheila?"

"New girlfriend. Come in and hang . . . hang out for a bit."

"Maybe another time. Thanks for today, Ed."

"I know you're staying at Bam's condo in Melrose. You want to be more local, I've got an extra room here. You're more than welcome to stay until this blows over. It should all die down in a few days."

Blow over, Mike thought. Die down.

Mike called information and twenty minutes later was driving down Vikers Street in what was called Old Town. The houses here were a big step up from the ones on Evergreen: duplexes separated by long, thin driveways; small, nice front lawns sectioned off by chain-link fences. Here, there was no stink of desperation. The houses had fresh coats of paint, manicured shrubs and freshly planted flowers, the street mostly quiet, everyone at work except for the few retirees out washing their cars or hosing down the windows on their houses.

Number fifty-three was a triple-decker with a front porch and steps and floorboards painted gunmetal gray. Mike parked on the street, got out and jogged up the flagstone walkway and up the stairs to the door on the left. He rang the buzzer, relieved to hear the sound of footsteps, of bolts being unlocked. The door swished open.

It was the woman he had seen that night inside Jonah's house.

"Mr. Sullivan," Terry Russell said.

"I'm sorry for dropping by unannounced, but I was wondering if I could talk to you."

"Of course," she said and opened the door.

Three steps and Mike was standing inside a large, rectangular room of hardwood flooring, bright yellow walls and a bluestone fireplace with bookcases built on either side of them. Lots of religious books in there with titles like *The Purpose Driven Life* and *Conversations with God;* lots of porcelain figurines too: Jesus hanging on the cross, St. Anthony, several of the Blessed Virgin Mary. Sunlight flooded the warm room, pouring in from the windows overlooking a backyard where a group of four or five toddlers took turns kicking a soccer ball.

"Would you care for something to drink?" she asked. She was dressed in jeans and a black cardigan sweater, the plain gold chain and gold crucifix proudly displayed over her white turtleneck. It was the only jewelry she wore. No earrings or rings—no makeup either. "I don't have any coffee, but I do have tea and some Coke."

"I'm all set, thank you."

She sat down on one end of a chocolate-brown couch, the only piece of furniture in the room. Mike sat down on the other end. The windows were cracked open, and he could hear kids giggling, screaming to one another.

"What can I do for you, Mr. Sullivan?"

"Please, call me Mike."

"And call me Terry."

Mike forced a grin. "I understand you were working with the police."

Terry nodded. "I've been working with Detective

Merrick, talking to him at the end of each day when Francis was alive."

Hearing her calling Jonah by his first name angered him for some reason.

"I take it by your tone Detective Merrick never told you about any of my conversations with Francis."

"No," Mike said. "He didn't."

"Detective Merrick was . . . well, he was rather specific in his instructions with me." She brushed at the tops of her jeans, wanting to tread forward gently and, he supposed, to choose her words with care. "I'm sorry about all of this," she said. "I just feel awful."

"You don't have anything to apologize for. I was just hoping——" Mike's voice caught on the word. "Did Jonah talk about Sarah at all?"

"Not to me. And I never asked him. Dr. Boynton was very specific on that point."

"Dr. Boynton?"

"A criminal profiler or psychiatrist, I'm not sure which. He's based out of Boston, I think. Anyway, when Detective Merrick approached me and asked if I would help in the investigation, he had me meet with Dr. Boynton. We discussed my conversations with Francis. We became quite close—Francis and myself, I mean. I know that may sound odd, even monstrous to some degree, but when a person is in a terminal situation, it's not all that unusual for them to open up—even to strangers. Francis didn't have any friends, unless you want to count his lawyer. But that's not really a friend, is it?"

"I suppose not."

"I think he considered me a friend," Terry said. "At the beginning, it was mostly chit-chat stuff. 'Good morning, Terry. You look very nice today, Terry. How's the world treating you?' That sort of thing. But over time, he opened up. He'd tell me stories about growing up here in Belham, about how he knew he always wanted to be a priest, how proud it made his mother."

"Did Jonah follow the news?" Mike remembered some TV shrink pegging Jonah as a narcissist, someone who took an avid interest in following himself on the news, using it to stay ahead of the police.

"He liked news programs. CNN and programs like *Crossfire*. If a reporter started talking about, you know, the case, Francis would switch the channel—at least that's what he did when I was there."

"So you never talked to him about it."

"No. If the subject came up, Dr. Boynton suggested I use what he called a third-person approach. You know, ask Francis something along the lines of 'What kind of person would leave a jacket up on the hill like that?' Dr. Boynton thought it might get Francis to open up, get him to talk about it in a safe way because he wasn't talking about himself. I remember Dr. Boynton saying something about how that approach was used on Ted Bundy. He denied he had anything to do with what happened to those young women, but when the FBI profilers asked Bundy his thoughts on what kind of person would, you know, actually commit that sort of atrocity, Bundy talked about it in the third person. 'This man would commit this crime in such and such a way.'" Terry sighed. "I tried to get him to open up. The problem was, Francis was deteriorating rapidly. During the day, all he wanted to do was sit in his rocking chair and go through his photo albums and play with his toys. They all do that—revert back to childhood. They'll want to look at pictures, play with toys, sing old songs, talk about people from their past. It's a way of comforting themselves. This one patient I had last year, Martha? She carried a football with her everywhere she went: bed, to the hospital, the bathroom, you name it. Wouldn't let it go. And all of a sudden she'd give me this real serious look and then she'd scream, 'Go long, Terry. For the love of Jesus, go long!' Martha was a real card. I miss her."

Mike wanted to hurry this up, get right to the heart of it; but another part, an overwhelming part, convinced him of the importance of being patient. It was clear Terry needed to take her time and not be interrupted with question after question—the way Merrick had probably treated her. Maybe this need to talk was her way of reconciling her version of Jonah with what the rest of the world thought; or maybe she just wanted to exorcise Jonah from her mind and talking was the only way she knew how to do it.

"Francis asked me to get down a couple of boxes of Christmas decorations from the attic. He wanted me to help him string lights around the living room and his bedroom. They were the plain, white lights—not the flashing ones. His mother kept some of the toys Francis had from when he was younger. Francis would just sit there and hold them. Sometimes he cried. He loved the

Christmas ornaments the best. Each one had a story. Francis loved to tell stories."

Mike couldn't picture Jonah as a person who had once been a child nursed by a mother, a boy who had turned into a man, into a monster.

"At night, Francis would sit in his chair and stare at those white lights. Just sit there and be quiet with his thoughts. The lights calmed him, I think. That and the medication. He cried a lot. He was such a lonely, lonely old man, and I know that hurt him." She shook her head, visibly sad.

"It sounds like you liked him," Mike said.

"I liked the parts he revealed to me. I know that must sound terrible, knowing what he, you know, did. But when people reveal themselves to you in those situations—in pain, knowing they're dying—sometimes it's impossible not to form an emotional connection. They teach you to block it out, but honestly, how can you? And I suppose I was drawn to him to a degree because he was a priest. That carries a certain amount of respect. I thought about attending his funeral today."

"Why didn't you?"

"The press. They don't know about me, and I didn't want to invite them into my life." Terry sighed. "Whatever side was capable of doing those things, Francis kept it hidden from me. How he acted after I left, whatever thoughts ran through his head? I couldn't tell you. When I was around, Francis acted as human as the rest of us."

"Did it surprise you that he committed suicide?"

Terry thought about it for a moment.

"At first, it did," she said. "For two reasons. Francis was a priest, and he knew it was a sin. Secondly, he wasn't in any physical pain—at least he didn't tell me he was. I've never lost a patient to suicide. It's almost unheard of. That being said, Francis wasn't like most patients. He had this . . . he had a lot of stuff inside his head—stuff I couldn't treat. The guilt, maybe. And like I said, he was so lonely. You can't medicate that."

"Hanging himself . . . it didn't seem his style."

Terry shrugged. "It's hard to say what goes through people's minds. I saw Francis that morning. On Sunday. He looked . . . he wasn't himself. He was all shaken up. I've had some time to process the whole thing, and the only answer I came up with is what I told Detective Merrick: I think Francis knew the police were coming to arrest him, and rather than die in jail, he decided to take his life."

Coming here wasn't about rekindling hope. Mike realized that now. The reason why he had gone to the funeral, why he was here talking to Terry—it was about closure.

"I'm so sorry for your loss," she said.

Mike nodded. There didn't seem to be anything left he wanted to say—at least anything he could think of, so he thanked her and stood up.

Terry reached inside her sweater pocket and came back with a business card and a pen. She wrote on the back of the card and handed it to him.

"The number on the back is my home phone number," she said. "If you have any questions, anything at all, don't hesitate to call me."

"I will. Thank you."

Mike thanked her. She walked him to the door. He took one last look at her gold crucifix, thanked her again and stepped outside.

"Mr. Sullivan?"

He turned back to her, Terry's face behind the screen.

"I'll keep you and Sarah in my prayers."

Mike was on his way home when, lo and behold, Merrick called and asked if they could meet.

"If it's about what the nurse told you about Jonah, don't bother. She was nice enough to fill me in."

"I have the autopsy report," Merrick said. "And we found some items in Jonah's house."

Mike tried to concentrate on the road, on where he was heading.

"Are you free right now?"

"What did you find?" Fear and hope mixing in Mike's voice.

"I'd rather discuss it in person."

CHAPTER 26

Dakota's was yet another example of a new downtown business that had sprung up overnight. It was located at the far end of Main Street, where Alexander's Shoes used to be, and had a parking lot full of high-end cars: Saabs, BMWs, even a Mercedes. Dakota's: Belham's first yuppie bar.

The inside sure looked like it. Lots of dark paneled wood and low lighting. A long bar filled with bottles that sparkled in expensive track lighting and just off to the right of the bar, a small dining area with white-linen tablecloths and votives on each table, the perfect place for trading and sharing secrets over dry chardonnay and overpriced gourmet appetizers. To the left of the main entrance, accessed by a glass door, was a cigar room with burgundy-colored leather chairs and couches and coffee tables holding copies of the *Wall Street Journal,* the *Financial Times,* and magazines like *Sailing* and *Vanity Fair.* Merrick sat in one of the leather couches that faced the bay windows overlooking Main Street, a snifter of port or some other high-priced booze cradled in one hand, the other flipping the pages of a magazine spread across his lap. His black suit and the drawn, haggard look on his face gave him the appearance of an undertaker relaxing after a long, hard day.

Mike plopped himself down in the leather chair across from Merrick and took out his pack of cigarettes. Merrick folded the magazine and gently placed it and his snifter back down on the glass coffee table between them. *Wine Spectator*. Jesus.

"It was definitely a suicide," Merrick said.

"As opposed to what?" Mike had seen the log lying sideways under Jonah's feet. It didn't take a brain surgeon to figure out that Jonah had stepped up on the log, tied the noose around his neck and then jumped.

"With suicides, you have to pay close attention. More often than not it's a homicide; a person is strangled and the body is moved to another place and hung to make it look like a suicide. When that happens, you always find two sets of ligature marks, and then you know you're dealing with a homicide. Jonah only had one set of ligature marks, and the marks matched the rope. He also had what's called petechial hemorrhaging—burst blood vessels you find in the white lining of the eyes. It's the distinctive evidence that someone died of asphyxiation. And fortunately, a lot of the snow was damp because of all the melting we've been having, and with air as cold as it was that night, it preserved some footprints. We were able to find several prints that matched Jonah's boots. We didn't find a note. But if you consider the audiotape with your daughter's voice . . ."

Merrick's face changed. He carried some unsettling piece of news and was now trying to figure out how to say it.

Here it comes, Mike thought, squeezing the ends of the armchair.

"The crime scene techs finished up with Jonah's house yesterday," Merrick said. "Underneath Jonah's bed we found a loose floorboard. We tore up the floor and found a decent-sized space underneath the boards. Sarah's snow pants were in there. So was a comb with some of Caroline Lenville's hair. Ashley Giroux's doll we found in Jonah's bed. His fingerprints were all over it."

"Bee-Bee Pretty," Mike blurted out, the doll's odd-sounding name popping into his head out of nowhere. Rose had shown him a picture of Ashley and the small doll with red plastic hair and one foot chewed off by her dog. Ashley had the doll in her backpack the day she disappeared.

"Jonah kept a Walkman next to his bed. We found an audiotape in it." A kink of sadness tainted Merrick's otherwise emotionless voice. "The others were in the drawer next to his nightstand. Sarah, Ashley and Caroline."

"You listen to them?"

Merrick nodded, and Mike again squeezed the edge of the armchair.

"What did Sarah say?"

"All three tapes were pretty much the same—the girls sounded lost, like they were in the dark and couldn't see." He spoke slowly, thoughtfully. "The one you heard out in the woods was spliced from the original Jonah kept."

Mike thought back to what Lou had told him about Jonah mentioning Sarah's name in his sleep. Jonah wasn't sleeping; he was making his . . . his what? His suicide tape?

"There were some sounds we didn't recognize, so we sent the tapes to the FBI for enhancement and analysis," Merrick said. "My guess is that Jonah had . . . I think he took them to someplace other than his house. Something could still turn up. If it does, I'll let you know."

"What about the dogs?"

"I don't understand."

"The morning after I found Jonah, I saw you guys with search dogs."

"Those were cadaver-sniffing dogs."

Mike fumbled for a cigarette, a part of him floating above himself, looking down at himself and watching while some other part of his brain was painfully aware of what was being said and was busy searching through Merrick's words for possible holes.

"The dogs didn't turn anything up," Merrick said. "We're still searching through Jonah's house for anything that might give us an idea where he might have . . . buried her. I'm sorry. I wish there was an easier way of putting it."

"What about Jonah's house? What's going to happen to it?"

"Jonah's estate will be turned over to St. Stephen's.

Father Connelly's the executor of Jonah's will. He wanted the money to go to a charity of Father Jack's choosing. The house is in terrible condition, so my guess is someone will come along, buy it and tear it down, build a nice Colonial or something. It will be cheaper than trying to fix it up."

All those rooms, all those possible secrets, waiting to be torn down and forgotten.

"I'd like to search the rooms. I might see something you guys wouldn't notice."

Merrick stared at him like he was lost and didn't have a clue as to how to get home.

"It's possible," Mike said. "And I want to listen to a copy of Sarah's tape."

"So you can punish yourself?"

"I want to hear it. There could be something there. You don't know my daughter the way I do. She's smart. She might have been trying to tell us something, you know?"

"I have the name of an excellent grief—"

"It can happen," Mike said. "Look at Elizabeth Smart. The police wrote her off for dead and the whole time she was alive, and if at any point the family had listened to the police and stopped believing, she would never have been found. But she was. She was found because the family kept on believing."

"I'll arrange a visit to Jonah's house if that's what you want. Give me a few days." Merrick glanced at his watch. "Unfortunately, I have to get going. Would you like me to call someone?"

It occurred to Mike that the last remaining member of his original family was a dog. That the only person he could call was Bill, his lifeline to the real world.

"I think I'm going to hang out here for a bit," Mike said. "Call me when I can go through the house."

"I will."

Merrick paused, then stood up and walked away, his shoes clicking against the hardwood.

"Merrick?"

"Yes."

"Ed told me about your father. I'm sorry."

"Take care of yourself, Michael."

Four o'clock now and the sunlight was hanging around longer, Main Street bright and busy. Mike remembered—this was years ago—he would stand right where he was now sitting and look out the window as his mother tried on shoes, the salesman smiling politely, trying not to stare at whatever lump or bruise was on her face. She was gone, dead, murdered by Lou. Sarah was gone too, most likely dead, killed by Jonah.

Mike saw himself on the morning of Sarah's anniversary date placing the lilacs on top of the Hill.

The act wasn't about remembering Sarah. It was about denial, his refusal to acknowledge the truth and let her go.

But let her go to where?

A waiter came inside the room, a young guy in his early twenties and dressed to the nines in a suit and a diamond stud earring in each ear. "The man who was just in here said dinner was on him," he said. "You mind me asking who he was? His face looks familiar for some reason."

"You know who Sarah Sullivan is?"

"No."

"Why would you? She's not on MTV."

"I'm sorry, did I say something wrong?"

Mike sighed. "No," he said. "It's not you."

CHAPTER 27

The time to do it, he knew, was when the daylight was still strong.

Mike drove down Anderson and saw the bouquets of flowers, the cards and candles and blown-up pictures of Sarah strewn over his front lawn and front steps. He didn't see any reporters; they had either given up for the moment or were still congregating over at Jonah's. He pulled into his driveway and parked his truck in the garage, out of view.

Inside, he unplugged the phone in the kitchen and his bedroom. He couldn't afford any interruptions; it might make him reconsider what he was going to do. He went to the basement, gathered up what he needed and then headed back upstairs.

Sarah's room was filled with a warm, soft light. The smell, that essence of her that had been trapped inside her pillows, her sheets and clothes, was long gone, dried away by time. Everything else remained the same: the drawing table by the window; the autographed picture of Tom Brady given to her by Bill; the stack of Barbie toys in the corner—Barbie's dream house and Mustang and private jet. Barbie even had her own private McDonald's right next to her mansion. Four framed pictures hung over Sarah's white four-poster bed: a picture of Sarah taken in the delivery room; one of Jess holding Sarah for the first time; Mike holding her; another one of Sarah sleeping in her bassinet. The pictures were Sarah's idea, Sarah amazed and fascinated that she had once been that small.

He started with the Barbie dolls. One by one he picked them up and gently placed them inside the cardboard box. The toys, the clothes and furniture he would donate. The pictures hanging on the wall above her bed would stay here until he was ready to deal with them. The items that held stories and special memories—like the bear with the words YOU'RE SPECIAL printed on its belly; he had purchased it at the hospital gift shop the day Sarah was born and had left it in her incubator and later, her crib—these items he would box up and bury in the attic, next to his mother's things.

CHAPTER 28

The next morning, Saturday, Mike had just recon-
nected the phone in the kitchen when it rang.
ELLIS, SAMANTHA flashed across the phone's caller ID
window. Mike picked up the phone. It was shortly after
nine.

"How are you doing?"

The question everyone was asking him, like he was a
terminal patient, the next one to follow Jonah into the
ground.

"I'm doing," he said, and poured his third cup of
coffee.

"What's your day looking like?"

"Lots of work. I'm under the gun." They were running behind on the jobsite in Newton. The addition
needed to be completed by the end of the week; Bill
had been shouldering most of the weight himself, log-
ging some serious hours. "What about you? You at the
office?"

"No work for me today. I've decided to do what normal people do for a change and take the weekend off. Last night I watched women-in-danger movies on Lifetime, and today I'm going to go to yoga and then watch more bad TV. Right now I'm watching three guys on ESPN having telephone-pole races."

"Telephone-pole races?"

"I'm serious. These big guys with these big leather belts around their waists are shimmying their way up telephone poles. I love sports, but this just seems stupid. Any ideas?"

"Is there a naked woman at the top?"

"That would be a no."

"Beer?"

"Not that I can see."

"Then your guess is as good as mine."

Sam laughed, the sound of it lifting something in him, making him feel lighter.

"You have any dinner plans for tonight?"

"Sam, you don't—"

"This isn't a charity call." Sam let it hang there to emphasize her point. "Look, why don't you go to work, do what you need to do, and if you feel like getting together tonight, give me a call. You can call last minute if you want. I'm here all day. You have my home phone number?"

"My caller ID flagged it."

"Okay then. Try not to work too hard."

"You too," Mike said and hung up with Sam's voice humming warmly through his thoughts.

Mike was looking out the opened window, at the lilac bushes in the corner of the backyard, when the phone rang again.

"So your plan is to just let me sit here and rot away," Lou said.

"What are you talking about?"

"You know goddamn well what I'm talking about." Lou's voice was out of breath, pinched, like a man who had just been rescued from the brink of drowning. "Knowing you, you probably read this morning's paper and jumped for joy."

Mike looked out the front window, at the mailbox at the end of the driveway. Still no reporters outside—at least not yet. He was sure they were still floating around Belham. The cordless phone pressed against his ear, Mike moved out of the kitchen and headed down the foyer.

"I don't give a rat's ass what they say," Lou said. "I'm telling you, I didn't do it."

Mike swung the front door open and then moved down the stairs and jogged across the front lawn, the air warm and breezy under the bright morning sun.

"You hear what I said? *I didn't do it.*"

He pulled out today's *Globe* and unfolded it. Right there on the front page was a color picture of Lou being escorted by two detectives. The headline above the picture read: BELHAM MAN ARRESTED FOR MURDER OF BODYGUARD.

"My lawyer retired to some other state," Lou said. "What about that guy you used? He got you a good deal."

Mike was speed-reading the article, words and phrases jumping out at him: evidence linking Lou to the murder of the bodyguard who had died due to complications from third-degree burns; arraignment pending; Lou's "alleged" connection to mafia figure "Cadillac Jack" Scarlatta; his "alleged" tie to several Brinks armored-truck robberies.

"Are you listening? I've only got five minutes."

Mike kept reading. "My lawyer died."

"Then you need to get me one."

Mike looked up from the paper. "What?"

"I need you to get me a lawyer."

His gaze shifted up to the attic. His mother's items—the few he had managed to save—were stored inside a shoebox. Shortly before Lou left for Paris, he had collected all of her clothes, the pictures—just about every personal item she had left behind—and burned them in an aluminum trashcan in the backyard.

"You rotten son of a bitch," Lou said and hung up.

CHAPTER 29

An hour later, Mike had figured it out.

When it came to the enigma that was his old man, Mike was sure of only one thing: Lou was terrified of tight, confined spaces. Lou had never come right out and said this—Lou never shared anything. Instead, it came to Mike in a sort of epiphany one rainy Sunday afternoon when he was watching *The Deer Hunter* on cable at Bill's house. Those scenes where DeNiro and Walken were stuffed inside cages, prisoners of war—that had once been Lou. Seeing the movie explained why Lou always insisted on taking the stairs instead of the elevator, why he didn't fly if he could possibly avoid it, why he absolutely refused to ride in small cars. ("There's no damn escape room. You get hit while in one of those, you're dead.")

Merrick wasn't at the station, so Mike spoke with Slow Ed. When Mike pulled into the station, he saw the reporters gathered around the front parking lot. Mike pulled behind the back of the station where Slow Ed was at the back door, holding it open.

"They put your old man in the holding pen with Brian Delansky," Slow Ed said as they walked down the hallway. "You know him? He's local."

"Doesn't ring any bells," Mike said.

"Picture a juicehead around Bill's size and twice as nutty. Two o'clock this morning we find Delansky lying on the floor in puke and blood, practically unconscious. Your old man's sleeping on his cot. Broken nose and the ER doctor had to drain the fluid from both of Delansky's testicles. Delansky's saying he slipped and fell. How old you say Lou was?"

"Coming up on sixty."

"I swear he'd give Hannibal Lecter a run for his money." Slow Ed stopped in front of the door leading to the holding cell. "Fifteen minutes, then we've got to get him ready for transfer."

"I remember the procedure."

"Only your old man's not going to make bail. Try and talk some sense into him. It will go easier if he co-operates with us." Slow Ed opened the door and Mike walked down the dimly lit hallway.

Lou was in the last cell, sitting hunched forward on his bunk, his hands wrapped around a can of Coke. His face was sickly pale and had an oily sheen to it. Despite the coolness of the room, dark rings of sweat were visible in the armpits of his blue T-shirt, the small room packed close with day-old sweat mixed with his fading Old Spice deodorant and smoke-filled clothes.

A folding chair had been set up. Mike sat down.

Two full minutes passed. Lou hadn't moved or spoken.

"I grew up with this guy Paulie Waters," Lou said. "He and I enlisted at the same time. This one time, it was at night, we stepped inside a village that was supposed to have been leveled. Paulie happened to be looking the wrong way when a gook with a flame-thrower turned Paulie into a walking candle. A man screams a certain way when he's burned. A sound like that never leaves you."

"And what sound do they make right before you blow their brains out?"

Lou's eyes slid off the Coke.

"The police found cigarette butts in Jonah's backyard, behind the shed," Mike said. "Want to guess whose prints popped up?"

"I'm not going to jail for someone else's mess."

"The prints were the same ones that matched the prints on the two shards of the glass bottle used in the Molotov cocktail. And to top it off, Jonah's neighbor is ROTC. As luck would have it, he was playing around with his night-vision goggles. Guess who he saw unscrewing the lightbulbs on Jonah's back porch?"

"They find any fingerprints on them?"

They didn't. Mike didn't answer him.

"Didn't think so," Lou said.

"They found your gold lighter in the snow."

"Last time I had it was at McCarthy's," Lou said. "Someone stole it out of my jacket. Go ahead and call George McCarthy, he'll tell you."

"Someone's trying to frame you?"

"You're goddamn right."

"I understand the police nabbed you just as you were getting ready to blow town."

"I was heading back to Florida."

"I think you're going to have a tough time selling that story."

Lou gritted his teeth, balls of cartilage popping out along his jaw.

"I made some calls," Mike said. After he hung up with Lou, Mike called Sam back, explained the situation and the idea he had in mind. She listened, gave some suggestions and agreed to help.

"Frankie Dellanno," Mike said. "You remember him?"

Lou nodded. "Old mob boss, ran his crew out of the North End."

"The lawyer I have in mind not only kept Dellanno out of jail, he also represented two of Dellanno's button men—Jimmy Fingers and some other guy by the name of Prestano. They never did any time."

"What's the lawyer's name?"

"Weinstein."

"Stu Weinstein? Has an office in Brookline?"

"No, this is a different guy, based out of Boston. He's next to impossible to hire, but I have a friend who can call in a favor."

"So call it in."

"He's very expensive."

"How much?"

"Fifty grand for a retainer."

No hesitation from Lou: "Make the call."

"The fifty's just for the retainer. Case like this, with the evidence they got against you, you're talking a figure that could run you, at a minimum, a hundred grand, possibly two. Guys like Martin Weinstein don't work on credit."

"I said go ahead and make the call."

"That part depends on you."

Lou's eyes narrowed.

"You help me," Mike said, "and my friend will contact the lawyer. You don't help me, you're on your own. That's how the deal's going to work."

"What do you want?"

"You're going to tell me what happened to Mom."

"My ass is on the line here and you want to rehash shit that happened in the past?"

Mike stood up.

"She left us," Lou said. "End of story."

"A month after she left, she mailed a package to Bill's house along with a note. That note said she would be coming back to Belham. How'd you find out where she was hiding?"

"I knew that, don't you think I would have brought her back home?"

"Not without giving her a good beating first. You remember those days, don't you?"

Lou took a long pull from his Coke.

"You went away for a few days, remember? On business? Of course you do. You came home and called me into the backyard and delivered a speech about how she wasn't coming home, that it was time for me to get over it. And maybe I would have bought it if I didn't happen to see your suitcase opened on your bed and decided to do a little investigating."

Mike reached inside his jacket pocket, brought out the yellowed plane tickets and tapped them against the bars.

"Tickets to Paris and a passport belonging to Thom Peterson," Mike said. "The guy in the passport photo bears a strange resemblance to you. Want to take a look?"

Got to hand it to Lou, he didn't buckle, didn't waver. He placed the Coke can on the floor and then leaned back against his bed and clasped his hands behind his head, acting like he was listening to a weather report.

"Thing is, you hate to fly," Mike said. "Yet you hopped on a plane and flew all the way to France— under a false identity. Now why is that?"

Lou's face was flushed with color and the thick, ropey veins in his arms were swollen with blood.

"You tell me what you did to her, I'll give you my word I'll do everything in my power to get you out of here."

"And if I don't?" Lou's tone carried a warning: fuck with me at your own peril.

"I hear the cells at Walpole are like POW cages."

Lou wouldn't speak, just continued to lie there with a gleam in his eyes.

The door opened and Slow Ed walked toward them.

"Time's up, Sully."

"No problem, officer," Lou said, a satisfied grin plastered on his sallow face. "Michael, since you're so interested in digging up skeletons, why don't you start with your wife—excuse me, your *ex*-wife. Ask her about the guy she was screwing at the bed and breakfast in New Hampshire the weekend before you got married."

CHAPTER 30

"You never told me about the tickets and passport," Bill said.

"It's not the sort of thing you go around advertising," Mike replied, and then helped Bill lift one of the custom-built cherry cabinets that were going into Margaret Van Buren's new gourmet kitchen. Her kitchen was a magazine showpiece with cabinets totaling eighty grand, granite countertops, two Sub-Zero refrigerators and, of course, the top-of-the-line Viking stove and oven. Only Margaret Van Buren hated to cook.

Bill said, "I'm surprised Lou never confronted you on it."

"He probably thought he misplaced them somewhere. Who knows? It was a long time ago."

"So you just held onto them."

"You think I should have given them to the police?"

"They thought Lou was responsible for your mother's disappearance."

"You and I both knew, even back then, that Lou had cops on his payroll. Father Jack confirmed that fact on more than one occasion."

"True."

"And plus, I was nine at the time. I thought that if Lou ever found out I had those tickets, I'd probably be lying somewhere next to my mother."

"You feel that way now?"

"I wouldn't put anything past him." Mike wiped the sweat away from his forehead. "I thought I had him. Lou's never been in a situation like this—you know, trapped and needing me to help him. Showing him the envelope in his state of mind, I thought I could have forced his hand."

"And instead he planted that crack about Jess in your head."

"Yes," Mike said as he worked the drill. "He certainly did that."

"You call her?"

"No."

"But you're going to."

For the next hour, they didn't talk. When they finished the cabinets, they went to work on installing the shelves in the walk-in pantry.

"Lou burning a guy like that," Bill said. "Don't seem right."

Mike stopped what he was doing, turned around and faced Bill. "We're talking about the same Lou Sullivan I grew up with? You were there when he bounced John Simon's head off a car bumper and almost killed him."

"Is Lou capable of burning a guy? No question. He's capable of that and probably a hundred other things you and I can't even think of. Hiding behind a shed and leaving cigarette butts and a gold lighter—it just seems sloppy, you know?"

Mike had thought the same thing.

"One thing I'll say about your old man, he wasn't sloppy. All those jobs he did, he was smart enough never to get caught. He never left any evidence."

That's because he buried the bodies where nobody could find them.

They didn't talk for the rest of the afternoon. Six o'clock rolled around and Bill decided to call it quits.

"You going to meet Sam in town for dinner?" Bill asked as he grabbed his coat.

"I'm going to finish up some stuff here and then head home."

"Good idea. Why go into town and have fun with a beautiful woman when you can spend a night fighting with your ex-wife?"

"I'm not going to Rowley." But he had gone out to the truck twice to call Jess. Still no answer. Her plane was supposed to have touched down at three. Maybe there had been a delay, or maybe she had taken a later flight.

"Patty's sister is taking the kids tonight," Bill said. "Patty and I are going to order up some Chinese and watch the new Adam Sandler movie."

"How'd you get her to agree to watch that?"

"Because last weekend she made me sit through this movie called *The Hours*. Said there were lesbians in it."

"Let me guess. No lesbians."

"There were, but not the hot kind." Bill sighed, shook his head. "Flush it out of your head, Sully."

"Could you?"

"If it came out of Lou's mouth? Yeah, I could."

"So if someone told you this about Patty, you'd just drop it."

"Patty and I are still married. You and Jess are divorced. What's the point?"

Mike picked up a large paper cup full of coffee. "What time you want to meet here tomorrow?"

"A week ago I was watching this program about how you can donate your body to cadaver research at medical colleges. You'd be surprised how easy it was. All it took was some minor paperwork. Your old man's going to make quite a specimen."

CHAPTER 31

At four o'clock the following afternoon, Mike rang the doorbell to Jess's house. A FOR SALE sign was posted on the front lawn.

Jess looked amazingly well-rested and put-together with her dark blue designer skirt and ivory shirt with a long, sloping V-neck. Her hair was different too, cut shorter and with highlights, and as he took her in, he was amazed at how this woman he had known since high school, this girl who once lived in jeans and a sweatshirt and thought a fun day was tailgating at a Patriots game with friends and beers, had now morphed herself into another woman, one who took great care in picking out her clothes and spent long weeks traveling through Europe.

Mike stepped inside the foyer and she immediately hugged him.

Holding her like this brought back the larger memories, the markers that had defined their lives together:

comforting her at her father's funeral; dancing together at their wedding; hugging each other after the neonatal specialist came in and told them that Sarah had fought off the lung infection. He felt all of the smaller moments too, the seemingly inconsequential moments that he had taken for granted every day: laughing at a movie, kissing her goodbye as he left for work. It made him feel frantic, lost.

"I'm so sorry," she said against his chest. "I'm so, so sorry."

He wasn't sure if she was sorry for him or sorry about Jonah, or for all of it.

Jess eased herself away from him and rubbed the corners of her eyes. She didn't know what to say—or maybe didn't want to say anything, at least not yet—and walked away from him and into the dining room. The majority of the furniture inside the house, he noticed, was already gone.

"When are you leaving?"

"Tuesday morning," Jess said.

Two days away.

"This is the best I could do," Jess said, making a sweeping gesture with her hand at the various plastic plates holding scrambled eggs, bacon, toast, sliced apples and melons.

Mike sat down. The sun pouring through the windows was warm on his face. He clung to that feeling, to the smell of the sweet, cool air blowing inside as he listened to Jess explain how the pots and pans—pretty much everything from the kitchen—was on its way along with a few select pieces of furniture. He vaguely heard her mention something about a moving company coming in and doing all the packing, how expensive it was.

Jess lies on her back, helping the pair of rough hands working the buttons of her shirt.

Mike kept his eyes on the cut-up pieces of honeydew melon as the number 10 flashed in his mind. He focused on the number, holding onto it as he took in a long, slow deep breath through his nose. Deep belly-breathing—that was the key.

Jess tucks her thumbs in the waistband of her jeans and panties and feverishly works them down over her hips and legs as though the denim is burning her skin.

Jess was saying something to him.

"What's that?" he asked.

"I asked you what's wrong."

In his mind's eye Mike saw Lou grinning.

"I packed up some of Sarah's room Friday night," Mike said. He kept his eyes focused on his plate of food, the bright colors of the melons and strawberries.

Jess folded her hands on the table, waited.

"It felt wrong. Like I was telling her I didn't have any room in my life anymore. The next morning I wanted to put everything back the way it was."

"Maybe you're not ready to say goodbye," she offered.

That's the thing, Jess. I don't know if I'll ever be ready.

He sighed, said, "How much do you know?"

"I read the stories on boston.com. The *Globe* did a very comprehensive job."

"You want me to fill you in on the rest of it?"

"Only if you want to."

Mike started with the night he had stood on Jonah's porch and took her through the rest of it, to his meeting with Merrick at Dakota's, and as he talked, his attention drifted out the window to the backyard, to the patches of greening grass and blooming flowers, to the different parts of Sarah's jungle gym—anywhere but Jess's face. He thought if he held her face in his eyes then the thoughts he had been carrying since yesterday's afternoon visit with Lou would boil over and he'd lose it, verbally tear into her like he did during their marriage.

"That morning out on the trail," Mike said. "I should have let him suffocate."

"You did the right thing."

He could tell by her tone that she didn't mean it.

"Is that why you're angry?"

"I'm not angry."

"Your neck is beet red."

"I'm hot. I think I'm coming down with the flu that's going around."

"Then why are you avoiding looking at me. You only do that when you're trying to avoid a fight."

She was right, of course. Jess recognized all the sign-posts of his moods, knew all of the emergency detours and exit ramps he used to back his way out of painful conversations.

"If you're angry about something," Jess said, "get it out in the open and we'll deal with it."

A diamond bracelet was on her wrist. Probably a gift from her new boyfriend. He stared at it

(as her fingers fumble for the man's boxers and when they find them, they grip the fabric and yank them down hard, maybe even ripping them, because when Jess Armstrong wants something, people, she goes right after it, it's always been about her needs, about what she wants—isn't that right, Mike?)

and felt Lou's words from yesterday sink their teeth deeper into the meat of his brain.

Mike looked up and into her eyes. "I take it you know what's going on with Lou."

"Yes," she said, then sighed. "I'm sorry you have to deal with that on top of everything else."

"You don't seem surprised. About Lou, I mean."

"When it comes to your father, nothing surprises me."

"I talked with him yesterday. At the jail."

"Jesus."

"He wants my help."

"Why on earth would you put yourself through that?"

"I ever tell you I thought Lou's claustrophobic?"

"What does that have to do with you going to visit him?"

"I thought I could use that weakness against him. Make him tell me what I wanted to know about my mother. I had him backed into a corner, and this time I had proof." Mike told her about the plane tickets and passports, how he found them.

"You never told me that story," Jess said. Her face looked wounded. "When the police came around asking questions about your mother, you should have told them."

"It wouldn't have done any good."

Jess thought about it for a moment, then said, "You're probably right. When it comes to keeping secrets, your father's a pro. Did he say anything?"

Lou didn't say anything about my mother, Jess. He did what he always did: deny, deny, deny. What he did, though, was cough up this tidbit about you being involved with some other guy the weekend before we got married. I'd dismiss it if the son of a bitch didn't look so goddamn smug when he said it, like he was daring me.

Mike had known her since high school. Any question about her fidelity would, even now, be the equivalent of a slap in the face. She held herself—and unfortunately, most everyone else—to a strict moral code of conduct. When one of Jess's best friends since high school revealed she was having an affair with a married man, Jess had hit the roof. Mike had been at home, listening to Jess from the kitchen: I don't care how much you love him, Carla, the man's married. It's wrong.

So why would Lou say it?

Jess is your only link to Sarah's memory. You ask Jess that question, just make sure you're prepared to say goodbye.

Jess put her hand on top of his and squeezed it. Whatever words he chose to share, she would help bear that pain along with him and, just as she had during their marriage, show him how to navigate his way through it.

"Tell me," she said.

"He denied having anything to do with it."

"Then why do you sound so surprised?"

"I really thought I had him. You should have seen his face. He's dying in there."

"Good," Jess said, squeezing his hand harder. "Good."

CHAPTER 32

In the months that followed Sarah's disappearance, Mike got accustomed to the phone ringing at all hours of the night. When he heard the phone ringing, he turned over and picked up the cordless from the nightstand, expecting the caller to be Jess, Merrick or yet another crank call from some mentally deficient, jobless loser who had nothing better to do than to call from a pay phone with some bogus story about having seen Sarah or professing to have knowledge of what had happened to her.

It was Rose Giroux.

"It's Ted," she whimpered.

Mike sat up in bed. He knew of her husband's three previous heart attacks, the last of which had almost killed him.

"He's accepted a research position at the University of California in San Diego."

"That's why you're upset?"

"He accepted the position without telling me."

That wasn't much of a surprise. He had never met the man personally, had only seen pictures of Ted Giroux, this big bear of a man with a full, thick beard and black-rimmed shop glasses, a chemical engineer who, according to Rose, spent the majority of his time either at work or holed up in his office in the basement. Based on the few stories Rose shared, Mike had the guy pegged as a cold fish.

"I told him I wasn't leaving—that I couldn't leave this house," Rose said, and then cleared her throat. "You know what he told me? He said, 'Do whatever you want, Rose, but I'm going.' It's his way of punishing me. Like keeping the dining table. Remember how I told you that I used to have Father Jonah over to my house for dinner?"

"I remember."

"He'd sit at our dining room table next to Ashley and our other children and after he left, every time—*every* time Ted would tell me what an odd duck he thought Jonah was. I told Ted he was being foolish. Ted doesn't go to church. 'Hocus-pocus,' he calls it. When he said those things about Father Jonah, I'd brush them off, and it infuriated Ted."

Rose blew her nose. Mike pictured her in his mind's eye sitting alone in the dark in some part of her house, wrapped up in a robe, a Kleenex balled in her plump fist.

"It was a different time back then," she said. "It's still a nice community, but back then, we knew all of our neighbors. Our kids grew up together. They hopped on their bikes and rode wherever they wanted. When you enrolled your child in the church's after-school program, you didn't worry about priests molesting children or the church covering it up. Even when the police told me they found Ashley's shoes in Jonah's office, when they told me about what he did in Seattle, I defended him, told Ted that there had to be some sort of rational explanation for this. You didn't question priests. You didn't question the church. And I had this man in my *home*. I confessed my sins to him. I *trusted* him." Rose blew her nose again. "Ted never forgave me, you know."

Rose had spoken at length of her daughter's disappearance but had never talked about how it had affected her relationship with her husband. Mike always had the impression that they were a united front, bonded by their grief and love for their daughter, committed to finding a way to move forward together.

"And you know what, Michael? Ted's right. He's right. A mother's supposed to protect her children. The signs were there and I chose to ignore them."

"It's not your fault," he said, then wished he could take it back. That was the stock response and besides, how many times had that line been used on him? How many times had he ignored those words, just flushed them away? Sarah walking up the Hill by herself—that was his fault. Apologize all you want but nothing would change that fact. Words couldn't erase grief.

"I still own that damn dining-room table," she said. "Ted refused to get rid of it. Ashley was gone less than a year and Ted went into her room and packed up all of her clothes and gave them away without telling me— told me that I had to move on. But the dining-room table? Oh no. We couldn't get rid of that. It didn't matter how much I hated looking at it, we just had to keep it because it belonged to his precious mother. I stopped eating there, but you think he cared? He wanted to punish me. For what happened to Ashley. For refusing to go with him to Cambridge when Harvard offered him a research position. There was no way in hell I was going to move, plus we had the kids to think of. I didn't want to disrupt their lives any more than they had been. But Ted, he pushed for a fresh start. I finally told him if he took that position, I'd leave him."

She sniffed away her tears and then said, "I deserve this."

"Nobody deserves this, Rose."

"The doctor said these things happened."

"How could you have known about Jonah's past?"

"I mean the baby."

"I don't understand."

"There was a baby before Ashley. Ted and I thought the pregnancy was going along fine," she said. The words came out sounding as if they were being torn from her chest. "The middle of the fourth month came along and we found out that the baby didn't have a brain. The doctor gave us two choices and Ted . . . Ted convinced me what the right thing, the humane thing was to do. Made it sound all so scientific and practical. The doctor was very gentle and understanding, but it didn't matter. In the eyes of God, I had committed murder. I knew that."

Rose was cut from the same die-hard Catholic mold of his mother—Rose a product of Catholic school from a time when nuns would crack you across your knuckles with a ruler. You went to Mass every Sunday, you took an active interest in the religious education and formation of your children—you followed the rules and did what you were told, and you *did not,* under any circumstances and for any reason, participate in or approve of the great evil known as abortion. Such matters were left to God.

Mike wanted to tell her what he felt to be true: that God didn't care. That the only person looking out for yourself was you.

"Under Canon law, anyone who receives an abortion is automatically excommunicated," Rose said. "I knew that, but I couldn't live with, you know, the burden of it. I wanted the Act of Contrition, but I couldn't confess it to Father Jonah. I was afraid he'd judge me. So I went three towns over and talked with Father Morgan."

Rose cried harder. "He screamed at me," she whispered through her tears. "Said that I had no right to make that decision, that I should have delivered the baby so the baby could have been baptized. Then he could have been properly buried and his soul sent to heaven, but I didn't do that. I took the easy way out and damned his soul to hell."

Navigating through these sorts of emotional landmines was Jess's specialty. She never had to fumble over the right choice of words, was never dumbfounded or speechless the way he was right now.

"Father Jonah . . . he knew something was wrong. I couldn't hold it in any longer. I told him. And you know what, Michael? He was so gentle with me. So kind. That was what I remembered when all that stuff about him came out. To be so gentle and kind and then to turn around and do whatever he did to Ashley, I just—I don't understand anymore, Michael. I just don't understand." Rose broke down, then pulled herself back a moment later. "I'm sorry," she said. "I had no right to call and dump this all on you. I don't know why I called, honestly."

"It's okay. Really. I just don't know what to say. I've never been good at this sort of thing."

"You're listening. That's more than Ted ever did."

"Is there something I can do?"

"Talk to me about Sarah. All these times we've talked, you've never really told me what she was like . . . before."

"What do you want to know?"

"Everything," Rose said. "I want to know everything."

CHAPTER 33

"It's a totally legit question," Bill said as he flipped over the hamburgers and hot dogs cooking on the gas grill set up on the driveway. It was a perfect spring evening, and everyone was outside, enjoying the pleasantly cool air filled with the shouts of a group of kids playing street hockey at the end of the street.

Mike bounced the yellow rubber lacrosse ball against the driveway to shake off the dog drool, and when the ball bounced back up, he grabbed it and chucked a grounder across Bill's backyard, Fang barking as he tore after it.

"Okay then. I'd be Spider-Man."

"You're an idiot."

"If I could pick one superhero to be, then yes, I'd be Spider-Man."

"But Superman can fly."

"So can Spider-Man. He's got web-swinging action."

Bill was shaking his head. "Swinging's not flying, bro."

"It's the same thing."

"No way. Spider-Man needs tall buildings, skyscrapers—you know, shit to attach his web to. Otherwise, he's stuck on the ground. How could he swing—excuse me, how could he *fly*—over a cornfield?"

"And why would Spider-Man want to fly over a cornfield?"

"Suppose he was called in to investigate crop circles."

"Crop circles," Mike said. Fang, the ball wedged firmly in his mouth, stopped near the grill, inspecting it with a sniff, before lumbering back over to Mike.

"Aliens leave them. It's part of their navigation system," Bill said through the smoke. "Didn't you see that movie *Signs?*"

"No. And by the way, what was with the argument with Patty about the grilling?"

"Because last time she did it, she snuck a tofu dog on the grill, thinking I wouldn't taste the difference. Damn thing tasted like feet. Rent that movie *Signs*. Dude who did that, M. Night? Pure genius."

Mike picked the ball back up and saw a silver BMW with tinted windows slide up to the front of Bill's house.

"You didn't tell me Bam was coming over."

"Bam just leased a Lexus," Bill said. "Hey, maybe it's the Publishers Clearing House people. Watch for a camera—and balloons. Balloons are always a dead giveaway."

"Those guys travel in vans."

The driver's side door opened and out sprang a young guy with platinum blond hair cut short and spiked with gel, his ungodly thin body dressed in, oh sweet Jesus, maroon pants with a black shirt. He pushed the black-rimmed sunglasses up his nose.

"Mr. Sullivan! It's me, Anthony!"

Bill picked up his bottle of Sam Adams. "Well, at least I know why I haven't seen you dating any chicks lately."

"It's Sam's secretary."

"Sam's got a dude for a secretary? You go girl."

Mike chucked the ball into the backyard and then walked down the driveway.

"We've been trying to reach you on your cell phone all day," Anthony said when Mike reached him.

"I forgot to recharge my cell phone last night. What's up?"

"Okay, here it goes: your father has retained Mr. Weinstein as his lawyer."

Mike felt the skin along his face stretch tight.

"Sam warned me you might have that reaction," Anthony said. "I know you two had some sort of deal in place. I don't know what went wrong. She told me to tell you she'd call you later."

"Sam in her office?"

"She's stuck in a meeting until eight. She'll call, I promise." Anthony reached in through the opened window, yanked a white envelope off the dash and handed it to Mike. The envelope was sealed. "This is something Mr. Weinstein wanted hand-delivered to you. The couriers we use don't come out this far, so yours truly offered his services."

"Thanks," Mike said. "I owe you a beer."

"It's a date," Anthony said and winked. He got back

in his car, his hand out the window and waving good-bye as he sped off.

Using his thumb, Mike ripped open the envelope. Inside were a house key and a folded piece of paper. He took out the paper, unfolded it and in the fading evening light read Lou's trademark scrawl written on the law firm's stationery.

Michael,

I was denied bail. They got me holed up in Cambridge until my trial. I'm meeting with my lawyer at 10 tomorrow. He's looking for $50,000 as a retainer. Money's in a floor safe. Peel back the carpet in your old bedroom closet and you'll find it. Combo's 34–26–34. Take out the money and leave the rest.

You said you wanted to trade. At the bottom of the safe you'll find some items that belonged to your mother. Drop off the payment tomorrow and I'll answer any questions you want. I can have visitors.

I had nothing to do with burning that man.

Mike folded the paper back up and walked up the driveway. He felt dizzy.

Bill pointed to the letter with his barbecue tongs and said, "That a love note from your fancy gentleman caller?"

Mike held the paper out. Bill grabbed it by a corner with his barbecue tongs and snapped it open.

"I sure hope your old man likes hot climates," Bill said and placed the letter on the grill. Mike watched the paper burst into flames, wishing he could do the same with all the questions inside his head, just put them one by one on the funeral pyre and walk away.

CHAPTER 34

The cell phone pressed against his ear, Mike leaned back in the front seat of his truck and said, "You said Weinstein wouldn't take the case unless he got the go-ahead from you."

"Your father left a message with Miranda—"

"Who?"

"Miranda is Martin's secretary," Sam said. "Your father left a message with her saying that if Martin took the case, he'd be looking at a twenty-five thousand cash bonus. If Martin got your father off, then he was looking at a bonus of a hundred grand. The operative word here is cash. You understand what I'm driving at?"

He did. In addition to whatever percentage the firm would give Martin Weinstein for taking on the case, he was looking at a potential $125,000 bonus—all of it tax free since Lou agreed to pay him in cash. No records, no way for the IRS to come knocking.

"And let me guess," Mike said. "Martin won't be

sharing any of that bonus money with the firm, will he?"

"Martin will throw some money Miranda's way to keep her quiet, and she will. She's been with him for a long time. Wherever Martin goes, Miranda goes. He pays her well for her loyalty."

"So far she's not doing a very good job at keeping quiet."

"Miranda didn't tell me any of this. Martin did."

"Martin care where this money came from?"

"No. He needs it. He's got his eye on a new Bentley."

"Sounds like a hell of a guy."

"Why didn't you tell me your father had that kind of money on hand?"

"I had no idea." Lou was never a flashy guy. Sure he wore suits, but he didn't dump money into fancy cars or big vacations. His house in Belham was a one-floor ranch, and there was a time, during those first few years back from Vietnam, when money was tight.

Sam said, "When you and I first talked about this, I said that if you used Martin's name as bait—and you clearly did—then there was a possibility that your father would pick up the phone and call Martin directly."

"Which is why I thought we had a deal in place."

"You didn't tell me your father was going to throw around wads of cash. If I had known that, I would have tried another tactic."

Mike wasn't pissed at Sam; he was pissed at himself. He had been so consumed with the idea of having Lou cornered that he hadn't thought about the money. Sure,

Mike knew about the armored car jobs, about the load that had totaled close to two million. His error had been in *ass*uming—incorrectly—that Lou had blown through the money. Mike hadn't figured Lou to be a guy who would have a lot of dough socked away somewhere.

And don't forget all that time Lou spent in Florida. What, you think he didn't do any jobs while he was down there?

Sam said, "Why is this bothering you so much? I thought you wrote him off."

"It doesn't matter now. How much I owe you for all of this?"

"No charge."

"Let me take you out to dinner then. I'll come into town and we'll go someplace nice."

"Nice could be dangerous to your wallet."

"What are we talking about here? Salads that cost fifty bucks a plate?"

"Oh no. Much, much higher than that."

"And I suppose I'm going to have to dress up."

"You bet your ass."

"Pick a time and place. I'll call you tomorrow."

Mike hung up and looked out the window at Lou's house—and make no mistake about it, it had always been Lou's house, mother and son nothing more than extended guests. The last time Mike was here, he was just shy of eighteen. After Lou had left for work, Mike packed up his stuff—what he owned fit into two boxes—and drove over to his room at the O'Malley house, the room vacated by Chuck and Jim O'Malley, the two of them enlisting in the army at the same time.

That was two decades ago and now the old neighborhood had undergone a conversion. The ranch homes had been leveled and replaced with nicely sized Colonials, a few of them with two-car garages. Two decades and during that time Lou hadn't spruced his place up, made it look a little cheery instead of like a brooding hideaway for a serial killer.

Mike sat in his truck, staring at his old home and thinking about Lou's note. Lou was giving him a one-shot deal. If Mike didn't show up with the cash tomorrow morning, it was over. Lou would gladly take all of his secrets with him to the grave. Like Jonah.

No good can come of this. You know that.

It was that rational, sensible voice that had kept him out of a good deal of trouble most of his early life. Sensible and rational. Just like his mother.

Mike stepped outside, shut the door and walked up the sloping lawn to the front door, fishing the key out of his jeans pocket. He unlocked the door and stepped inside the living room, his right hand sliding up the wall on his right for the light switch.

The living room still had the same low-pile tan carpeting, the walls still painted white, not a mark on them. No pictures, no framed prints. Beyond the living room was a small kitchen—same white linoleum floor, clean and polished, spotless as always, the green counters, sink and kitchen table absent of any clutter. The air lingered with traces of ammonia and bleach—harsh, antiseptic smells that went right along with the cold furniture: hard, functional pieces that could have been plucked from a hospital room, places where you were forced to ponder your bruises and scars.

Mike shut the door behind him. Six steps and he had walked through the living room and part of the kitchen. He flipped another wall switch and moved down the narrow hallway, about to head to his old bedroom when he passed by Lou's opened bedroom door and caught a glimpse of what looked like picture frames displayed on top of a bureau.

Mike turned around, walked into the bedroom and flicked on the light.

The framed pictures were of Sarah.

Four of them, all taken outside, all of them capturing Sarah at various ages: Sarah wearing a sundress and walking barefoot next to Fang, her hand on the dog's back for support; Sarah smelling a dandelion; Sarah playing with Paula O'Malley at the jungle gym at the Hill; Sarah dressed in her pink snowsuit, holding Mike's hand as they waited for their turn to go down the hill.

The pictures looked familiar and unfamiliar at the same time. Mike had never given his father any pictures—and neither had Jess. No way in hell. Mike was the designated family photographer, Jess having no patience with cameras, more concerned about keeping her hands free to catch Sarah in case she fell.

Mike hadn't taken these pictures. Lou had. Lou had been told to stay away and instead had watched Sarah through a camera lens and stolen these moments.

There had to be more photos of Sarah, more rolls of film.

Mike searched through Lou's bureau drawers first. When he came up empty, he moved onto the nightstand drawers, the shoeboxes on a shelf in Lou's closet and then finally under the bed. Nothing.

Maybe the pictures were in the safe.

Mike walked into his old bedroom and flicked on the light. The room was completely empty. So was the closet. He removed the Swiss Army knife from his front pocket, a Christmas gift from Bill's kids last year, and after selecting the blade, got down on both knees and used the knife to pry up a corner section of the carpet. Once he got a strip, he grabbed it and gave it a good, hard yank.

Lou had gone all out with the floor safe. Mike knew a thing or two about safes. A few years back, when Jess wanted to store some important documents inside the house instead of making trips to the safety deposit box, Mike had a guy from Trunco Safe in East Boston come out and run through all the different models and options. While Lou's safe appeared to be a similar model—square, made of solid steel with a flush cover plate that was perfect for concealment under carpet—Mike was willing to bet Lou's model had drill-proof plates and was built to provide protection against forced entry with something like a sledgehammer. The safe had been set in concrete, making it impossible to pull out unless you happened to have some serious heavy machinery.

This safe hadn't been here when he was a kid. It was also less than five years old. When Sarah disappeared, and before Jonah became a suspect, Merrick and crew had locked their sights on Lou and had ripped apart every square inch of this house, the thinking being that Sarah was kidnapped because of one of Lou's past associations. Slow Ed had never mentioned anything about finding a safe full of cash—or pictures of Sarah for that matter.

Mike worked the dial. The combination entered, he turned the hinge and heard the safe click open.

Two rows, two stacks each of crumpled hundred dollar bills bound together by elastic. Mike grabbed one stack, counted through it. Ten grand—and that was just one stack. There'd be a hell of a lot more, depending on how deep the safe was. Five minutes later he knew.

"Holy shit."

Half a million—in *cash*.

Of course, a voice said. *If he placed it in a bank, the government could come in and freeze the accounts.*

An insane thought flashed in Mike's head: Donate it. *Yeah, Lou, I found the money, only I got to thinking about how it would be better off in someone else's hands. You know, give it to someone who really needed it. So I gave it to the ASPCA. They're a group that works with lost and runaway dogs. No need to thank me, Lou. The look on your face is thanks enough.* Priceless as that moment would be, if he did that, Lou would stick around and haunt him forever.

At the bottom of the safe was an elastic-wrapped envelope. Mike reached inside, pulled out the envelope and removed the elastic.

Pictures, but not of Sarah. The top picture, the colors

slightly off and yellowed with age, was of people walking through a crowded alley of brick and white buildings filled with lights. At first Mike thought the place might have been Faneuil Hall in Boston. But this area was more enclosed and had a foreign feel to it.

Like Paris.

Mike studied the faces in the pictures. He didn't recognize any of them. By the way people were dressed, it was either spring or summer. He turned the picture over and saw the developer's date stamped on the back: July 16, 1976.

July. The month Lou went to Paris. Next picture: a woman with frosted blond hair sitting at an outdoor table under a white awning covered with ivy, a pair of round black sunglasses covering her eyes as she read a newspaper. People sat around her, reading newspapers and books, talking, drinking coffee. Mike flipped to the next picture, a close-up of the same woman, only she had taken off her sunglasses and was smiling at the man now seated across from her. The man's back was toward the camera, but the woman's face was as plain as day.

It was his mother.

He flipped through the rest of the pictures. His mother was in every one of them, as was her companion, this unknown man who was a good deal taller than her and had a very sharp, hawk-like nose, long sideburns and thick, wavy black hair—a banker or investor of some sort given the suit. Hard to say. What was clear was how much his mother cared for him. In every picture she either held his hand or arm. In the last picture, the man had his arm wrapped around her shoulder as they walked down a crowded street, his mother's wide smile turned away from him, his mother safe and happy, relieved to be back in Paris, lost in the streets of her birthplace and hometown.

CHAPTER 35

M ike had been expecting someone along the lines of the male version of Sam: a tall, conservatively dressed guy with a thin body shaped by early morning runs and afternoon squash matches, a guy who liked to kick back on the weekends with his pals Preston and Ashton on his sailboat docked near his summer home in Hyannis. Martin Weinstein, with his olive skin and thinning black hair combed straight back, the gold Rolex and pinkie ring, looked every inch the bada-bing crowd.

"You're wondering how a Jewish guy ended up looking like Tony Soprano, right?" Weinstein smiled, flashing his big, capped teeth. His weight clocked somewhere in the neighborhood of three bills, his body thick with hard fat. "My mother's a hundred percent Italian, my old man's a hundred percent Jewish. Me and my two younger brothers came out looking like her and got our father's smarts. I marry an Italian woman and my two kids are as pale as Irishmen. The miracle of genetics, I tell you."

"Here's the money you wanted," Mike said and tossed the cash envelope to Weinstein. "I want to meet him alone."

"No BS, just like your old man. I like that. Come on. I'll bring you to him."

Two guards—old grizzled hands with beer guts and jowls—told Mike to empty the contents of his jean pockets into a plastic bowl.

"And your belt and shoelaces," the guard said.

Weinstein said, "Potential weapons. Don't worry, you'll get it all back."

After Mike handed everything over, the guard worked him over with a metal-detection wand, then asked him to take off his boots, examining the heels and insides thoroughly before handing them back.

The guard nodded to his partner, and a buzzer sounded, the gate sliding back, clank-clank-clank-clank.

A series of corridors and locked gates followed, locks releasing and then bolting home, Weinstein leading the way and Mike reviewing again how he was going to approach Lou.

The prison guard saw Weinstein, nodded, and then took out his keys to unlock a door. Through the glass panel, Mike could see Lou sitting in a chair and dressed in his orange prison jumpsuit, his head bowed, studying the handcuffs secured around his wrists, the chain wrapped around his waist.

"You've got fifteen minutes," Weinstein said, then leaned in closer with the peppermint reek of his breath mint. "And be nice, okay? Your father was up all night throwing up, the chills, the shakes—I'm talking the whole nine yards. They had to call in a doctor. Looks like a bad strain of the flu."

Not the flu. The correct diagnosis is claustrophobia.

The lawyer opened the door. The room was small, holding a desk and two chairs, and smelled of soap and shaving cream. Lou kept his head down as he spoke.

"He give you the money, Martin?"

"We're good," Weinstein said. "Lou, you need anything, I'll be standing just outside the door."

Weinstein shut the door. Mike slid out the chair and sat down.

"Start talking."

"About Jess or about the pictures you found inside the safe? You did find them, right?"

"You know I did," Mike said. "I also found pictures of Sarah on your bureau. When did you take them?"

Lou's eyes tightened at the mention of his granddaughter. "So what did Jess say about her weekend getaway?"

"Who's the guy in the pictures?"

Lou looked up, grinning. In the fluorescent lighting, he looked withered, the skin under his eyes bruised from lack of sleep, his thin lips bloodless. Drops of perspiration ran down his forehead. "Didn't have the balls to ask her, did you?"

"We're going to talk about Mom, and you're going to start by telling me how you found out where she was hiding."

"Hiding," Lou repeated. "Are you seriously that re-tarded?"

"I swear to Christ, if you try and back out of—"

"Arnold Mackey."

"Who's that?"

"The O'Malleys' postman. Mackey was a regular at McCarthy's every Friday night. One night he comes in and asks me why your mail is getting delivered to the O'Malley house. He sees I'm totally confused and then tells me about the package you got from Paris. We get to talking, I buy him a few beers, and I ask him to keep an eye out for any more mail with your name on it, tell him that if he hand-delivers it to me instead, I got two one-hundred-dollar bills with his name on them."

"So she sent a second package."

"More like a note. It was written on one of those heavy, expensive note cards. Then again, your mother always valued expensive things. Did I ever tell you how your mother almost bankrupted me? In the beginning money was tight but that didn't stop your mother from treating herself to fancy dinners, nights on the town in Boston. When she bought things, she'd hide them around the house. You ever see her do anything like that?"

"What did this letter say?"

"Who'd she say that blue scarf of hers came from?"

"I don't remember."

"I thought you came for the truth, Michael. Or are you looking for me to verify your version of it?"

"She said her father gave it to her."

Lou leaned back in his chair and folded his hands over his flat stomach. "Her father was a waiter who could barely afford the groceries. Her mother died when Mary was four."

Mike searched his memory for stories his mother told him about her parents, something to verify it against what Lou was saying, prove he was lying. When he couldn't come up with anything, he said, "Tell me what the letter said."

"I don't remember her exact words, but it was something along the lines of how much she missed you, that she carried you in her thoughts—you know, all that happy horseshit."

"That's it? That's all she said?"

"You mean did she say when she was coming home to get you? I do remember her mentioning an address but no phone number. I wonder why she wouldn't leave you her phone number." Lou wore his prize-fighter's smile, that lustful look of satisfaction when he knew he had you cornered. "I still have the note, you know."

Mike felt his pulse quicken.

"Would you like to know where it is?" Lou asked.

Lou giving him a choice: either back out now or go forward, you choose.

"Go home, Michael."

"Where's this note?"

"It's downstairs in the basement," Lou said. "Top drawer of the Gerstner."

The Gerstner was a solid oak tool chest made by H. Gerstner and Sons. It was where Lou kept all his precision tools. Mike said, "So in this second letter, she included a return address. That's how you found her."

Lou winked. "You got it."

"And once you had her address, you just hopped on a plane to Paris."

"Correct."

"With a fake passport."

"There was a misunderstanding between me and the authorities at the time. They believed I had something to do with the theft of certain electronics items from a warehouse in South Boston."

"Only you hate to fly because you're claustrophobic."

"I don't fly because I don't trust planes."

"So why not call her? You had her address; you could have found her phone number. Why bother hopping on a plane?"

"Boy needs his mother," Lou said, Mike feeling the heat in Lou's voice, words coming together and forming a fist.

Why is he acting so confident?

He's setting you up.

But for what?

"You've always viewed your mother as a saint," Lou said. "What about all the things I did? The ball games, the bikes and the car, your tuition at St. Stephen's. When you and Bill started your business, I offered you money, even steered some clients your way. Anything you ever needed, you got."

"Including getting hit."

"You needed toughening up. Parochial school and all that church nonsense were making you soft. That's the problem with your generation. You love to hoard every little hurt life throws at you and spend all your time whining about it. It's no wonder we got so many faggots running around these days." Lou shook his head, then leaned forward, his chains rattling. "You ever hear me bitch about my situation? About losing my brother to that shit war or spending over a year in that POW camp?"

"Tell me what you did to her."

"I tried to talk her into coming home."

"You're lying."

"Did we get into it? Absolutely." No apology, no remorse in either his face or tone. "Accidents happen, right? Like that night you went over to Jonah's. I'm sure you didn't go over there with the intention of beating the living shit out of him, but you heard him lie to your face and you just couldn't contain yourself—or do I have it all wrong?"

"Talk to your best friend Cadillac Jack recently?"

"I didn't hurt her. You don't want to accept it, then that's your problem." Lou's tone was calm—way too calm, Mike thought.

"Who's the guy in the pictures?"

"Jean Paul Latiere."

Surprise bloomed on Mike's face before he could hold it back.

"Yes, I know who he is," Lou said. "They grew up together. They were very, very close, those two—thick as thieves, you could say. Jean Paul and your mother were quite an item when they were young. Inseparable. Then your mother moved to the States. She was fifteen and hopelessly in love. She and Jean Paul kept in touch by mail, by phone—only Jean Paul had to do the majority of the calling since your mother's father—your grandfather—wouldn't have allowed phone calls to France. As Jean Paul got older, nineteen or so, he'd fly here and meet your mother. He could afford to do it. He was working at his father's paper mill business when your mother left, you know, being groomed to take over the family business. Latiere Paper. Big company over there. And Jean Paul, he just loved to shower your mother with expensive gifts. Like her scarf. Expensive gifts popped up from time to time around the house."

Unconsciously Mike rubbed his forehead, found it slick and greasy.

"Having a hard time believing your perfect saint of a mother could possibly be involved in something so seedy?"

"If she was having an affair, I don't blame her for it."

"An affair? She was in love with him the day we met."

"Then why'd she settle for you?"

"Jean Paul's family was very successful, very rich. Prestigious background, lots of inventors and politicians—you know, all that pedigree nonsense that gets some panties wet. Nothing got your mother more excited than money. Problem was, Jean Paul's old man wasn't going to let him get involved with common-variety trash, even if that trash was someone as beautiful as your mother—got to think of the bloodlines, you know? Your mother was a lot like your wife—excuse me, your ex-wife. They both valued the finer things money could offer, only your mother wasn't a patient woman. And I didn't know she was still holding out hope for Jean Paul, even after we married. I always knew those pictures were bullshit."

"What pictures?"

"Your mother kept photo albums of pictures of Jean Paul's family. She must have showed them to you."

The photo albums she hid in boxes in the basement—the ones she packed up and took with her—Mike remembered how she would sit down alone in the basement and go through them, the few times he caught her there crying and she would bring him over, go through all the pictures with him and narrate the story of her family. *Her* family.

"No," Mike said. "She didn't."

"He was around Belham a lot when I was away during the war. Even after I came home, Jean Paul came to Boston a lot. All those secret missions you two shared, surely you must have met him."

As Lou talked, Mike searched through his memories for the man he had seen in those pictures. The Frenchman's face didn't ring any bells. It was a long time ago.

"I never met him," Mike said.

"Huh. Now I wonder why that is. Any ideas?"

"So you knew about the affair?"

"I had my suspicions. Fresh flowers every now and then—she said she bought them at the florist. Nice item like a silver picture frame or a nice pair of shoes pops up, a nice dress, your mother says she found them at Goodwill or some place like that. Your mother could be very persuasive with that soft gentle voice of hers—you know that better than anyone. Smoothest liar I ever met, your mother. Did you know she kept a post office box downtown? That's where Jean Paul sent the gifts and money."

Mike tried picturing her getting dressed and made up and driving into Boston to meet this guy, this Jean Paul, at a place like the Four Seasons; but Mike couldn't picture her beyond her frumpy clothing, her penny-pinching ways and dime-store makeup she used to cover her bruises. That image was fixed in his mind because it was true—and here was Lou trying to destroy it with his lies. To believe Lou would ever come clean about anything had been both stupid and foolish. Lou lied for a living, and he was lying now.

"Your mother knew I took those pictures," Lou said. "And God knows I wanted to—"

"Let's get one thing straight. You and I are through. The next time you see me will be when I'm on the witness stand, telling everyone about that night you came by and told me about how you'd been inside Jonah's house. I bet the police haven't found the listening devices."

Lou's eyes had taken on a heated, watery glow. "Martin?" he called out. "Martin, we're done in here."

Mike leaned across the table. "You're never going to see daylight again. That's a promise."

The door swung open and Lou said, "The problem was that Jean Paul loved your mother but didn't love children. So he gave her a choice: life in Paris or life in Belham. Which one you think she chose, Michael?"

CHAPTER 36

The oak tool chest, the Gerstner, was exactly where Lou had said: in the basement, stacked at the bottom of one of those self-assembled plastic shelving units. It was locked. Rather than wasting time searching for a key, Mike grabbed a drill and drilled a hole through the lock, remembering that when Lou wasn't working, or when he got into a particularly nasty fight with Mary, he would come down here and putter around on some project. He had a talent for cabinetry but didn't have the patience; he once built a hutch made of solid oak, but it had taken him three years to do it. It was here, using Lou's tools, that Mike made the birdhouse he had given his mother.

The chest opened without a problem. Sitting inside the walls of green felt were six neat stacks of envelopes bound together by elastics. They were all addressed to Mary Sullivan in Lou's trademark chicken scrawl. Most of the paper had yellowed, and the stamps in the corners had curled, about to fall off.

Lou's war letters.

Odd that he would keep them, Mike thought. It was such a sentimental act, and Lou was hardly sentimental. Even odder that he'd write them in the first place since he rarely talked about what had happened over there.

Mike removed one stack and set it down on top of the long counter that stretched its way down one length of the wall. He lit a cigarette, unfastened the elastic and picked up a random envelope. This letter was one page, written in pencil.

May 13, 1965

Dear Mary,

The sun here doesn't let up, and everywhere I go there's this thick, wet heat. Mail over a fan when you get a chance, ha ha.

Things have been heating up here. The other day we were choppered into Dodge City and immediately we were in the middle of a firefight. Thank God I had my helmet and flak gear otherwise I wouldn't have made it. The gooks had us pinned down for two hours. I couldn't even raise my head and see where they were—that's how bad it was. I've never been so scared in my entire life. I don't believe in hell, but if there is one, this place must surely be it.

Keep talking to my brother. I don't want him over here.

Please write me. Your letters will get me

through this. How is Michael? What is he doing?
The two of you are always in my thoughts. Send a
picture of Michael if you can.

> Love,
> Lou

Scared and *love*. Words Lou never used but had written here.

Mike opened another envelope. This letter was dated
a week later.

They have us guarding a road next to a grave-
yard. Every night I'm sleeping next to a tomb-
stone. We're losing about a man a day, most of it to
the damn heat.

I love you, Mary. I know some words were exchanged before I left. And I know money is tight
and things are tough for you and the baby right
now, but I'll come home and make it up to you.
Don't give up on me. Don't give up on what we
have. I'm coming home. That's a promise.

There were a dozen more letters like that, all of them
written in an almost identical way: Lou describing the
hell around him and asking Mary to write to him. The
last letter read:

I'm sure you already know about Dave Sim-
mons. He was standing right next to me—right
next to me, Mary—and after he sneezed he was

shot in the head. Goddamn weirdest thing. Please check on Dave's wife, see if she's doing okay.

Please stop punishing me with your silence and write to me.

A card-sized envelope was on the bottom of the chest drawer, resting on top of sealed flaps of old Brick's Photo envelopes (THANK YOU FOR TRUSTING US WITH YOUR MEMORIES was written across the flap). The card was addressed to Michael Sullivan at Bill's old address—just as Lou had said. This card had a return address in the corner.

Mike removed the envelope from the pile and flipped it around. The back flap's seal had already been torn open. He lifted the flap and peeled out the heavy note card.

Dear Michael,

I'm sorry it has taken me so long to write back to you. I've been actively searching for a place big enough for the both of us. Paris is incredibly expensive, especially here on the Île St-Louis. There's first and last month's rent to consider, and security deposits. I'm working as a waitress at a café, but money is slow coming in. Looking back, I should have taken the money I withdrew from the bank and used it to set us up here, but there was your tuition to consider. After all the setbacks you've had, I didn't want you to have to endure moving to another school and away from your friends.

I'm coming for you. I know it has taken longer than I've said, and I know you've been patient. I need you to keep being patient. You can write to me at the address on the front of the envelope.

Don't let your father find this address. Hide this letter where he won't find it. If your father finds out where I'm hiding—I don't have to remind you what your father is capable of.

The restaurant where I work has a wonderful view of Notre Dame church, and as I sit here and write you this letter, I can look out the window and see the gargoyles you loved so much.

No matter how bad it gets, always remember to have faith. Always remember how much I love you.

> God bless,
> Mom

Mike slid the note card back in the envelope. His throat felt raw when he swallowed.

You've always viewed your mother as a saint. What about all the things I did? The ball games, the bikes and the car, your tuition at St. Stephen's.

Mike removed the Brick's Photo envelope and opened it, expecting to see more pictures of Sarah or his mother. He didn't expect to see Jess—a much younger Jess—climbing inside the passenger seat of a car. Mike flipped through the pictures and saw—

He flung the envelope against the wall; pictures exploded across the floor.

Mike opened the bulkhead, walked up the steps and stepped into Lou's sun-filled backyard. He took out his wallet and found, tucked behind his money, the folded yellow Post-it note with Jess's new address and phone number. She had given it to him this past Sunday just as he was leaving. *If you need anything, Michael—anything, you can call me.*

Goddamn right I will. He dialed the number, pressed the phone up to his ear.

"Hello," Jess said.

The words felt swollen inside his throat. He opened his mouth but no sound came out.

"Hello?" Jess said again.

Mike snapped the phone shut and wiped his face.

You've always viewed your mother as a saint. What about all the things I did? The ball games, the bikes and the car, your tuition at St. Stephen's.

Mike called information for St. Stephen's rectory and asked the operator to connect him.

"This is Mike Sullivan," he told the secretary who answered the phone. "I need to speak with Father Connelly. It's important."

The secretary put him on hold for a moment and then Father Jack's voice came on the line. "How are you doing, Michael?"

"I was hoping you could help me with something. A quick question about my mother."

"I'll do my best," Father Jack said, Mike hearing walls go up in the priest's voice. Mike knew his mother had been close to Father Jack, the priest all too well aware of

Mike's home life with Lou. And Mike remembered how shocked Father Jack had acted when asked if he knew anything about where his mother had gone. If it was an act, it was worthy of an Oscar.

"Is there any way to find out if she paid for my tuition?"

"Your tuition?"

"I know it's an odd question, but I just had a talk with Lou and he told me that he had paid for my tuition. Is there any way of finding out if that's true?"

"It's true."

"You're sure."

"Positive. He came to me personally and paid me in cash not long after your mother left. Every year he paid in cash. He's the only parent who ever did that."

Mike didn't know what else to say. "Okay then. Thanks."

"Is there anything else I can help you with?"

"Not right now." Mike thanked him again and hung up.

Looking back, I should have taken the money I withdrew from the bank and used it to set us up here, but there was your tuition to consider. After all the setbacks you've had, I didn't want you to have to endure moving to another school and away from your friends.

His mother's words from the note, only it was a lie. Lou said he had paid for the tuition, and Father Jack had just validated it. She had lied to him. Why?

"This has got to stop," he said to no one. "At some point this has got to stop."

You asked for this, remember?

A memory of Sarah: the two of them driving to the Main Street Diner a couple of weeks after Bill's mother had died. Sarah must have been five at the time. Bill's mother treated Sarah as one of her own grandchildren, so he and Jess sat Sarah down and told her that Nana Jane had died, Jess taking the lead then and explaining to Sarah that death meant that the body had stopped existing, and that while her soul had gone to heaven, all the good things people loved about Nana Jane, all those good times everyone had shared with her—those memories would continue to live on in everyone who had loved her.

Sarah asked a couple of questions and then left to go play with her Barbie dolls, the questions pretty much stopping as the days wore on, the two of them figuring that Sarah had come to grips with it—until that day in the truck when she announced that she was still sad.

"I still miss Nana Jane," Sarah said.

"We all do, sweets."

"When will the sadness go away, Daddy?"

"It takes time."

"How much time?"

"It's different for everyone. You need to give your heart time to make room for it."

"And what happens if my heart runs out of room?"

Impossible, he had told her.

Now though? Now he wondered how much grief a heart could hold, how many truths it was forced to accept before it ruptured.

CHAPTER 37

The few memories Mike had of Beacon Hill were hazy ones from his younger days—drunk nights spent running from bar to bar with Wild Bill and the rest of the Belham pack, Beacon Hill boasting some of the best-looking women in the city. He remembered the place as being a brick-lined haven for elitists and the superrich, complete with bad parking and lantern-like streetlights. Beacon Hill seemed small until you actually walked through it and then it resembled a hedge maze, its narrow one-way streets lined with brick sidewalks and tall brick-faced condos and town houses, the price of one the cost of three or four nice homes in Belham.

The narrow streets and bad parking still held true, and so did all the brick. But as Mike walked up Charles Street, he was surprised by the neighborhood feel of the place. Sure, you had a Starbucks on each corner, and he spotted a Store 24 on the block, but other than that, Beacon Hill seemed to have resisted the whole brand-naming effort that had infected downtown Belham. And a part of him enjoyed the fluid busyness of this warm spring evening, the distraction of watching people coming in and out of stores, on their way to dinner, the college students with backpacks drinking coffee and talking on cell phones, parents out pushing strollers.

Mike took a left onto Sam's street, found the number and then climbed the steep front steps. After leaving Lou's house, Mike wanted an unbiased perspective on what he was thinking of doing next and, already knowing what Bill would say, called Sam at her office.

Mike found Sam's name on a brass panel listing the names of the people who lived here, rang the buzzer and after a moment heard the door buzz. Sam's place was on the third floor. He walked up the winding staircase and found Sam waiting for him at the door, dressed in jeans and a black collared shirt. She was the only woman he had known who could dress in something so simple and basic and yet make it look both sexy and elegant.

"You cut your hair," he said. "And highlighted it."

"Anthony convinced me to do it."

"It looks great." It really did.

"I needed a change. Anthony also tried to convince me into getting my navel pierced with him, but I drew the line there. Come on in."

Her third-floor condo was a wide, rambling space bursting with sunlight and high ceilings. A surprisingly big gourmet kitchen dominated the left half of the room. The table was set for two, nice china and crystal, a bottle of wine already opened. A plasma-screen TV hung on the brick wall, and to the left was a den with soft leather couches and mahogany bookcases packed with books.

"This is . . . wow," Mike said. He thought the place would be much smaller. The space in here, you could raise a family, no problem.

"Thank you. I had a friend help me decorate. Dinner's warming in the oven."

"You made dinner?"

"Takeout from Antonio's. Best Italian food in the city. When you called and asked to get together, I forgot to ask. I hope chicken parm is still your favorite."

He was surprised—and touched—that she had remembered.

Sam said, "What would you like to drink?"

"A Coke would be great if you have it."

Sam walked into the kitchen in her bare feet, opened the fridge and handed him an ice-cold can of Coke.

"We can eat now," she said, "or we can sit, talk, whatever you want."

"Sitting sounds good."

Sam grabbed her wine glass from the kitchen counter and Mike followed her to an alcove holding two oversized, overstuffed chairs that faced each other, an ottoman between them. A big picture window overlooked her street and a long, oval, gated area of grass and trees that was vaguely familiar to him for some reason.

"What's that area over there?" Mike asked.

"That would be Louisburg Square. If you have eight

million to spare, I can get you a great deal on a fixer-upper."

"Eight *million*."

"And don't forget the property taxes that can run as much as fifty thousand a year."

Mike placed his Coke on a small end table next to his chair and then removed the envelope from his back pocket before sitting down. Sam sat down, propping both legs up on the ottoman, her feet inches from his knee. They used to sit like this, Mike remembered, Sam always wanting to face him when they talked about something serious, Sam sometimes putting her feet on his leg, Mike rubbing a foot as they talked.

"I don't even know where to begin," Mike said after a moment.

"Start at the beginning."

"If I do that, we'll be here all night."

"If that's what it takes."

Then he remembered.

Louisburg Square. Christmas. Every year his mother had taken him into the city to see the big, brightly lit tree on the Common, and after that, they would head over to Beacon Hill for the holiday stroll where a tour guide would give them a walking history tour that always ended at Louisburg Square. The condos and town houses weren't open to the public, but sometimes, if the first-floor curtains weren't drawn, you could see inside the big windows and see the huge Christmas trees of the insanely wealthy. Thing was, his mother had seemed more interested in watching the people around her than hearing the history of the multi-million-dollar town houses where Louisa May Alcott and the Kennedy family had once lived.

He remembered something else too. During their last Christmas together, his mother had seemed especially distracted, wanting to linger after the tour had broken up. It was snowing, and while he didn't mind that, he did mind the cold. The air was raw, the wind biting into his skin, and he wanted to get going. His mother said they couldn't, not yet, because she was waiting for a friend. Yes, a friend. That was the word she used. *Friend.* It surprised him since his mother didn't really have any friends—at least, she never spoke of any. He had been even more surprised when he found out that this friend of his mother's was a man.

Was this man Jean Paul? Mike didn't know. He couldn't remember what the man looked like or how he dressed, but he did recall something about shaking the man's hand, the gentle way this man put his hand on his mother's back and ushered her to a corner where they seemed to talk forever, the man glancing every once in a while in Mike's direction.

"Don't feel you have to talk, Sully. We can just sit here and relax, enjoy the evening."

Mike touched the envelope resting on his thigh. "You still friendly with your ex-husband?"

"God no."

"So it ended badly between you."

"That's putting it mildly."

"You mind me asking how it ended?"

Sam sipped her wine, then said, "Well, for three years we

tried to conceive a child, and when we couldn't do it naturally, we started the whole fertility process. The pills, the hormone shots—I even tried in vitro three times. No luck. So we dealt with it the way all mature adults do: we both worked longer hours and stopped talking. We began to drift apart and then he came to me one day and said that he wasn't happy, I said neither was I and we agreed to divorce. Matt desperately wanted children, and since I couldn't give him any, he wanted to go, you know, go looking elsewhere. Adoption was never an option with him. I always suspected that was the reason he was cheating."

Mike wanted to say he was sorry, but didn't want to disrupt the flow of her thoughts.

"I caught him—twice," Sam said. "Both times in a motel. Both times it was raining and I'm sitting in my car with a pair of binoculars, watching him as he opens the door and then kisses his bimbo goodbye. Such a cliché, right? And as pathetic as that was—and it was extremely pathetic—I topped myself by taking him back both times, buying into his promise that he'd stop seeing her. I made a commitment for better or for worse, so I figured the cheating came under the worse category. And I think on some level I thought I deserved this because I had faulty eggs." Sam drank some more of her wine and when she was done, went to work on rubbing out a crease on her jeans. "Her name was Tina. She was a lawyer at another firm. One of Matt's lazy sperm hit the jackpot. That's why he wanted the divorce. He had a woman who was going to give him a family."

"I'm sorry, Sam."

She shrugged. "Life."

"So you knew."

"About the cheating, yes, I knew. I didn't find out Tina was pregnant until after the divorce papers were signed. It was a quick divorce—he basically gave me whatever I wanted. But the pregnancy—Matt managed to keep that very hush-hush."

"You ever call and ask him about why he had done that to you?"

"Matt is a self-absorbed asshole. What's the point in calling to confirm something I already know?"

Mike leaned forward and felt Sam's toes brush against his stomach. He placed the envelope on her lap. "These pictures were taken by Lou," he said. "The week before I got married."

Sam put her wine glass on the floor and then delicately opened the envelope. As she went through the pictures, he pretended to watch the people move up and down the street and tried not to think about the photos—thirty-six snapshots that told a story of Jess getting into a Volvo with a man Mike had never seen before, the two of them driving up to New Hampshire (Lou having taken multiple pictures of the car driving on Route 128 North and then Route 3 North), parking in a bookstore parking lot and then walking across a busy street to climb the steep concrete steps of a blue house, the bed and breakfast Lou had mentioned. The last three pictures of the roll culminated in Jess and this man walking down the stairs together, getting back into his car and then kissing.

Out of the corner of his eye, he saw Sam tuck the pictures back inside the envelope. "These pictures don't necessarily mean she had an affair."

Mike turned to her. "What about the last picture, the one where they're kissing?"

"The focus isn't that good. To me, it looks like they're hugging."

"Still."

"And your father just gave these to you out of the blue today?"

"I found them at the bottom of a toolbox along with a note from my mother that Lou had intercepted. You remember what happened to my mother?"

"I remember you mentioned something about her running off."

Mike started with the day his mother left and the reasons she did; took Sam through his last three encounters with Lou and ended with the second letter found in the toolbox, Mike telling Sam what the letter said and the lie about St. Stephen's. When he finished, the sun was gone, the lantern streetlights on.

"So now you're thinking your mother never had any intention of coming home?" Sam's voice was low, almost fearful, like she was afraid to ask the question.

"Did Lou go over there and take pictures of my mother with this guy? Yes. Do I think she was having an affair? Looks that way. Do I think Lou tried to talk her into coming home? I doubt it. People who cross him disappear. That's a fact."

"He was telling the truth about paying for your tuition. The priest confirmed it."

"Sam, this is a man who lies and kills for a living. My mother wouldn't just vanish. If she's alive, she'd have written a letter or called. She'd have done something."

Sam nodded, listening.

"When my mother disappeared, the police came around. A lot," Mike said. "He had those pictures. He knew where she was, who she was with. All Lou had to do was hand them over and he'd be free and clear."

"And what if you found out about the affair? Imagine what that would have done to you. How old were you? Nine?"

"Something like that."

"As for the pictures of your ex-wife," Sam said, "my only guess is that your father found out something about her and thought that if he showed you the pictures, you would leave her."

"Only he didn't."

"Maybe he didn't show you these pictures for the same reason he didn't show you the pictures of your mother," Sam offered. "The fact that he didn't, that's rather admirable, don't you think?"

"One time I saw Lou work a guy over with a lead pipe. The guy was big into debt with Lou's buddy Cadillac Jack. Guy's on the ground, crying, begging for his life, and Lou keeps whacking him. What's Lou do afterward? Goes home and takes a nap."

"Sully, I'm not going to sit here and play the armchair shrink and tell you that I understand your father. I don't. From everything you've told me, he sounds like a real son of a bitch. That being said, there's obviously this other side of him. It's possible that instead of showing you the pictures of your mother, he decided to shelter you from the truth."

"That's what you think?"

"Why else take pictures? Honestly, I can't imagine what that news would have done to you at that age. And maybe . . . this is just a thought, but maybe, on some level, he thought that having you hate him would be easier than knowing the truth."

Mike shut his eyes, rubbed them. He saw Jess kissing this other man. He saw Lou wandering through the streets of Paris, following his wife and her longtime love, snapping pictures and thinking about how he was going to get Mary alone. Mike kept seeing all these things and wanted to shut the door on all of it and walk away, only he couldn't.

"Maybe I have it all wrong," Sam said. "I don't know what makes your father tick. Quite frankly, I still don't know what makes my own father tick. All I know is that people are messy."

"I called Jess today."

"What did she say?"

"She said hello and I hung up."

"The day you met Jess for lunch, why didn't you ask her?"

Mike had thought about his reason for days now. "I

was afraid that if I asked her and she said yes, it would strip away those good times we had together. Change the way I think about and remember her."

Sam remained quiet. Mike thought back to this new memory he had just discovered, this Christmas memory of his mother and this man in Beacon Hill. Was it true? Had that man been Jean Paul? Or was his mind coughing up something out of fear? The memory felt true, but he wasn't sure anymore.

Sam said, "Walk away from it."

"Could you?"

"Depends."

"On what?"

"On how many more doors you want to open."

Mike nodded. "The second letter from my mother," he said. "There was an address on the envelope."

Sam waited for the rest of it.

"I called your friend Nancy and asked her to see if she could find out anything about that address, about my mother and this guy Jean Paul. I figured Nancy would have a better shot at finding her than I would."

"So you've decided to try and find her."

"All this time I thought, you know, Lou had done something to her. Buried her somewhere. Now I come to find out she might be alive. I can't turn away from that."

"And if your mother is alive?"

"I don't know, Sam. Honest to God, I don't know."

CHAPTER 38

For the next three days Mike buried himself in work. They finished with Margaret Van Buren's addition and kitchen renovation on Monday and then moved to the next jobsite, the one in Newton—The Urn Lady. Dotty Conasta was retired and very old ("Seriously, when you babysat Moses, was he a bad kid?" Bill always asked her); borderline senile (she repeated the same stories about her late husband Stan over and over again); and clearly lonely (she followed them room to room). Normally having a customer hovering around them every second sent Mike over the edge; but listening to Dotty was a welcome distraction from the constant, grinding process of sifting and sorting thoughts about his mother, about Lou and Jess and the newest addition, this guy Jean Paul.

After they kicked off from work, he would go home with Bill and drown himself in the chaos of Bill's house. Movement was important. Constant movement would exhaust him, so he helped Patty clear the table and clean the dishes, helped bathe the kids—a major project with the twins, who liked to get into splashing fights. He helped Paula with her homework and invited her on walks with the dog. They talked about nonsense stuff really—why TV shows totally sucked now, why boys were so confusing, why tennis rocked. At night he'd head downstairs to Bill's basement office and go over estimates or watch ESPN, MTV, whatever Bill wanted to watch, Mike forcing himself to stay up as long as possible before heading upstairs to sleep. Bill knew what was going on and didn't ask any questions.

Then Nancy Childs called.

"I have a lead but my French is a little rusty," she said, and then, as if reading his mind, added, "Yes, some of us Revere girls actually took a foreign language other than Spanish."

"What'd you find out?"

"Let me get everything together first and then I'll tell you. The reason I'm calling is that I was thinking of getting Sam involved in this since she speaks fluent frog. You okay with that?"

He was. Sam knew everything anyway.

It was during these stretches of quiet, usually when he was in bed, that he would start to wonder exactly what Nancy had uncovered. And the stuff about Jess was chewing its way through him. The pictures floated through his thoughts from one moment to the next, and sometimes he would pick up the phone and start dialing Jess's number and then hang up, usually before a first ring. Did he want the truth? Or was he looking for a whipping post? He wasn't sure.

Friday afternoon came and Mike made a promise to himself that he was going to enjoy the evening with Sam. No talk of Lou or Jess, none of it.

He owned one suit, black, perfect for both weddings and funerals. After he finished dressing, he came downstairs into Bill's kitchen and saw the twins sitting at the table, the two of them dressed in shirts and shorts and slurping grape popsicles that dripped over their hands and plates.

Bill whistled. "Looking good, Louis."

"Feeling good, Todd."

The phone rang. "Slap a Zima in your hand and you're good to go," Bill said as he jogged down the hallway to retrieve the cordless from the family room.

Grace popped the popsicle out of her mouth. Her lips and tongue were purple.

"Are you getting married?"

"No," Mike said. "I'm just going out to eat."

"In a suit?"

"It's a very nice restaurant."

"Daddy doesn't wear suits to restaurants."

"This is true."

"Mommy said Daddy's got bad table manners."

"That is very true."

"Is Daddy going with you?"

"No, I'm going with a friend of mine."

"A girl?"

Mike nodded as he searched for his car keys in the mess of newspapers and coloring books piled high on top of the island table.

Grace said, "Your tie is ugly."

"You think?"

"Daddy has a better one. With Snoopy on it. Girls like Snoopy." Grace turned to Emma: "It's in Daddy's closet. Go get it."

This time, Emma did what she was asked and scurried off.

"You should bring her flowers," Grace said. "Girls like flowers. Mommy likes flowers but says Daddy never brings her enough and when he does they're the wrong kind."

Mike found his keys. "Hey sweets?"

"Yes, Uncle Michael?"

"Don't ever change." Smiling, he planted a kiss on her forehead.

Grace smiled back. "Girls like it when you share popsicles too."

Traffic on Route 1 South was a mess. Mike forgot this was late Friday afternoon—rush hour—and just as many people were anxious to leave the city as they were to get in. He sat in his truck, bumper to bumper with everyone else, inching forward toward the tolls for the Tobin Bridge.

A plane had taken off, and as Mike watched it climb in the air above the skyscrapers of downtown Boston, he thought of Jess again, thought about how she, like his mother, had packed up her life and flown away to leave their problems. Only that wasn't true. You never really left your problems; you just moved them to another place. Fly halfway around the world and you were still who you were. Yet it amazed him how many people packed up and left everything they knew, tried rooting themselves in some new location, thinking they would be someone other than themselves. Like Jess with her clothes. Maybe dressing the part was the key. And buy yourself some distance. And time. Yes. Time and distance could make you forget anything, even a son or a daughter. *Just ask my mother,* Mike thought. *Just ask my ex-wife.*

Dinner was a three-hour production that ended with a bill that cost more than his monthly truck payment. When they stepped back outside, it was dark, the evening air cool and charged with an almost electrical current of excitement, the pure joy that comes from being able to be outside after enduring another horrendous New England winter.

"You really should have let me split the bill with you," Sam said as she wrapped around her shoulders some piece of fabric that was a cross between a scarf and a cape. She wore black high-heels and a stunning black dress that had a slit that ran all the way up her right thigh.

"I said I'd take you out anyplace you wanted. That was the deal."

"I know, but to get you all dressed up—and to a gourmet restaurant, no less. Michael Sullivan, you positively shocked me."

"I'm trying to branch out as I approach middle age."

"So are you ready to go dancing?"

Mike scratched the corner of his mouth.

"The look on your face is priceless," Sam said. "I was just teasing. I couldn't go dancing in these shoes. They're killing me."

"Let's take a cab."

"And waste a night like this? No way."

She led him down Newbury Street, Boston's equivalent of Rodeo Drive. It was after nine and the street was jammed with traffic, the sidewalks crowded with young people who looked very serious, acting like they were on their way to important places. Watching some of these couples got him to thinking of the pictures of Jean Paul and his mother—his new and improved mother in the pictures.

"You remember that time we went to Marty's Crab?" Sam said.

Mike smiled. It took two hours to drive to this shack in the middle of some neighborhood in Ogunquit, Maine. To date, it was the best seafood he had ever had.

"We had some great times," Sam said.

"That we did. That we did."

"So why'd it end?" Sam smiling even after she said it.

Mike shoved his hands in his pockets, jingling his change and car keys as he looked down the street.

"I'm just curious," Sam said. "I promise I won't beat you up."

"You promise?"

"Pinkie swear."

"Well, if it's a pinkie swear." His eyes bounced from the ever-present lights of downtown Boston to the traffic wrapping its way around the Public Garden on Arlington. "The truth," he said, "was that I was scared. You were going to college and onto greater things, and I was going back to what was familiar and safe. What can I say? I was nineteen and stupid."

They crossed the street and entered the Public Garden, walking past the bronze statue of Paul Revere riding his horse.

Sam said, "How are you doing with everything that happened this week? You didn't say much at dinner."

"I'm to the point where I'm sick of hearing myself talk."

"Talking's good."

"Not when you're dumping your problems all over the other person. It's nice to hear someone else talk about their life for a change."

"You're not dumping on me, and, for the record, the other night when you came by? I was glad."

They walked across the bridge overlooking the lagoon. Below, on the dock where the swan boats were chained up, a little girl was pointing to the real swans and saying something to her father. Mike felt his stomach clench, his breath hitching in his throat.

"Nancy called me while I was stuck in traffic," he said. "The address that was on the letter belongs to a café in Paris, only my mother never worked there—at least, not under the name Mary Sullivan. Nancy said you were the one who called and spoke to the owner."

Sam nodded. So she knew about the café having been owned and operated by the same family for two generations, the family having also branched out and built two very successful restaurants in the same area, none of which Mary Sullivan had worked in—at least under the name Mary Sullivan. It was possible that she was going by another name when she arrived in Paris, maybe even had legally changed it for fear of Lou finding her.

Mike had now caught his mother in two lies: about paying for the tuition at St. Stephen's and working at the café.

Mike said, "What else do you know?"

"Just the restaurant stuff."

Mike took a moment and sorted through what Nancy had told him.

"Jean Paul Latiere is still alive. He's still the owner and operator of his father's paper company, Latiere Paper. He's fifty-eight, same age as my mother, and he still lives on the island of—I forget the name."

"Île St-Louis."

"That's it. Jean Paul's been married only once. He

married a woman named Margot Paradis about two years before my mother married Lou. Then Jean Paul divorced Paradis in November of 1977—that's about a year after my mother moved there. He never remarried. No kids either."

Sam didn't say anything, already knowing of Lou's comment about Jean Paul not wanting children.

"This guy seems to be constantly on the move," Mike continued. "He has multiple phone numbers. Nancy finally managed to get him on the phone by pretending to be the vice president of some big-name paper company here in the U.S. You mind if I smoke?"

"Just as long as you share."

"You smoke?"

"I quit four years ago, but I like to dabble every now and then."

Mike pulled out his pack, lit hers first and then his.

"So back to Nancy," he said after a moment. "She didn't ask him anything about Mary Sullivan. She thought I might want to, you know, talk to Jean Paul directly myself. He speaks very good English."

They walked past the bronze ducks that Sarah thought came alive at night and stopped at the intersection of Beacon Street and Charles, Sam grabbing his arm as they darted across the street and then releasing it when they reached the sidewalk.

Sam said, "Are you thinking of calling him?"

"Jean Paul?"

Sam nodded.

"I've got to do something else first."

"Jess," Sam said.

"I thought I could walk away from it."

"It's a hard thing to walk away from." Sam paused, and then said, "When are you going?"

"Tomorrow morning. I called Jess and asked her if she was going to be around."

"What did she say when you told her you were coming out to New York?"

"I told her I was coming out there for a couple of days with this friend of mine, Bam-Bam, and wanted to get together and talk. We're meeting for lunch."

Sam nodded, seemed to be considering a thought.

"You need anything, you call."

"I will." Mike saw the sign for Mt. Vernon, turned right and headed up her street. He got about six steps before Sam called for him.

"Where are you going?" She stood at the corner, in the shadows next to the liquor store.

"I thought I was walking you home."

"Grandpa, it's nine-thirty. Are you tired—or are you afraid of breaking curfew at the nursing home?"

"They let us stay out till eleven these days. And no, I'm not tired."

Mike walked up to her, holding her eyes in his own for a moment. Those old feelings he had for her were still there—dented and bruised and maybe a little different from all this time apart, but they were definitely still there. And Sam knew it too. He could tell by the way she stared back at him now.

Sam said, "You want to go home?"

"Not really. You?"

"Not really."

"Any ideas? And please, no dancing."

"I was thinking of cannolis."

"I haven't had a good cannoli in a long time."

"Then you're in luck. I know this great spot in the North End. You in?"

"I'm in."

They walked down Charles Street, Sam slipping her arm through his.

CHAPTER 39

New York was Boston on steroids: taller and wider, meaner, ready to devour you if you were careless or clumsy or just plain stupid. Rule number one of city life mandated that you made every effort not to look like a tourist. That meant keeping up with foot traffic and watching where the hell you were going; but this country bumpkin across the street (by the looks of him, probably from some cornfield town in Iowa, a-yuck) was trying to divide his attention between reading the street signs and finding his location on the city map he held spread out in front of his face like a newspaper. A mental patient stood on the corner with a big white sign that read THE TIME FOR REDEMPTION IS NOW, ASSHOLES!

That was the great thing about cities like New York. They were never short of free entertainment.

It was a gorgeous spring day—Tanqueray season, as Bam-Bam liked to say—the afternoon sun warming his face and bringing to mind those weekend afternoons spent on Bam's boat with a few stiffies, laughing away the day. Mike sat at an outdoor table at a restaurant across the street, watching as Mr. Iowa ran headfirst into a Magilla Gorilla clone who dwarfed even Bill, when he caught sight of Jess heading his way. As he watched her approaching, he could see the smile on her face, the kind of automatic, good-natured happiness that came from enjoying the warm air and sunshine—or being a nobody— in a city where people didn't stop to stare.

"I can't believe you're actually here."

Jess stood next to the table.

He forced a grin. "I'm here," he said. His tone sounded strong, in control.

Jess slid her sunglasses up across her forehead and parked them on the top of her head.

"Where's Bam?" she asked.

"Something came up and he couldn't make it. It's just you and me."

No sooner did Jess sit down than the waiter sidled up to the table, eager to please, Mike supposed, or maybe the guy just wanted to get a good, up-front look at Jess, Mike remembering how time had been more of an ally to Jess than an enemy. She ordered a white wine, and after the waiter ran off, she placed her purse on the ground next to her, Mike again trying to place himself back in the time period frozen in the pictures. Back then, Jess had still been fun—although the caution that would later rule his life and Sarah's had started to seep in when Jess learned she was pregnant for the first time—

that caution about to become a permanent resident after the second miscarriage.

"So," Jess said, smiling as she leaned back in her chair and crossed her legs, "what are you and Bam doing for fun tonight?"

Looking at her, he thought back to her "I'll never lie to you, Michael" and "There will never be any secrets between us, Michael" philosophies of life and marriage. Having an affair went against everything she was—or, at least, everything she had pretended to be during their life together. Cheap words or did Jess practice what she preached? Time to find out.

There was no gentle way of doing it. He slid the envelope across the table, knowing full well he was about to torpedo the good will between them.

"These belong to you," Mike said.

Jess tried to read his eyes for some hint of what was going on, and when she failed to find anything, she picked up the envelope and gently shook the pictures onto the table.

The front picture was that of her and her boyfriend or fuck buddy or whatever he meant to her walking hand-in-hand down the front steps of the bed and breakfast. Mike had made sure he put that picture on the top before sealing the envelope shut. Seeing her face would tell him the truth about what had happened.

Jess's lips parted and the blood drained from her cheeks. She continued to stare at the picture of her former self, trying to prevent what she was seeing from penetrating the shell she had built over the past five years after losing Sarah. Jess swallowed, her eyes narrowing as if saying, I won't let you break me. It was the same look she had given him the night in the kitchen when he had come home from the Hill dripping wet and told her that Sarah was missing.

But it *had* broken her, and he knew it when she slowly turned her head away from the picture and to the street, the look of total abandonment on her face reminding him of the high school girl he had fallen in love with standing by her bedroom window, watching as the police car pulled into her driveway and already knowing that the two cops slowly advancing up the front steps were there to tell her why her father, three hours late, hadn't come home from work.

"How long?" Mike said, and felt something hot and sharp break away inside him and sink. He had mentally prepared himself for this possibility, but having it unfold right in front of your eyes—that was a different thing altogether.

The waiter came over and placed the white wine next to Jess, asked if they were ready to order lunch. Mike shook his head no and the waiter stormed off, miffed at the small tip this bill was going to generate.

"How *long?*" he said again, Jess flinching from the anger in his voice.

As much as you want to flip over this table and get into her face—totally justified, I might add—you've got a decision to make, and you've got to make it right now: Do you want to know what happened, or do you want to punish her? Because you can pick only one. You can't have it both ways.

Mike started over. "I stumbled on these by accident."

Jess laughed bitterly. "I doubt that. When it comes to Lou, there are no accidents."

"You *knew* he took these pictures?"

She didn't answer. She kept her attention focused on the street, her eyes bouncing from one object to the next.

Mike said, "You going to talk?"

"What for? I'm sure Lou told you everything already."

If he said no, he hadn't spoken to Lou and instead came here to hear it from her instead, would that give her the room she needed to maybe lie and escape? She had no obligation to volunteer the truth, but if she believed Lou had already filled him in . . .

"Why are you here? To gloat? To have the satisfaction of rubbing my mistake in my face?" Jess met his gaze and Mike saw in her eyes that stony resolve starting to gain footing. She was starting to close up.

"I came here for an explanation," he said as calmly as he could.

"No, you didn't. You came here to use me as a whipping post. Well, guess what? That's not my job anymore."

"Jess, I—"

"No. I'm not doing this. I made a mistake—a huge mistake—and it has torn me up in ways you'll never understand. But I've forgiven myself. It was a long road, but I've forgiven myself, and I've moved on. As for that part of my life—" she pointed to the pictures on the table—"*that* part of my life is over."

"Don't I deserve the right to move on?"

She snatched her purse off the ground.

"Just tell me what I did wrong. What made you run to this guy?"

Jess moved her chair back and stood up. Mike stood up too, moved around the table and grabbed her arm.

"I didn't ask to find this out," Mike said, "but I did. Now I've got all these questions bouncing around in my head. I don't have any room for them. Not after what happened to Sarah."

Jess hadn't moved away, but he could tell she was still contemplating an exit.

"All I'm asking for is an explanation," Mike said. "I think that's fair."

Mike thought her face had softened a little. He was right. She released the grip on her purse and put it back down on the ground. He let go of her arm.

"Thank you," he said, and they sat back down.

"I want to be clear about this. I'll talk about it now and that's it. After I leave, the subject's closed."

Don't worry. After you leave, I have no plans to ever talk to you again.

Jess picked up her glass of wine, settled herself in her chair and crossed her legs, her face indignant, a woman getting ready to face cross-examination.

"I know this guy?" Mike asked.

"No."

"What's his name?"

"I thought Lou told you everything?"

"He didn't mention a name."

"Does his name matter?"

"I suppose not."

Jess drank some of her wine.

"Rodger," she said. "The summer you and I were engaged, I rented that house in Newport, remember?"

He did. It had been a busy summer for him, the business with Bill going well, starting to pick up. Jess was a special-needs teacher and had her summers off with the exception of the occasional waitress work at The Ground Round in Danvers. A friend from college asked her if she wanted to go in on a house in Newport with four other girls. Jess asked if he had a problem with it and he had said no, said it would be fun to slip down there every other weekend, take a day off and hang out on the beach.

Jess said, "You didn't come down one weekend and I met Rodger at this party. He was in his late thirties and worked in Boston's financial district. He was so different from the people you and I grew up with. He was so smart in that . . . that bookish way I guess you'd call it. Every morning he read the *New York Times* and the *Wall Street Journal*. My father only read the sports section of the *Herald*, and my mother, well, you know she could have cared less about what was going on in the world outside of Belham. Rodger was an investor, but he was passionate about art and architecture. He rented a villa in Tuscany one summer. He had all these stories about traveling through Europe. He loved sailing."

"So you're saying, what, you were attracted to him because he was rich?"

She shot him a look. "I'm not that shallow and you know it."

Mike held up his hands and said, "So what was it then?"

"Rodger was . . . he was just so well put together. I didn't know anything about investing, and the farthest I had ever traveled was to Rhode Island. But he was interested in me and I was attracted to that. Into discovering why he could like me, I suppose. I didn't understand why. And I didn't plan on falling in love with him."

He heard the word *love,* and flinched as it twisted its way through his gut.

I thought you didn't care? a voice asked.

Jess saw the reaction on his face. "It was a very confusing time in my life," she said by way of apology. "Rodger knew about you. He knew I loved you. I didn't hide anything from him. He knew I was afraid of losing you. Of losing what we had."

Mike dug a fingernail into the callus on his palm, aware of the heat climbing into the back of his neck, starting to spread across his face.

"That summer you spent at Hampton Beach, you told me you met someone. Cindy or someone," Jess said. "I remember you told me you thought you loved her."

"You and I weren't engaged at the time."

"At that time in my life, I believed that your heart was only built to love one person. And I thought that person was you. I chose you because I thought that was where I belonged, but Jesus, Michael, we were so young when we were married. We were practically kids. We didn't know what we were doing."

"So why'd you decide to break it off with Rodger and settle for me?"

"I didn't settle."

"Then what would you call it?"

Jess propped an elbow on the armrest, rubbed her forehead as if trying to massage back a migraine. As he waited for her to speak, he took in several deep breaths, praying that he could stifle his growing urge to rip into her. He wasn't sure where that need came from, exactly—Jess describing an event that happened, what, close to twenty years ago?

"September came around and it was time to go back to work," Jess said. "I had convinced myself that someone like Rodger couldn't be interested in me in any serious way, so I told myself it was a mistake and broke it off."

"Only he didn't want to break it off."

Jess stared at him the way you did when you bumped into people you once knew and no longer cared to see.

"He kept coming around," Mike said. "So when did you decide to start screwing him full-time again?"

"There's no need to be crude."

"Well what would you call it?" He had come here and had validated what he thought was true. Fuck being nice now.

"I call it a mistake. A big mistake," Jess said. "I tried being friends with him—just friends—but we were attracted to each other and— What I did was wrong. You and I were going to get married, and it should never have escalated the way it did. But it did, and I knew I had to put an end to it. No matter what Lou told you about that night, I was in the process of breaking up with Rodger."

"What night?"

"The night I saw Lou at the restaurant." Jess searched Mike's eyes. "He didn't tell you?"

"I only had a few minutes with him. He didn't get into too many specifics."

"I met Rodger for dinner at a restaurant in Charlestown. I told him that it was over, that I couldn't deal with it anymore. I went to the ladies' room, and there was Lou standing in the hallway with this big smile on his face. He escorted me over to a table in the back, started in on how nice it was to see me, how good I looked, and then he drops the pictures on the table, just like you did."

Jess took a sip of her wine. "He told me to break it off with Rodger, which I was going to do anyway. He said if he saw me with Rodger again, he'd show you the pictures. Then your father told me that I should, you know, be the person to make peace between you and him. I said I'd try, and your father stressed how it would be in my best interest to make sure it worked out."

Mike tried to remember back to that time but couldn't ever recall Jess talking about Lou in any positive way.

"Every day when you came home I worried that Lou had said something to you," Jess said. "And then your father got mixed up in that business with the armored-car heists, and when I heard he left for Florida, I felt I could breathe again."

"How lucky for you."

"Don't."

"Don't what?"

"Don't look at me like that. You have no right to sit there and judge me."

"You'll have to excuse me if I'm having a hard time swallowing your load of shit about how you felt confused and weren't in touch with your feelings."

The skin on Jess's face stretched tight, that stony resolve fighting to stay front and center. "You've got a lot of goddamn nerve after what happened to Sarah."

"That hasn't got anything—"

"You were the one who let her go up that hill by herself, remember? But did I ever turn around and say that what happened was your fault? *Did I?*"

Mike's eyes slid off hers. The women from the other table were stealing glances this way.

"You're goddamn right I didn't," Jess said. Tears spilled down her cheeks, but her voice remained clear and strong. "I wanted to. I blamed you for what happened and I hated you for it and you'll never know how many times I wanted to scream it at you. But I never did, Michael. I never did because I knew how those words would cut you to the bone. Accidents happen, and what happened to me was an accident. When I found out that I was pregnant, as much as it killed me, I had to do it. It was wrong and immoral and I knew that

I was committing murder but I had to do it. I couldn't bring this other man's baby into our marriage. It was wrong, but I did it. I did it because I wanted to stay with you. Because I loved you."

Mike saw himself leaning forward in his chair, as though he had slipped out of his skin and was now watching this unfold from the sidelines.

"It was a mistake," Jess said, her face crinkling, about to break into sobs any second now. "Everyone should be allowed one big mistake in their life. You shouldn't have to pay for it forever, but I did. The doctor screwed up the procedure—it was a miracle Sarah was even born—and then God punished me and took my baby away. *My* baby. *My* Sarah."

Mike couldn't stand up fast enough. The top of his thigh hit the underside of the table; it tipped, and before he caught it, the wine glass and the coffee cup fell onto the floor and shattered. Jess hadn't moved.

"I forgave you that day at the cemetery. Now it's your turn. Tell me you forgive me."

Stumbling forward, Mike plowed his way around the spaces between the chairs and tables and into the street. He looked left, then right, unsure of which direction to go, his legs wobbly, weak.

"Say you forgive me," Jess screamed. "Say it."

He picked a direction and moved.

"Say it," Jess screamed. *"Don't leave without saying it."*

Don't look back, a voice said. *Whatever you do, just keep walking forward and don't look back.*

CHAPTER 40

When Mike stopped walking, beads of sweat were running down his face, and his back and armpits were soaked. He didn't know how long he had been walking or where he was. He was standing next to a bank, and the streets were surprisingly free of foot traffic, the afternoon sun shielded by tall buildings and skyscrapers.

What had just happened with Jess was exactly what had happened with his last visit with Lou: Mike had gone there expecting to uncover one thing only to get sucker-punched with something much, much worse. He had expected Jess to confirm what he saw in the pictures, but the pregnancy?

The first pregnancy he had discovered by accident. They were renting out the second floor of a duplex and he was using the spare room as an office. He misplaced a good-sized check that he needed to deposit to cover their rent, and when he tore up his office and failed to find it, he thought the check might have been accidentally mixed in with the trash. He went out to the garage and started picking through his trash bags and found the check stuck to the bottom of one bag along with three boxes for pregnancy tests. He found one of the plastic test strips, then the other two. All three were positive. He knew this from the pregnancy scare they had back in high school, Jess driving to his house and saying that her period was three weeks late. They bought two pregnancy tests—"They're not always correct," Jess had told him—and then drove to her house, since her mother wasn't home. Both tests came up negative. No pregnancy. Jess's period came two days later.

Now he was holding three pregnancy tests that read positive.

He remembered feeling moderately surprised. They had talked about starting a family at some point, wanting three, maybe even four kids, but they hadn't started trying yet. Then again, they weren't exactly being careful. And Jess had never been on the pill, had some sort of allergic reaction to it.

Miscarriages happen, she had told him later that night—nervously, he now remembered. During the first trimester, especially when you were pregnant for the first time, it wasn't that uncommon to have a miscarriage. She had taken the tests and wanted to wait a few more weeks before telling him. And then, as if by some great omen, she had a miscarriage.

Only that was a lie. She was pregnant, yes, but not

with their baby, and the baby hadn't miscarried at all. She had lied to him, and he bought the lie.

You had no reason not to believe her.

Right, because when you came right down to it, how could you ever really know another person? Say your vows in front of God and pledge to each other that you would be honest and open, but the real truths were the ones you didn't speak to anyone, maybe not even to yourself. What the other person saw was what you allowed them to see: truths mixed with half-truths, little white lies and sometimes all-out fabrications. In the end, you had to buy into the whole smoke-and-mirror show, roll the dice and give it your best shot—unless you wanted to spend the rest of your life alone.

The moments sealed inside those pictures weren't about cheating; they were about comfort. Rodger wasn't kissing her; he was hugging her, consoling her after her . . . procedure.

Mike reached inside his shirt pocket for his cigarettes, took one out and lit it, thinking about what would have happened if he had seen those pictures years ago. Would he have stuck around? No way. No fucking way. There are some things in life you can't forgive.

But she forgave you.

Mike thought about Sam's comment about people being messy. No shit. Everyone he knew leading double lives and burying these sharp-edged secrets—even someone like Rose Giroux, Rose as holy as they come and admitting to having an—

Mike stopped walking.

Two women with missing children had their pregnancies terminated.

Clue or one hell of a coincidence?

He removed his cell phone from his belt, cycled through all the numbers he had programmed, found Rose's number and hit the speed-dial button.

"I'm so glad you called," Rose said. "I feel so horrible about the other night."

"We've all been there, Rose. The reason I'm calling has to do with that . . . you know, that thing you had done. I know this is going to sound like an odd question, but can I ask you where you had that done?"

He heard her take in a long breath.

"I know this is personal, Rose, but it might be important."

"I don't mind you asking. It's just since I blurted it out the other night, I've been trying to forget about it." Her voice sounded stiff, cold. There was a long pause, then she said, "Concord, New Hampshire."

"Describe the place to me."

"It looked like a house. That's the first thing I remember. And there wasn't a sign out front. Back then, if you had that . . . done to you, you had to do it in secret. It's not like it is nowadays, where you can pick up the yellow pages and find places proudly advertising it. The inside was so cold, and the people there—"

"Describe the outside. What did the outside look like? Was it blue?"

"White," she said without hesitation.

"You're sure?"

"I remember everything about that day. I had to climb this really steep set of concrete steps. I'll never forget those steps. It was like I was climbing up a mountain. When I came out, I was in so much discomfort and still woozy that Ted had to hold onto me, help me down the steps. I kept feeling like I was going to fall."

Just like in the picture. Rose was describing the same place.

Mike said, "Rose, do you know Suzanne Lenville's phone number?"

"Her last name isn't Lenville anymore. It's Clarkston. She changed her name when she remarried—even changed her first name to Margaret. Margaret Ann Clarkston."

"Right, I forgot. You have the number?"

"She won't talk to you, trust me. When Jonah died, I wanted to call and tell her I was sorry. I knew she had an unlisted number, and I knew she probably wouldn't want to talk to me."

"But you called her anyway," Mike said. Rose the constant mother, wanting to make sure people were doing okay.

"I know it was wrong of me, but I had a friend from the phone company give me her new number. I called her to . . . I guess I wanted to reach out, talk to her the same way I talked with you. She nearly bit my head off. Said that this number was unlisted for a reason and hung up on me."

"Give it to me anyway."

"Can I ask you why? You've never wanted to talk with her before."

"I know, but . . ."

"Does this have to do with Jonah?" Rose's tone jumped, brightening.

"Look, I'm probably grasping at straws here."

"Tell me anyway."

"I need to speak with Suzanne first. If what I'm thinking pans out, I'll call you first thing tomorrow."

"Can you hold on for a moment? I have to go searching for it."

"Take your time."

Rose opened the door and clunked the phone down on something hard. As he listened to the soft, slightly far-away sounds of her shoes clicking across the floor, of drawers being opened and shut, he thought about how he would approach Suzanne Lenville/Margaret Ann Clarkston. Everything pointed to the fact that she didn't want to talk about what had happened to her daughter. If she had caller ID, she would have recognized Rose Giroux's name when it flashed on the caller ID screen. But Suzanne had picked up and ripped Rose a new one.

Suzanne wouldn't have that attitude if a police officer was calling.

Merrick wouldn't do it. In his mind, the case was closed. Slow Ed might. It probably went against some sort of rule, but maybe—

Rose came back on the line. "Here it is," she said and gave him the number.

"Thanks, Rose."

"Promise you'll call me if you find out anything."

"Cross my heart," Mike said and hung up.

By the time he found a pay phone two blocks away, he had formed a solid—and hopefully, workable—story. He dialed the number

(this is insane)

relieved when the phone on the other end picked up.

"Hello," the breezy female voice asked.

"Mrs. Clarkston?"

"Yes."

"Mrs. Clarkston, my name is Detective Smits. I'm sorry to bother you, but I need to speak with you for a moment. I just have a quick question."

"I don't want to talk to you people anymore. You've been here day after day, and I told you everything I know about that goddamn monster. I'm done with all of it. Do you understand? I'm *done.*"

She didn't have caller ID. She was assuming he was calling her from whatever city she was living in.

But your face—your voice—has been all over the TV, even CNN. What if she recognizes your voice?

Too late to turn back now. He launched right into it: "Mrs. Clarkston, are you Catholic?"

"That's your question?"

"I know it's an odd question, but it's important."

"I was Catholic. Emphasis on *was.*"

"Did you . . . I know this is extremely personal, but I need to know if you ever had an abortion before Caroline was born."

A dead, ringing silence came from the other end of the line.

"I know this has been an extremely difficult time for you," Mike said. "Believe me, if there's anyone who understands what you're going through, it's me. I wouldn't ask if it wasn't extremely important."

"My daughter's been dead for twenty-four years." The tough edge to her voice was gone; now it was teetering between crying and full-blown anger. "I'm not reliving it anymore. I've had it with you people. I changed my name for a reason. You're not going to steal this life away from me too."

"So that's a yes?"

The sting of the dial tone came next. Mike dropped the phone and moved out to the street, one hand in the air to wave down a taxi, the other on his cell phone, dialing Merrick's number.

CHAPTER 41

So you told Merrick," Bill said to Mike. "Let him take it from there."

"I'm pretty sure he's going to blow it off."

"Sully, he said he'd look into it."

"I'm not holding my breath."

Bill went back to working a sudsy sponge over the hood of Patty's new bright yellow Ford Escape. He wore shorts, flip-flops and a short-sleeve shirt that showed off the biohazard tattoo on each meaty bicep. The silk shirt was imprinted with hundreds of miniature covers of *Playboy* magazine.

It was closing on six, the sunlight fading but the air still warm. Mike had just returned from Merrick's office. After touching down at Logan, Mike had gone straight to the police station to see Merrick, who had agreed to a meeting, Mike telling the detective everything except the part about playing a police officer.

"Nice color," Mike said. "The pink ones all sold out?"

"Patty picked it out," Bill said, his voice flat. "I had nothing to do with it."

"That the reason you're pissed off?"

"It's been a long day. The twins." Bill shook his head. "There are moments when I wish I had been sterile."

"I'll bet anything Margaret Clarkston had that procedure done in New Hampshire."

The strained look on Bill's face was the same one Merrick wore just moments ago: Don't talk, just nod, and hopefully this person will shut up and walk away.

Mike put down his Coke on the driveway and walked over to Bill. "You don't find it the least bit odd that all three women had abortions?"

Bill shrugged. "It happens more than you think."

"And if all three women had it done at this same place?"

"Okay. Let's say what you're saying is true."

"Let's."

"What's the connection to Jonah?"

"I don't know. That's why I forwarded it to Merrick. It's called a clue."

Bill dropped the sponge in the bucket and picked up his bottle of Sam Adams from the hood.

"Say it."

"I was just thinking back to Friday night when you came down to the kitchen all dressed to the nines. The next morning, Grace comes up to me and says, 'Uncle Michael's smiling again.'"

"I didn't ask for this."

"Yeah, you did." Bill pointed the beer bottle at Mike as he spoke. "You were the one who went to Lou and kept squeezing his cherries until he spit up this stuff about your mother. So now you got that bouncing around your head, and if that isn't enough, you go to New York and dig up all this crap on Jess. Bottom line? It's got nothing to do with nothing."

"I think it's worth something."

"Yeah. It's a nice distraction."

"From what?"

Bill propped both forearms on the Escape's hood. He picked at the beer label as drops of water dripped off the SUV.

"What I say, I say out of love. Let Sarah go. You want to cry, scream—you want to go and get drunk, fine, you name it and I'll be there with you, if that's what you want. But all this digging . . . it's got to stop, Sully. At some point you've got to move on and enjoy your life."

Mike lit a cigarette, turned his face away to the front lawn where Grace and Emma sat, playing with their Barbie dolls. Paula sat on the front steps, a cordless phone pressed against her ear, her free hand rubbing Fang's belly, the dog on his side, passed out.

Paula saw Mike staring at her, waved hello. Mike waved back.

"She's really grown up, hasn't she?"

"I'm sorry, Sully. I know that's not enough, but that's all I can say."

"I'm going to head out for a bit."

"Stay for dinner. Patty's making steak tips. No Alka-Seltzer needed."

"Another time. Thanks again for watching the dog. Enjoy your night with your family," Mike said and walked over to get Fang.

CHAPTER 42

Mike was on the way home when, for a reason he couldn't explain, he felt a need to go over to the cemetery. Without questioning it, he turned around, and he now stood in an almost trance-like state at Jonah's grave. Fang remained in the truck, too tired to move.

The morning he had lost it out here on the phone with Jess—he had cried for Sarah, absolutely, but he hadn't been able to *release* her. Even later, when he listened to Merrick more or less say that Sarah was dead, a part of Mike still refused to give up hope. When he packed up her room, a cry of hope rose up and told him that what he was doing was wrong. Now, as he stood here at the gravesite, he found the hope still there, still digging in its heels. *I'm not leaving and guess what? You can't make me.*

Maybe Bill had a point. Maybe digging up all this stuff was a distraction.

Jonah lay six feet under, sealed behind wood, preserved in embalming fluid. The grass had recently been cut. Mike saw wet grass clippings stuck to the sides of his shoes, and he remembered how Sarah loved to run around barefoot and would sometimes come back in from outside with the bottom of her feet stained green, clippings all over the carpet, driving Jess crazy. He remembered how she loved to scoop the cheese off pizza—"Daddy, it's the best part, and I only want to eat the best part"—and he remembered how she would throw a fit if she wasn't allowed to pick out her own clothes or decide the amount of blueberries she wanted in her pancakes or put in the number of chocolate chips she wanted in the cookies she and Jess baked together. When he thought of Sarah, it was always these moments of toughness that came to him, these small ways she had of trying to control her world, to prove that she was independent and had a mind of her own and God help you if you got in her way. Remembering Sarah in this way—this spirited toughness she used to move through life—maybe that was a distraction too. Maybe he didn't want to see her as willingly walking off with Jonah, no matter how upset she was.

Why didn't you kick and scream when Jonah picked you up, Sarah? Why didn't you have one of your patented meltdowns? I would have heard you. Why did you just walk away and leave me?

That coffin held not one body but four. And it would be that way forever—unless he wanted to hold a separate service for Sarah, maybe bury her snow jacket and snow pants when the police released them. Only you didn't bury things. You buried people. You prepared them for their journey into the ground and whatever lay beyond it. You didn't say goodbye to a snow suit. *He* couldn't.

How do I say goodbye to what I don't even know? When was the right time to give up on the people you loved?

Mike turned around and stared down Evergreen Street. Two boys were having a sword fight with sticks, going at it hard, the mother or babysitter sitting in a plastic patio chair on the porch, flipping through the magazine spread out on her lap.

Maybe if he went through with a service of some sort, maybe it would tell his circle of friends that he had finally accepted Sarah was gone. I love you, Sarah. Goodbye. Now everybody leave me the fuck alone.

Some time later, he took out his phone and dialed Sam's number.

"Your ears must be burning," Sam said. "I was just talking about you."

"Oh yeah? With who?"

"With Nancy. I just got off the phone with her. She called to tell me about her blind date last night."

Mike thought of Nancy coming at some guy with that truck driver mouth of hers. Poor bastard.

Sam said, "How'd it go in New York?"

"It's been . . . You in the mood for some company?"

"Sure. You eat yet?"

"No. How you feel about dogs?"

"I had terriers growing up."

"What about big dogs who drool?"

"I've got plenty of towels."

"One last question: If Nancy's free, you mind if I ask her to stop by?"

"Not at all. What's going on?"

Mike turned his attention back to Jonah's gravesite. "I'll explain when I get there."

Over dinner, Mike filled Sam in on New York, Merrick and Bill.

"You probably know why I asked Nancy to come over," he said.

"Makes sense, especially after what you just told me."

"So what do you think?"

"It doesn't matter what I think. If you need to dig into these things, then dig. Dig as far as you want to go, and if you decide that you want to stop, then stop. There's no right answer here. Who gives a shit what anyone else says or thinks?"

"You always knew how to get right to the point, Sam."

"It's better than living life in those pesky gray zones."

They ate in silence for a moment. Mike said, "I had a good time the other night."

"The cannolis were good."

"I was referring to the company."

Sam smiled. "I know."

It had been a good time. Nice and effortless. No pressure to act or say anything in a certain way. That comfortable rhythm that they once had was back again and he didn't want to ruin it.

"My life is a bit messy," he said.

"Everyone's life is messy, Sully."

The doorbell rang and Fang popped his sleepy head up off the floor. Sam buzzed Nancy in, and when she stepped into the dining room with a bellowing *"Howyadoin?"* Fang scrambled over to meet her, tail wagging, sniffing madly around her body.

Mike said, "You want me to pull him away?"

"Are you kidding? This is the most affection a man's shown me in weeks." Fang followed Nancy as she walked over to the table and sat down. "So," she said to Mike, "what are you so anxious to talk to me about?"

Mike told her. When he finished, Nancy was quiet, digesting all of it, Mike supposed. Sam's windows were open; a cool evening breeze, mixed with the sounds of traffic and people, filled the room.

"Okay," Nancy said. "Margaret Clarkston didn't come right out and admit to having an abortion."

"No, she didn't come right out and say yes," Mike said, "but I know the question hit home."

Sam said to Nancy, "Can you find out if she had the procedure?"

"Normally, I'd say yes," Nancy said. "Nowadays, health insurance picks up the tab. And everything's stored on MIB."

Mike said, "What's MIB?"

"Medical Information Bureau," Nancy said. "Basically, it's a computer network that stores all of your medical records. Insurance companies generally use it."

"I thought medical records were private."

"Welcome to the digital age. Forget MIB. I doubt you'd find any information there. Margaret Clarkston's somewhere in her late sixties, right?"

"Sixty-six," Mike said. Her age had been noted in a recent *Globe* article.

"That meant she had Caroline when she was twenty-seven—real old for back then. So let's say she had this procedure done when she was, oh, I don't know, twenty. That's forty-five years ago—1958. Your dad wore a cardigan sweater and smoked a pipe while your mom was just oh so happy to be playing Susie Homemaker. You didn't mention the word abortion, let alone have one."

Sam added, "If she had one done, chances are it was done in secret."

"And hopefully by a doctor who didn't botch the job," Nancy said. "Pay your cash, get it done and pray that you'd be okay. It was a completely different time back then. No yellow page ads, no pro-life commercials on TV. Before sixty-seven, abortions were illegal."

"And no computers either," Sam said. "At least, no personal computers. Back then, everything was stored on paper."

Mike said, "So there's no record of the procedures."

"For Clarkston? I doubt it. Even when Rose Giroux

had the procedure, I'm willing to bet it was still secretive," Nancy said. "A lot of women probably gave anonymous names, paid in cash. No records. And even if a file did exist—I'd say it's next to impossible, but let's say that a paper file does exist somewhere. The only way I'm going to get my hands on it is to bribe someone who works at this clinic. I think that's a dead angle anyway. I'm willing to bet that place in New Hampshire wasn't even around when Margaret Clarkston had it done."

"So what you're telling me is that there's no way to find out," Mike said, feeling defeated.

"The best way is to ask directly, which you did. If Merrick calls her, my guess is she'll say no to him. Cops generally don't call over the phone. They show up to your house unannounced and shove a badge in your face and make you talk until you give them what they want. What'd he say about this?"

"He said he'd look into it."

"And you don't believe that," Nancy said, "which is why I'm sitting here."

"You got it."

"Can I be honest here?"

"Is it possible for you to be any other way?" Mike asked.

A grin tugged at the corner of Nancy's mouth, then disappeared. "My sources told me the police already found personal items belonging to all three girls inside Jonah's house, under a floorboard in his bedroom. And we know about the blood inside the jacket hood, and we know Jonah committed suicide."

Mike took in a deep breath.

"I'm sorry," Nancy said. "I guess I don't understand the point of trying to investigate something that's a dead end and is only going to prolong your pain."

"Why am I the only one who finds this odd?"

"Women get abortions. Not all women, but when a woman decides to get it done, they don't go around advertising it. Maybe they confide in a friend or two, but mostly they keep quiet and go on with their lives, try to come to grips with what they've done.

"Which brings me to my second point," Nancy said. "You're Catholic. As a fellow die-hard Catholic myself, I speak from firsthand experience when I say that us Catholics, practicing or not, are terminally obsessed with shame and guilt. I'm not trying to play armchair shrink here, but have you ever considered that your need to continually poke around despite the overwhelming facts might have something to do with you trying to correct what happened that night on the Hill?"

"What if there's a connection to Jonah buried in all of this?"

"Such as?"

"I don't know," Mike said. "But that doesn't mean there isn't some sort of connection."

"I hate to say this," Nancy said, "but I think you're grasping at straws here."

"So you're not even willing to entertain the idea?"

"I bill out at one-twenty an hour, plus expenses. You want me to dig, I'll dig. It's your tab."

"I think this warrants some digging."

"Okay then," Nancy said. "I'm officially on the clock. Let me grab a pad of paper and we'll get started."

CHAPTER 43

M ike's phone rang at 6:45 the next morning.

"Nadine's having a palm-reading party tonight at Bam's," Wild Bill said.

"Bam know about this?"

"Knows about it and is going to be there. So are you and I. We'll take turns videotaping Bam as he gets his aura read. What are you doing right now?"

"Lying in bed next to a big wet spot."

"That's my boy."

"It's dog drool. What's all that yelling?"

"That would be the twins. They're running around the house—I swear Patty puts caffeine in their milk. I'm sitting here at the kitchen table with my box of cereal. For the record, Lucky Charms are no longer magically delicious. You eat breakfast yet?"

"Some of us like to sleep in on Sundays."

"Come on over. Bring the dog—and Father Jack. The twins need an exorcism."

Mike hopped in the shower. Nancy Childs's plan for today was to attend her goddaughter's baptism in Wellfleet, a town at the uppermost tip of the Cape, and then head back sometime later in the afternoon and hopefully talk with Jonah's hospice nurse, Terry Russell. Nancy promised to call and update him sometime midweek. That was how they left it last night.

Now, though? Mike didn't see the point in waiting. Nancy didn't know any more than he did about what was going on—in fact, she probably knew less, so why wait? Why not get the ball rolling? The best time to talk was in the morning, after a full night's rest, when your mind was relaxed and fresh.

After he finished dressing, Mike grabbed the leather writing pad from his office and headed out to Terry Russell's house.

Two cars were parked in her driveway. Mike parked against the curb, got out and climbed Terry's stairs. The front windows were open but the blinds were drawn, and there was a two-inch gap between the windowsill and the shades. He wanted to check and see if she was awake—it was 8:30—so he bent down and peered through the screen, relieved to see a shadow moving across the far wall where he saw two rows of neatly labeled boxes. Terry was home, and judging by the faint *chink-chink* noise he heard, she was probably unloading her dishwasher.

He stood up and rang the doorbell, expecting to hear footsteps. He waited a full minute and then went back to the window and bent back down. Terry's shadow was no longer moving, Terry standing absolutely still.

"Terry, it's Mike Sullivan. Can I talk with you for a moment?"

A pair of legs came out from the kitchen. By the time Mike stood back up, Terry had cracked open the front door.

"Sorry, I thought you might have been a reporter," she nearly whispered behind the screen. She wore jeans, sneakers and a plain gray Champion sweatshirt, her gold cross, as always, on display. Her hands were covered by the same kind of yellow rubber cleaning gloves Jess wore to clean the bathrooms and stove. "Come on in."

The cool air inside the apartment was heavy with Pine Sol. The bookcases were naked, the contents packed in the neatly stacked and labeled boxes near the window.

"I didn't know you were moving," he said.

"Neither did I until a few days ago. This amazing opportunity came up and, well, I decided to jump on it."

"Judging by that smile on your face I'm guessing it has nothing to do with the hospice business."

Her smile gained some wattage. "A good friend of mine works at this spa in Phoenix, Arizona. She called the other night and we got to talking, and she started telling me about how the spa's looking for a new massage therapist. Sally—that's my friend—knows I used to be a massage therapist years ago. So we get to talking, and Sally is telling me about how nice the weather is out there, you know, warm and sunny all the time— great weather if you suffer from fibromyalgia."

Mike looked at her, puzzled.

"Fibromyalgia is . . . well, doctors don't know exactly what it is for sure, but it's like having a really bad flu and your muscles ache all the time. It's worse in the winter, and this was a really bad winter. Anyway," she continued brightly, "Sally's single like me and owns this really nice house. She's going to let me stay with her until I find a place to rent—or she said I could stay with her for good."

"Sounds exciting."

"I'm really looking forward to it, especially after everything that's—" She stopped herself. "I'm sorry. I didn't mean to sound insensitive."

"You're not. I'm happy for you."

"Thank you. So what brings you by at such an early hour? And with a notepad no less."

"I'm sure you're probably sick and tired of answering questions."

Terry's smile was polite. "I'd be fibbing if I said no."

"Reporters still bothering you?" Mike asked. They hadn't bothered him, or maybe they had just grown tired of trying to chase him down all the time and had given up.

"The calls have pretty much tapered off, but every now and then they'll drop by here unannounced— please don't take that the wrong way."

Mike waved it off. "Believe me, I understand where you're coming from. It's just, well, I've come across some information and I didn't want to wait for Nancy Childs—she's the investigator—to stop by. She'll probably be calling you sometime this afternoon. You going to be around?"

Now Terry looked puzzled. "I thought the case was closed—at least, that was what Detective Merrick told me."

"Sorry. This woman Nancy is a private investigator. The question I have, I know it's going to sound a little off the wall, but just bear with me."

"Let's sit down."

Mike sat in the same spot he did the other day. "Yesterday, I found out that my wife along with the women from the other two families, Rose Giroux and Margaret Clarkston, these three very Catholic women had—" he didn't want to use the word *abortion* in front of Super Catholic here—"they elected to have their pregnancies terminated."

The shock on Terry's face barely masked her disgust.

"I'm not sure about Margaret Clarkston," Mike said. "But I know for a fact that Rose Giroux and my wife had it done at the same clinic in New Hampshire. Rose Giroux—that's Ashley's mother—she told me she had spoken to Jonah about it."

"For confession?"

"Yes. The first priest, he didn't take too kindly to the news and said—"

"As well he shouldn't. What that woman did was murder."

"Jonah forgave—"

"It's murder. Some priests forgive that sort of thing—just as some priests and cardinals knowingly shuffled sexual predators to other parishes and then covered up their disgusting actions. To use your power to hide such a thing is an absolute disgrace. It's a sin. But God will deal with them properly, just as He'll deal with Father Jonah properly."

The room had an awful stillness to it.

"I'm sorry," he said after a moment. "I didn't mean to upset you."

The indignation set in Terry's face slowly melted away, her features softening, slipping back into the bright and pleasant woman who had greeted him at the door.

"I should be the one who's apologizing," she said. "I didn't mean to go off on a rant. It's just . . . What happened here in Boston with Cardinal Law, and now what you just told me about Father Jonah—it makes it hard to keep believing."

"In God?"

"No, not God." *No, of course not God, you fool—and how dare you even think such a thing.* "When I was growing up, I never considered the Catholic Church a political organization," she said. "But that's exactly what it is. It's a business. It's always been that way, I suppose, but it didn't sink in until my sister tried to get her first marriage annulled. She was married for a year with a baby girl when her husband just packed up and left. Wanted nothing to do with her anymore. The church wouldn't annul her marriage on account of the baby. Now take that example and compare it to the son of senator you-know-who who was married for something like twenty years and had four children. The priest granted that annulment right away. It's disheartening, but that's the way things get done in life—and in the Catholic Church. You wouldn't *believe* the stories Father Jonah told me."

"Like what?"

"He just talked about how political the church was. I'm sure some of that—well, maybe even all of it came from his bitterness at being defrocked. He missed it. Being a priest, I mean."

And the cloak of secrecy it provided him, Mike added privately.

"I know Father Jonah spoke to Father Connelly a lot," she said. "He's a priest at St. Stephen's. Father Jonah spoke very highly of him."

"Father Jack's on my list. Is there anything else you can tell me? Anything at all?" Mike grasping now.

"I've told you everything I know. That side of Father Jonah that hurt those girls and kept those items hidden under the floorboards of his bedroom—I didn't know anything about that man. I just knew the man who had cancer." She shrugged. "I'm sorry."

"I'll let you get back to cleaning," Mike said and stood up. "Thanks again for your time."

CHAPTER 44

O n the way home, Mike called Nancy's cell phone and left a brief message giving the highlights of his conversation with Terry Russell, and then made a pit stop at Mackenzie's Market. Mackenzie's had become a hot spot ever since a local guy bought the winning lottery ticket for a $30 million jackpot about three years ago. Mackenzie's also had a deli that made great Italian and meatball subs, and in the morning, breakfast sandwiches.

Mike ordered a fried egg and bacon sandwich on whole wheat along with a coffee and picked up the Sunday editions of the *Globe* and *Herald*. He ate his sandwich inside the truck and read the *Globe* sports— too much baseball coverage; then again, 'tis the season. Ten minutes later, he tossed the paper onto the passenger seat and saw a group of mostly teenage boys walking up Delaney with their Wiffle-ball bats. Probably on their way to Ruggers Park. You didn't go to the park at night, not unless you were looking to score some drugs, and most mornings you'd find condoms mixed with the cigarettes and empty booze bottles scattered on the grass and in the dugouts where hookers often took their johns.

It hadn't always been that way. Back when he was a kid—and, when you got right down to it, it hadn't been that long ago, right?—local bands would put on free concerts at the park during the summer. He played touch football there, and back then the worst thing you had to worry about was broken glass. One summer afternoon—the last summer with his mother, in fact—he had fallen on a jagged bottom piece of a beer bottle and cut his knee right open, the pain so bad he was sure shards of glass had made their way underneath his kneecap.

He couldn't ride his bike home, so Bill and this wiry, buck-toothed spaz named Gerry Nitembalm helped him walk back to Mackenzie's. Mr. Demarkis, a neighbor of Gerry's, saw the bleeding gash on Mike's knee and told him to get his butt in the backseat of the car, Bill hopping in along with him.

Because of his age, Mike needed a parent or legal guardian to sign a form authorizing the hospital to administer care. He called home for over half an hour but his mother never picked up.

"She said she'd be home all day," Mike told Bill.

"You're going to have to call your dad."

"Are you insane?"

"You want to sit here in pain all night?"

Bill called the garage, got Cadillac Jack on the phone and explained the situation. Lou showed up fifteen minutes later, his face flushed and getting darker by the second as he listened to Bill explain what had happened at the park, Bill stressing the word *accident*.

"How many times I told you not to play down there because of the glass?" Lou said. "You messed up that knee, that's it. You won't be playing Pop Warner in the fall."

Bill said, "It was my fault, Mr. Sullivan. Mike didn't want to go and I made him."

"Get your butt on home, Billy," Lou said.

Bill paused at the emergency room doors, turned around and mouthed the words "I'm sorry" to Mike before leaving.

Two hours later, his knee bandaged and stitched with staples, Mike leaned on his crutches and watched as Lou peeled off three one-hundred-dollar bills from his money clip to settle up the hospital bill. When Mike hobbled outside the ER doors, Bill and his father were sitting on the stone stoop.

"Sully," Mr. O'Malley said. "How's the knee?"

Lou said, "Just some bad cuts. He's goddamn lucky he didn't ruin his knee."

"Accidents happen," Mr. O'Malley said, and then shifted his attention to Lou. "You remember those days, right, Lou? Like that summer you were horsing around in Salmon Brook Pond and you slipped and broke your wrist. You were sixteen, remember?"

Lou walked right by him without answering.

Mike sat in the backseat on the way home, Lou in the front, smoking, grinding his teeth. Mike tried to hold it together, tried to steer his mind away from what was going to happen the second they got home and felt his insides get all knotted up and turn to water.

Nothing happened—not to him, anyway. But when his mother stepped inside the door? He heard the screaming, the broken dishes and the cries for help behind his closed bedroom door, through the pillow he stuffed over his head. Lou was pissed off because his wife should have been the one down at the hospital—not him. At least that was what Mike had always believed that fight was about.

The pay phone at Mackenzie's was still there, still near the Dumpster, the phone one of those new Verizon models with a bright yellow receiver that would have gone nicely with Bill's new Ford Escape. Mike stared at the phone, the memory from the hospital teetering in his mind, unsure of where it belonged now—that memory one of dozens.

I thought you came for the truth, Michael.

Lou's words from their visit at the jail.

Mike got out of his truck and walked over to the pay phone, one hand reaching back for his wallet. The piece of paper with the phone numbers was wedged in against the slot holding a calling card he used for times when his cell phone crapped out. He picked up the receiver, hit zero for the operator.

"I want to make a call and charge it to my calling card," Mike said after the operator came on.

"And the number you'd like to call, sir?"

"It's in France," Mike said. "Can you dial it for me?"

"Yes sir. Just provide me with the number."

Try the home phone number first and work your way down.
Mike recited the series of numbers, then his calling-card number, and the operator told him to hold on. A moment later, Mike heard the connection go through, heard the ring bring life to a phone in some house halfway around the world, Mike's stomach clenching at the sound of it, a part of him wanting to hang up.

The phone on the other end picked up. *"Allô,"* the male voice said.

Mike's breath caught in his throat.

"Allô."

"Jean Paul Latiere."

"C'est Jean Paul."

"I'm sorry, I don't speak French."

"This is Jean Paul."

"I'm calling you about Mary Sullivan."

"I'm sorry, but I do not know—"

"My name is Michael Sullivan. I'm her son."

A slight pause from the other end and Mike spoke into it, spoke quickly: "I have pictures of the two of you together in France. I know she moved out there to be with you. I know all about you, your connection to her." The words were tripping over each other in their rush to get out. "All this time I've thought Lou—that was her husband. Lou Sullivan. I'm sure she talked about him. About what he did for a living."

Trickles of silence as Mike drew in a breath, picturing Jean Paul dressed in a sharp suit and sitting in some fancy antique chair in his mansion or whatever they called them over there, Jean Paul debating whether or not he should answer the questions or find a polite way to hang up.

"I just have a few questions. Five minutes and I'll let you get back to your life."

"Jésus doux et merciful."

"Look at it from my point of view," Mike said. "You'd want to know, right?"

On the other end of the line Jean Paul sighed heavily against the receiver. "This is . . . I would rather not have this conversation."

"I need to know," Mike said, and tightened his grip on the receiver. "Please."

It was a full minute before Jean Paul spoke.

"Francine Broux. Your mother changed her name. She was terrified of your father."

"I know for a fact Lou flew over there and found her."

"Yes." A heavy sigh, then Jean Paul added, "I know all about it."

"What happened?"

"He beat her. He broke her nose and two of her ribs."

Mike propped his left arm against the top of the pay phone and leaned forward, rubbing his tongue against the top of his mouth, finding it dry.

"She had a very nice life here," Jean Paul said. "I loved her very much."

There was a hitch in Jean Paul's voice that told Mike to hang up and run.

"It happened about a year ago," Jean Paul said. "She woke up with chest pains. I rushed her to the hospital . . . I'm sorry."

All this time his mother had been alive.

Mike felt the sting in his eyes and tried to blink it away. "I met you once, didn't I? In Boston? I was with her, doing a Christmas tour in Beacon Hill, and she pretended to bump into you, introduced you as a friend of hers."

A pause, then Jean Paul said, "Yes. That was me."

"Only you didn't plan on her showing up with me."

Jean Paul didn't say anything.

"So that night," Mike said. "That was about, what, her trying to convince you to take me in?"

"Early on, I knew one thing about myself for sure: I knew I wasn't parenting material. I'm very selfish. Very self-centered and self-absorbed."

"She never had any intention of coming back for me, did she?"

Jean Paul didn't answer.

"She made a point of telling me to make sure Lou didn't find out where she was hiding," Mike said. "Only it didn't matter whether or not he did. She had no intention of coming back. She dropped those letters in the mail, and when she didn't come for me, she knew I'd blame Lou."

"I didn't agree with your mother's choice."

"But you don't regret it either."

"We were young," Jean Paul offered. "When you're young, you do foolish things. You don't stop and think about the consequences. How you'll have to live with them."

"She ever regret her decision?"

"I can't speak for your mother."

"You just did." Mike hung up and felt the St. Anthony medal, the one his mother had given him that night at the church, bounce against his chest.

CHAPTER 45

M ike was pulling out of Mackenzie's parking lot when his cell phone rang.

"Last time I checked I didn't have a partner," Nancy said.

"You were busy today, so I thought I'd help out, get the ball moving," Mike said.

"If I wanted help, I would have asked for it last night. You just don't go barging in and—"

"Nancy, I'm warning you, I'm not in the mood."

There was a sharp intake of air on the other end, then Nancy said, "Your message said she freaked out when you mentioned the abortions."

"A little, yeah."

"Give it to me word for word. Don't leave anything out."

For the next five minutes Mike explained what had happened with Terry.

"That's a rather strong reaction," Nancy said when he finished.

"The woman's Catholic with a capital C. She wears a cross outside her shirt."

"I'm Catholic."

"But not with a capital C. Trust me, there's a big difference."

"I still wouldn't rant like that in front of a stranger. What else?"

"I told you about her moving to Arizona."

"Because of the fibromyalgia?"

"That's part of it. I got the impression it's more to do with her friend."

"What's the friend's name?"

Mike thought about it for a moment.

"I don't remember the name," he said.

"Jesus Christ."

"Who cares? She's not a suspect, Nancy."

"Hold up. Were you or were you not the person who last night asked me to dig?"

"Yes, I—"

"My job is to talk with people, ask them questions, look for holes in their stories. When things don't add up—when something seems off—that's when I dig deeper. Now, would you like me to do my job, or would you like to handle this yourself?"

"No," Mike said, gritting his teeth. "I want you."

"Okay then. Now, did Terry mention anything else about Jonah?"

"No. In fact, she made a point of emphasizing she didn't know that side of him."

"That's what she said? Those were the words that came out of her mouth?"

"She said something like, 'The side of him that hurt those girls and kept those items hidden under the floorboards of his bedroom—I didn't know that part of him.'"

"She said the items were stored under the floorboards of his bedroom."

"That's what she said."

"You're sure?"

"Positive."

"That information hasn't been in the papers or on TV."

Mike hadn't been following the news on TV or reading the papers. "So maybe she heard it from Merrick," he said.

"Merrick wouldn't go into that level of detail with her."

"He did with me."

"That's different. He did it to convince you—" Nancy stopped herself.

"Convince me that it was over? Is that what you were going to say?"

"When was the last time she talked with Merrick?"

"I have no idea. You want me to go back and ask?"

"No, but since you're so eager to play private eye, you keep an eye on her until I get there," Nancy said. "Keep your ass parked in the truck and call me if she leaves the house. I don't want her disappearing before I get a chance to talk with her. I'm heading back."

CHAPTER 46

Mike found a curb spot about a block up from Terry Russell's duplex, a spot under the shade of a tree that offered a good view of the nurse's front door and porch. He tilted his seat back and lit a cigarette and smoked and watched Terry's front porch and driveway. He saw himself at nine pedaling up the driveway on his new bike—a birthday gift from Lou, no less—and Mike tried to turn away from the memory and heard Lou calling him from the backyard and then saw Lou sitting on the back steps, Lou freshly showered and dressed in a clean white undershirt and a pair of jeans, not a crease on them.

"Take a load off, chief," Lou said, and slapped the step next to him. "Me and you need to have a talk."

It was a humid evening in July, the air thick with heat and the smell of fresh-cut grass and bark mulch. Mike sat down on the opposite end of the step, a good arm's length between them—the space he needed in case he needed to run. Lou didn't seem angry—at least not yet. At the moment his eyes were fixed on their neighbor, Ned King, on all fours and working on his garden, his tan shorts and the hard, peach-colored plastic of his artificial limb streaked with mud.

"A mine did that," Lou said. "Stepped on it and blew his leg clean off. Now the poor son of a bitch is fighting cancer. Agent Orange. You'd think God might smile once in a while, give us a break."

Louis Sullivan, Purple Heart recipient, shook his head and sighed, sad or angry, maybe a mix, Mike could never tell. His father's moods, what made them fluctuate and erupt, were about as easy to predict as the New England weather.

"Your mother's never coming back," Lou said. "Not a week from now, not a year from now. She's gone, understand?"

"Gone where?" Mike asked, but he already knew the answer.

The month after she left, a padded envelope addressed to Mike arrived at Bill's address. Inside the envelope were a silver key chain and a note card. *The next time I write, I'll have an address where you can write me,* his mother had written. *Soon you'll be with me here in Paris. Have faith, Michael. Remember to have faith, no matter how bad it gets. And remember to keep this quiet. I don't have to remind you what your father would do to me if he found out where I was hiding.*

Paris. His mother was living in Paris.

Lou took a pull from his beer bottle and when he was

done, let the bottle hang between his legs. Mike paid close attention to Lou's hands, waiting for them to clench up—the sure sign that a beating was on the way.

"It doesn't matter where she went," Lou said. "She left us. That's what matters. And praying isn't going to bring her home. God doesn't give two shits about your problems. He doesn't care that your leg got blown off from a mine or why your brother died in some shit war or why your mother ran away. He takes and keeps on taking because underneath it all, God's a sadistic prick. Remember that next time you listen to Father Jack mouthing off about the great, divine plan He's got for everyone."

Mike toyed around with the idea of unleashing the truth on his father, imagining how it would hit him. But if Lou found out where she was hiding, Mike knew his father would hunt her down and kill her. Mike had heard the stories about how his father made people disappear. Not only that, he had witnessed his father's anger firsthand. Those experiences were practically tattooed on his skin.

"You want to cry, go ahead and let it out. Ain't nothing to be ashamed about. I cried when I found out my brother died in the war, and I cried when I buried my mother." Lou searched his son's eyes for a reaction.

"I'm okay."

"You want to be a man about it. I respect that." Lou gripped Mike's neck and squeezed hard. Drops of sweat ran down Mike's back. "Don't worry, Michael. It's gonna be okay. You'll see."

Mike asked if he could get going; he was supposed to meet Bill down at Buzzy's. Lou nodded, and Mike bounded down the hallway to his room. As he passed by his father's bedroom, the door partly open, he caught a bright metallic blink that made him stop.

On top of Lou's opened suitcase was a camera—a real sweet one by the looks of it. What was Lou doing with a camera? And where had he been for the past four days?

Mike looked through Lou's bedroom window. His father was still sitting on the porch steps. Mike stepped inside his father's bedroom, and when he picked up the camera, he saw an envelope stuffed in the corner of the suitcase. Inside were plane tickets to Paris, only the name on the tickets was Thom Peterson—the same name on the passport, the one with a picture of Lou with a beard and a mustache.

Sitting in the truck, Mike thought back to that night in the church with his mother: *Real bravery—true bravery—involves the spirit. Like having faith your life will turn out better when it looks like it won't. Having faith—That's real bravery, Michael. Always have faith, no matter how bad it looks. Don't let your father or anyone else take that away from you.*

The setup, followed by the first letter: *And remember to keep this quiet. I don't have to remind you what your father would do to me if he found out where I was hiding.*

And now the second: *I'm coming for you . . . I need you to keep being patient . . . Don't let your father find this address . . . If your father finds out where I'm hiding—I don't have to remind you what your father is capable of.*

Mike pictured his mother dropping each of these letters off at a mailbox or whatever they called them over there in Paris—his mother knowing exactly what she was doing.

And yet . . . and yet on some level, even before he found out about Lou's trip to Paris, hadn't he known his mother wasn't coming home? Hadn't he known that, over the course of the five months she was gone, if she had really wanted to come get him, wouldn't she have made some sort of arrangement? Some sort of effort? She would have tried *something*.

Your mother could be very persuasive with that soft gentle voice of hers—you know that better than anyone. Smoothest liar I ever met, your mother.

Funny thing about the mind—how it could take each experience and trauma and shave off the parts it didn't need or want. Easy to store that way, he supposed. Or maybe it was a survival mechanism. Maybe the brain simply couldn't handle cataloging the polarizing depths of how some of us could love and hate and kill in equal measures. Maybe the reason he couldn't see himself as an alcoholic with a violent temper that mirrored his murderous father's was the same reason he couldn't see Sarah willingly walking off with Jonah, Jess being unfaithful, his mother never coming home because she didn't have any room for him in her new life. To accept the truth was to accept all of it, and he could feel his mind crumbling under the sheer weight of it.

Mike pictured Lou lying back in his bed, his hands clasped behind his head and beads of sweat running down his forehead as he stared at the bars of his jail cell.

Admit it, Michael. Your life was much simpler when you were busy hating me.

A blue-gray Volvo came to a stop at the corner of Dibbons Street, and then banged a left and made a quick right into Terry's driveway. At first, Mike thought that the Volvo was going to back up and turn around; then Terry came rushing out of her door and down the stairs, one hand clutching both a bulky black leather briefcase and her purse. She looked up the street as if expecting to find someone. Mike had already sunk further down in his seat.

This is ridiculous. He took out his cell phone and after he dialed Nancy's number, he inched back up and peered over the truck's dashboard. Terry was still leaning into the passenger side window of the Volvo. The briefcase, he noticed, was no longer in her hands. Just the purse.

"What's up?" Nancy asked.

Mike explained what was going on, watching as the driver stepped out of the Volvo.

Nancy said, "You recognize the guy?"

Salt and pepper hair, kind of tall—around six one—wearing a white shirt and chinos with sneakers. Mike was positive he had never seen this guy before. "No," he said. "Right now he's running up the stairs to Terry's house."

"And what's Terry doing?"

"She's getting behind the wheel of the Volvo. . . . Now she's pulling out of the driveway."

"Can you see the license plate?"

"Yeah."

"Give it to me."

Mike did, and right as he finished, Nancy said, "Follow her. I want to know where she's going."

"Don't you think we're being—"

"Just do it. She know you drive a truck?"

"I have no idea." Terry had pulled out of her driveway and was now driving down the opposite end of the street, away from him. Mike wedged the phone between his ear and shoulder and started the truck.

Nancy said, "You ever follow someone?"

"Yeah, I do it all the time, pick women out, stalk them for fun." He drove down the street. The Volvo was at a STOP sign. No directional was on.

"What you want to do is to stay as far behind her as you can without losing her," Nancy said. "If she's checking around to see if she's being followed, she'll be looking two or three cars behind. Since you're in the truck, you're sitting higher up, you have a better view of the road and don't need to be as close. You got a friend who can keep an eye on her house until I get there?"

"Don't you think you're being a little extreme here?"

"That a yes or no?"

"I have someone in mind." Mike was at the STOP sign now.

"Have him call me. Stay on Terry, and whatever you do, don't lose her." Nancy hung up.

The Volvo had turned left and was now driving up Grafton. A mile or two down the road were the exits for Route 1.

So Terry was going out for a drive. So what?

Why would she take this man's Volvo? Why not take her own car?

He started to rattle off possible explanations: Maybe there was some mechanical problem with her car. Maybe— Who the hell knew? There could be a dozen explanations, all of them perfectly valid.

Still, as he drove, he felt Nancy's paranoia mixing with his own. Okay, Terry *had* acted weird, even a little fanatical about the whole abortion thing. And yes, when she came out of her house, she *had* looked around the street, checking it out. Why? Was she looking for him? The police?

And let's not forget her mentioning the items Jonah stored underneath the floorboards in his bedroom.

Mike called Bill.

"I need you to do me a big favor, and I don't have the time to get into the reasons why," Mike said. "I just need you to do it, okay?"

"Lay it on me."

"You got a pen?"

"I'm in the kitchen next to the chalkboard. Shoot."

Mike gave Bill a brief explanation of what was happening, then rattled off the address and Nancy's cell-phone number. "Watch the house," Mike said. "Call Nancy, tell her you're there, keep her updated."

"I'll keep my cell phone on," Bill said. "Where are you going?"

"I wish I knew."

CHAPTER 47

For the next two hours, Mike followed Terry as she drove north on Route 93 and then 89, passing through a good chunk of New Hampshire and now heading into Vermont with no signs of slowing.

Tailing someone was hard—much harder when there were no cars between you. Right now they were traveling on a quiet, two-lane stretch of highway lined with trees on both sides, the Volvo a good ways ahead of him but still visible and still driving a steady sixty-five. Terry hadn't sped up once. Either she wasn't in a rush to get to her new destination, or she was being a stickler for the speed limits because she didn't want to take the chance of getting pulled over.

Terry, what the hell are you up to?

And what was the connection to Sarah? The question kept buzzing around in his head, searching for an answer as he drove.

Mike checked the fuel gauge. The first tank was

about empty, but the second tank, thank God, was full. Terry was going to have to stop and get gas at some point. She had to be getting close to a quarter of a tank by now.

His cell phone rang. Nancy.

"Sorry it took me so long to call, but the computer friend I use just finished going through Terry Russell's phone records. No phone calls either to or from Arizona on the house phone or from her cell," she said. "And the fibromyalgia? That's a lie too. Checked the medical databases and came up dry."

"Who owns the Volvo?"

"That would be Anthony Lundi, owns a home in Medford, married, two kids, used to be a cop and took early retirement about six years ago—don't know why yet. I do know two things about the man. First, he was arrested for disorderly conduct—this was after he retired—for, get this, protesting at an abortion clinic."

First Terry's wacko reaction, now this information on her friend.

"Second," Nancy said, "the man's quite the cleaner. For the past half hour, I've been watching this guy through my binoculars. Right now he's scrubbing down the walls in Terry's apartment. I'm thinking of hiring him to clean my place."

"He could be just helping her with the move. When you leave an apartment, you're supposed to clean it." Mike said the words but didn't fully believe them.

"Or, if you're like Ted Bundy, you meticulously clean your apartment and car to get rid of evidence."

"Of what?"

"That's what we're going to find out. What's Terry doing?"

"Still driving."

"This is really starting to stink. Stay on her and don't lose her," Nancy said and hung up.

The warm sun that had greeted him this morning was now gone, replaced by dark gray clouds. Mike watched the Volvo dip over the horizon. He stepped on the gas a little to catch up.

Was she heading to Canada?

You'll find out soon enough.

Mike saw a long stretch of empty road. The Volvo was nowhere in sight.

Panic gripped him. On the far right were a Mobil station and a Burger King. If she hadn't pulled in there, she must have taken the exit after the station.

Check the gas station first.

Mike floored the gas and headed straight into the Mobil parking lot. *Let her be here, Jesus God, don't let her have taken an exit—*

The Volvo was parked at one of the full-service pumps. He didn't know whether or not she was in the car; maybe she had left for a bathroom break and to get something to eat. But it was her car. He recognized the license plate.

Mike did a three-point turn and parked the truck at a pump three lanes over, figuring he might as well get gas since he didn't know how much longer Terry was going to be driving. His truck wasn't exactly concealed, but Terry would have to look behind her in order to see it. He was in the middle of refueling when he saw Terry walk out of Burger King's front doors. She couldn't see him. Her back was toward him, and as Mike watched her, he noticed she took her time walking back to her car, and she wasn't looking around like she had when she left her house. She seemed relaxed. Good. She climbed back inside the Volvo and started the car.

Mike waited a moment, wanting to give her a head start, and when he climbed back inside the truck, he saw that Terry had pulled up next to a pay phone and was now standing outside, making a phone call. He turned around and drove to the opposite end of the lot and backed into a space near the air hose. Terry, he could see, had hung up and was walking back to her car.

Only she didn't drive away.

Two minutes passed. Five. Terry was still there.

Could be eating her lunch.

Or she's waiting for someone.

And then another thought, this one new and alarming: If Terry was, in fact, waiting for someone, what would he do after this person or persons showed up? He could only follow one.

Call the police.

And say what? Hello, my name is Michael Sullivan. I'm the father of Sarah Sullivan, the girl who's been missing for five years. What I need you to do is to come and arrest Terry Russell, Francis Jonah's former hospice worker.

And what is the emergency, Mr. Sullivan?

The emergency is that Terry Russell is acting very strange. She's lied to me and now she's using a friend's car and is driving through Vermont and heading only God knows where—Canada would be my guess. And she just used a pay phone to call someone. I don't know who she called, but I do know she has a cell phone. Very suspicious, don't you think?

Maybe her cell phone has bad reception.

Or maybe this has something to do with Jonah—and Sarah. Why else would she hop in her friend's car and drive north?

I see your point, Mr. Sullivan. While I have you on the phone, can you please give me your chest size? We like all of our mental patients to feel comfortable when we fit them with a straitjacket.

I'm serious.

Of course you are. Those voices in your head can be so darn convincing! Now when the doctors come, Mr. Sullivan, don't you worry. It's just a shot, just a tiny sting, and all those nasty voices in your head will float away. Now where did you say you were again?

Right now Terry was alone.

Take a chance now or wait it out?

Mike grabbed his cell phone, got out of the truck and started running.

CHAPTER 48

Mike opened the passenger side door and threw himself inside. When Terry saw him, she jumped, and the burger and fries spread out on the waxy yellow paper on her lap fell on the floor, the paper drink cup sliding from her hand and spilling against the console separating the two seats.

"What are you—"

"Merrick never told you where the items were found," Mike said, "and yet you knew they were found under the floorboards under Jonah's bed. That's pretty specific, Terry."

"I never said—"

"Cut the bullshit. It's over."

She made a move for the door. He reached across her chest and pounded her door lock shut.

"Stop it, you're crazy—"

He clamped his hand over her mouth. "You scream and the police will come," he said. "I don't think you want that, do you, Terry?" He shook her. "Do you?"

Her nostrils flaring, sucking in air, she looked at her rearview mirror. Mike glanced over his shoulder out the back window. People were walking across the lot of the gas station to Burger King but nobody was looking in this direction. On the backseat was the black leather briefcase she had carried with her out of her house.

"We're not going to stick around for your friends," he said. "I'm going to remove my hand and you're going to keep your voice down, got it?"

She nodded.

Mike slid his hand off her mouth. Terry licked her lips, her eyes wide and scared.

"I overheard the police talking about it," she said, her voice low, trembling. "They said they found a doll and your daughter's snowsuit. That's the truth, I swear to you."

"Then you won't mind talking to the police. Now drive."

"I'll do whatever you want. Just don't hurt me."

Terry started the car. Mike sat half twisted in his seat, watching her face as she put the car in gear. Her door was locked; he was in no danger of her trying to leave.

She stopped at the end of the parking lot. "Where do you want me to go?" she asked.

"South. I'm sure you're anxious to get back home and get this car back to your police friend Anthony Lundi."

No change in Terry's expression. "May I please put my seatbelt on?" she asked.

"Go ahead."

Very calmly, she put her seatbelt on, then used the power buttons on her door to roll up the windows. She turned left and drove back down the highway, never driving over sixty-five, both hands on the wheel—ten and two o'clock, just like the rules said.

"Your friend Anthony Lundi," Mike said. "What's he doing inside your house?"

"Knowing Tony, he's probably cleaning."

That took him by surprise; he had been expecting to catch her in another lie.

Terry continued: "I'm in a lot of pain right now, so I called Tony and asked him to come over and help me clean. He's going to help me finish packing and then help me move the boxes."

"The pain from your fibromyalgia."

"Yes. Tony was kind enough—"

"You don't have fibromyalgia."

Still no change in Terry's expression.

"And you never received any phone calls from Arizona," Mike said. "I had you checked out."

"Okay."

"You're not going to try and deny it?"

"My friend Sally lives in Nashua, New Hampshire. She just got a job down there."

"I know about your friend Tony's arrest for protesting an abortion clinic."

"That was a long time ago. He doesn't do that anymore. I told him there isn't any point in protesting. God will deal with those people when it's time."

She said *those people* with acid, but the rest of the words calmly rolled off her tongue, the nervousness gone, the expression relaxed now, as if she were alone in the car, enjoying a leisurely drive through the countryside.

Keeping an eye on Terry, Mike reached into the backseat, unzipped the pouches of the briefcase and found what felt like a laptop computer. It was—one of those thin, lightweight models. He held it near her face.

"Why'd you drive all the way up here with this?" Mike said.

"My hard drive has crashed. I can't retrieve any of my files, so my friend offered to take a look at it for me. He's an expert at retrieving data from corrupted disk drives, so I drove up here to meet him."

No hitch in her voice, no hesitation.

"His name is Larry Pintarski," she said. "I can give you Larry's name and address if you want to call him. But we'll have to stop and use a pay phone. I couldn't get a signal on my cell phone."

"So you dropped what you were doing and drove all the way up here."

"This is the only time he can work on it."

"Why'd you borrow this car?"

"Because I've been having transmission problems with my car, and I didn't want to risk taking it on such a long drive. I have an appointment at the garage on Monday."

Mike glanced quickly out the back window. No cars behind them.

"There's no conspiracy here," Terry said. "My checking accounts, my resume—my entire life is on this computer and I need—"

"Why didn't you drive to this person's house?"

"Because his house is very hard to get to. Last time I was there was two years ago and I got lost. I'm awful with directions. To make it easier on me, Larry told me to meet him at the gas station. That's what I was doing when you abducted me. Go ahead and call him if you want."

Terry answering all the questions so smoothly, making it all sound so rational, he found a part of himself responding to her.

"Mr. Sullivan, you're under a great deal of stress—and understandably so. I don't have any children myself, so I won't pretend to know what you're going through. What I do know, what my area of expertise is, is grief. I know that sometimes grief can be so powerful it can blind you. I understand that, and I want to help you. Just tell me what you want."

"I'm going to find out the truth about my daughter, and I'll do whatever it takes, understand?" Mike trying to scare her now.

"I can't give you what I don't have."

The same words Jonah used that morning out on the trail.

"The person responsible for what happened to your daughter has since passed on," Terry said. "I can't change that, and I can't change the fact that those three girls are with God now."

"You knew about the items under the floorboards."

"I told you, I overheard—"

"I already talked with Merrick," Mike lied. "He never said anything to you. Nobody did."

"I overheard it."

"Bullshit."

"I don't want to argue with you. We'll sit and talk with Detective Merrick, if that's what you want. And I'm not going to press charges. That's a promise."

The resolve that had fueled him for this entire trip was now crumbling. Why was Terry being so agreeable? Nothing he said tripped her up. She had an answer for everything. Was it possible he was wrong? *What am I missing?*

Terry turned her head and flashed him a look of sympathy. "You have to let your daughter go. If you don't, it will destroy you."

Mike opened up her laptop. "You won't mind if I take a look on your laptop and verify your story, would you?"

"The power button is on the far left, the one with the green square in it."

He placed the laptop on the top of the console between them and pressed the button.

Terry slammed on the brakes.

CHAPTER 49

Mike was sitting sideways when Terry hit the brakes. He felt the side of his head slam against the windshield and white balls of pain exploded across his vision. He tumbled back against the seat, the sound of squealing rubber filling the air as the car skidded across the highway.

Terry hit the gas. His head spinning and screaming, he tried to gain some footing when she hit the brakes again. Right before his eyes clamped shut, he saw the glowing blue numbers on the radio clock. His forehead slammed against the radio and more balls of white light exploded. He fell back against the seat, dimly aware that the car had pulled off the highway and was now bouncing its way down the grassy slope of the median strip.

Then, some time later, stillness.

Pain signals flared all the way up his spine; every muscle felt twisted and bruised. But he was conscious.

He thought he heard a door open, yes, it *was* open; a steady ding-ding-ding chime filled the car.

(She's getting out hurry you've got to get up and move and get her or she'll do something else Jesus she knows something about Sarah has to has to know she knows what hurry she knows)

Mike opened his eyes and saw Terry's blurry shape still in the car seat. He blinked, his eyes focusing a little better, clear enough to see that her seatbelt was off, the laptop clutched against her chest along with what looked like her purse, one hand in it, digging.

Mike groped for her. She turned and screamed and violently slammed her fist into his face, two, three more blows before he managed to grab hold of her wrist. Terry twisted her body, trying to fight him off, and the laptop tumbled outside her door and dropped to the ground. Her free hand, the one digging in her purse, came out *oh shit,* she was holding a gun.

Mike lunged forward with everything he had.

The shot was deafening; it blew out the front windshield, and shards of glass rained down on them. He was lying sideways on top of her, all of his strength going into holding the hand with the gun while her other hand beat about his face. He pushed the back of her hand against a shard of glass stuck in the window and Terry screamed—a high-pitched, rabid sound that tore down his spine and scared him. *Normal people don't scream this way, this woman is crazy and she knows what happened to Sarah oh God she KNOWS.*

The gun dropped and tumbled to the floor, near the

gas pedal and brakes. Mike went for the gun. Terry broke free and ran outside.

Gun in hand, Mike tumbled out of the car and rolled against the ground. Terry had picked up the laptop only to put it back on the ground, the laptop open and Terry stomping on it with her sneakers.

"Stop," Mike screamed. "Stop or I swear to God I'll shoot."

Terry ignored him and continued kicking. Using the car as leverage, Mike got to his feet and almost fell back down. His equilibrium was off, like he was drunk.

Not drunk, a voice corrected him. *It's a concussion.*

The laptop's screen was gone, and dozens of plastic keys and pieces were scattered across the ground. He staggered over to her, and when she saw him with the gun, she turned and ran into the woods.

He aimed low, meaning to fire off a couple of warning shots. He had never fired a gun before, and when he squeezed the trigger he was surprised to feel the gun kick. He fired again.

Terry screamed and he saw her legs buckle.

When he caught up to her, he saw three blurred versions, Mike waving his gun at all three of them, relieved when, a moment later, the three bled back into one. He kept blinking, making sure Terry was still there. She was. A dark red spot was on the leg of her jeans, her hands clutching at it, her hair wild and messy. The sleeve of her sweater had been torn.

"What did you do to Sarah?"

Terry ignored him. She folded her hands and started to pray.

Mike pressed the gun against her temple. "My daughter," he said. "Tell me about my daughter."

Terry continued to pray. Her eyes were glazed over, staring in that vacant way that reminded him of a dark, empty house. Was it a trance? Wherever she was, she wasn't here.

"The police are already involved," Mike said. His mouth was bone dry, and he was finding it difficult to form thoughts into words. Blood dripped down his face; he could feel it sliding down the back of his head and forehead, saw a drop hit the sleeve of his shirt. He was bleeding, but how badly? "This thing you're involved in—"

"Is so much bigger than you," she said, snapping her head to him. "You can't scare me. I am acting by the will of God and God alone will protect me."

Mike dug the gun harder into the side of her head, tilting it. "Tell me where she is," he said. "Tell me and I'll let you live."

"I don't bargain with sinners. Sinners will be punished. You, your whore of a wife—you'll all face judgment just as Father Jonah did. When the rope was slipped around his neck, he didn't fight it because he knew he had sinned by forgiving those murdering whores. He will face God's punishment because God's punishment is swift, it is—"

"You killed Jonah." That wasn't right. Jonah committed suicide; Merrick said so himself, right? Yes, of course he did. Yes, at the restaurant in Belham, Dakota's. Mike remembered—at least he thought he did. He wasn't sure.

"Your daughter's dead," Terry said.

Mike blinked, almost stumbled.

"We killed her."

"You're lying."

"Deliver me," Terry said and wrapped her mouth around the gun, her lips forming a gruesome smile around the barrel.

Mike felt his finger pressing against the trigger.

Don't do it, a voice screamed at him. *Don't turn this nut into a martyr, that's* exactly *what she wants you to do.*

He yanked the gun out of her mouth and then used his other hand to push Terry to the ground. She didn't fight it, even when he rolled her onto her stomach. Terry's face was turned to the side; her eyes were shut and she was mumbling what sounded like a prayer. Mike stood back up, planting his foot on the small of her back, and after he switched the gun to his left hand, he removed the cell phone from his back pocket. He was about to dial 911 when he realized he couldn't see the numbers. They were blurring in and out. So was Terry's face. So was everything around him.

Mike blinked and kept blinking until everything snapped back picture perfect and then dialed 911.

"I've got her," Mike told the male operator.

"Got who, sir?"

"Terry Russell. Francis Jonah's nurse. She knows

what happened to Sarah—Sarah Sullivan, that's my daughter. I'm her father." The words came rushing out of him, bordering on a scream. "I'm her father, Mike Sullivan. You need to get here. You need to get here right away."

"Mr. Sullivan, I need you to slow down and—"

"Listen to me. You've got to send people here *right now*. We don't have a lot of time."

"Tell me where you are."

Mike gave the operator the directions and then made him repeat them back. "I've got a gun to her head," he said. "I've already shot her once. Do you understand what I'm saying?"

"Yes. I understand." The tone in the operator's voice jumped, and he started speaking slow and loud so there would be no mistake. "Help is on the way, Mr. Sullivan. Just stay on the phone with me. You don't want to do something you'll regret for the rest of your life."

"Then you better hurry." Mike hung up. It was becoming even more difficult to concentrate, to fight off that urge to sit down, maybe close his eyes for a bit. Not to sleep, just a rest.

THAT'S THE CONCUSSION TALKING DON'T DO IT YOU'RE SO CLOSE YOU'VE GOT TO FIGHT IT IF YOU SIT DOWN YOU'LL SHUT YOUR EYES AND YOU'LL LOSE SARAH AGAIN DO YOU WANT THAT?

No. No, he didn't want that—couldn't bear the *thought* of it. Sarah was alive. No matter what Terry said, Sarah was alive and he wasn't about to let her down again.

The urge to sit down and rest came at him again and he fought it by thinking of Sarah about to head up the Hill, only this time when he offered his hand she grabbed it and he could feel the softness of her hand, and she was smiling, her glasses crooked on her face, he could see her face, her beautiful face, he could see it clear as day.

"Don't worry, Sarah. Daddy's not going to let you go, I promise."

"She's gone," Terry said. "You'll never find her."

Terry smiled—at least Mike thought she did. Her face, the ground, everything around him wasn't swimming away, it was melting. He blinked three, four, five times. The melting wouldn't stop.

Terry was praying again; he could hear her mumbling.

Mike pressed the gun against her temple.

"Tell me," he said and cocked the trigger. "Tell me right now."

CHAPTER 50

Mike's eyes fluttered open. He saw a wall-mounted TV playing an old episode of *The Simpsons*. For some reason Homer's ass was on fire; he ran around, screaming, trying to find a spot to put out the flames.

Mike heard a soft chuckle and his eyes cut sideways to a young, attractive woman with short blond hair who was busy making a note on a chart. She wore a white lab coat and had a stethoscope around her neck.

A doctor or a nurse. He was in a hospital.

(Terry)

(who?)

he moved a hand to his face and when he touched his forehead

(Terry is Jonah's nurse)

he felt thick gauze bandaging packed along the right side of his head.

(I was following Terry. I followed her to a gas station and then I climbed inside her Volvo and Terry freaked out and—)

"Sarah," he croaked.

"No, Mr. Sullivan, don't lift your head up."

Spikes of pain flared and his head crashed back against the pillow. Oh Jesus. Oh Christ. He turned on his side, wanting to throw up.

"That's it, just lie back and relax," the woman said, and stepped up next to him. "I'm Dr. Tracy."

"I need to talk to the police."

"Slow down, Mr. Sullivan."

"You don't understand."

"I do understand. The FBI is here."

Mike blinked, stared at her.

"That's right. There's an agent posted outside your room who is very anxious to speak with you, but before he does, I need you to answer some questions for me. Tell me your first name."

"Michael."

"And where do you live?"

"Belham. Belham, Massachusetts. It's just outside of Boston. Where am I?"

"Vermont. Do you know how you got here?"

"I remember being in the woods."

"Were you alone?"

"No. I was with a woman. Terry Russell. She was Jonah's hospice nurse. Please, I need to speak with the FBI right now."

"Just stick to answering my questions for the moment, okay?"

The doctor launched into a list of seemingly ridiculous questions: what was today's date; the year; the name of the president. Mike answered all of them correctly, and then the doctor went on to explain that he had suffered a grade-two concussion. The CT scan they ran came back fine: no intercranial bleeding.

"We're going to keep you for the night," the doctor said. "Tonight a nurse will come in and wake you up. If you don't wake up easily, if you become confused or if you start vomiting, we're going to keep you here, run some more tests. I think you'll be fine, but for the next couple of weeks, you're going to have to give your brain some time to heal. That means no physical activity, no work, lots of rest."

"I can't remember how I got here."

"Sometimes with a head injury patients experience what's called spotty amnesia. It's completely normal. Your head took quite a few knocks."

No argument there. Behind whatever drugs they had given him, Mike could feel, very faintly, tiny throbs along the right side of his skull.

The door swung open again and in walked a suit-and-tie guy with neatly trimmed blond hair and an all-business look on his face.

"Mr. Sullivan, I'm Special Agent Mark Ferrell."

"My daughter," Mike said again.

Ferrell's face changed slightly—closed up, Mike thought, and he felt his heart skip a beat.

"We'll get into all of that," Ferrell said. "You feel up to talking?"

Before Mike could answer, the doctor said, "Go easy on him."

"I will," Ferrell said. "Scout's honor."

"Good," the doctor said. "Then you won't mind me hanging around, see if you live up to your word."

Ferrell sat on the heating register and Mike said, "Terry Russell."

"In custody. She gave the state police one hell of a highway chase."

Mike remembered Terry on her knees, praying. He remembered cocking the trigger, wanting to scare her. *Now that's not exactly true, now is it?* No. He *did* want to scare her, yes, but that other part of him had wanted to put another bullet in her. The thought hadn't scared him so much as made him sleepy, and he remembered taking a step back from her, and then another, and then . . . *Shit.* What was he missing?

The doctor said, "Are you okay, Mr. Sullivan?"

"I don't remember what happened in the woods."

"I'm sure it will come back to you," Ferrell said. "I have agents speaking with Terry Russell right now, and the FBI is assisting with the investigation in Belham. Her buddy Lundi's in protective custody. He's looking to trade information for a lighter sentence. And we have Terry's laptop. Now, we've barely scratched the surface of what's going on, but I'll tell you what I know so far. You don't understand something, you've got a question, just jump right in and ask, okay?"

Mike nodded. Why was Ferrell speaking so slowly?

He's not, a voice answered. *It's your head. It was used as a pinball and now you're loaded with drugs, so make sure you pay attention. You might only have one shot here.*

Ferrell said, "What we know at this point is that Terry Russell and Anthony Lundi are part of a radical pro-life, ultra-Christian group that called themselves The Soldiers of Truth and Light. We believe this group has been operating for the better part of two decades. What this group does is kidnap young children from parents who've had abortions, brainwash these kids into thinking their parents are dead, and then these kids are placed into the Christian homes of adults who, for one reason or another, can't have kids of their own. The new parents of these abducted children also belong to the group—that's how they've maintained this level of secrecy for so long—and a good majority of them live in other countries, mainly Canada. This group operates in an Al Qaeda–like fashion strictly through encrypted email. They had members working in abortion clinics all over the country, gathering data on various women, who they were—"

"Terry told you all of this?" Mike couldn't believe Terry would turn over this information. She had refused to talk with a gun pressed to her head, why would she talk now?

"Terry's refusing to cooperate," Ferrell said. "Now her friend Lundi? He's an ex-cop, so he knows how the game is played. At first he didn't want to talk, but when we told him we had recovered the laptop, well, he practically started singing."

"No."

"No what?"

"She broke the laptop. I saw it. The screen was gone."

"Ah. My fault. I assume everyone's familiar with computers. Yes, technically, she broke the laptop. But she didn't break the most important piece, which is the hard drive. We took that baby out, transferred it into another computer and once our boys hacked their way past the security, we were good to go. What we've uncovered so far is Terry's address book with the names of all these people, addresses and phone numbers. And we have copies of her emails from the past three months. She didn't know it, but her email program was set to auto-archive every email she received or sent."

That explained why Terry had been in such a rush to move the laptop out of the house. *I told her about the abortions and she panicked, figured that it was only a matter of time until the police came knocking—and if they did, if for some reason they took the laptop into evidence, then they'd be able to examine her hard drive, see what was stored on it.*

"Terry made some phone calls on a cell phone during her drive," Ferrell said. "It looks like she called some of the members of her group, who then turned around and alerted the families—you know, got them moving. You feeling okay?"

"Just a little sleepy. Don't stop talking." He was afraid that if Ferrell stopped talking, he would fall back asleep and his hope would evaporate and when he woke up someone would come in and say this was a dream, I'm sorry, Mr. Sullivan, so sorry.

"There was quite a lot of information on Jonah in these emails," Ferrell said. "The first girl he allegedly molested all those years ago? The mother of the girl was a part of Terry's group, and she convinced her daughter to go along with it. The little girl conveniently dropped the charges right before it went to court, but it didn't matter. The seed of doubt was already planted."

"I'm not following."

"Terry's group hated Jonah because they knew he granted forgiveness to women who had had abortions. Jonah represented—and I'm quoting here—'the continuing moral decay of the Catholic Church.' They believed Jonah had no business being a priest, so what this group did was pin the disappearance of the three girls on him."

Wait. Was Ferrell saying Jonah was innocent? That couldn't be right.

Mike said, "Merrick found the items underneath the floorboard in Jonah's bedroom. He found audiotapes."

"Terry planted all of it," Ferrell said. "And Lundi planted the jacket on the cross. It was pure coincidence that Jonah walked around the top of the hill that night, but it didn't matter if he found the jacket or if someone else did. When the jacket was found, you would ID it, and then the police would head straight to Jonah's and put him under the microscope again."

Jonah's voice from the night he had called: *I'm going to die in peace. You're not going to take that away from me. Not you, not the police, not the press. You stay away from me or this time I'll send you to rot in jail.*

"So why go through all this when Jonah was already dying?" Ferrell said. "They wanted to prolong his suffering. Jonah admitted to Terry that he was terrified of dying alone in a jail cell. All he wanted was to live out the last part of his life in peace, to die in his home. When it didn't look like the police were going to arrest Jonah, Terry and Lundi concocted the idea of burning him. Of course, Lundi knew the police would start an investigation, so they had to pin it on someone."

"Lou," Mike said.

"You got it. Lundi knew your old man was poking around Jonah's house, so Lundi set him up. It was Lundi who was waiting behind the shed that night, Lundi who threw the Molotov cocktail. Lundi drops your old man's lighter and some cigarette butts and guess who the police are going to nail to the wall? We've already contacted your father's lawyer."

Mike's attention was still focused on Jonah. "So Jonah was . . ." He couldn't get the words out.

Ferrell nodded. "Innocent. His suicide was staged. Terry loaded him up on morphine, and Lundi slung Jonah over his shoulder—not hard to do since Jonah was so emaciated at this point. Police come in, find the tape with your daughter's voice on it, do their work and find the single ligature mark around Jonah's neck and given Jonah's history, it looks like they have a suicide on their hands. Case closed. The extra morphine in his system didn't raise any red flags because Jonah was using it to treat his cancer."

Then Mike remembered Terry's words about Jonah: *When the rope was slipped around his neck, he didn't fight it because he knew he had sinned by forgiving those murdering whores. He will face God's punishment because God's punishment is swift.*

Mike pictured Jonah struggling against the noose tightening around his neck as the knowledge of what had really happened to him screamed inside his head. Mike tried to imagine how Jonah confronted that last moment of his life.

Only God knows what is true.

Innocent. All this time Jonah had been innocent. All this time he had been telling the truth.

And I tried to kill him—twice.

Mike felt a cold sweat break across his skin.

Ferrell said, "They made this poor son of a bitch suffer right up until the very end. When Lundi fitted the noose around Jonah's neck, Lundi confessed to Jonah what they had done to him and then kicked him off the stump. It's all detailed in the emails between Terry and Lundi."

Ferrell's cell phone rang.

"This whole operation is so amazingly simple it borders on brilliant. Excuse me for a moment," he said and then walked over to the far corner of the room, Mike watching as the agent pressed the phone against his ear and spoke in whispers.

Only God knows what is true.

Mike's eyes felt heavy. He shut them and kept himself awake by focusing on the agent's voice, the clicking of his shoes. They were going to find Sarah. Mike knew that. No God would bring him this far, this close, only to make her disappear again. God wouldn't be that cruel twice.

Mike fell asleep.

"Mr. Sullivan?"

The FBI agent's voice. Mike opened his eyes and saw that the room was dark.

"I just got the word," Ferrell said, and broke into a smile. "We've got her. We've found your daughter."

Faraway, So Close

CHAPTER 51

I'm not one of those, you know, nature dudes, but even I appreciate a view like this."

Bill was right. The view *was* impressive. Everywhere you looked were valleys of blooming trees. The Vermont farmhouse, with its sprawling maze of rooms, was completely isolated. It was a safe house, Special Agent Mark Ferrell had explained, a place generally used as a temporary shelter before people were placed into the Witness Protection Program. With the media frenzy surrounding Sarah's story, the FBI thought it would be better to have the reunion here, someplace without cameras and microphones, give Sarah some time to adjust.

Behind him, coming from inside the house, a phone rang. Mike whipped his head around and through the windows saw Agent Ferrell walking across the hardwood floor as he talked on a cell phone. The woman dressed in the black suit was the child psychologist, Tina

Davis. Mike had spent yesterday afternoon and a good portion of last night talking with Davis, listening as she explained how to approach Sarah, what to expect.

The most important person in all of this is Sarah, Dr. Davis emphasized. *She's going to be very confused right away. There's a lot she has to adjust to: that her parents are alive, that you and your wife are divorced. She may even be angry. She may not want to talk. That's all normal. The Myer family has been very good to her.*

The Myer family. Catholic, no children, Dina Myer unable to conceive and unable to afford adoption, Dina and Albert Myer part of Terry Russell's radical pro-life group. It was the lead story on every news program, every newspaper—and, according to Ferrell, was only going to get bigger. Mike couldn't absorb what was going on; he couldn't imagine how Sarah was dealing with all of this.

Bill said, "You talk to Jess yet?"

"Not yet." Jess had been halfway through her twenty-four-hour flight to Australia when the news about Sarah broke. When the plane touched down, the Australian police came on board and explained the situation. Right now Jess was on a flight back home. Her plane was due to touch down sometime later tonight.

Mike's cell phone rang. He was keeping it on in case Jess decided to call.

It was Sam's office number.

Nancy Childs came on the line: "How you feeling, Daddy?"

"Excited. Terrified. You name it."

"It's all going to work out."

"That's what they keep telling me."

"It will. Now, as I'm sure you're aware of, this thing you've uncovered is huge. You're going to be inundated with phone calls—Oprah, Diane Sawyer, literary agents wanting to tell your story and sell it as a movie of the week. My advice is to get a media rep to handle all of this so you can focus your attention on your daughter. I've got the name of one who's excellent. Her name is Lucy Waters. I'll have her call you later on your cell. Is that okay?"

"That's fine. Nancy, I want to thank you—"

"I kept digging because you asked me to. Everyone, including myself, told you to quit and let her go, but you didn't. You, Mr. Sullivan, kept on believing, so if you want to thank someone, go look in a mirror."

"Can't let a man get a word in, can you?"

"Another thing Sam and I have in common. Speaking of which, here she is. Hold on."

Sam came on the line: "I don't want to keep you. I just wanted to tell you how happy I am for you."

"I couldn't have done it without you. Thanks, Sam. For everything."

The back door opened and Agent Ferrell stepped out, his suit and tie gone, replaced by jeans, a white shirt and a fleece vest.

Mike said, "I've got to run. Can I call you later?"

"I'm not going anywhere."

"Neither am I," Mike said. He thanked her again and hung up.

Ferrell was smiling this morning, his blue eyes bright and unclouded. Mike liked Ferrell. No question seemed too stupid or too repetitive. The first two days, Mike kept asking, between Ferrell's questions, "You're sure the girl you found is Sarah? You don't have any doubts?" and Ferrell would always flash a smile and then reaffirm what he knew: *There's no question it's your daughter. We matched her fingerprints, and as we like to say, fingerprints don't lie.*

Still, Mike felt that creeping fear bleed back into him. *I'm sorry, Mr. Sullivan, but there's been a mistake.* And then they would drive him back to Belham, back to his empty house where the reporters would be waiting, and he would get up in front of those microphones and have to say, *Sorry, this was all just a big misunderstanding.*

"Your daughter's en route," Ferrell said. "She'll be here in an hour. Mr. O'Malley, you understand that—"

"I know, strictly family, we don't want to confuse her because she's going to be confused enough. Dr. Hot Legs in there already gave me the four-one-one."

"Car's waiting for you out front," Ferrell said, then turned his attention to Mike. "Dr. Davis would like to speak to you, go over a few things before your daughter gets here."

Your daughter.

Sarah was on her way here.

To see him.

To come home.

And the joy filled Mike up to the point where he thought he was going to burst.

With the joy came a new set of fears.

"What if she doesn't recognize me?" Mike asked Dr. Davis.

"She might not at first. She was six when she was taken."

"And a half."

"Excuse me?"

"Sarah was six and a half when she was taken."

Dr. Davis smiled. She seemed genuinely empathetic to the situation and wanted to help. Mike found himself wanting to open up to her, put his heart on the table and dissect it—anything she wanted.

They were sitting in the living room, Dr. Davis in a chair facing a window overlooking the long, winding driveway. Mike sat on a couch, leaning forward and rubbing his hands between his knees as he stared at the floor.

"How many memories do you have from when you were six?" she asked.

Mike could only cough up fragments: wandering across the street to the neighbor's yard; getting into a rowboat with Lou; arguing with his mother at a store, wanting two coloring books instead of one.

"Sarah may have memories of you and your wife, but they're most likely buried," she said. "But that's temporary. These memories will come back to her, but you'll have to give it some time. What Sarah's going through right now is very traumatic. She was brainwashed—all those kids were. That's why this group only took young children. Sarah was told by Dina and Albert Myer that you and your wife died. She's living with a new family in a new country and then, out of nowhere, the police barge in and take her away. Not only does Sarah find out that you and your wife are alive, she also finds out that the Myer family kidnapped her. It's possible Sarah overheard bits and pieces about the Myers being a part of this radical Christian group. In any case, it's a lot to absorb. And Sarah may not want to absorb it right now. That's okay. Remember how you felt when you found out the news of your mother."

Mike nodded. He had told Dr. Davis all of it yesterday.

"What if she wants to go back to them?"

"That's not going to happen," she said. "They're going to jail."

"But she may want to go back to them. It's possible, right?" Mike raised his eyes to hers.

"You're her father," Dr. Davis said, her tone gentle but firm. "Nothing is going to change that fact. Yes, there will be some bumps along the way. Yes, there may be times when you get frustrated and angry at the unfairness of what has happened. But it *will* work out. She's coming up on twelve. She's still young. You can still have a childhood with her. You have time. That's a gift that some of the other families don't have. Remember that."

Mike thought of Ashley Giroux in her late twenties, a graduate student living in Italy; Caroline Lenville was in her forties, married with two kids, living a mile down the road from her adoptive—was that even the right word?—family in New Brunswick, Canada. Would he rather be in that position, trying to reconnect with an adult?

"They're here," Dr. Davis said.

Mike turned and saw two black Lincolns come to a stop in the driveway.

He stood up, his heart pumping so fast he was sure it was going to quit on him. He could see the headline now: FATHER OF MISSING GIRL REUNITED ONLY TO DROP DEAD OF A HEART ATTACK.

Why was he so scared? He had prayed for this moment how many thousands of times, and now it was here, right in front of him, just beyond the front door, and his skin was clammy, his stomach doing double flips.

Deep, slow breaths. It was going to be fine. It was going to work out.

"Mr. Sullivan?"

Mike wiped the sweat away from his forehead. He tested his legs. A little wobbly, but okay.

"You're her father. Don't forget that."

And with that Mike opened the door to meet his daughter.

CHAPTER 52

Sarah was tall—much taller than he had imagined.
And thin—not from lack of food but from all the growing she was doing.

Her glasses were gone.

So was the pigtail. Her hair was cut short, shoulder-length, just as he imagined. Her hair was so blond, so fine, the sun made it seem white.

No earrings. No jewelry. She was very plainly dressed, jeans and white Keds, a pink, long-sleeve T-shirt with a small bow printed on the center.

What he loved most—what made him almost crumble right there in front of everyone—was seeing her face. He could still see the stubborn traces of the six-year-old girl who had refused to grab his hand that night on the Hill.

Sarah stood among the three agents, her hands folded in front of her, her head bowed, staring at the tops of her sneakers. She was upset. When she knew she had done something wrong, she would bow her head and stare at her feet, the floor, anything to avoid looking in your eyes. Seeing her like this made him want to run over to her, grab her, hug her close, take the fear and pain and all the questions she carried in her eyes and transfer them to him—like he did when she was little, when she was his.

Only it wasn't going to work that way.

Mike gripped the railing and took the steps one at a time, wanting a chance to absorb her but more afraid that if he moved any faster, he'd trip and crack his head open, have the reunion in a hospital room. When he stepped onto the gravel, he kept his hand on the railing, squeezing it.

Dr. Davis addressed the crowd: "Why don't we give them some room."

Everyone nodded and moved away, Sarah's eyes coming up and tracking a chunky woman in jeans and a powder-blue shirt. Probably the psychologist, Mike thought. The woman had moved only a few feet, stopped and leaned against the hood of the Lincoln.

Mike walked over to his daughter but didn't get too close, wanting to give her some breathing room from all these eyes pinned on her—and him.

"Hi," he said, pleased that his voice sounded confident, strong.

"Hi," she said softly.

Hearing her voice for the first time made him want to reach out and touch her, make sure she was real.

"How was your ride?"

"Long," she said quietly, her eyes still downcast, locked on her sneakers.

"You want to stretch out, go for a walk?"

Sarah's gaze cut to Mike. Those eyes had once looked up from her crib into his, had once sought him out in their house, been excited to see him when he came home—these eyes he had helped create and shape now stared back at him, studying him, wondering who he was.

Sarah, remember our last Christmas together, you were so excited that you came and woke me up at four and whispered in my ear, "He came, Daddy, Santa came again!" Remember how we didn't want to wake Mom up so you and I went downstairs and made pancakes and burned them and you tried one and said yuck so you gave it to Fang? Remember how you don't like olives but you always kept trying them and kept making that grossed-out face? Remember that Saturday morning when you brought all your dolls and stuffed animals downstairs into the TV room and seated them on the couch and then stood up on top of the coffee table because you thought it was a stage?

He had hundreds of little memories like that. But they didn't mean anything right now. What she had were the memories from the Myer family—memories and stories and events he didn't own.

Sarah remained quiet.

Tell me you remember, Sarah. Please. Give me something.

"I could use a walk," Sarah said.

★   ★   ★

Behind the house were a barn and a stable for horses. No horses though. There was also what Mike believed to be a small skating rink. Sarah was eyeing it too, probably wondering the same thing.

As they walked down the slope, heading toward the trails, he debated whether he should talk first or wait for her to say something. Right now she seemed to be enjoying the peace and quiet. She probably hadn't had much of it during the last few days, so he decided to wait for her to initiate the conversation.

Ten minutes passed, and then he decided he couldn't bear the silence any longer.

"I know you're probably very confused—maybe even scared. That's okay. If you don't want to talk, I understand. This is about you. What you're feeling."

Sarah didn't nod, didn't respond; she kept walking, eyes straight ahead. He wanted to take the ache he had been carrying inside him for these past five years and shape it with words she would understand, words that would form a bridge she could travel across, see the hell he had gone through.

"They said you died," Sarah said.

Mike nodded, trying to keep the anger and judgment from reaching his face.

"I remember sitting in their kitchen and both of them telling me that you died and that bad men were looking for me," she said. "That's why they changed my name to Susan Myer. It was the only way to protect me from these bad men. And they said if I told anyone my real name, then the bad men might come looking for me, hurt me and them both."

Listen. This is about Sarah. Your job is to listen.

"Mr. and Mrs. Myer were always so nice to me," she said. "They never yelled at me. They took me to Disney World. I went to church with them. Why would they lie to me?"

They're religious fanatics, Sarah. They all share the same sick belief that God spoke through them—not priests, no, they're as morally corrupt as the rest of us. That's why they punished Father Jonah. He had the audacity to forgive women who played God.

Mike's thoughts momentarily turned to Jonah, his body cold in the ground now. Jonah had suffered right up until the very end.

He didn't see the need to tell any of this to Sarah.

"Sometimes you can believe in something so much, with such intensity, that it blinds you," he said. "When that happens, when you believe with all your heart and mind that what you're thinking or doing is right, it's all you can see. In their minds and in their hearts, Mr. and Mrs. Myer believed that what they were saying and doing was right."

"But they *lied*," Sarah said.

"I know. And I wish I could change it, but I can't. As you get older, you'll find out that people will lie to you—sometimes people close to you. It's sad, and it hurts, but it happens. That's why it's important to think about the good things. Like this."

Mike reached into his back pocket and handed Sarah a small stack of loose pictures.

"Sorry they're a little wrinkled," he said. "I forgot I was sitting on them."

Sarah slowed her steps as she studied the picture of Jess.

"Your mother will be here sometime later today."

Sarah studied the picture for a moment, Mike waiting, ready to answer questions if that was what she wanted. Sarah flipped to the next picture.

"Oh my gosh," she said and stopped walking. "Is that a baby bear?"

"That would be your dog, Fang. He's a bull-mastiff."

"He's *huge.*"

"And he drools, big time. Flip to the next picture and you'll see him as a puppy."

Sarah did. She wasn't staring at Fang though; her eyes were locked on the girl with the glasses and crooked teeth sitting next to the sleeping puppy. Mike had chosen it hoping it would trigger a memory.

He moved in closer, debating about whether or not to put his hand on her shoulder when she flipped to the next picture, a grainy newspaper color photograph taken of Lou Sullivan as he left prison. Bill had given him the news clipping this morning; Mike had folded it up and stuffed it in his back pocket, meaning to read it later.

"Who's this?"

"He's . . . he helped me find you."

"His name is Lou Sullivan," Sarah said. "That's your last name."

It's your last name too.

"He related to you?"

Mike nodded. "He's my father," he said. "Your grand-father."

Sarah held out the pictures.

"They're yours," he said. "You can keep them."

"Can you hold them for me? I don't want to lose them."

Her face was closed up. He had pushed her too far.

"Sure, no problem." Mike smiled, but it was forced and holding it was an effort. He took the pictures and tucked them in his back pocket.

"I'm hungry, so I think I'm going to go back and get something to eat."

"Okay," he said. "You mind if I hang out here for a moment?"

"No."

"Okay."

"Okay then. Later." Sarah turned and jogged away from him, back up the slope toward the house where Dr. Davis and the other psychologist were waiting.

Later.

It was okay, he reminded himself. They had time now. At least they had that.

CHAPTER 53

At eleven o'clock that night, Mike stepped out onto the porch for a smoke. The sky was black, bursting with stars, the air still hanging onto its winter chill. He lit a cigarette, sat in the rocking chair and put his feet up on the railing, feeling the weight of the day in his bones.

Dr. Davis and the other shrink had spent a good part of the afternoon with Sarah, who suddenly didn't want to talk anymore, just wanted to hang around her room with the door shut.

"She's overwhelmed," Dr. Davis had explained to him. "It's a lot to digest. Just give it time."

He had given it five years. Sarah didn't need all this talking. What she needed was to be home, not here in this sprawling farmhouse full of strange rooms and strange faces. She needed to be back in *her* house, in *her* room and sitting on *her* bed, and he would sit next to her and the two of them would go through the pictures from the day she was born until the day she was taken from him—go through all the pictures and all the home movies over and over and over again until Sarah finally turned to him and said—

"Smoking's bad for you."

Mike turned around. Sarah was standing on the porch.

"You're right." He mashed the cigarette out on the floor, then flicked the butt into the darkness and removed his feet from the railing.

Sarah stepped up next to him. She wore gray sweats and a denim jacket over a T-shirt. Mike wondered who had bought the jacket, if it was a birthday gift or something she had picked out herself, a reminder of her home for the past five years now comforting her as she waited in this strange house, about to go to another strange house with another strange bedroom.

"Can't sleep?" he asked.

"No."

"It's been a long day."

Sarah nodded. There was a problem; it was written all over her face.

She's here to tell me that she wants to go home to her other family.

Only that wasn't going to happen. Sarah wasn't going back to Canada, but the warm, good feelings she held for the Myer family were very real and weren't going away.

"This scar," Sarah said, then pointed to the skin near her right temple and leaned in so he could see. The scar was faint, about an inch long and jagged. "I can't remember where it came from. Do you know?"

He thought about the dried blood he'd seen in her hood.

"No," Mike said. "I don't."

Sarah nodded. She seemed on the verge of tears. He resisted the urge to reach out and hold her. *Don't force it,* Dr. Davis had said. *Let her come to you. And most importantly, listen. Listen without judgment, without anger.*

Mike said, "I'm sorry you have to go through all of this."

Sarah stared out at the trees, the leaves rustling in the wind.

"Today when we were walking we saw the skating rink," she said. "At least it looked like a skating rink."

"I think it was."

"I was in bed thinking about it—about the skating rink, I mean. At your house, was there a pond out back?"

Mike nodded. "Salmon Brook."

"It's out in the woods, right?"

"There's a trail in the back of the house. You saw figure skating on TV, and you wanted me to teach you how to skate."

"You put these, like, crates or something on the ice."

"Plastic milk crates. I'd stack two of them together and you'd hold onto the top as you skated. You didn't like them after a while. You wanted to skate on your own. You'd fall, and I'd rush over to pick you up and you would get so mad. You wanted to learn to get up on your own. Skating, swimming—especially sledding."

The last words came out before Mike realized what he had said, and he wished he could take them back.

It was okay. The words washed right over Sarah. She kept staring out at the trees with a faraway, dreamy look, as if the memory he was describing was being played for her.

"But then I got better."

"Oh yeah," Mike said. "You really took to it."

"And we played a skating game. You held me up in front of you while we skated."

A chill washed through his body. He wanted to speak, wanted to urge her on but was too terrified to say or do anything that might break her connection to this hazy fragment of a memory.

"You held me up and I'd call out names," Sarah said. "And they were silly names, right? Hungry Caterpillar or something like that."

Mike swallowed. "Something like that."

Sarah nodded slowly, lost again in a time they had built together and once shared.

"Yeah," she said with a shy smile. "I remember."

**ATRIA BOOKS
PROUDLY PRESENTS**

**THE MISSING
CHRIS MOONEY**

Coming soon in hardcover
from Atria Books

Turn this page for a preview of
The Missing. . . .

CHAPTER 1

The first time Darby almost died was the night of her sixteenth birthday. Early that evening, her parents had taken her out to dinner at a nice restaurant and when they came home, Darby opened her gifts: clothes, a couple of records and, the one thing she really wanted, a silver ID bracelet with her name etched on the front in really elegant letters. She had shown the bracelet to her mother one day at the mall who, typical Sheila, had said it was tacky, which made Darby want it even more. Darby suspected her father had bought it for her. He gave her a wink as he slid the small, gift-wrapped box across the table.

Stacey and Mel thought the bracelet was cool. That night, the three of them were sitting in the living room of Stacey Stephens's house, talking about the looming eight-page paper on the most boring writer of all time,

William Shakespeare, when their conversation shifted to their favorite show in the whole world, *The Love Boat*. Stacey said they should make strawberry daiquiris and celebrate Darby's birthday in style. Problem was, Mr. Stephens didn't have any liquor in the house, and the only person they knew who was old enough to buy for them was Darby's brother, Sean, who was away at a military school in Vermont.

"We could have a beer," Stacey said. "My Dad has some in the downstairs fridge."

And boy did he have lots of it. All three shelves were packed with cans of Miller High Life and Busch. Apparently Mr. Stephens was running a bar down in his basement.

"We can't drink it here," Stacey said. "If my parents decide to skip the movie and come home early and catch us drinking, my father will have a fit."

Darby thought about Stacey's father, his good-natured smile and the gentle way he called Stacey and her mother "cookie" and "sugar pie." Lingering behind the smile and kind words was a crackling, high-tensioned energy that, if you weren't careful, had the potential to break bones. Both Stacey and her mother often shared the same kind of bruises.

"I know a place where we can go," Stacy said. "You in?"

"I'm in," Darby said, and, along with Stacey, looked at Melanie. Mel thought it over for a moment, and when she finally nodded, a mischievous light sparked in Stacey's eyes.

Stacey's backpack had a big rip in it, so Darby grabbed hers from the car and packed six cans—two beers each—and headed out into the darkening street. It was after eight on this first Saturday in May, the air still warm and the sidewalks still busy with people.

Twenty minutes later, they crossed Route 4, the one-lane highway that took you straight into downtown Belham, and headed into a stretch of woods with no trails. Nobody came out this way; the real attraction was behind them—the trails in and around Salmon Brook Pond where people went jogging and took their dogs for long walks.

Darby dropped her backpack in front of a sloping bank of dead leaves, cigarette butts and empty beer cans. Not wanting to ruin her new Calvin Klein jeans, she tested the ground to make sure it was dry before she sat down, but Stacey, she just plunked her butt right down in the dirt. There was something inherently grubby about Stacey, with her hand-me-down jeans and T-shirts worn always a size too tight, the way she laughed too hard when boys were around—none of it was ever quite able to mask the sense of desperation that hovered around her like Pig Pen's dirt cloud.

Darby had known Melanie since, well, since *forever* really, the two of them having grown up on the same street. And while Darby could recall all the events and stories she had shared with Melanie, she couldn't for the life of her remember how she met Stacey or how the three of them had become friends. It was as if Stacey had just appeared one day, suddenly with them all the time—during study hall, at the football games and parties. Stacey was fun. She told dirty jokes and knew the popular kids and had gone as far as third base whereas Mel was a lot like the Hummel figurines Darby's mother collected—precious and fragile things needing to be stored in a safe place.

Stacey handed out the beers, then cracked open her can and drained half of it in one long, thirsty gulp. Darby took a small sip. Melanie sniffed her beer first; Mel sniffed anything new before she tasted it.

"Yuck," Melanie said. "It tastes like soggy wet toast."

"Keep drinking, it will taste better." Stacey wiped her mouth on the back of her hand, lit a cigarette and pointed to a black Mercedes snaking its way up Route 4. "I'm going to be driving one of those someday."

"I can totally picture you as a chauffeur," Darby said.

Stacey shot Darby the finger, then said, "No, somebody's going to be driving *me* around 'cause I'm going to marry a rich guy."

"I hate to be the one to break this to you," Darby said, "but there are no rich guys in Belham."

"No shit, Sherlock. That's why I'm going to Boston—or some place like New York City. All I know is, I'm not hanging around this dump forever."

At least we have that in common, Darby thought. No matter how hard you tried to pretty her up, with nice trees and nice parks like The Hill and places like the trails around Salmon Brook Pond, Belham would always be Chelsea's ugly twin sister. And the people who lived in Belham seemed lost—like Stacey's father. Mr. Stephens was always parked in a chair with a beer, not watching TV but staring through the screen, as if the life he had always envisioned or one damn close to it was just beyond, on the other side.

"And the man I marry is not only going to be gorgeous, he's going to treat me right," Stacey said. "I'm talking dinners at nice restaurants, nice clothes and any kind of car I want—he's even going to have his own plane to fly us to our fabulous beach house in the Caribbean. Maybe I'll even take you guys—if you're still nice to me." Stacey winked at Darby, then blew a long stream of smoke into the air. "What about you, Mel? What kind of guy are you going to marry? Or is your heart set on being a nun?"

"I'm not going to become a nun," Mel said in that shy, quiet voice of hers.

"So did you finally give up the goodies to Michael Anka?"

Darby nearly spit out her beer. "You've been making out with *Booger Boy?*"

"He stopped that back in the third grade," Melanie said. "He doesn't, you know, pick it anymore."

"Lucky for you," Darby said, and Stacey howled with laughter. She had one of those infectious laughs, and Darby found herself laughing too—only this laugh felt different. This one carried that floating sort of bubbling joy, and for some reason it made her think of her father, the way he would sometimes wrap his big meaty arm around her chest and pull her close to his rough, whiskery cheeks with their smell of Old Spice.

"I haven't been making out with him," Melanie said as she fingered the dozens of charms on her bracelet. "He's just, well, he's nice."

"Of course he's nice," Stacey said. "All guys are nice until they get what they want from you. Then they treat you like yesterday's garbage."

"That's not true," Darby said, thinking about how her father always held open the door for her mother; how after they came home from dinner on Friday nights, the two of them smiling and happy—and this was funny—they would head into the living room and put on a Frank Sinatra record. Sometimes Darby caught them dancing cheek-to-cheek, her father singing along with Frank about flying to the moon or how those were the days.

"Trust me, it's all an act," Stacey said. "That's why you've got to stop being so goddamn mousy, Mel. You keep acting that way, they'll take advantage of you every time. You know what my mother says? Act just like them. Stand up and speak your mind. And never, under any circumstances, take their shit."

But apparently Mrs. Stephens didn't mind taking a fist every now and then, Darby thought as she opened her second beer. She had caught more than one shiner on Mrs. Stephens and a bruise or two on Stace—Stacey always willing to swear on a stack of Bibles that her latest bruise or cut was due to her clumsiness. She and her mother were always running into things, always tripping. Some people were just accident prone, Stacey had said.

Stacey started in on her lecture series about boys and

all the sneaky things they did to trick you into giving them what they wanted. Darby leaned against a tree trunk and looked out at the cars zipping along both lanes of Route 1. She thought about the people inside all those cars, interesting people with interesting lives off to do interesting things in interesting places. How did you become interesting? Was it something you were born with, like your hair color or your height? Or did God decide for you? Maybe God chose who was interesting and who wasn't and you just had to learn to live with whatever you were handed.

The more Darby drank, the stronger and clearer that inner voice of hers grew, the voice that sometimes whispered with a sense of authority that she, Darby Alexandra McCormick, was destined for bigger things—maybe not the life of a pop star or a big-name actress, but something definitely better and a whole lot bigger than her mother's Palmolive world of cleaning, cooking and cutting coupons. Sheila McCormick's biggest thrill was the greedy hunt for bargains on the clearance racks. This bigger life, whatever it was, would be far away from her mother's small world here in Belham.

"Listen," Stacey said.

Ripped from her thoughts, Darby turned and saw Stacey on all fours, her head poking up past the slope of ground. The sun had gone down a while ago, and the woods were dark. Darby checked her watch. Wow. It was coming up on ten-thirty.

Snap-snap-snap—the sound of dry twigs and branches being crunched by footsteps.

"Did you hear that?" Stacey whispered.

"It's probably a raccoon or something," Darby whispered back. Why was she whispering? And why was she feeling afraid all of a sudden?

"Not the branches," Stacey said. "The *crying.*"

Darby put her beer down and poked her head up over the crest of the slope. She saw nothing but the faint outline of tree trunks. But that dry, snapping sound was growing louder and moving closer. A sharp chill raced up her spine, making her scalp tingle.

Oh please, Darby. First of all, you're drunk. Second, you're acting exactly like that time last year when you were home alone with the flu.

Sheila had run out to grab the medicine and do a few quick errands, leaving Darby alone in the house. Darby had almost drifted off to sleep when she heard glass shattering downstairs. Someone had smashed through one of the windows to get inside the house. Darby opened her bedroom window and in her bare feet climbed onto the back-porch roof, dropped into the backyard and ran to a neighbor's house to call the police.

Her father responded to the call. After he searched the house, he clasped her hand inside his meaty fist and walked her to the living room where Nana Kay's big mirror lay in hundreds of shattered pieces. The wire holding the mirror to the wall above the fireplace had snapped, he explained. Not a burglar, Darby, just a broken wire.

And do you remember what he told you?

That when you got scared you started to panic—and when you panicked, you got your mind worked up to a point where it stopped thinking rationally. Your imagination took over, convincing you that a burglar who looked *exactly* like Michael Myers from the *Halloween* movies had entered your house in broad daylight and was climbing the stairs with a huge butcher knife in his hands. There was no burglar and there was no crying woman out there in the woods. What was happening right now was the direct result of watching too many movies like *Halloween* and *Friday the 13th*.

"I heard a woman crying," Stacey said. "I swear to God I'm not making it up."

The snapping and cracking sound stopped and then they all heard it, faint but clear:

"Please," a woman whimpered between tears. "Don't hurt me, please."

CHAPTER 2

Very real, what was happening was very real and not the product of her imagination getting in a little scare workout. There *was* a woman here in the woods and the woman *was* crying and the woman was *terrified*.

"Take it," the woman pleaded. "There's over three hundred dollars in there, and a credit card. Take it, I won't tell anyone, I swear to God."

Stay calm, the rational side of Darby urged. *If you don't stay calm you won't be able to think.*

Darby thought of her father—Big Red, they called him, just like the gum, her father a tall man with a dark-red buzz cut who always had to wear short sleeves, even in the winter, because of his big arms that reminded her of telephone poles. His whole body seemed that way—solid and unbreakable, his mind just as tough in its ability to soak up every little detail and, when needed, recall it right on the spot.

This was a mugging—scary, without a doubt, but not

the worst thing in the world. The fact that the woman wasn't putting up a fight or trying to run away meant only one thing: the mugger had a weapon. If he had a knife, she might risk running away. That wouldn't be the case with a gun.

You better hope he doesn't have a gun. If he hears something and starts shooting—

Darby grabbed Stacey by the arm and pulled her back behind the slope. They huddled close together, Mel wedged between them, her hand clamped over her charm bracelet to keep it from making that jingling sound.

"It's just a mugging, but I think he might have a weapon," Darby whispered. "A knife or something."

"What if he has a gun?" Melanie asked.

"All the more reason why we need to keep quiet," Darby said. "She'll hand over her purse and then he'll run away and it will be over, so let's just keep quiet, okay?"

Stacy nodded. Mel did too. As scary as it was, Darby knew she had to poke her head back up over the slope. When the police came with their questions, she wanted to be able to recall everything she saw, every word and sound. She pictured the proud look on her father's face. *That's my girl,* he'd tell his police friends. *Not only is she brave, she's smart as hell. Because of her, we got this mugger behind bars.*

Slowly, Darby slid her head back over the top of the slope and searched through the curtain of darkness for the mugger and the woman. They weren't far away, Darby knew, but she couldn't see much of anything. Stacey had poked her head back up and was looking around too.

"Take it," the woman said. "Here, just take it."

The mugger whispered something Darby couldn't hear.

"Okay." The woman started crying. "Okay, just don't hurt me."

The sound of branches snapping filled the cool air.

"I promise I won't tell." The woman was sobbing now. "I swear to God I won't, please don't hurt me."

Stacey looked to Darby for an answer, but Darby didn't have one. Why was the mugger stalling? Was he getting his jollies by making this woman cry? On TV, the mugger always took the lady's purse and ran.

A gurgling noise filled the warm air, the sound instantly reminding Darby of that time during lunch last year when Billy Preston almost choked to death on a chicken wing.

Stacey got right next to Darby and in a panicky voice said, "What are we going to do?"

What could they do? Activate their Wonder Twin powers? This wasn't a TV show and they weren't part of the Justice League of America. This was real life and real life didn't have superheroes or butt-kicking, crime-fighting sixteen-year-old girls. If the mugger had a weapon, he certainly wouldn't hesitate to use it. What if one of them got shot or stabbed? What if one of them actually got *killed?* What would her father say then?

A car was coming up Route 4. Out of the corner of her eye, Darby saw the car's headlights form eerie yellow circles of light that slid across the tree trunks and the slope ground, full of rocks, leaves and downed tree branches. Darby heard music—Van Halen's "Jump," David Lee Roth's voice growing louder along with the worrisome voice in her head telling her to look away.

She didn't, though. She wanted to—God knows she wanted to duck back behind the slope and close her eyes and wish this away—but some other part of her brain had taken control. The headlights washed over them as David Lee Roth's booming voice sang to go ahead and jump and Darby saw a woman dressed in jeans and a gray T-shirt on her knees, her face a deep, dark red, eyes wide, bulging almost, her fingers desperately clawing at whatever was tied around her throat. The mugger stood behind the woman, shaking her violently

(*not shaking, he's strangling her*)

and when Darby's eyes slid up to the mugger's face, the headlights disappeared, plunging the woods back into darkness.

Stacey stood up and knocked Darby backward against the dirt. Her head hit a rock hard enough to make her see stars. Darby rolled onto her side and saw Stacey pushing her way past branches, running out of the woods and heading toward Route 4. Mel was running too; Darby heard the jingling sound of her charm bracelet.

A woman screamed—not the woman in the woods, no, this scream came from the car, and right on the heels of it came a wave of laughter. In that moment, Darby would have given anything in the world to be in that car, on her way someplace else, even back home where her mother was no doubt cutting out coupons and planning tomorrow's meal.

The woods became quiet again. Darby was too terrified to move. She sat in the dirt, her heart pumping madly in her chest, a greasy sweat working its way down her armpits.

Next came the dry crack of branches and twigs snapping—the mugger was running this way, running toward *her.*

(not a mugger he's a killer a murderer GET UP *NOW—)*

Darby scrambled to her feet. As she ran after Stacey and Mel, she was sure she heard the woman start coughing.